The Vicar's Daughter at the Lodging House

BOOKS BY NATALIE MEG EVANS

The Wartime Lodging House series

The Irish Nurse at the Lodging House

Standalone Novels

The Dress Thief

The Milliner's Secret

A Gown of Thorns

The Wardrobe Mistress

The Secret Vow

The Paris Girl

Into the Burning Dawn

The Italian Girl's Secret

The Girl with the Yellow Star

The Locket

The Paris Inheritance

The Vicar's Daughter at the Lodging House

NATALIE MEG EVANS

bookouture

Published by Bookouture in 2026

An imprint of Storyfire Ltd.
Carmelite House
50 Victoria Embankment
London EC4Y 0DZ

www.bookouture.com

The authorised representative in the EEA is Hachette Ireland
8 Castlecourt Centre
Dublin 15 D15 XTP3
Ireland
(email: info@hbgi.ie)

ISBN: 978-1-80550-378-1
eBook ISBN: 978-1-80550-377-4

1

The earth shook as a bomb fell. Sickeningly close. A shudder ran through the curved ribs of the Anderson shelter where Jess sat hunched in her coat, a blanket about her shoulders. She'd been alone in the house when the sirens went, her landlady and housemates having left her – supposedly – to a quiet night in. She'd come out in the dark with a torch, a thermos and the book she was reading, hoping the raid would be short.

She wasn't entirely alone: she'd brought her landlady's hens in with her and was cradling the most fragile of them, a little black Dorking. The bird's heart hammered against her palm, fast and shallow. From the park, anti-aircraft guns boomed and she imagined them as fists swinging in the dark, flailing at the waves of incoming bombers – until a fluting whistle cut through the din and her heart faltered.

After three weeks of sustained attacks, she knew that if the whistle dulled in tone as the bomb fell, the impact would happen elsewhere. This one held to a single note.

She shut her eyes and dug her chin into her chest. As if that would save her or the little black hen.

The impact was volcanic, the earth heaving as if it had

folded in on itself. The roof sagged inward, striking her skull. Her torch toppled and went out.

There followed a moment of absolute silence.

Jess thought she knew darkness. Like the cellar at home when the power failed, or the London blackout with every glimmer of light smothered in drapes or pitch-paint. Neither was as black as the void that now engulfed her.

She wasn't certain if the world outside existed still, or if it had been blown away. The hen's feverish movements against her breast told her that at least she wasn't dead. Though she might soon be. The roof was a finger's width from her scalp, forcing her into an angle that made every breath a labour. Panic tightened her chest: would anyone realise she was missing before she suffocated? Her lips shaped a cry, then closed. No one would hear through whatever material – bricks, timber, part of the house? – had fallen on top of her. She was trapped with four anxious chickens and the absurdity of this fact did nothing to lessen her dread.

Would Mrs Kesgrave, Grace or Betony remember that she'd stayed at home? They had their own concerns. Mrs Kesgrave had gone down to Brighton. Grace and Betony were chasing love in their different ways. What if they stayed away for days, forgetting her altogether? And what if a fire took hold, and there were timbers around?

'What ifs' fed on fear. What if the shelter couldn't hold and became a burial pit?

The awful irony was that she was only here in bomb-stricken London because she'd set out to rescue someone else.

Charlotte. Her lost sister.

But for one chance find, she'd have stayed at home in the vicarage, passing the war in modest usefulness. Going to work in an office, helping out in the parish, keeping the household accounts and peeling potatoes for dinner. Instead, she'd rushed headlong to a city too vast and loud for her in search of a ghost.

She had slept in the cold, gone hungry, mistaken friend for foe, yet she'd pushed on, her mission to find Charlotte whatever it cost.

This, then, was the cost. Two lives wasted, Charlotte betrayed and herself no wiser. 'I just wanted the truth.' At once, the hens settled as if the admission soothed them. Jess found a better way to breathe, in through the nose, out through the mouth.

It became hypnotic and after a while she began to see faces. Charlotte's first. Sleek raven hair, shadowy eyes, skin too pale. Then Mrs Kesgrave, brows like sweeping strokes of ink, always ready with comfort and counsel. Betony next, fair hair glossed and curled, mouth painted the newest shade of crimson. A fashion-plate smile, vain one instant, surprisingly kind the next. And lastly Grace, eyes of blue, red hair, a wounded soul. Ready for battle or to laugh at herself...

If anyone could pull her up from here, it would be those women, though none of them had set her on this path. It was her own doing.

Fate had brought her to this.

A locked door, a letter and a name with no context. Alder Grove.

The memory took her back to Ramsgate, to a morning in mid-July.

Three months earlier, St Saviour's Vicarage, Ramsgate, Kent

The typewriter had sat untouched in the box room for months. Jess stared at it, like a treasure hunter who has unearthed a long-lost casket.

It was Charlotte's old Remington, glossy black with keys like liquorice drops and it was the only trace of her sister left in the house. Everything else, clothes, books, childhood toys, had gone. Anything deemed to be of no value such as her school reports, poems and stories had been burned at the top of the garden. Jess had kept the typewriter against the odds, claiming she needed it to practise her skills for her job. Her father, Reverend Gresham, had agreed reluctantly – then locked the typewriter in the box room. When Jess asked for the key, he'd told her it was lost.

That was last winter, the first of the war. Each time Jess passed the box room, she imagined the Remington waiting for her. She would conjure Charlotte's face, remembering the impatient energy that had made her sister such fun to be with. Jess sometimes even saw Charlotte leaning over her when she woke in the morning. The hazy image always had a smile, and Jess would hear the beloved voice:

'Get up, lazy bones, chickens to feed, words to weave.'

Jess told no one, of course, least of all her father, who tolerated no mention of the daughter whose loss was too painful to admit. Denied the expression of grief, life in the vicarage had grown stifling to Jess. She longed to leave but hadn't the courage.

Then, last night, months after she'd given up looking for it, she'd stumbled across the missing piece. Hunting for the spare potato peeler, she'd emptied one of the biscuit tins her father kept for odds and ends. No peeler, but the box room key. Feeling like a housebreaker, she'd turned it in the lock. The Remington sat on a broken chair with its hard case on top. Jess shot the catches and lifted the lid. 'Hello you.' Some of the gold cyphers on the keys were worn faint with use. A sheet of paper was caught in the rollers.

It was a letter, typed on the vicarage's embossed stationery to the editor of the *London Mercury*. Fleet Street, EC4. Jess began to read it, her breath catching.

Dear Sir, my name is Charlotte Gresham,

It was the date that hit Jess like a slap. Twenty-third of December 1939.

Impossible. Charlotte had been dead for two days by then.

Squeezing up to the tiny window to get the best of the light, Jess read her sister's letter all the way through.

> Dear Sir, my name is Charlotte Gresham, and I wrote to you over a month ago in response to your advertisement for a newsroom typist. I am so, so keen to start a career in journalism. Please reply. I leave home tomorrow and I will come to your offices in person. I hope by then

The letter broke off mid-line.

Jotted in ink, hurried but not careless, was a name: Alder Grove.

It meant nothing to Jess but she couldn't shake off the idea that Charlotte had left her a message, hastily penned in the midst of typing.

That week in December, the run-up to Christmas, was graven in her mind. Two days before the date on this letter, Jess had gone to work, leaving Charlotte in bed. Unwell. She'd struggled home through the blacked-out streets eight hours later, hindered by a fast-falling sea fog and found Charlotte on the floor of their bathroom in a pool of blood. The scream she'd let out lived inside her still. Her father had come home almost at that moment, and she remembered him thundering up the stairs, shouting, 'What is it?' A tiny detail – his glasses were misted and he'd had to wipe them on his gloves before he could properly view the scene in front of him. The parish secretary, Miss Hillingdon, had come in behind, a constant shadow.

After that – shock. Towels, water. Jess sent down to make a telephone call. An ambulance pushing through the fog. A stretcher brought up. Urgent questions – 'Does she take medication, have a history of seizures, has this happened before?'

Questions Jess could not answer. The ambulance had left with Charlotte and their father inside. Miss Hillingdon had seen Jess onto the last train to Faversham. She was to stay with Miss Hillingdon's sister. And then – nothing. No news. No explanations. Just Miss Hillingdon's cool words on Christmas morning:

'Your sister passed away in the ambulance, Jessica. A brain haemorrhage, which explains the blood. Yes, I know... but apparently young people can suffer them. Take comfort that your father was with her.'

As if that would make up for the loss. As if it closed the door on everything.

Miss Hillingdon had few doubts as to the cause. 'Forever dashing up to London, chasing the folly of a career... I warned her. City air is so unhealthy. Setting herself up for disappointment. Girls of your background do not become news reporters. It's an unsavoury profession.'

Unsavoury or not, it had been Charlotte's dream. Not her folly. She'd been clear-sighted about the path ahead: for a young woman, it meant starting in the typing pool, and for that you needed lightning-fast speeds. Every Saturday for a year, Charlotte had raced to catch the 7.20 to London to attend a secretarial college on the Charing Cross Road. She'd come home and practise her skills obsessively, yet Jess had always suspected there was more to those trips. Charlotte had changed, become secretive in ways Jess couldn't quite pin down.

That last London trip had been on a Wednesday. Charlotte had stolen off from her job in a bookshop on Ramsgate High Street with the excuse of a family emergency. A lie.

Jess rolled the letter back into the typewriter, replaced the lid on the machine and quietly locked the box room door. Her father was in the bathroom. She could hear the taps running as he shaved. She went quietly downstairs. Nobody seeing her would guess the jumbled emotions behind her pale, grave features. In the breakfast room, she laid places for herself and her father. She wouldn't mention what she'd stumbled across because she'd get no straight answers and the typewriter would be removed.

Not for an instant did she doubt the letter. It radiated Charlotte. Screamed her name.

So, so keen to start a career in journalism.

'You never did, though, did you?' Jess whispered. Her father's feet creaked on the stairs, measured, unhurried, bound for the front door and the morning paper. 'It all stopped for you, and I need to know why.'

She poured his tea, placing it ready for him... bade him good morning. He echoed an answer, sat down and unfolded his paper.

As their morning routine unspooled, an urgent question rose up through the polite hush between them. Alder Grove.

What do you want me to find there, Charlotte?

2

After washing up the breakfast pots, Jess left the vicarage and walked the couple of miles to Ramsgate High Street.

She worked for a firm of accountants as the lowest-grade clerk, paid fifteen shillings a week. She typed letters, did the filing. At eleven she made tea for her supervisor. Today, as every day, she passed through several offices to reach the kitchen and was ignored. Not unkindly: the staff at Hedgley & Co. simply didn't see little Jess Gresham in her cotton skirt, neat blouse and cardigan. They bracketed her with the office furniture, the duplicating machine and the kettle.

They thought her dull, meek, pliant.

They were wrong.

At midday, instead of heading out with her and her father's ration books to queue at the greengrocer's, she rolled a fresh sheet of paper into her typewriter and began a letter:

To the Recruitment Officer, Civil Service Commission, Burlington Gardens, London W1

Dear Sir or Madam,

I wish to apply for clerical work in London. I am nineteen years old and can type at almost forty words a minute and have office experience. I am willing to accept any posting available. As I intend to come to London very shortly, I shall be in need of paid employment.

Respectfully,

Jessica Gresham

Charlotte had been planning her own move to London, if that letter to the Fleet Street editor proved anything. Their father would never have allowed it. He'd have forbidden Charlotte to rent a room or move into lodgings, sharing with girls of no known family. He'd try to stop Jess in exactly the same way. So she wouldn't tell him.

After signing the letter to the Civil Service, Jess wrote one to the senior partner of Hedgley & Co. – her resignation. A risk, yes, but she had a little money saved and a burning determination to find her sister. To know if Charlotte was dead, or miraculously still alive. After standing a moment in the corridor, listening in case any of her colleagues were returning early from lunch, Jess crept into her supervisor's office and lifted the telephone receiver.

This was a crime, a personal call without permission. Perhaps even a sacking offence.

She dialled 100.

The operator answered quickly. 'Number, please, caller.'

Jess cleared her throat, suddenly afraid. 'Um, I don't have a number but I'm hoping you can put me through to Alder Grove.'

There was a pause. 'You mean the nursing home in Dover?'

That didn't sound right. 'I assumed it was a hotel. Is there one of that name? It might be near London.'

'Hold one moment.' The operator went silent. Jess's palms began to sweat. From downstairs came the click of the street door, footsteps on the stairs.

At last, the operator returned. 'I have an Alder Grove in Surrey. It isn't a hotel, though. Did you realise that?'

Jess's hand tightened on the receiver. 'What is it?'

The operator gave the answer. Jess pressed the receiver back into its cradle as if it burned and hurried to the ladies' toilets and locked herself in, fighting a desire to be sick.

Three days brought a reply with a London W1 postmark.

19 July 1940

Miss J. Gresham,

Madam,

In reply to your application for clerical employment, you are requested to attend the Civil Service Commission, Burlington Gardens, W1, on Thursday next, 25 July, at 10.30 a.m. Please report to Room 14, Miss Trevelyan, in connection with vacancies for clerical officers required at the Ministry of Information.

Bring any proofs of qualification.

Yours faithfully,

for the Secretary,

Civil Service Commission

Ministry of Information. Jess read the name several times over, pulse thudding as if she'd won a prize. The first hurdle was leaped. The chance of a London job. Now all she needed was somewhere to live.

3

The Civil Service Recruitment Office was half-hidden behind sandbags. A sign nailed to one of them directed interviewees inside. Her gas mask in its cardboard box clumping against her hip, a stiff, brown envelope pressed to her chest, Jess followed a couple of women who seemed to know where they were going.

She felt woefully under-prepared. She had her School Certificate as proof of educational attainment, but nothing to show beyond that. She'd got her job at Hedgley's because the senior partner was one of her father's parishioners.

In Room 14, she found all the chairs were taken. Women clutching manila envelopes like hers sat in earnest silence. Some were matronly, some young. All wore gloves. Except her.

A door opened, and a tense-looking woman emerged. A stern voice rang out:

'Next, please. Miss Pauline Dunkerly.'

A girl about Jess's age disappeared into the interview room. She'd dropped her envelope as she stood up and Jess felt sorry for her. Nerves were the world's worst saboteurs. Still, at least there was now a seat free. Jess had brought a novel to read, but everyone else was sitting with hands folded in laps.

After an hour, Jess was invited into a room and asked a series of questions.

'Who is our current Prime Minister?'

Easy. 'Mr Churchill.'

'Who is our current President of the Board of Trade?'

She dredged it up. 'Mr... sorry... *Viscount* Lyttelton.' She blessed Father's daily newspaper, always spread like a barricade between them at breakfast. Next came a maths test, after which she was sent back to the waiting room.

Another hour crept by before a frayed voice called, 'Miss Jessica Gresham.'

Jess clutched her envelope so tightly, when she put it down in front of a woman in an immaculate grey jacket, it showed her handprint in perspiration.

'I'm Miss Trevelyan.' The woman confirmed Jess's name. 'Follow me.'

She led Jess into an office containing a desk, typewriter, two chairs. A tall window half-covered by blackout cloth offered a view of blank sky. Miss Trevelyan sat, gesturing for Jess to do the same. 'I'll read your credentials in a moment. You are applying for Clerical Assistant, Records Department,' she said. 'You passed the aptitude tests. However, your typing speed is listed as forty-plus words per minute. We need to verify it.'

Jess swallowed. Forty-plus was a highly optimistic figure.

'Over there.' Miss Trevelyan gestured to the Remington on the desk. At least that was familiar. 'You will type from my dictation. Begin when I say.'

Dry mouthed, Jess shifted over to sit in front of the typewriter and positioned her fingers – which seemed to have swollen to twice their normal size – on the keys. Touch typing was essential. No looking down.

Miss Trevelyan began. 'On the eighth of January this year, sugar, bacon and butter came under ration following an edict from the Ministry of Food, in a memorandum sanctioned by the director—'

The test was dense with names, dates and statistics. Jess strove to keep her fingers moving in rhythm, but the keys felt different to those she was used to. Stiffer, heavier. She faltered. Did 'commodities' have two 'm's or one?

'Stop.'

Thank heavens. Having hardly breathed for the last hundred and twenty seconds, Jess glanced down at the keys and found they were swimming. Miss Trevelyan took her page and examined it.

'Thirty-one words per minute,' she said finally. 'Neat enough, though "commodities" has two "m's" and one "t". However, your speed is below the minimum requirement for Records work.'

'I'm practising every night.' Jess heard the note of pleading in her voice. She had to get this position, or how would she support herself in London?

'During wartime, efficiency isn't a preference, it's a necessity.'

Jess flushed at the rebuke. She'd taken today off as unpaid leave, telling her supervisor at Hedgley & Co. that she was attending a training course on what to do in case of a gas attack. Not entirely a lie: the training was at seven tonight in her father's church hall. At some point, her story would unravel. Only a firm offer of employment from His Majesty's Government would shield her from disgrace and, inevitably, curbs on her freedom.

'You are otherwise sound,' Miss Trevelyan said, having glanced through Jess's paperwork. 'The references from your former headmistress seem satisfactory. I expect your current employer will write one on request?'

'I'm sure they will.' *If they can remember who I am.*

'Would you consider reassignment to a department where typing speed is less critical?'

Jess nodded so hard, the hairgrips securing her Alice band dug in.

'The Ministry of Information has vacancies in Censorship. You would report to a Mr Brinkworth.'

'Censorship?' Jess weighed up the word. 'You mean, telling people what they should and shouldn't write?' She imagined Charlotte screwing up her face, hissing, '*You can't*. Walls with eyes, and everyone spying on everyone else.'

'You would be reviewing civilian correspondence,' Miss Trevelyan said briskly. 'Your responsibility would be to identify and flag content that might compromise national security.'

Despite feeling disloyal to Charlotte, Jess said it sounded interesting.

Miss Trevelyan's response was tightly pursed lips. 'It is repetitive and strictly confidential. You would not be permitted to discuss what you read with anyone, not even a parent or spouse, under penalty of the Official Secrets Act. Do you understand?'

Perfectly. Jess was getting to be good at secrets.

'Very well.' Miss Trevelyan slid a fresh form across the desk. 'Sign this, and we will expect you back in a month. Initial salary is thirty-eight shillings per week.' She stopped, seeing Jess's reaction. 'Sorry, you expect more?'

'No!' It was more than three times what Jess was earning now. 'I've never had so much.'

'London is expensive, you will find. However, there's the possibility of promotion after three months.'

Jess signed the form with an unsteady hand. She had passed. A job – seven pounds and six shillings a month and the freedom after hours to follow Charlotte's trail. She needed only to find a place to live.

She barely remembered leaving Miss Trevelyan's office.

Faces in the waiting room turned as she went by, her giddy smile challenging the drabness of the walls and the scratched linoleum.

Outside, the roar of traffic startled her. Almost at once, there came an air raid siren, jarring as the sopranos in a choir going wildly off-key. Jess couldn't think what to do – run or stand still. Nobody else seemed to be reacting. The pedestrians crowding the pavement kept walking at the same pace.

A false alarm, then, most likely. Though the war was almost a year old, very few actual bombs had been dropped. The occasional German plane strayed over the Channel, always seen off by the RAF.

Still, she decided to head straight back to the train station and worry about finding accommodation later. There would be agencies and hostels she could write to.

Her immediate task – the one she was least looking forward to – was breaking the news of her new job to her father.

4

Thursday, 1 August 1940

She let a week go by, losing her nerve each time, though she'd rehearsed the words often enough. It was the first of a new month and, waking from a guilt-ridden dream, Jess decided: *Today or never.*

Breakfast was the obvious moment as it was the only time she could rely on her father being home and sitting down with her in the same room. The table was set, tea poured. Reverend Gresham came in, dressed for the day ahead in a lightweight summer suit, grey shirt and dog collar.

Jess moved quickly before he could raise his newspaper, placing a cup and a folded letter by his elbow.

'What's this?'

'Read it, please, Father.'

He slid on his glasses. Cleared his throat. 'Dear Miss Gresham, following your recent interview and having perused the references provided...' His face fell into stony stillness. Jess's stomach clenched. She'd hoped the crown and shield on the letterhead might smooth her path, sparing her explanations. Evidently not.

Reverend Gresham refolded the letter and pushed it across the table without a word.

Jess could never endure silent reproach and a confession spilled out. Yes, she'd gone secretly to London, taken time off work and applied for a Civil Service job. 'With a salary and prospects.'

'Without my permission.'

Yes. Without his permission.

The lines between his brows deepened. 'When did you apply?'

'Two weeks back.'

'Who supplied your references?'

'My headmistress and my supervisor at Hedgley's.'

'And nobody thought to tell me.'

'No. I'm sorry.'

'As Charlotte before you, a lying child is a father's heartbreak.' Reverend Gresham got up leaving his tea untouched, picked up his newspaper and walked out.

Jess stared miserably into her cup. Her first instinct was to dash off a refusal to Miss Trevelyan, then beg her father's forgiveness. But when she heard him leave, she stayed seated. Charlotte's rebellious spirit must have taken root. For once in her life, Jess wasn't going to back down, appease or apologise. Putting on her hat and jacket, she went to work without clearing the table. By the time she'd reached the High Street she knew that today, she would formally hand in her notice at Hedgley's. She had a start date at the Ministry of Information of 26 August.

If her father pressed her to rethink, she would look him in the eye and say, 'I'm sorry, but King and country outranks even your hurt.'

That little speech was never needed. Reverend Gresham

made no further reference to the letter or Jess's plans. But if her father said too little, Miss Hillingdon said too much.

She cornered Jess after Sunday service. 'So. You are abandoning your father. How will he manage, alone in that enormous house?'

'He must get a housekeeper.'

Miss Hillingdon, unused to hearing Jess speak so plainly, shook her head. 'I never thought you hard-hearted, Jessica. I must have been deceived by those meek looks.'

Yet, a housekeeper did make sense. A capable woman who could cook and clean, and with time to queue for groceries each day. More to the point, someone her father needn't trouble himself to talk to.

When it became clear nothing would shake Jess's resolve, Miss Hillingdon tried another tack.

'The question of where you'll live... don't bother with an accommodation agency. They'll either place you somewhere too expensive, or miles from where you work. Not to mention unsuitable companions.' No, Jessica must stay in a Christian women's lodging. Miss Hillingdon knew of one in Paddington. 'I'll write to the matron and explain that this is your first time away from home. She'll offer proper supervision.'

Jess refused. The whole purpose of going to London was independence. She explained she intended to write to the Girls' Friendly Society. 'The one in Westminster. I can stay at their hostel.'

'Do they have room?'

'They're bound to and it'll be just as respectable as your place in Paddington. More central.' She couldn't resist adding, 'More in the swing of things.'

Miss Hillingdon dropped the subject, only to insist on inspecting Jess's suitcase, which she'd dragged out of the box room and begun to pack. 'Too few warm things and too many books. You won't be able to lift it. Besides, if your new job is as important as you say, you won't have time to read. And what's this?' Miss Hillingdon pounced on a notebook.

'Don't – it's private.'

Too late. Miss Hillingdon read out loud, '"Act One, the Drawing Room of a Country Vicarage." It's your hand. Are you writing a play?'

'Trying to,' Jess said, snatching the notebook back.

'Not about us, I hope?'

'I don't know yet,' Jess answered truthfully. 'There isn't much plot so far. I haven't lived enough life to give my characters anything to do.'

'Does your father know?'

'No. But I expect you'll tell him.' Jess shut her suitcase and shot the catches. Miss Hillingdon was right in one thing. It was heavy but she wasn't intending to take half the books she'd packed. They were place-savers, to be swapped at the last minute for something far more important.

Saturday, 24 August

'Jessica?'

Her father's voice rose up the stairs. They'd both woken at dawn, jerked from sleep by the sounds of heavy aircraft. The war was getting closer and she was leaving.

Jess stood at her window, suitcase ready, her coat folded neatly across it. In the small hours she had slipped into the box room and removed Charlotte's typewriter. Most of the books were back on the shelf, the Remington in their place.

Charlotte's last letter was still trapped in its frame, with its cryptic message. *Alder Grove.* Not a hotel. Nor a guesthouse.

A destination. A cry for help. The first place she meant to go.

'Jessica, are you ready?'

'Yes, Father.'

'Then why aren't you down?'

'Coming.' Not moving from the window, her gaze followed the grey shapes of enemy bombers swarming inland. Their targets were the RAF stations of Manston, Lympne and Hawkinge deep in the Kent countryside. Every bomb unleashed sent tongues of flame into the sky and rattled her dressing table mirror.

'It's past ten o'clock and you know we have to walk to the station.'

Her father sounded tense, and he was right. She mustn't miss the 11.08. Jess knew what kept her dawdling up here. Fear. There was a question she had to ask before she left. She'd flinched from it at breakfast but it was now or never.

She cast a final look around the bedroom she'd occupied for as long as she could remember, always with Charlotte. Precious things were being left behind. The bedspreads knitted by their mother, who had died so long ago, Jess had no real memory of her.

So many objects were imprinted with a childhood shared with her sister but it was time to tear free. She'd be in London by mid-afternoon, and on the hunt for somewhere to stay. The Girls' Friendly Society hadn't answered her letter, but she was a member so they had to take her in. Her induction at the Ministry of Information began in forty-eight hours. Monday, eight thirty sharp. Between now and then lay Alder Grove.

She had the address: Hook Road, Epsom.

'Jessica?' Her father's voice in the doorway made her jump. 'You're still standing about? Miss Hillingdon is late too. Honestly, women.'

'She's not coming with us?' Couldn't they have this last morning to themselves? Her trust in her father had sustained a blow but she still loved him. She wanted to say her goodbyes privately. And ask that question, also in private. As her father reached for her suitcase, Jess sprang forward.

'Don't. You take my coat.' She thrust her old school gabardine at him, smiling to hide the strain of lifting the case herself. A gift from her father's parishioners, it was made of leather and still smelled of the saddler's shop. A generous present but even empty, it weighed a ton. Full, as it was now, it felt like two.

Jess bumped it downstairs step by step. In the front hall, she checked herself in the mirror. She was travelling in a mustard-brown cotton dress, a matching jacket, short socks, solid shoes and her straw boater hat. With her battered satchel and gas mask slung over her shoulder, she felt less like a young woman setting out into adulthood than a convent schoolgirl heading back after the holidays.

Still, that might work in her favour. Invisible Jessica Gresham, slipping through the world on a mission that no one would guess.

Her father came down carrying her coat and nudged her aside so he could straighten his dog collar – until the roar of a plane passing so low overhead made him jump, his fingers at his throat. An explosion shook the fanlight above the door.

'The town's not being bombed, surely?' Jess asked in astonishment.

'No, still Manston, I think,' her father said, having walked to the window. 'Our boys are seeing them off. That sounded like a plane hitting the ground. One of theirs, I hope, God forgive me.'

The thought of death happening close by, on a fine summer's day, acted on Jess like a prod. 'Father, there's something I need to ask before I go.'

He turned a stern expression on her. 'No more shocks, please. I've agreed to this escapade. Isn't that enough? Right. We shan't wait for Miss Hillingdon.' He picked up her suitcase before she could stop him and immediately put it down. 'What's in here, bricks?'

'Books and clothes mostly. I said I'd carry it.'

He shook his head. 'I wish I hadn't had the tyres taken off

the Austin 7.' He pointed to the kitchen door. 'Fetch string; we'll lash this to my bicycle.'

As Jess searched the kitchen dresser, she heard Miss Hillingdon arrive and returned to the hall in time to see the woman unfastening the suitcase catches.

'Leave it!' Jess yelled. 'I've packed it just as I want.'

Miss Hillingdon stood back, checked by the rebuke – for a second or two. 'Anyone would think you're moving to Australia. You must still have too many books in there. Why, when London has libraries? Your hostel is quite a distance from Victoria station – I've checked – and you won't be paying a porter or taking a taxi, I hope.'

'I'll be fine.' Jess handed her father the twine.

They secured the suitcase between the seat and handlebars of his bicycle. He wheeled it down the path, Jess and Miss Hillingdon falling into step behind. Out in the countryside, plumes of smoke and pillars of flame marked each new impact.

Jess spared a last look at the handsome, shabby vicarage. The unkempt garden, the walnut tree with the rope swing. 'Here I go, Charlotte. I'll pick up your trail and God willing, I'll find you at the end of it.'

'Who are you talking to?' demanded Miss Hillingdon.

'Only to myself. Are you all right?' Miss Hillingdon was plucking at her collar, as if regretting her choice of outfit. She was married to tweed, Jess thought. Even in a summer frock, a staunch green jacket was buttoned over the top. For their walk to the station, Miss Hillingdon had tucked her greying auburn hair under a felt hat: she must be boiling. The morning was growing warm, promising another sticky, airless day. Not waiting for an answer, Jess walked faster, placing a hand on the suitcase to help her father. They made it to the station with a few minutes to spare.

Her train was already in. Miss Hillingdon went ahead to ensure her a seat.

'Return fare or single?' her father asked as he took out his wallet.

'Single,' Jess said firmly. There was no coming back. Well, not until she had some leave. 'But I'll pay.'

'Nonsense. A man cannot launch his only daughter into the world free of charge.' Turning away, Reverend Gresham headed for the ticket window.

Only daughter. It could have been a slip-up, in the stress of the moment.

While she waited, Jess counted the money in her purse. She had almost five pounds made up of her final wage packet from Hedgley's and the last of her savings. Then, last night, her father had silently passed over two pound notes. Looking at him now at the ticket window, slightly stooped and wearing the faithful trilby, she felt a surge of emotion. You could love someone though you no longer trusted them. When he returned and handed her a single ticket, she seized the moment. 'Daddy...' The word felt dangerous. He'd been Father since she was twelve. 'Tell me where Charlotte went.'

'To heaven, of course.'

'I mean in the ambulance. Miss Hillingdon said St Mildred's, but I don't believe it.'

'Don't believe it? What nonsense is this, child?' His voice sharpened, eyes narrowing, and Jess bit back her question about Alder Grove. One wrong word and he might forbid her to leave.

She forced out a different question. 'Where is she buried, then?'

For an instant the mask faltered, then snapped back into place. 'Why on earth are you asking?'

'Miss Hillingdon told me she died on the way to hospital.'

'On the way to St Mildred's. Whether you believe it or not. Let's change the subject.'

'No – we won't see each other for ages and I can never have

a proper conversation with you. Either you're busy or Miss Hillingdon is lurking.'

'That is disrespectful and unfair.'

Hardly, but there was no time for that argument. 'Charlotte is buried somewhere, so tell me. I want to visit.'

Reverend Gresham glanced away, and Jess sensed he was willing Miss Hillingdon to come back and rescue him. Affection curdled into frustration. 'Father, *please*. Just say.'

'We told you what happened to Charlotte... to her remains.'

'Because of the emergency measures. Everyone who died that month had to go in a communal grave.'

'And you doubt my word?' The ice in his voice was almost enough to make her back down. But the roots of rebellion had forced their way even deeper over the preceding days.

'I doubt the story, if that's what they told you. Why isn't she buried in our churchyard at home? You're the vicar; they wouldn't have said no to you.'

Her father laid a hand on her arm. A surprisingly gentle touch, a lesson in the mastery of emotion. 'You'd have me use my position to gain a privilege out of reach to others? We must not be selfish, Jessica. Charlotte may not be with us physically but she's in our prayers. Yes?'

Jess didn't answer. She no longer prayed.

'Ah, here's Miss Hillingdon.' His voice rose in relief.

Miss Hillingdon looked pleased with herself, though her expression sharpened, as if she detected tension. She had saved Jess a seat in a compartment with two ladies, she said. 'They have agreed to chaperone you. Soldiers are on the train, already drinking, would you believe. The ladies will keep you safe.'

Boarding her train, Jess met a couple of the soldiers. They were smoking in the corridor. One winked at her; another helped stow her suitcase on the rack, grunting with effort.

'What's in here, sweetheart, paving slabs?'

Her father appeared at the open compartment window.

'Call when you arrive. Let us know you're safe. Got your gas mask?'

Jess tapped the strap over her shoulder. She wished she'd made their last minutes together more loving. It didn't stop her being angry.

Her father was warning her to look out for pickpockets. 'Miss Hillingdon says London's riddled with them. And... dear... you will be careful when it comes to strangers. I couldn't bear to lose another child.'

The break in his voice pierced her, pity flooding in and washing anger away. Her father didn't lie. Charlotte was gone. Charlotte was dead. The letter meant nothing – the date a mistake. Alder Grove was just another of the dramatic flourishes her sister thrived on.

There was still time to jump off—

The train began to move, and steam billowed past the window. Her father walked alongside, lifting his hand for a final wave.

'I love you, Daddy,' she shouted.

What Jess saw in his face shocked her. Not love returned, but something implacable: pride and a refusal to yield.

As her train steamed across the water-veined landscape the sky became a huge, blue canvas. Droves of German bombers cut across it, harried by British fighter planes. Jess hunkered in her seat as dogfights took place overhead.

Incendiaries dropped in clusters, innocent-looking until they hit their targets. The ladies into whose company she'd been forced hid their eyes behind cream net gloves.

One of the British fighters – a Hurricane? – dipped and spurted smoke from a wing. She didn't see it come down but felt it in the shuddering of the window glass. A bend in the track blanked out the last view of home. Today, the bombing had come much closer than at any other time, but Jess was confident the Germans wouldn't waste their fire on a small seaside town. The thought comforted her, though alongside it, another voice whispered that nothing – not even love or childhood memories – were safe now.

Her train pulled into Victoria shortly after three. The heavy bombing of coastal Kent had not reached towards London where everything looked untouched. Jess placed her suitcase in left luggage, and with money in her purse, defied Miss Hillingdon and queued for a taxi.

For the first time in her life she gave a driver a destination: 'Waterloo station, please.'

The cab moved along freely, very little private traffic around. It was Saturday, and the only delays were caused by buses pulling up, or the occasional delivery van stopping to offload. It felt good to stare out of the window and see women in bright dresses with shopping baskets. There weren't many civilian men about, of course. Plenty of soldiers lounging on corners, or in sandbagged doorways. More uniforms than she'd ever seen at home. They must be on leave, she thought, and waiting for the pubs to open.

At Waterloo, she paid the fare and joined a thin tide of travellers heading for the concourse. Overhead, the great clock struck four. The queue was brisk at the ticket desk.

'Third class return to Epsom, please.'

'That's one shilling and sixpence, miss.'

The ease of it unsettled her as she boarded her train. Alder Grove was twelve miles up the line, and by supper time, the riddle would be solved, the lies laid bare. Could it really be so simple?

Getting off at Epsom, Jess waited her turn to pass through

the barrier and have her ticket clipped by a woman in navy serge.

'Hook Road, d'you know it?' Jess leaned forward so the people behind her wouldn't hear. 'I need the hospital.'

'Which one? There's five. Manor, Horton, St Ebba's—?'

'Alder Grove.'

'That one.' Pity flickered. 'Out the forecourt, love, bear left under the railway bridge, then it's a straight walk. Look out for the big chimneys. Fifteen minutes, no more.'

5

Hook Road soon left the town behind, narrowing into a country lane lined with hedges, tangled with traveller's joy and late honeysuckle. Jess saw chimneys, then slate roofs, before the buildings came into view. At first glance it looked like a grand country estate: red-brick mansions looming over rows of accommodation blocks, with water towers and washhouses and great iron gates.

The Horton Cluster.

In Ramsgate library, she'd sat hunched over *Kelly's Directory*, to find out what she could about Alder Grove. The directory gave little other than names and addresses. Only when the librarian dug out a stack of London County Council reports did reality dawn. The Horton Cluster was a ring of asylums built at the turn of the century to ease pressure on London's older madhouses. From the sprawl of buildings Jess could see, there must be hundreds – thousands – of patients confined inside. This was no cosy St Mildred's where she'd been born and where her sister had supposedly been taken in an ambulance. This was a walled city, built to separate the troubled, the difficult, the lost, from the rest of the population.

White steam spooled from a chimney, sharp with the smell of boiled cotton and soap. The idea of Charlotte pacing a room, or lying drugged and forgotten among strangers, was more horrible than that of her being dead.

Jess approached a gate with ALDER GROVE welded into its tracery. She faltered. Surely, you couldn't just walk in.

It seemed you could. A side gate gave to her push. Her shoes crunching on gravel, she trudged up a driveway and climbed the steps to a pillared entrance where she turned the brass doorknob. That yielded too, oiled and smooth. She wiped her feet on the coir mat before walking up to an empty reception desk, her steps echoing off wood panelling. The reception desk had a hotel-style bell, the kind you press with your palm. Jess hovered her hand over it, wondering if she might be accused of trespassing though that fear was nothing to the real one: what she might learn.

She glanced towards the exit. If she fled now, nobody would ever know...

A man came in from a corridor, double doors swinging in his wake. He wore a white coat and had a sheaf of papers tucked under his arm. Seeing Jess, he stopped and frowned, as if she'd materialised out of nowhere. 'Yes?'

Jess opened her mouth and abandoned the speech she had rehearsed on the journey. 'It's my sister. Charlotte Gresham. I'm looking for her.'

'One of our nurses, is she?'

'No – no, she's a—' The word stuck and Jess had almost to prise it out of her throat. 'A patient. I think, anyway.'

The man, a doctor presumably since he'd referred to 'our nurses', gave a short laugh. 'Do you have any idea how many patients we have here? You'd do better to write to the registrar.'

'Does the name not ring a bell?' Jess repeated, 'Charlotte Anne Gresham.'

'Didn't you hear? I treat hundreds, as do my colleagues. We couldn't possibly remember them all.'

The words fell like a dismissal. Coming here was a misjudgement that might cost her dear. It was getting late and she had nowhere yet to stay in London. Why hadn't she brought a photograph of Charlotte along with her? She could have shown it to this man. Instead, she thought back to that morning, staring into Charlotte's wardrobe, mentally refilling it with the clothes Miss Hillingdon had cleared at Father's request. After Charlotte's death, her things had been taken away – only, two pieces had gone missing long before. Jess had noticed their absence on her return from her bleak Christmas exile at Miss Hillingdon's sister's house. A plain black felt hat, and Charlotte's coat. Red as a London bus, tight-waisted, wide-collared, buttons like ripe cherries. A coat cut to flare as its wearer moved – impossible to forget.

'You may not recall Charlotte,' Jess said, 'but you'd remember her coat.' She described it. 'Striking against her black hair. She looked like a duchess in it.'

For a heartbeat she thought she saw recognition, but the doctor looked away. 'As I said, miss – registrar.' With that, he was gone.

Jess made for the door and was grappling with the handle when someone caught her arm. She spun around to see a nurse, a girl younger even than herself, eyes bright with urgency.

'I was in the back office and couldn't help hearing. Red coat, you say, black hair?'

'Her name was Charlotte. Charlotte Gresham. You remember her?' Jess asked, her voice shredded with disbelief. To her disappointment, the nurse shook her head.

'They may have changed her name when they admitted her. They do that, to protect the families.'

'The coat—'

'Yes.' The nurse nodded with absolute conviction. 'Red and smart enough for a duchess, you said. I know that coat.'

'Then tell me' – Jess had to force herself to breathe slowly, not to gabble – 'is she here still?'

The nurse shook her head. 'No. She left. Ran.'

'What – ran away?'

'Reckon so, though they cover that up when it happens. The whisper was, she got out of a window on New Year's Eve, when the staff were having their midnight tipple. I'll never forget her coming in, though, a couple of days after Christmas. It was dark, an atrocious night, freezing rain. She fought. Kicking, shouting, and they had to drag her in. Then she collapsed like a clockwork doll that needs winding up again.'

'She got away, you said. New Year's Eve.' Jess worked it out. 'Three days later.'

'Yes, bless her. God knows where she went. Like I said, the weather was filthy and she didn't have her coat.'

'Didn't take it?'

'No. Nor her hat or shoes. Matron sold them on.'

For a moment, Jess was speechless. 'Sold – for profit?'

'Sold to a dealer. Wait.' The nurse darted off, through a door in the panelling. Jess shifted from foot to foot, fear prickling. Any moment, someone might come in and question her, summon orderlies to remove her. Telephone her father. There was something clandestine and repressive about this place.

The young nurse reappeared, clutching a ledger, which she opened for Jess. 'It records clothes and personal belongings. Anything deemed unsuitable for a patient to keep, they're logged here and passed on. The money goes into the patients' savings accounts, though most of them never get to spend it.' She flipped pages, then pressed her finger to an entry.

Jess read out the number. 'AG/1939/865.'

'That's Alder Grove, year of entry, admission number. But look.' The nurse pointed. 'Hat, black felt, medium brim, pinched crown. Shoes, black court, Cuban heel. Coat, red. No maker's label.'

'Charlotte bought it from Debenham & Freebody,' Jess said. 'My father thought the colour too bright.' Miss Hillingdon had been outright shocked: 'Cardinal red, Charlotte? And your father a Church of England vicar.'

'Maybe she cut the label out,' said the nurse. 'I can tell you where it was sent for sale.'

First, Jess had to know if patient No. 865 was her sister. 'Are names recorded anywhere?'

'Yes, but not in any filing cabinet I can open.' The nurse suddenly glanced to the side and muttered, 'Oh, crumbs.' Footsteps were approaching along the corridor, clipped voices drawing near. 'Here, take this.' The girl tore the page free, thrust it into Jess's hand, and vanished.

Jess hurried out. Sunlight the colour of brandy had brought the hedgerows alive and they thrummed with bird song. Honeysuckle scents in the air warned her that evening was drawing on.

This trip had not yielded proof that Charlotte had been brought here, but the nurse's description of a girl fighting her jailors, then escaping, felt convincing. Charlotte must have known she was going to be put away. Committed to a secure hospital, which was why she'd written the name of the place on that letter. A final, urgent communication.

Jess paused at a field gate and scanned the page the nurse had torn free.

Black hat, shoes, red coat. Buyer: Madame Renée,
Elegant Exchange, Grafton Way, WC1

She had two addresses now. Grafton Way and Fleet Street. London was where she'd find Charlotte and the certainty propelled her back to the station.

The train left on time, rattling out into the Surrey countryside, but soon the rhythm faltered and it slowed to a standstill as the roar of engines swept overhead. Through the grimy glass Jess glimpsed planes banking low, golden sunset outlining their wings. A guard's shout ran down the carriages – 'Take cover' – and everyone bent forward, covering the backs of their heads with their hands. As if that could shield them.

When the all-clear failed to come, the train edged on in jerks, halting in cuttings and under bridges whenever the sky grew loud. The half-hour run to Waterloo turned into a three-hour crawl and by the time the train drew in, darkness had fallen.

Jess had no bed for the night.

6

Charlotte had loved travelling on the London Underground, claiming she could navigate her way with her eyes closed. Jess, a complete novice, found it bewildering and took three wrong trains before managing to board one to Westminster.

She arrived at the Girls' Friendly Society hostel on Francis Street shortly before ten. At least, she thought she had the right place... using a torch whose beam was reduced to meet blackout regulations, she was making an educated guess. She rang a bell, knocked at an unforgiving door. Nobody came.

Frightened now by the prospect of a night in the open, she walked on until her torch picked out the reassuring outline of a policeman. Crossing the road, she asked for directions to Victoria station. It turned out it was only ten minutes' walk.

'Do you happen to know if there's a hotel there?'

'The Grosvenor, very nice, I believe. Good luck, miss.'

Good luck? She had money, so why would she need luck? She would redeem her suitcase and have a porter wheel it to the hotel. An extravagance, just this once.

Left luggage had closed at 8 p.m.

The entrance to the Grosvenor Hotel was on Buckingham

Palace Road, next to the station. A doorman trained a torch on her, its beam dulled by strips of brown muslin, before guiding her inside.

'Watch the curtains, miss.'

She pushed between swathes of thick felt, blinking in the glow of lamps as they fell shut behind her. A clerk in a dark suit looked up from his register.

'Good evening, miss, can I help?'

'A single room, please,' she said, hoping she sounded like someone who stayed in classy hotels as a matter of course.

The man's gaze passed over her. 'Your luggage, miss?'

'Oh, it's at the station. Left luggage was closed when I got there. I'll collect it in the morning.'

The clerk's expression cooled. 'I'm afraid we can't accommodate single ladies without their baggage.'

'Why on earth not?'

'House policy.'

'But my train was slow, and I missed—' She stopped. Charlotte would never have stooped to explanations. She'd have given this uppity clerk a piece of her mind. 'I can pay, if that's what you're worried about,' Jess said, hoping she sounded less daunted than she felt. 'Do you have space or not?'

The answer was succinct. 'No luggage, no room.'

Jess lingered, heat rising in her cheeks, the burn of panic. She couldn't be facing a night outdoors? The clerk had turned away, and in a swift, desperate change of tack, she asked, 'Do you know of another hotel that might take me?'

This time, he gave her a slow once-over and Jess cringed. Message received. A day spent getting in and out of dirty train carriages, walking country roads and London streets had done nothing for her appearance. 'I'm respectable,' she blurted out. 'My father's a vicar.'

'I'm sure he is, dear. And I'm sure you are. Respectable.' The clerk glanced at the school satchel on Jess's shoulder, its straps wound up in the strings of her gas mask. Something approaching sympathy glimmered in his eyes. 'There are places off Vauxhall Bridge Road, if you care to walk.' He reached under his desk and took out a skimpy paper map. 'Try the Arcadia. They take in all sorts.'

As Jess stumbled out, it struck her that Vauxhall Bridge Road might as well be on the moon since she couldn't read a map in pitch darkness. Not unless she held her torch between her teeth. The doorman had vanished, so there was no one to ask. She drifted along empty streets, praying for a policeman. Now and then shadowy figures loomed, slowing as if to size her up, and she hurried on, stumbling on the uneven pavements.

Ahead, a pinprick of light flared, and Jess halted by a deep doorway. In the dim glow she made out a woman. A patterned dress under a moth-eaten fur shrug was doing little to protect bare arms and a goose-pimpled throat. Her hair was set in curls, her mouth painted primal red. A spray of flowers at her breast concealed a miniscule torch. She took Jess's measure and snapped the beam off.

'My patch, sweetheart. Move along.'

'Sorry. I'm... I'm looking for the Arcadia Hotel. D'you know it?'

The woman let a second or two pass. 'Staying there, are you?'

'Hoping to.'

'Got the money? Hotels round here don't come cheap.'

Jess drew back, wishing she'd kept going. Except, this person seemed to know the area. 'Is it near?'

The woman stepped from her niche and slipped an arm around Jess. Squeezed her in a motherly gesture. ''Bout ten minutes' walk if you get a wriggle on. Bottom of the street, left, then left again. You'll see it ahead. Good luck, love.'

'Thanks. You too.'

A dry laugh followed. 'It ain't luck. It's learning the rules of the game and applying them.'

Despite the directions, Jess ended up back at Victoria station. She couldn't keep circling aimlessly. The streets felt unsafe and a blister had come up on her heel. For the first time in her life, she might have to sleep on a bench.

At least the station had a ladies' toilet where she washed her hands and face, combed her hair, and studied her strained reflection in the mirror. The woman in the doorway might once have come to London with hopes and prospects, only to end up like Jess was now. Hungry, thirsty, stranded.

She'd passed a Women's Voluntary Service wagon outside the station, still open for hot tea and buns. Dragging herself there, she joined a queue. When there was just one person ahead of her, she reached down to open her satchel.

How odd... one of the buckles was undone.

She felt inside. Oh no. She dug around frantically, then checked her jacket pockets, but knew before she finished that her purse was missing. Her savings, the two pound notes her father had sent her off with – everything had gone with it.

Leaving the queue, she returned to the ladies' loos and tipped out the contents of the satchel. Her book, notebook, pencil, comb, handkerchief. Pointless. She knew who had taken it, and when.

It ain't luck... it's learning the rules of the game and applying them.

Jess was no longer simply alone in London. She was destitute.

7

'Board a train without a ticket? Certainly not, miss, it's unlawful.' The railway employee Jess had stopped as he strode towards one of the platforms frowned down at her. 'Not without a travel warrant. You won't get one of those without official permission.'

Why hadn't she asked her father to buy her a return fare? She'd been stupidly confident this morning, no idea what lay ahead.

She explained to the railway guard that she was stranded and that her father – the *Reverend* Gresham, she emphasised that – would meet her off the train and pay. She was going to call him, reversing the charges, and ask him to make things right with the stationmaster at Ramsgate. He would do it, course he would. The reproaches would come later.

She wasn't prepared for the guard to say, 'Ramsgate? We're not running civilian trains down to Kent for the foreseeable. Only military ones. It's too dangerous after the hell that broke loose—' Jess's look of blank horror made him pause. 'You don't know? Ramsgate took a hammering. Half the town's rubble.

Miss...?' He caught her arm as she swayed. 'Easy now. I can see it's a shock. But you're safe enough here.'

She wasn't safe here, but that was no longer her concern. 'I have to go home. I *have* to.' If there was even a chance her father, her friends, her old colleagues, were hurt – or worse – she couldn't stay put. 'Are you sure – how d'you know?'

'It's my job to,' the man said succinctly. Seeing the despair in her face, he suggested she try London Bridge, as trains from there used a different line into Kent. 'You might get to Canterbury and a bus in the morning. Would that suit?'

Jess nodded miserably. 'If that's the only way.' She had put her father in harm's way, making him walk her to the station as the bombing started. They'd assumed it was just more of the same, the enemy targeting RAF bases. Maybe overflying the town by accident.

Clearly not and he might have been caught outside, unprotected.

Why Ramsgate, a place of seafront hotels, fishing boats and sandcastles?

The guard offered to put her on the right bus for London Bridge, but without sixpence for the fare, that was no help. Somehow, catching back sobs, she told him.

'There, there. Don't cry. Let's get you started.' Ushering her to a telephone booth, he took some pennies from his pocket. 'Here you go. That should get you through, assuming the phone lines are working.'

Lifting the receiver, Jess held the first penny against the slot, fingers shaking.

'Number, please,' came the operator's voice.

Jess gave the vicarage's telephone number, saying, 'I'm praying the lines aren't down.'

'They were earlier but the chaps fix them pretty fast. Have your coin ready, miss. Connecting you now.'

Far away in Kent, a telephone shrilled. *Answer. Please,*

answer. Forty rings later, Jess hung up. At least she could be sure that the vicarage was still standing, but why wasn't Father answering? He rarely went to bed before eleven, sitting in his study, writing or reading.

The penny rolled out of the slot. Jess repeated the process, dialling 100 and this time asking for St Saviour's church hall.

Two rings later, the call was answered.

'Reverend Gresham speaking.'

'Daddy, oh Daddy, you're there!' In her relief she reverted to her twelve-year-old self. 'Thank heavens you're all right.'

'Yes, I do thank heavens. Today more than ever.' He sounded exhausted. 'Where are you calling from?'

'Victoria station. Oh, Daddy, it's all gone wrong. I couldn't find—' She almost said *Charlotte,* catching the name back. 'I couldn't rouse the Girls' Friendly Society hostel, and they wouldn't let me into the Grosvenor Hotel. I got lost after that and this awful woman...' Wait, was he even listening? A muffled conversation was going on and she imagined him with his palm over the receiver. 'Daddy, are you there? I've only got tuppence left.'

A different voice came on the line. Unwelcome. Bristles on raw skin. 'Miss Hillingdon, please put my father back on.'

'I'm afraid he's had to go, Jessica. Someone important has arrived.'

More important than his stranded daughter? 'Who, the King, the Lord Mayor?'

'This isn't the time for jokes. It's Mr Hodgekiss, the undertaker.'

Jess rocked. She'd persuaded herself that as her father and Miss Hillingdon were safe, so must everyone else be. 'Have people...?' She couldn't bring herself to say it.

'There are many dead, if that's what you mean,' Miss Hillingdon replied tersely. 'It was a sustained strike on the centre of town.'

'But didn't people go to shelter?' For all it was no obvious target, Ramsgate had prepared for war with a network of underground tunnels. People were used to taking cover when the sirens went.

'It all happened too suddenly,' Miss Hillingdon told her. 'Your father and I were lucky to be near the station, or we'd have been caught too.'

'Good. So I am some use.'

Miss Hillingdon either didn't hear or chose not to dignify the remark. 'Our church hall is a temporary mortuary. Your father and I are helping with identification and offering comfort.'

'Then I need to come home,' Jess said. 'To help. Only... I haven't any money.'

'What about the two pounds your father gave you? Don't say he didn't. And as I've said before, indulgence did your sister no good.'

'Indulgence? Anyway, it's none of your business—'

Miss Hillingdon cut in. 'It *is* my business, Jessica. I know what you asked your father this morning, raking up his grief over Charlotte. Shame on you. From now on, I will see to his welfare, his ministry, his peace of mind. He rightly relies on me and I won't see him troubled by your demands.'

For a moment Jess couldn't speak. She'd stepped out of her father's life to seek her own path and had just heard the door slamming behind her. She was on her own. Truly on her own.

Miss Hillingdon's voice came down the line, softly spiteful. 'This is the time for courage, Jessica. And if you have none... too bad.'

A cleaning woman shooed Jess out of the ladies' waiting room where she'd taken shelter.

'Sorry but we don't allow overnights, love.'

The thought of sitting on a hard station bench for hours, under the eyes of patrolling railway policemen, was unendurable. Jess stared at the woman's mop and bucket and it crossed her mind to offer to help in exchange for being allowed to stay.

As if she guessed, the cleaner shook her head.

Jess was crossing the station, her thoughts in a tangle, when the friendly railway guard spotted her.

'No luck, then, miss?'

She was hardly able meet his eye. 'Do you know where I could stay?'

'With no money?' He sucked in a breath. 'Why don't you ask at the WVS van. Those ladies know a thing or two.'

Jess seized the suggestion. She hovered by the tea stall where, a bare hour ago, she'd discovered her purse was gone. The WVS women were packing up, putting teapots in boxes and spoons into empty biscuit tins. One of them looked her way and asked if she was all right.

'Nowhere to stay,' Jess admitted, walking up to the hatch. 'And...' This was hard to say. 'I haven't any money. It got stolen.'

'Rotten luck.' The woman turned to consult her colleague, and the upshot was a cup of tea, the last dregs from a pot – and two Bourbon biscuits. Just as welcome were the directions to a refuge near St Paul's Cathedral.

'Church hall off Carter Lane,' the woman said. 'You'll find other girls there, war workers mostly. It's basic, but safe enough. Tell them Mrs Chadwick sent you.'

Jess went out into the night, confident she'd recognise St Paul's easily enough. A landmark even in the blackout. A beacon of safety.

Yet somehow, it eluded her.

After an hour of solid walking, she spotted the great dome shining like polished pewter under a moon that was one day past full. She aimed straight for it, but a maze of narrow streets drew her away each time she thought she was in touching distance.

And then the dome dropped out of sight, leaving only a line of lightless Georgian houses, their steep roofs silvered by moonlight. It was so bright when the clouds parted, she could read her watch. Surely it couldn't be nearly midnight. Where was she and where was Carter Lane?

Street signs had been removed, a precaution in case of invasion, and soon she was so lost, she abandoned all hope of reaching sanctuary, unless by pure accident.

At last, she saw a wall plaque someone had forgotten to take down. She reached up and traced the name. Gresham Street.

Wondering vaguely at the coincidence, Jess turned down one pitch-dark road and then another. Her heart leaped as she saw another street sign. It began with 'C'.

Colman Street. She could have wept. But hang on... at its far end rose a church tower. That might be the refuge. At any rate, somewhere to rest.

Come on, Jess. A few more yards. Just a few more.

It was a time for courage, and she had that, whatever others might think.

She set her shoulders, aware that it was only her footsteps breaking the seal on the sleeping silence. Then, out of that silence, a sound began to rise. A thin moan that might have been the wind, until it rose to a sustained pitch. *No. Please, no.*

She gazed upwards to where searchlights struck the moon's face. The silhouette of a plane appeared, then vanished, then roared back low.

What was it the prime minister before Mr Churchill had said? *The bomber will always get through.*

It felt as though they were seeking her out in London because she had slipped away from Ramsgate just in time. Jess dropped into a crouch, her hands over her ears. Through the siren's wail came a high-pitched whistle, followed by a blast that threw her off her feet. She lay stunned, her cheek against the cold pavement, until a blinding flash made her sit up. Flames bloomed at the end of the street. The church. The place she'd been making for.

Smoke rolled past. The tower was engulfed.

Every instinct said, *Run!* but her legs were jelly. She pulled herself up somehow, using iron railings for support. They belonged to one of the flat-fronted houses that lined the street, enclosing the shallow well where servants would once have walked down, and coal would be tipped. A set of steps rose towards a door whose brass knocker reflected the flames.

Clutching her satchel, her gas mask, Jess walked up and steadied herself against the door. It swung inward on silent hinges and she stumbled across the threshold, pulling it shut behind her.

For a moment she stood reaching for breath. The fanlight above the door let in enough flickering light for her to see she was in a hallway that ended in a moulded arch and stairs. There was a small table for letters, an umbrella stand, a coat on a hook. It was someone's home. She was trespassing.

And she'd been discovered. A glimmer at the top of the stairs revealed a man. He was descending, holding what looked like a beer bottle with a candle pushed into the neck. Its flame wavered, revealing him in fragments – a shoulder, a cheekbone, the gleam of an eye. He seemed young, perhaps a few years older than she was: lean, wiry, with a narrow face and straight brow. His hair was brown, with a hint of copper that might have been candlelight.

'Who's there? I can see you – who are you?' He peered in her direction.

He'd rolled out of bed, roused by the Armageddon at the end of his street: the round-necked undershirt and pyjama trousers he wore said as much. The drawstring was knotted at his navel. He moved carefully, one hand on the banister rail. Unsteady, as though the blast had caught him as it had her.

'I know you're there.' The voice was not unpleasant. The faint burr in his 'r' told Jess he wasn't a Londoner, though she couldn't place the accent. She opened her mouth to explain that she'd been escaping and that the door had opened on its own, when the house seemed to shudder.

For a heartbeat she thought it was her own fear, some deep instinct warning that she'd walked into danger. The crack that followed was real – a deafening report from above. She looked up, and before she could shout more than 'Watch out!' the ceiling over the stairs came down. The man and his candle vanished in a choking fog of dust.

8

Silence followed, except for the eerie trickling of rubble from a gaping hole above the staircase. Jess edged towards it, coughing violently. Her shins struck something sharp. She bent to feel – it was a splintered lath from the fallen ceiling. Her fumbling hands encountered debris. It was everywhere. The darkness was total.

'Are you all right, can you hear me?' she rasped. She wanted to ask, 'Are you still alive?' but the words stuck. What if he was lying there broken, or already dead? The thought turned her cold. A second shudder seemed to run through the house. *Oh, heavens.* What if the whole structure gave way and buried them both? Nothing in her quiet country life had prepared her for this.

Courage. *If you have any.*

Still coughing, she began to clear the rubble piece by piece. Plaster dust coated her fingers and every shift of weight sent little avalanches sliding. Then her hand brushed something smooth and warm. A foot. He must have fallen and slid to the bottom of the stairs.

'Hello?' she whispered. A faint groan. Thank God.

'I'm going to try to free you,' she said, her voice shaking. She clawed at the rubble with both hands, plaster and grit raining over her shoes. Stopping wasn't an option. He was alive and that was all that mattered.

He was trying to move, to help, and at last he sat up, gasping. Jess felt for one of his arms and gripped it. He shouted in pain.

'Sorry. Can you stand up?'

'Just about.' The words seemed to come through tight teeth. 'Let me grab the stair rail...' A long-drawn-out 'ahh' got him to his feet and he placed his other hand on her shoulder. 'God. Bloody hell.'

Jess couldn't blame him for the outburst. 'Lean on me. Where shall we go, out into the street?'

'Need to sit down. Living room. There.'

Taking as much of his weight as she could, Jess edged sideways until her fingers found a doorframe. She pushed the door open and stepped into darkness, one arm outstretched, until her hand brushed the worn curve of an armchair. He all but fell into it, breath rasping.

'Is it safe to put the light on?' she asked.

'You can try.'

Jess felt along the wall. She found a switch and flicked it. Nothing. 'There doesn't seem to be any power.'

'That bomb will have taken out the overhead line or a substation. It wasn't working upstairs, but I hoped it was the circuit.'

He was speaking in complete sentences now, which steadied her. The fact that he knew how electricity worked was oddly reassuring. It made him seem human and real. 'Is there anyone else up there?' she asked, realising she should have thought about that sooner.

A pause, then: 'No. Just the two of us.'

The words struck her with unexpected force. Alone

together in a ruined house. That simple fact meant she'd broken the solemn assurance she'd given her father, within twelve hours of leaving home. 'Where will I find a candle?' she asked breathlessly.

'Fireplace. Other side of the room. There's a lamp and should be matches nearby. I hope you've a strong stomach.'

'For the oil lamp?'

His laugh was a snatch of breath. 'Me. I'm not pretty.'

'We're neither of us looking our best,' she said lightly.

'Not what I mean.'

Something in his tone made her stomach tighten. In the minutes it took to find the lamp and coax the wick to life, Jess steeled herself. *Not pretty* had sounded like classic British understatement. What was she about to see?

As the light spread, the room took shape – long, narrow, divided by double doors pinned back. Green wallpaper, a dark oak table with its leaves folded down, a piano with candle sconces. An empty birdcage. Oddly old-fashioned for a man his age. Someone else had made this a home once.

And now she had no excuse but to look at him.

He sat in a velvet armchair, his head bent forward, and he seemed to be clawing at his scalp. For a moment, she thought he was in unbearable pain. Only when she forced herself closer did she realise he was combing the muck from his hair with his fingers. Fingers that were vivid with blood.

He lifted his head and she caught her breath. Beneath the dust, raw burns made a tracery down the left side of his face and neck, fading into the fabric of his vest. A thin line of blood ran from his brow to his chin and dripped, scarlet, onto his chest. Jess's mind scrambled for something to say. Anything. Under the mat of brown hair lay a deep gash to the scalp. That was the source of the blood. Panic fluttered. A handful of school first-aid lessons hadn't prepared her for this.

As if he scented her fear, he looked up and she discovered

he had hazel eyes, framed by dark lashes. If he was unsettled by her reaction, he wasn't showing it.

'I did warn you.'

'You need a hospital,' Jess said tightly.

'How, with an air raid on?'

He probably thought she was squeamish, but that wasn't it. Since finding Charlotte lying in a pool of blood, Jess had come to doubt her own judgement in a crisis. Miss Hillingdon had seen straight through her: no courage, no backbone. Yet even as she quailed inside, a sliver of resolve took over. Fate – or plain bad luck – had brought her here, and this man deserved more than her paralysis. 'Should I fetch water? Try to clean you up?'

He gave a grunt she took for yes.

'I'll have to take the lamp,' she said apologetically. 'Leave you in the dark. I'm sorry.'

'Don't be. What's your name?'

'Jess. Well – Jessica.'

'Jessica what?'

She could almost see her father grimly shaking his head. Not the sort of conversation a decent girl had at midnight with a stranger. She said it anyway.

'Gresham,' the young man repeated. 'Like the street?'

'I only discovered that tonight. What's yours?'

'Rafael Taverner. Rafe to friends. Not that I have so many now.' His chin dipped, and Jess, after a moment's hesitation, picked up the lamp and went.

Squeezing past the rubble at the base of the stairs, she found a long passage, which took her through a small parlour where a daybed stood ready. Eying tartan blankets and plumped pillows, she imagined sinking down on it. Oh, if only…

The kitchen was unexpectedly tidy, even the breadboard brushed clean and propped against the upstand. A search turned up a large tin bowl, which she held under the tap. Water sputtered out in a thin stream, the pipes coughing. She swirled a piece of carbolic soap through it until the sharp, medicinal smell told her it was enough. She didn't want to sting that raw face. He *really* needed a hospital. She hadn't been exaggerating. But for now, she was all he had. Poor man.

Carrying her soapy water back to the living room, she found the armchair empty. 'Rafe – Rafael? Mr Taverner?'

A movement drew her eye to the far end of the room. He was fastening the shutters.

'St Giles has gone,' he muttered, turning towards her.

'The church at the end of the road? I was heading there. If I'd been a few minutes earlier…'

'Then you're lucky.' He took a step towards her, then caught the edge of the table as his balance faltered. Jess hurried to him, careful not to spill the water.

'You should have stayed where you were,' she said, setting the bowl down. She eased him onto a dining chair, then pulled out one for herself, sitting with her knees angled to the side. She could hear the distant clang of fire engines and flinched as another bomb landed somewhere distant. 'I wish I knew where they're falling,' she muttered. 'Then I'd know whether or not to be terrified.'

'They've switched to the other side of the river,' Rafe told her. 'Probably jettisoning what they've got left before they fly home.'

'The planes? I wish they'd hurry up, then. Or realise what they're doing and give up.'

He didn't answer. The words had sounded childish the moment they left her lips. Of course the Germans wouldn't give up. They wanted to invade. A creak somewhere above her head sounded like the second before a collapse. 'Will the house fall down?' she asked. She wouldn't forget how the stairwell had dropped away before her eyes.

'Probably,' Rafe said.

'What – you mean it will?'

'Another near miss and it might. These Georgian town-houses were built in a hurry for fashionable people on a budget. Corners cut, literally so.'

'Then we ought to get out. Do you have anywhere else to go?'

'Yes.'

'Where?'

He looked at her, his injured features unreadable. 'War.'

Jess dropped a wad of lint she'd found in a kitchen cupboard into her bowl, lifted it out and wrung it dry.

Rafe flinched at the smell. 'God, coal-tar soap.'

'It's antiseptic.'

'I know. The Navy runs on it.'

Ah, made sense. She saw that his side-hair had been cropped short not so long ago. It was growing out faster at the top. The undamaged side of his face had a windburned look. Something awful had happened to the other side. 'Is that where you were before... on a ship?'

'Uh-huh.'

Was that a way of telling her to shut up? She didn't want to pry. Or offend him.

He withstood her scrutiny while his eyes, not brown, not green, held hers with an intensity that made Jess conscious of each beat of her heart.

'Are you going to sit there waving that lint at me all night?'

'Sorry. Deep breath.' She shifted his hair where the blood pooled and gently cleaned a gash an inch in length. 'Lean forward.' She asked him to hold the bowl under his chin before trickling water over the cut to flush out the grit, stopping only when he choked.

'Swallowed some,' he muttered. 'Carry on.'

'I've finished that bit. Let's do your face.'

She started on the uninjured side, discovering a faint, silvery scar that followed the line of his cheekbone. After returning to the kitchen to change the water and rinse her cloth, she gave her attention to the raw-looking side.

'It looks sore,' she said. 'What...'

'Flash burn,' he answered. 'Yes. Hurts like hell and having a load of masonry falling on me hasn't exactly helped.'

She waited for him to explain 'flash burn' but he seemed to have said all he meant to. As lightly as she could, she mopped away the blood and dirt. 'I hope you got first aid when it happened,' she said. 'Cold water to stop the burn penetrating.' She remembered learning that.

'There was plenty of cold water about, don't you worry. After I was rescued, I was in hospital for over a month. I've been discharged.'

'To live alone in an unstable house?' She paused, surprised at her scolding tone. She must not become Miss Hillingdon. 'Not my business. Apologies.'

'Accepted. I was recovering well, till this.'

Jess lifted the lamp to study her handiwork. The burns extended over his shoulder, upper arm and around the back of his neck. Probably his back too. He needed proper nursing, or these half-healed injuries would get infected. She said as much.

Rafe held her gaze, saying slowly, 'You have eyes dark as the Silent Pool, Jessica. Wise eyes.'

That was the sort of thing men said when they couldn't come up with anything better.

'I don't feel very wise.' With dry lint, she blotted his face.

He took it from her. 'What are you doing out, so late?'

'I got lost,' she said. 'I've come to London to work but couldn't find my lodgings.' She wasn't going to admit to being robbed and homeless.

Rafe asked what she'd come to do.

'A government job. Lowest rung.'

'Don't you have to be at least eighteen for the Civil Service?'

'I'm nineteen. Emergency intake, Section C.' He'd taken her for younger. People did. Alerted by the sounds of shouting, Jess went to the window and put her ear to the shutter. Whoever was outside, and whatever they were telling each other, was lost under the clang of an emergency vehicle and the distant roar of flames. Rafe joined her, moving hesitantly. He brought the lamp.

'Sounds like the fire tenders are attacking the blaze from this side now,' he said. 'There's an ambulance pulling up so there may be casualties. That Heinkel was way off target.'

He even knew what kind of plane it was. Jess was impressed he could tell so much from random noises. To her, it was simply a cacophony. Perhaps it was shock catching up with her, but a wave of faintness passed over her.

Rafe extinguished the lamp so he could open the shutters without showing an illegal light.

Thinking he meant to lean out, she raised the window sash. Smoke rolled in, acrid and heavy.

Rafe shut the window with his good arm, then steadied her as she sagged into a chair. 'That wasn't clever,' he said. 'I wanted to see if we needed to evacuate. A hand on the glass would have been enough.' His touch lingered a moment on her shoulder. The touch of someone who knew what fear felt like.

'Do we? Need to go, I mean.' She felt stupid. Unfit for this new existence.

'Not now. The fire isn't spreading this way. The wind's in the opposite direction and to my knowledge, there are no fuel dumps or gunpowder warehouses close by.'

'There'd better not be.' Jess hadn't imagined anything like that. 'Was St Giles a lovely church?'

'St Giles-without-Cripplegate. Eight hundred years of history destroyed in a matter of minutes. Are you all right, did you swallow smoke? It's horrible if it gets into your lungs, as I know.'

'I'm fine.' She dislodged his hand from her arm. Sympathy *and* physical contact was a step too far.

'Fine, you say. There's something of the lost soul about you, little Jess. You creep in from the midnight dark, like a shadow. Well, not a shadow exactly, since I heard you. I was coming down to challenge you when the ceiling fell.'

'That wasn't my fault.'

'If you hadn't walked in, I wouldn't have been on the stairs at the wrong moment.'

'You'd have been trapped on the first floor with the stairs blocked.'

He gave a short, raspy laugh. 'My guardian angel, is that what you're saying?'

She shook her head. 'Hardly angelic. Not much good at all except—' She broke off.

'Except?' His voice had a natural warmth. Odd, to feel kinship with a stranger, though she told herself it was because he'd expressed interest. Rare, in her experience, and tempting her to open her heart.

'What I mean is, I'm not good at much except being loyal.'

'That's a talent and not universal. Who are you loyal to?'

'Someone I love. Someone who's missing.'

'Ah.' His voice dropped. 'Missing believed dead or missing in action?'

'Missing. That's all.'

'Then you have my heartfelt sympathy.'

He was a gentleman; he knew what to say, how to say it. It spurred her to a confidence. 'It's hard when keeping faith with one person means deceiving another.'

His manner shifted, cool suspicion creeping in. 'You're saying you've left one man for another?'

'No, it's not at all like that. No man has ever wanted me; they never get past the front door.' The words landed awkwardly and Rafe turned away, as if uncertain what to make of her candour.

'The fire crew will be sucking everything out of the mains, which means the water pressure will drop to zero in a minute,' he said. 'Why don't you make us a drink?'

'A cup of tea?' Only then did she realise why she'd almost fainted earlier. She was famished.

'Can't boil a kettle, I'm afraid,' Rafe answered. 'I turned the gas off when I arrived, as a precaution. There's barley water in the kitchen cupboard, and biscuits too. Do you mind? It takes me ages to do anything.' He relit the lamp and handed it to her, then closed the shutters in slow movements.

In the kitchen, Jess leaned her hands on the edge of the sink. What had possessed her, confessing she'd never been loved? It wasn't even true. A few years ago, she'd met a boy who walked the same stretch of beach each morning before work. For a week or two they'd met at the same spot, as if by accident, to stroll and talk about nothing much at all. She had certainly sipped at love – the butterflies in the stomach, the flutter of pleasure when she saw the familiar pale jacket and cap in the distance. And the wrench when one day he wasn't there and never was again. Charlotte would have called it a crush. Yet it had shown Jess she was capable of falling for someone, of groping towards passion. Perhaps 'grope' was the wrong word as they'd done no more than hold hands. She'd still not been kissed nor ever had a Valentine's card.

No wonder she'd embarrassed Rafe Taverner, who must think her gauche and unsophisticated. She found two bottles of barley water in a larder cupboard, different flavours, and a tin of arrowroot biscuits. She lingered after she'd put tumblers on a tray because she had no idea what she ought to do next. Share a snack, then leave? The prospect of venturing back into smoke and danger was worse than staying with a man she knew nothing of.

'Sorry I took so long,' she said as she opened the sitting room door with her foot. 'I couldn't decide between lemon or lime. I hope—'

The room felt thick with silence. She turned slowly around. He wasn't there.

Putting down the tray, carrying only the lamp, she went back into the passage. 'Rafe?' Her voice rose then dropped flat, deadened by the debris on the stairs. 'Rafe, are you there?'

She didn't expect him to reply.

He had gone.

9

GRACE

Sunday, 25 August 1940

At six o'clock, Grace stepped into a London morning thick with smoke and brick dust. She had one simple aim: find the money to keep the roof over her family's head and still make it to work on time. To the west, the skyline glowed red where a bomb had fallen in the night. London's first.

She'd woken around midnight to the roar of a plane. Moments later, the eerie cry of the air raid sirens followed by a sound like the earth tearing open. The blast had come as she stumbled to a window, pulling back the blackout blinds to see. A huge red rose of a detonation had flowered somewhere within the City's square mile. The window glass, and the thin walls of the Whitechapel flat, had shuddered though the impact was maybe a mile away. She stood, her face and throat bathed in moonlight, thinking, *The bombers have finally come.* London had flinched.

On Whitechapel Road, she boarded the Number 8 bus, moving to the front of the lower deck where the air was generally less thick with cigarette smoke. Other passengers looked up and smiled, nodding hello, though their smiles fell once they saw that Grace Whelan, Mary's girl, sported a nasty-looking black eye. Grace was a familiar face in her nurse's blue, someone from their own streets, but even so, they looked away. If they had their suspicions it was her brother Cormac who'd landed that Victoria plum on her, they weren't going to say.

Finding a seat, Grace turned her face to the window. The chatter started up again as the bus pulled away and the same refrain was on everybody's lips.

What a night. London's properly copped it this time.

No more phoney war.

Let's hope it don't get worse, else we can forget a decent night's sleep.

That'll be the least of it, ducks. Spent a night in a public shelter yet?

The conductress moved up the bus, winding out tickets, offering words of comfort. 'We'll get you to work, my loves, don't you fret. Nothing stops a London bus.'

She spoke too soon. As the dome of St Paul's came into view, they were brought to a halt and after a brisk conversation with an air raid warden, the driver leaned round and called out, 'All this part's closed off. Cripplegate took a hit last night.'

After reversing some distance, the bus diverted down narrow Carter Lane before dipping down toward Blackfriars. The river opened up before them, a wide, pink ribbon in the sunrise. They turned up towards Ludgate Hill, on to Fleet Street where their driver called out, 'Next stop, the Strand. Anyone for Trafalgar or Piccadilly, you'll have to hoof it from there.'

Grace got out, glad to feel solid ground under her feet. It might have been all those sharp turns, but she'd started feeling sick... course, it could have been because all she'd had that morning was a cup of black tea. No food in the house.

Or were her nerves getting ready for what she was about to do?

Last night, listening to the thud of guns and the distant clang of fire engines, her decision to call in at Smith's Court, Soho, this morning had seemed reasonable. Now? She touched her sore eye. Cormac owed her but would he see it that way?

The money she wanted from him wasn't for her but that wouldn't mean much if she caught him in a bad mood. Walking through Covent Garden, crossing Leicester Square, she reflected that if September's rent had still been in the tin where it should be – if her mother hadn't spent it on a bottle of gin – she could be heading straight to work with nothing worse to look forward to than a day on her feet, nursing a difficult patient. Mam and Ricky were afraid the landlord would throw them out. Grace knew darn well he would, since it wasn't the first time they'd been late paying. Nor the second or third either.

When she reached Brewer Street, the dread of seeing her brother had built to such a pitch, it brought on a headache. She drew breath at the mouth of Smith's Court. Cormac lived somewhere down there – above a club, that was all she knew. The alley was narrow, its cobbles littered with cigarette ends. An odd choice for a man who dressed sharply and polished his shoes to a shine, but perhaps that was the point. You had to know where to find Smith's Court and if you didn't, you wouldn't find him.

Stepping over litter and broken bottles, trying not to inhale through her nose, Grace made her way to a brown door. A tarnished plaque was hard to read in the gloom, but she ran her finger along the lettering and leaned close.

THE RING AND RABBIT CLUB.

A rabbit wearing boxing gloves was etched under the name. This felt like the right sort of burrow for a man who was quick with his fists.

On her second knock, bolts scraped back and the door opened to reveal a woman in a pink dressing gown that strained across a generous bosom. She blinked at Grace, giving the impression that daylight, and a knock at the door, had come far too early. Gemstones – as red as the hair wound around a stack of curlers under a net – flashed as she pulled her belt tighter.

'What is it?' She noted Grace's uniform, grey cape, the work bag and neatly braided hair. 'I don't think anyone's been took ill.'

The lady of the house, thought Grace. *House with a capital 'H' if I'm not mistaken.* 'They haven't,' she said. 'Been taken ill, I mean. I'm looking for Cormac Whelan.'

'What d'you want with him?' The tone was curious, not hostile, and the eyes that travelled over Grace held a measure of kindness. 'You ain't his usual sort. He's got a girl on the leash at the moment anyway.' The woman leaned forward, chins wobbling, the better to see Grace's black eye. 'Who put that shiner on you, then? Left side... That's a wallop from a right-hander.'

'Cormac. He did it.'

'No! You must have found him in a rotten mood...' A pause, a knowing wink. 'Or were you a naughty girl?'

'He's my brother, if you must know. Sorry – but I need to see him urgently.'

The woman gaped a little. 'His sister? I knew he had one—'

'He has two,' Grace cut in. 'I'm the one he doesn't get on with.'

'Not sure you ought to wake him then.' The woman glanced behind her. 'He's upstairs, dead to the world, I shouldn't wonder. Didn't roll in till God knows what time. Can't it wait?'

'No. I've got to get to work and won't be off till seven tonight, if I'm lucky.'

'All right. Suit yourself.' The tone suggested that Grace was barmy. 'Upstairs, second on the right.'

Grace murmured her thanks and stepped inside. The woman followed her to the foot of the stairs. 'Mind yourself.'

'I'm fine,' Grace said, though when the woman left her to it, shutting doors behind her, she slipped off her shoes and crept the rest of the way in her stockings, every muscle braced. She found Cormac's room, recognising the pinstripe jacket draped over a chair. He'd been wearing it three nights ago when he lumped her.

Silently, she put down her shoes and entered. The room was semi-dark, a mothy-looking blackout curtain dragged across the window. Little enough light would come in at the best of times, but she could tell that the bed was occupied. Grace made out a man's shape. He was lying on his front, one arm stretched across the width of the bed, the other crooked under his brow. Coal dark hair, a naked back. Glistening. Hair grease and sweat. The room was airless and too warm.

Grace held her breath and listened. The even rasp, in and out, confirmed what she'd been told. The night owl was catching up on sleep.

Relieved but also guilty at what she was about to do, Grace slid her hand inside the jacket. Found the hidden pocket. Her fingers met the edge of a wallet... and something else, smooth and tapering – ouch!

She tore her hand free, sucking the blood from the end of a finger.

Expecting to see Cormac roll over to confront her, she counted her heartbeats until it was obvious there was no change in the pattern of his breathing. With exquisite care she reached once more into the pocket and eased out the wallet. She opened it.

Lord above, what a wad; business must be booming. Grace peeled off five one-pound notes.

A movement brought her head up. The bed covers were moving, someone stirring. Someone who, until this moment, had been hidden, pushed to the edge of the mattress by Cormac's spreadeagle.

The figure sat up. It was a girl, dark-haired, clutching a sheet to her chest. So young.

For a long second, they stared at each other. Then Grace put a finger to her lips.

Shh.

'Who are you?' The girl shaped the words, barely above a whisper. Fear flickered as her gaze fell to the wallet Grace still held.

Grace replaced it, hesitated, then drew out the thing that had cut her finger. Cormac's little secret. She carried it over to the girl's side of the bed, hunkering down so their eyes were level. The girl was older than she'd first supposed. Twenty-two or -three? Lost-soul eyes in a pale face made her seem childlike. She was thin, her cheeks hollow. Grace remembered what the woman downstairs had said:

...got a girl on the leash at the moment.

Did this waif have any idea what she was up against?

'You should go,' Grace muttered in the girl's ear and held up the object. It was the handle of a carving fork filed to fit nicely in the palm of a hand, its tip fitted with a razor blade. 'He doesn't carry this for fun.'

Dark hair without a scrap of curl in it swung as the girl shook her head. 'I know, but I can't. I haven't anywhere.'

'Even so.' Grace looked across at her brother, at the muscular shoulders tapering to a narrow waist, the knuckles of his spine twitching as he chased down some dream alley. 'Leave while he's spark out.'

The girl glanced fearfully at the sleeping man beside her. 'I don't know... he helped me when I had nobody.'

'He's still a bad apple.' Grace straightened up and retreated. She slipped the weapon back into Cormac's pocket and left.

She'd done what she came to do, and the girl would have to choose her own path.

Out again in the daylight, Grace walked off, like a prisoner who's shimmied out between the bars and knows the alarm will go off in one minute. She reached Regent Street which, on any other day, would have swarmed with office workers and shop girls hurrying to start their day. But it was Sunday, and except for a road sweeper and a few early window shoppers, she was the only pedestrian. She kept up her pace, hardly glancing at the storefronts, or the goods behind sandbags and gum-taped windows. London had never felt so dangerous as now and not only because a German bomber had got through last night. Five stolen pounds smouldered in her pocket.

Cutting across Grosvenor Square towards Upper Brook Street, where her ailing charge would be waiting, watch in hand, temper ticking, Grace thought of the waif with the penny-black eyes.

The girl had seen her steal. Would she blab?

Time would tell.

Grace knocked at the grand front door of Ventnor House and waited for the butler to admit her. Her life wasn't easy, not by a long stretch, but at least she wasn't alone in London, with no one to turn to but Cormac Whelan.

God help any girl in that state.

10

JESS

She'd slept on the daybed, wrapped in the plaid blanket and woken with no idea where she was or what time it might be. Her ears were ringing from the detonation that had sent her sprawling last night. The window she peered out of was thick with ash and smuts and offered no clues.

A bomb had fallen. A church had been hit.

The moment Jess stumbled into the pile of debris at the foot of the stairs, details rushed back.

Colman Street. Rafe Taverner.

She'd made him something to drink, returned to find him gone. Two questions – why and where – sat like lumps in her throat. Only he could say.

After a wash at the kitchen sink and two glasses of barley water, she packed some biscuits into her pocket and found her satchel and gas mask. Time to go. She had to survive another day and night without money or lodgings.

At the front door, she discovered three pound notes on the mat and at first assumed Rafe had dropped them as he left. He must have been in a hurry. But when she bent to pick them up, she saw her mistake. They hadn't been left; they'd been placed. For her.

Along the edge of one, in neat, slanted writing:

Pay me back when you can. Good luck with your search. R.

Jess wept. A miracle – yet she was angry. What kind of girl did he take her for? When she stepped out into the new dawn, she couldn't close the front door properly. A closer look showed that somebody had forced it quite recently. Rafe, perhaps. Maybe he was as much a vagrant as she was. In which case, the gift of money likely came from the good side of his heart. She would keep it, use it and pay him back if ever she could.

Jess began to walk. The air smelled of cinders and hot pennies, which must be molten lead from the church roof.

By eight o'clock, she'd found her way back to Victoria. Breaking into a pound note, she bought breakfast at the station café and redeemed her suitcase from left luggage. Half-carrying, half-dragging it the mile or so to Westminster, a blister opened up on her palm. It hurt to knock at the door of the Girls' Friendly Society, even more so when nobody came. She tried the door but it was locked.

Course it was. It was Sunday. As a Christian organisation, the boarders would be attending church service. Jess tried one last time, and a moment later, the door opened. A woman wearing a matron's uniform peered at her.

'May I help?'

Jess explained her predicament. She was starting a job with the Ministry of Information in the morning and needed a room here. 'I arrived rather late yesterday,' she said, and mentioned the bombing in Ramsgate, expecting it would soften the matron's expression. 'I'm a society member,' she added, 'and I wrote a few days ago, but got no response.'

'Because we're run off our feet.'

'I understand, but I need to stay until I sort some other accommodation. A couple of weeks, maybe?'

'Weeks?' From the matron's tone, Jess might have said 'For the duration'. 'We've got twenty girls more than we've beds for. They're on mattresses on the floor. Everyone and their sister is coming to work in London so unless you're on my list as having booked, or have a formal letter from your local chapter—'

'I'm with the Ramsgate branch,' Jess said hastily. 'You know we were bombed yesterday?' Yes, she was repeating herself, but if the only way in was to evoke pity, she'd do it.

The matron asked to see her membership card.

'I'm afraid I haven't got it with me.' The card been in her purse and was now in the possession of the streetwalker who'd robbed her.

'National Registration card, ration book, then?' the matron asked impatiently.

'Yes, course.' Jess fumbled at the straps of her satchel. She'd tucked those into an inner pocket. Only they weren't there.

She took out the book she'd brought to read on the train, her bookmark and the money from Rafe. Shaking the bag upside down, the stub of her train ticket to London fluttered to the pavement.

She couldn't have lost her identity documents too. Life couldn't be that cruel.

'You realise, you're legally obliged to carry ID at all times?' Matron was growing visibly impatient.

Jess nodded distractedly. She needed to think... only, a malicious hand was scribbling over her thoughts, like a toddler with a crayon. 'I had them this morning.'

Matron's patience ran out. 'I cannot admit you without seeing your identity papers and as I said, we're chocka. Come back in a week if you can't find anywhere suitable.'

A week? What was she supposed to do, bed down on a park bench? 'Wait.' Jess's mind cleared. 'I've just thought...'

At left luggage, she'd displayed her National Registration card to the man behind the counter. Her ration card was with it, as they were bound with a rubber band. She must have left them. 'Could I please use the telephone?'

'Certainly not. This is a hostel, not the GPO.' Matron shut the door.

It felt crueller even than Miss Hillingdon's rebuke on the telephone. Even more than Rafe Taverner's vanishing.

Nobody wants you, Jessica Gresham. You're no use to God nor man.

She couldn't start at the Ministry of Information without her ID, so it was back to Victoria. Unable to face dragging her suitcase all that way, she calculated how long Rafe's loan would last if she took another taxi. Friday was the month's end and hopefully, she'd get her first wages then. So perhaps she could treat herself again... It was hardly going to become a habit.

The absence of any available black cabs in Westminster made the decision for her. She would have to take the Underground. As she walked down the stairs, the stink of disinfectant and warm brake dust heightened her sense of rejection. This was a place where people moved quickly on, where you might stumble or fall and not be seen. Where would she sleep tonight now that the Girls' Friendly had failed to live up to its name? She was already bone weary. So much so, she fulfilled her own prediction, misjudging the last stair, her suitcase thumping onto the concrete passageway.

Other travellers shot glances at her.

'Oops, they'll think you're tipsy. On Sunday morning, too.' Charlotte's voice came into her head for the first time since leaving home. 'You've got in a muddle but be thankful you're homeless in summer. You can't imagine what London's like in the depths of winter.'

Go away, Jess silently projected. *You're not real. I only hear you because it stops me accepting that you're dead.*

'Am I, though? I could be around the next corner. That's why you're here. Because Father won't say which.'

Jess hefted her suitcase, then put it down because of the pain in her hand. This talking to herself had to stop. 'I'm tired. In shock. You're not real.'

'Doesn't make me the *late* Charlotte, does is? If I'm dead and buried, where's my grave?'

'Father explained.'

'Oh, that's right. The convenient public pit next to the hospital. Tell me this. How did I write a letter two days after I expired in an ambulance?'

Jess put her hands to her ears. 'You wrote it before you got ill and post-dated it.' Why had it taken so long to arrive at the most rational explanation? 'You're gone, Charlotte, and I'm in this fix because I couldn't accept it. Now, leave me alone.'

Lugging her suitcase over to a large map of the Underground, Jess plotted her route to Victoria. Two stops, westbound. Finding the platform and slumping on a bench, her eyes closed. A moment's doze till her train came in...

Next thing she knew, somebody was touching her face. Lifting her chin.

A man. A total stranger, mid-twenties, in a tobacco-brown pinstripe suit. Smart. Striking dark hair, slicked back off his forehead. Eyes stridently blue under black brows. Jess's first thought was that he was handsome. Strong-jawed, with a street toughness beneath the white collar and silk tie. His fingers had a possessive weight, yet when he spoke, his tone was almost gentle, as if he knew he frightened her.

'Got you, sweetheart. That note you let me wake up to... what was that about?'

The voice had an Irish lilt, flattened and scraped thin by London.

'I didn't leave any note,' Jess stammered.

'Exactly.' His tone hardened. 'Not a word. Off like a cat. What's going on, what do I need to know, Charlotte?'

Jess screamed and knocked his hands away. 'Leave me alone or I'll find a policeman.' Was her mind playing tricks? She lurched to her feet but her suitcase was in the way. She couldn't leave it.

'All right, all right.' He spread his hands, scarred knuckles catching the light. 'I know I've got a side to me, but we can talk, can't we? I was there when you needed me. Don't say I wasn't. Why did you leave?'

A rumble and a blast of warm air announced the train. But was it her saviour or a trap? He'd follow her on board. Grabbing her things, she hoisted the suitcase with Titanic effort and hurried along the platform, daring him to come after her.

He did, following a pace behind, murmuring, 'Charlotte, talk to me.'

'I don't know you.'

'Oh, really? I'm Cormac Whelan, the fool who put clothes on your back and kept you from the gutter on the coldest night of the year.'

The train pulled in. A group of workmen stepping off – shovels and picks on their shoulders – gave her precious seconds. She reached the far end of the platform, stumbled into an empty carriage, and slammed the door. If the train didn't move now, she was done for.

Frozen, she watched the man striding along, peering into windows. The guard's whistle sliced through the Sunday quiet. The carriage jerked. Wheels shrieked against the rails as the train began to move slowly. The door was wrenched open.

'Charlotte!' He was coming in. 'You don't do this to me!'

'Oi! Stand clear there!' The guard's shout cracked like gunfire, followed by a fierce blast of the whistle. The brakes bit. The carriage jolted to a stop. Jess was thrown forward, clutching the metal pole to keep from falling. For a heartbeat, she thought her pursuer would jump aboard anyway, but he stepped back. The guard slammed the door, twisted the handle home, and gave two sharp blasts of his whistle.

'All clear to depart!'

As the train entered the dark throat of the tunnel, Jess pressed a hand to her chest. Her pulse hammered so violently she thought she might faint. That face, those blue, burning eyes. They were branded on her own.

Even when they pulled in at the next station, St James's, she half-expected him to be waiting. Cormac Whelan. Had Charlotte ever mentioned that name? She thought not.

He'd shouted a last message as the train pulled away: 'London's big, but you can't hide from me.'

Jess collapsed onto a seat, drained and boneless. A complete stranger had seen her and not hesitated. He'd spoken her sister's name with tenderness and hate.

If it was recognition, then Charlotte was alive. She'd escaped from Alder Grove and made it to London.

But what danger was she running from now and would it engulf Jess too?

11

At Victoria station, the man at left luggage recognised her at once.

'Good thing it's Sunday, miss,' he said, returning her documents. 'On a weekday I'd have passed these to a bobby. Not so many about today. You're wanting to dock your case again?'

He leaned over the counter, eyeing the suitcase. He knew how heavy it was, but his look went further, as if he felt the raw sting of her blisters.

'I think so,' she said, thinking how quickly you spent money in London. 'Maybe till Tuesday evening.'

'Very good. We'll keep it safe till then.'

At the station newsstand, she bought a sixpenny map and sat on a bench, working out where she must go tomorrow. Senate House, where she'd be working, was on the London University campus. Malet Street, off Gower Street. Her job in Censorship loomed like an exam she hadn't studied for. But the hours before, they were the problem. No bed, no room, no friends. The house on Colman Street might still be open, but what if someone reported her as a trespasser? She couldn't face the Girls' Friendly hostel again – not another refusal. Home was locked against her. What about the refuge on Carter Lane, the one the WVS lady had mentioned? Maybe, except it lay in the shadow of St Paul's, an easy, accidental target if another bomb fell on the City.

In the end, she spent most of the night shivering on a bench in the station concourse beside two coughing women, warming her hands on a cup of tea from the WVS team. The volunteers recognised her and this time, their kindness was touched with dismissal. The first night they'd seen a stranded girl. The second time, she resembled a problem that hadn't gone away.

At 4 a.m., a railway official prodded her and her companions awake.

'Come on now, ladies. No loitering.'

Jess tramped the dark streets until the first streak of dawn, when it felt safe to sneak back. At seven, she was first in line at the station café. Tea and jam sandwiches. She waited by the left luggage office to reclaim a few things from her suitcase – her coat, clean clothes, hand cream and a comb. In the ladies' toilets, she tidied herself and put on her blue velvet Alice band to keep her hair off her face. With that in place, she looked like Jess again and not like Charlotte.

She'd survived her second night in the capital. Feeling a tiny bit proud despite her stiff muscles and tired, dry eyes, she bought a postcard of the River Thames. On the back, she wrote:

Dear Father, sorry if I worried you with my call. I'm relieved you're doing all you can to help those who need it at home. I am fine, having moved into a shared dormitory at the Girls' Friendly. My welcome dinner was potato and cheese pie. It's fun, being in company. I'll write again soon but you're not to give me a second thought. Yours, Jessica

She didn't post it, the untruths so blatant, any self-respecting post box might spit it out.

It was Monday, 26 August and Jess crossed the river for her first day as a civil servant. At 8.29 a.m. she was outside Senate House, the London branch of the Ministry of Information. *Oh, the irony,* she thought, *for someone steeped in half-truths and evasions.*

Jess and the other new recruits were handed over to a clerical officer, Miss Cartwright. Tall and reed-thin, like a plant forced to grow without sunlight, she wore spectacles that squeezed her nose to the point of a sneeze. She ticked their names off on a clipboard before announcing, 'Your induction begins now. Afterwards, you will be bound by the Civil Service code. If anyone feels unable to proceed, leave the building at once.'

Nobody moved.

'Good. Then, follow me, please.'

As they trailed Miss Cartwright down strip-lit corridors, a girl Jess's age nudged her and whispered, 'Like school, isn't it? I wonder who'll be the first to tie that one's shoelaces together. I dare you.'

Jess stiffened. This job was her lifeline. The last thing she needed was to be drawn into larks and escapades. 'I don't like pranks,' she muttered.

'Suit yourself.' The girl fell back into step beside someone else. A muffled giggle followed.

They were escorted to a windowless room where they sat down to a lecture. Jess hardly heard a word. It was so airless, she could barely keep her eyes open.

'We are the Postal and Cable Censorship Office,' Miss Cartwright intoned. 'Censor clerks in Section C, which you have joined, are the first line of defence in the battle against loose talk, hostile agents and sabotage.' Miss Cartwright did, finally, sneeze. Twice. She dabbed her nose. 'We can't read every letter, so we take random samples from the sorting office.

Your job is to examine those letters for anything that might aid the enemy or threaten national security.'

Their hours of work were eight thirty to five thirty unless required to stay longer, under wartime Emergency Directive Number...

Jess lapsed into a moment's sleep. She woke when her chin touched the top button of her blouse.

The next two hours covered the rules and methodology of censorship. They would develop an instinct over time for what was innocent and what was not. They must repeat nothing they saw or heard within Senate House unless formally instructed to do so by a senior ranking staff member. 'And now, please follow me...' Miss Cartwright was out of the door, leaving the new emergency intake to scramble to their feet.

In another blank-faced office, Jess was handed a paper to read carefully then sign. A phrase cut through the fog:

> Loose talk amounts to treachery which, in extreme cases, may merit imprisonment or the death penalty.

Jess signed the Official Secrets Act with a shaky scrawl that barely resembled her usual signature. Being told to fill in her address on a card launched her out of her stupor. What address had she given during her interview?

St Saviour's Vicarage, Ramsgate.

That wouldn't work now. Nor would 'A bench, Victoria Railway Station'.

She wrote the address of the Girls' Friendly Society. *Please God, let nobody check.*

Her photograph was taken for her door pass.

That done, she and the others were directed down to a basement canteen where, for a penny ha'penny, Jess bought tea in a thick-rimmed cup and a wedge of sugarless carrot cake.

She sat alone as the others split off into groups, effortlessly avoiding her. She told herself it was better that way.

Section C's wing lay in the bowels of Senate House. Desks, ranked four across and stretching deep into the room, stood beneath unforgiving lights. Jess counted heads – forty, fifty female clerks, some of whom looked up to check out the newcomers. As that girl had said to Jess, it wasn't so different from school. The air smelled of dusty parquet and menthol sweets. Jess learned later that the clerks sucked them to keep their throats from drying out. On the wall nearest the door, a Ministry-issued poster warned in bold letters:

CARELESS TALK COSTS LIVES: A WHISPER TODAY, A FUNERAL TOMORROW.

Miss Cartwright told them to find a vacant desk. Jess took one between two women who looked to be in their forties. One gave a swift nod; the other muttered, 'Don't look so scared. It's not that bad.'

She drew comfort from their ordinariness. Cotton blouses, subdued lipstick, greying hair and wedding rings. She surveyed her desk, finding an in-tray, an out-tray, a letter opener, a blotter and a rubber stamp marked PASSED BY CENSOR. Miss Cartwright buried another sneeze and from the front of the room said in a voice that carried to the back, 'You are now examiners. Prepare to receive your first batch of twelve letters to review.'

A man came in, pushing a trolley piled with bundles of post. A stack was placed in front of Jess. She stared at it. Was she really meant to pick up that letter knife and slice into the one on top?

To examine and read a stranger's words?

'Go to it, it won't bite,' said the more talkative of her neighbours. Jess picked up the blade, hoping nobody would see that her fingers were shaking. She hacked rather than sliced open the letter.

It had been sent by the secretary of a London doctor, inviting a patient in *for a confidential chat. Following tests, we have reasons for concern.*

Jess's stomach clenched. *I shouldn't be reading this.* What would the poor man think, if he knew?

But nobody else on her row seemed troubled by their task. She reached for the next letter, reminding herself she was only checking for anything that might endanger national security. She was helping the war effort – and, in her quieter moments, serving another cause entirely.

Finding her sister, who had vanished between the lines of an unfinished letter.

12

At twelve thirty, they broke for lunch.

'Coming to the canteen?' asked her neighbour, who introduced herself as Phyllis. 'It's subsidised, and not too bad, all told.'

'Thanks, but I need fresh air.' Conscious of sounding ungrateful, unfriendly at best, Jess escaped onto Gower Street. From a café on nearby Grafton Way, she bought a dripping sandwich for threepence and six carrot sticks for a penny, turning down the offer of a currant bun at half price. She'd overheard two of her fellow recruits bemoaning the fact that they wouldn't get their first wages until the end of September. Thirty-three days away.

Rafe's gift, now down to two pounds ten shillings thanks to the taxi fare, would have to last all that time. Was that even possible?

Jess had meant to find the garden square she'd passed that morning and enjoy her lunch in the shade, but when she got there all the benches were taken. She backtracked along Grafton Way, thinking, *Why is the name familiar?*

She ate as she walked and could almost hear Miss Hillingdon tut-tutting at her shoulder.

'Consuming food in the street, Jessica? Dropping standards so soon.'

Charlotte's voice followed, light as laughter. 'Ignore her. But seriously, you'll have to call home for funds. Take it from one who knows, you can't survive London on one shilling and sixpence a day.'

Call home, after the way Miss Hillingdon had hung up on her? Not likely.

She stopped, remembering why the name of this street rang bells inside her head. Reaching into her pocket, Jess unfolded the page the young nurse had torn out for her.

Black hat, shoes, red coat. Buyer: Madame Renée, Elegant Exchange, Grafton Way, WC1.

Charlotte's possessions, seized. Jess's only lead from her visit to Alder Grove. She'd come away intending to follow it up immediately – only to forget in the emotions of a bombing, of meeting Rafe, a night on the streets and the shocking incident on the Underground. No wonder her thoughts were scrambled.

But here she was, by chance or fate.

On a street that was mostly offices, shops and modest lodgings, Charlotte's stolen possessions had come to be sold. The woman who'd acquired them might, at this very moment, be stitching a hem or brushing a sleeve ten feet from where Jess stood.

She might even know where Charlotte was. A long shot? Not necessarily. The Charlotte Jess knew would have fought tooth and nail to reclaim her property. Not only the red coat with the buttons like ripe cherries, but the black shoes that made her calves look long and slender, and the hat that lent her the air of a serious, grown-up woman.

'You were kicking and screaming as they dragged you into Alder Grove,' Jess said quietly to the sister who had become her unseen shadow. 'They must have torn those things off you.'

'They did. Two nurses held me while another stripped me.'

'Why did Father allow it?'

'You tell me, Jess.'

Maybe Father hadn't known what had befallen Charlotte. Once someone was carted away to hospital and handed over to doctors, anything could happen.

'I might have done him a terrible injustice,' Jess murmured, willing it to be true. Perhaps he really believed Charlotte lay in a communal grave. If so, he deserved pity, not her anger. And she – this would be a severe test – *she* must tell him the horrific truth.

She'd have to phone the vicarage again.

But not now, she told herself. Not while he was conducting funerals, supporting his shocked and broken-hearted parishioners. Let him have a few more days of peace.

Jess moved slowly up Grafton Way, scanning each window, reading the nameplates beside every door. Her thoughts turned inward. *Life used to be so ordinary. When did it go wrong?*

She couldn't find an answer, so tried another question. 'When did the lies start, Charlotte?'

Charlotte's voice, throaty and teasing, replied inside her head:

'Months ago. When I first decided I had to pursue my dream to write for the press. Little white lies at first, because Father could never let us go, could he? But later I doled out some massive, juicy fibs. You had no idea at home what I was getting up to in the big, bad city. Not only on Saturday for my typing course. I'd sneak off work during the week, pretending I was needed at home by my widowed father and dependent little sister. Wicked.'

Jess walked down both sides of the street, doubling back on

herself without seeing a sign of Madame Renée or Elegant Exchange. Popping into a newsagent on the corner with Gower Street, she bought a stamp and dropped the postcard to her father into the letter box. It landed with a soft thud. More lies winging their way to the vicarage.

'Cheese and potato pie and a friendly dormitory,' she sighed. Her imagination had shown itself cruel. She couldn't face another night on a station bench, but where could she go where nobody would move her on or lay a hand on her?

By mid-afternoon she was desperate enough to ask Phyllis, her neighbour in Section C. 'I've, um, had to leave my lodgings at short notice. Bomb damage... we've all had to go. I just need somewhere cheap and decent. Somewhere I can think.'

Phyllis shook her head in sympathy. 'I wish I could offer you a bed, but my husband's parents are living with us now. Try College Hall, the women's hostel on Malet Street. They've a noticeboard in the foyer and there's always someone needing a housemate.'

The moment her day's work was done, Jess acted on the advice. By nine that evening she'd found a room. Of sorts. A broom cupboard at the back of a boarding house near Paddington station, where the bed shook whenever a train went by and the ceiling light swung for minutes afterwards. The mattress was hard, the sheets stale, but it cost only five shillings a week.

The English-literature student who sublet the room had demanded a month's rent up front but Jess had found the nerve to refuse, saying she'd pay just to the end of August. They haggled, and eventually settled on two weeks' rent down, the rest if she stayed on.

She hoped she wouldn't have to.

Of Rafe's three pounds, only two now remained. The end of September and payday felt a long way off.

Still, she'd made it through one more day. Tomorrow, she'd

have another stab at finding Elegant Exchange and as soon as she felt able to ask for a little time off, she'd visit Fleet Street, where the newspaper offices were. Charlotte's last letter had named the *London Mercury*. She'd been writing to its editor. Maybe, just maybe, he would remember the girl in the red coat with the cherry buttons.

13

BETONY

Tuesday, 3 September 1940

Laughing a little too loudly at something her escort said, Betony Styles passed beneath the unlit letters of The Rialto on Coventry Street and into a muted lobby. While he paid their entry fee, she glanced towards the marble stairwell. After midnight, there was always a table or two for the smart, the glamorous.

With the rest of her party following behind, she descended to the crowded club. Inside the Café de Paris, the word 'blackout' was banned. Mirrors reflected the ceiling lights. Glasses on white linen twinkled as champagne bubbles turned to mist. You'd almost think it was still 1938.

The band was in full swing, Ken 'Snakehips' Johnson driving his men through the brass riffs of 'Tuxedo Junction', his tap shoes snapping out the rhythm. The maître d' found them a table. Betony's date pulled out a chair for her, saying, 'I'm guessing Veuve Clicquot, Betty?'

'As always,' she said, smiling, while her eyes slid towards the next table where a group of RAF officers were holding a loud conversation over the music. Handsome in slate-blue, their wing badges glinted. One of them met her gaze for a heartbeat.

She knew him. His name was Owen Henderson.

Seeing the dark blond hair slicked back, that cool, assessing look, her stomach flipped. They'd met here a few weeks earlier, danced twice and clicked at once. He'd asked to see her again and she'd said, 'Why not? I'd like that.'

Then she'd done the worst thing in the world. Given him the address of a house a few doors down from her parents' in Bruton Street, a house she knew to be unoccupied. Why? A dozen reasons, and none of them worthy.

Amazing he even spared her a single glance.

It must be obvious that she'd come here tonight with another man. One who was probably – no, definitely – the most attractive being in the room. In any room, frankly. Winter Macpherson, attaché to the Canadian High Commissioner, had thick black hair with a rebellious wave and eyes as clear as snow under sun. He had status, style, and a thoughtful Canadian drawl. Tall, spare, perfectly self-possessed – the sort of man who seemed to come with his own spotlight.

And yet...

Briar Etherington, one of her party and an old schoolfriend, poked Betony and hissed, 'You won't hog Winter all night, will you?'

'I'm sure I won't.' Betony had noticed the glances Briar had been sending Winter since they'd all got into the same taxi. As though he were the last chocolate in the last box to come out of Cadbury's.

And yet. For Betony, he wasn't quite enough. However edible he looked in evening clothes, her desires were all for the men in uniform. The ones who'd signed up to fight Hitler. *Really, I should let Briar have him. It's not fair to string him along when my heart isn't in it.*

Her gaze drifted back to Flight Lieutenant Owen Henderson, who was now behaving as if she'd ceased to exist. Did he guess why she'd snubbed him so cruelly? It was because everything about him from his cufflinks to his off-the-peg uniform shouted 'middle class'. 'Grammar school'. The sort of upbringing her parents would dissect within minutes, though she herself couldn't have cared less.

'Who are his people, dear? The Cheshire Hendersons? No... Then who?'

'Where did the chap go to school? Say again. Never heard of it.'

It always seemed to happen with the men she brought home and each time she was left raw with humiliation. She liked Owen – more than liked – but there was only one path: secrecy.

Betony wanted more than that. She wanted to be married. It was her only escape from home, from the feeling of being a flower set in aspic. Pretty to look at, sealed off and trapped.

The champagne was poured; they all clinked glasses. The band softened its tempo, a lick on the clarinet leading into 'A Nightingale Sang in Berkeley Square'.

'Oh, I love dancing to this,' cried Briar, pitching it straight at Winter.

Betony's pulse tripped. She wanted to dance too. With Owen. But he was already on his feet, hand extended to a girl in WAAF uniform, one of his crowd.

'Shall we, Betty?' Winter's fingers brushed her bare arm. 'Seems a shame to waste a slow song and a gorgeous gown.'

He meant the midnight-blue Vionnet she'd chosen for tonight: simple, narrow-waisted, the skirt flaring when invited to move. A refugee had smuggled it out of Paris hours before the Germans arrived and Betony had modelled it for *Practical Modes*, the magazine she worked for. She'd then sold her grandmother's pearls to make it hers. She hadn't yet told her mother.

'Go on, then,' she said, rising. She might crave another man, but she wasn't about to let Briar pinch this one off her, uninvited.

Winter led well. The band made the song into a slow foxtrot and his hand rested lightly on her back. His breath brushed her hair. Owen and the WAAF girl were almost touching distance away on the crowded floor. The girl's eyes were closed, lost in the tune. Owen looked distant, as if counting the steps.

Winter's mouth dipped close. 'Say, Betty, you and I dance kinda well together. So maybe it's time—'

The lights went out.

A gasp, a burst of chatter, nervous laughter. The band kept playing.

'Ain't no more than a power cut,' Snakehips called into the mic, smooth as ever. 'God's way of tellin' you – dance close, babies. Dance close.'

Winter's arm tightened around her. Somewhere close by, glass shattered.

'Somebody's wasting champagne,' Winter murmured. 'Don't move.'

They were jostled apart in the uneasy stir that followed. A shift of bodies, a brush of shoulders and then a different voice rumbled in her ear.

English. Polite. Very.

'Thanks for the duff address, Miss Styles. Nice touch.'

She gasped. 'Wait – Owen, please…' Snatching in her eagerness, her fingers found the rough nap of a uniform sleeve as he pulled away. 'Owen? Don't go. I want to explain.'

The reply was a kiss. Warm, hard, restrained until she answered it, pressing close. A spark ignited. *You. I want you.* Then a jostle, breathless laughter nearby and the kiss broke.

Her wrist was caught, lifted. The nib of a pen grazed the underside of her arm.

He was writing on her skin. Before she could draw breath it

was over and he was gone. Candles arrived and Winter was there again, ready to usher her back to their table. He murmured something about the local substation failing because factories on nightshift were drawing so much current. He could talk about substations when her life had tilted on its axis? If ever she needed proof why Owen Henderson won over Winter Macpherson, this was it.

Owen was back at his table too, standing behind the WAAF who was smiling up at him through inviting, poppy-red lips. He didn't look Betony's way. He didn't need to.

She looked down at her left arm where a telephone number had been inscribed in blue ink, tightening as it dried. She quickly draped her silk stole across her elbows so nobody would see.

Shortly after two, they tumbled out into the street, a knot of uniforms, dinner jackets and silk gowns. The blackout held out here, of course. No streetlamps, only the muffled swing of the doormen's torches.

Someone suggested coffee and they found a place off Leicester Square serving tarry brew in cups designed for workmen's hands. The café owner rustled up some fried bread but Betony didn't touch hers.

She was a model, a *mannequin* if one wanted to be French about it. Keeping a twenty-three-inch waist was necessary torture. Besides, she was drunk on the memory of that kiss. Owen and his RAF friends had followed them into the café and were doing most of the talking. Winter was teasing Briar for retouching her lipstick before reaching for her fried bread.

'You'll have to do the job all over again, surely.'

'Or you could do it for me,' Briar invited.

Betony watched the interchange, Briar fluttering her lashes, leaning close so her hair brushed his sleeve. Winter giving his slow smile, saying, 'If you want. Can't promise you'd like the result.'

'You're so nice, Winter.' Briar's voice slurred. Honey and champagne. Too much of the latter. 'Nice, nice, nice. You let Betony walk all over you.'

'I do?'

'You do. I bet if she punched you, you'd say thank you.'

Winter's smile held. 'Where I come from, we save our fighting strength for the real battles.'

Owen glanced over, saying lightly, 'There's one going on right now unless I've been asleep these past three months.'

'I know that.' Winter's tone wasn't combative. It didn't invite a quarrel. It was simple agreement.

Betony saw Owen nod. Something had shot between the two men that made her feel as if the war somehow didn't include her. She wasn't like the WAAF girl with her vivid lips and disciplined curls. She, Betony, was a face in a magazine. A frame for the latest fashion. Feted in certain circles. Yet at this moment, she felt irrelevant.

It was time to go. Out on the pavement, the group scattered – the servicemen and their girls heading for the car they'd borrowed, piling in for the journey back to RAF Hornchurch.

Winter offered to walk her and Briar home. They lived not far from each other, Betony on Bruton Street, Briar in Dover Street. Owen joined them. He wasn't returning with his companions. His intention was to walk to Ealing and call at his mum's place for breakfast.

'Ealing?' Briar squealed. 'That's ten miles at least!'

'Not quite. But what else? I'm not waiting around for a train or a bus. Anyway, I left my motorbike there.'

'Even so.'

'Even so. A quiet walk in the dark suits me. And I've got a torch.'

Betony, having flinched at his casual reference to 'mum' –

another social signal her own mother would seize on – said, 'In that case, you can light our way to Mayfair, and we'll point you towards Bayswater Road from there.'

They walked through the silent streets, crossing Piccadilly. A siren wailed somewhere, but it didn't rise to a warning pitch. A factory klaxon most likely, signalling tea break for a weary nightshift.

The air had the metallic tang that comes before rain.

'London's a strange place in the dark,' Owen remarked. 'Everything looks half-finished.'

Winter said quietly, 'Better than half-destroyed. What d'you say to what happened in Ramsgate ten days back?'

Owen gave the question some consideration. 'Was it thirty people dead? Next night, our bombers went to Berlin and did the same to them. Poor devils on both sides. People running for shelter are the victims, whatever their names.'

Betony wanted to add something – anything – to sound as if she knew what they were talking about. Shame prickled. What had happened in Ramsgate? The newspapers hadn't mentioned anything... or perhaps they had. Her reading ran to fashion pages and light novels.

They walked on, conversation spent. Owen's torch was regulation-dimmed, so they went carefully, missing kerbs and crossing side streets without realising. With cars and bicycles blacked out too, it felt less like a pleasant stroll than an obstacle course. One that promised drama from every shadowy corner.

Which was exactly what happened on Berkeley Square. They had delivered Briar to her front door, Winter gallantly taking the key from her wavering hand and seeing her into the front hall. Five minutes it took him to disentangle from Briar's goodnight.

He, Betony and Owen were now a few yards short of the right turn into Bruton Street.

Behind them, an engine revved and a van swung into the

square. Too fast. Its driver tried to correct and mounted the kerb, the blackout slits on its headlamps flashing briefly before hitting the railings in a shatter of glass and crunching metal.

Vapour rose from its crumpled front end.

'Christ.' Winter ran towards it. Owen too.

Betony followed more slowly. It looked like a Women's Voluntary Service van, the kind whose side dropped down to allow tea, sandwiches and sympathy to be served through a hatch. What if...

She dreaded the sight of blood.

Voices rose, someone – Winter or Owen, she couldn't be sure – promising to get those trapped inside safely out.

The driver's door appeared to be jammed. Between them, Owen and Winter forced it open.

A figure – a body? – rolled out into their arms. Betony, steeling herself, came forward and saw it was a woman in a herringbone tweed suit. Middle-aged, her green felt hat still anchored in place in a stoic refusal to budge, though there was blood on her face. The men carried her to the opposite pavement.

'Can you get my jacket off?' Winter presented his back to Betony.

'Why?' The night was warm, but not close.

'To put down. This lady doesn't strike me as the kind who's used to lying on the sidewalk.'

'Oh, I see. Course.' She eased his dinner jacket off one shoulder, then the other, and placed it lining side up on the pavement. *Don't look, Savile Row.* She removed his wallet and ID card, to look after them for him. 'All ready.'

She ought to kneel beside the casualty, like a caring soul, and at least wipe the blood away. But the fear of having someone die in front of her was making her giddy. Instead, she asked, 'Is there anyone else in the van?'

Owen had already gone to look. Betony joined him as he

climbed into the driver's side and heard him say, 'It's all right, ma'am. Hold on.' He turned to say in a low voice to Betony, 'We won't get her out except by brute force and I don't want to do that. Somebody should dial 999.'

'I'll run home. We have a telephone—' But before she could prove herself useful in that way, they both heard the peal of an ambulance. Somebody living on the square must have rung already.

Within a minute, a volunteer ambulance pulled up alongside, offloading stretcher bearers with Red Cross armbands.

As they got to work, a shrill, confident voice rang out in the darkness. 'What's going on?'

A torch beam danced, and behind it, a woman in overalls. She wore a steel helmet, a white 'W' on its front.

They explained what they'd witnessed. A WVS van took the corner too fast. 'Driver rescued, passenger trapped.'

'We'll need a lorry with a tow rope to pull it off the railings,' Winter called across. He'd stood back to let the Red Cross medics tend to the woman in the felt hat. 'That or several strong men.'

'How about several strong women?' suggested the girl with the helmet. And she *was* a girl, Betony saw. Couldn't be more than sixteen.

Responding to a whistle, three other tin-hatted young women arrived and sized up the situation. Helped by Owen, Winter and two stretcher bearers, they pushed the van back across the pavement. Owen had handed Betony his torch and she shone it at the front of the vehicle, in a last desperate bid to be of some help.

'Hold it higher,' ordered the young warden in a voice so resonant with authority, Betony was instantly back at school being told off by the head girl. 'Higher. I need to see whoever's trapped. No, not that high,' the girl snapped, throwing a scornful look. 'You're not the Statue of Liberty. Yes, that's better. Well done.'

Well done, Styles – a rare display of intelligence. For a fashion model.

Berkeley Square was filling with emergency workers. More ARP wardens, men this time, police constables and another ambulance.

'I guess we can go.' Winter wiped a smudge of blood from his palm and told Owen he'd see Betony home. 'You've still got a trek ahead of you.'

To her disappointment, Owen didn't argue. He wasn't really looking at her anyway, but at the girl wardens clustered on the corner, watching the ambulances move off. Baggy overalls buckled at the front, tin hats like saucepan lids – he was regarding them as if they were the chorus line at the Windmill Theatre.

'Pretty magnificent, aren't they?' Winter said to Betony, taking his wallet and ID from her, slipping it back inside his jacket.

'The girls? I suppose so. Though heaven knows, I'd pay for the job of redesigning those hideous uniforms.'

Somehow, the last part of her sentence carried to the corner.

'Pardon us, milady,' one of the girls called back. 'Government issue and they were right out of ball gowns when it was our turn.'

Betony wanted to say she hadn't meant it as a criticism. What she'd meant was that a softer shoulder line, a dart or two, would work wonders. But nobody was listening. She trudged toward Bruton Street, thoroughly dissatisfied with herself. Winter stayed beside her until they reached her door. He watched her turn her key in the lock, then bade her goodnight.

She knew he was waiting for her to say something, but her thoughts were keeping pace with Owen, off to his mother's house.

Correction: *his mum's place.*

'See you whenever, Betty.' A brisk kiss on the cheek, and Winter was gone too.

In the downstairs hall, she switched on a lamp. Her reflection in a scrolled Venetian mirror showed a stranger. Still elegant, despite her brush with danger, a silk stole across her shoulders. Fair hair piled up for the swan neck look. Cheeks waiting to be cleansed of powder, light blue eyes too wide. Letting the stole drop, she read what was written on the inside of her arm.

TRA 9876.

TRA – Trafalgar – was a telephone exchange. Owen had given her his number. *A* number, not an Ealing one, so perhaps he had a flat somewhere. That would be nice. It meant he'd forgiven her and wanted her to call.

She was sure he'd have kissed her again had Winter not been there. What an evening. She hoped the WVS ladies were all right. Splendid types, giving up their sleep to serve tea and comfort in a harsh city.

Bone-tired, Betony climbed the stairs, thinking only of bed. Muffled sounds took her in a different direction, however, and she found her mother in her suite, bustling among half-packed trunks. A large suitcase lay open. Scents of lavender drifted from an open wardrobe.

'Mummy, what going on? It's gone three.'

'I could say the same to you. What time is this to roll in? Obviously, I'm packing. We're leaving first thing.'

Leaving? Why?

Lady Styles rolled her eyes. 'Because of the bombing, obviously, but also because your father has offered this house to one of his Ministry departments. They're dreadfully short of space, apparently.'

'He's given our home away?'

'We do have another,' Lady Styles pointed out. 'We'll stay at Styles Court for the duration. Not a bad swap, as we'll only have to heat one property. Go and pack your things.'

Betony gaped, not believing what had been decided over her head. What about her job at *Practical Modes*? What about her and Flight Lieutenant Henderson? Walled up at Styles Court, she might as well order her grave clothes and die.

She glanced down at her arm. The ink was already smudging. 'I can't, sorry,' she said. 'Rather a lot depends on me being here.'

Her mother appeared not to hear. Told her again to run along and pack what she needed. The rest could be boxed up and sent down later.

'No.' If she disappeared into the country, Betony thought desperately, she'd never see Owen again. Never get the chance to show him she could be more than a frivolous deb. She'd shown so little compassion for that poor WVS lady. Too squeamish, too self-absorbed to be properly human and he'd seen it all. As had Winter. 'Please understand, Mummy, I have to become somebody better.'

'What on earth are you talking about?' Lady Styles said, exasperated, a fur coat in her arms.

'If this house is being given up, fine. I'll find a flat.'

'You couldn't possibly afford one on what you earn.'

'A room, then. Or a cupboard at the end of a corridor, if need be.'

'You're talking nonsense. Go and pack.'

In her own room, Betony drew back the blackout curtain and put her cheek to the glass. Somewhere out there the Café de Paris slumbered, keeper of her great secret, the kiss that had changed everything.

'I'll start looking for a place the moment it's light,' she murmured. 'London's the only place that sees me. So how can I leave?'

14

JESS

Jess was finding her work as a censor strangely relaxing. Having overcome her reluctance to read other people's mail, she was enjoying the idea of being on the front line, scanning for security breaches, fishing for spies.

She knew not everyone felt the same, not if the sighs in the canteen and cloakroom each morning were anything to go by. But life as a vicar's daughter, watching, listening and being overlooked, had schooled her in patient observation.

Miss Cartwright would nod approvingly whenever she passed Jess's desk and saw her wielding her letter opener and censor's stamp with brisk confidence. Even Mr Brinkworth, the Section Chief, had stopped by on one of his daily rounds to remark, 'Ah, you're the Miss Gresham I hear so much about. The one with the natural zeal.'

Only one thing clouded her thoughts.

The rent on her room was due. She had to find somewhere else. There were mice behind the skirtings. Though to be fair, mice apart, nobody bothered her once she'd put the catch on the door. The other women in the house, undergraduates with complicated personal lives, hardly seemed to notice her existence. She was eking out her remaining money. Fortunately, the Ministry canteen was cheap and tea and carrot sticks filled the gaps.

Eleven days since she'd arrived in London. Her first weekend had passed in a blur, the result of a wretched head cold she must have caught on that station bench. She'd dragged herself to work yesterday, Monday, thankful that censorship required quiet concentration more than conversation.

Illness had put a temporary brake on her mission to find Charlotte, but this morning she'd woken clear-headed and determined. Two tasks lay ahead, and the first fitted neatly into her lunch hour.

The minute the bell sounded at half twelve, she plunged outside, shrugging on her jacket as she went. Today, God willing, she'd track down Madame Renée. Her prize: a cherry-red Debenham & Freebody coat – a thread that might yet lead her to Charlotte.

Most of the doorways on Grafton Way carried multiple nameplates or brass plaques, the houses sliced into lodgings, offices and consulting rooms.

Jess read each one, finding a roll call of masculinity. J. M. Redgrave, Solicitor. C. A. Morton, Surveyor. Kershaw & Pelham, Accountants and Auditors. Ugh, that swept her straight back to Hedgley's.

No dress shops, haberdashers' or milliners' and no sign of a second-hand clothes dealer either. There was a hairdresser's, though. If anyone would know... She was reaching for the door handle when a card in the window drew her eye.

ELEGANT EXCHANGE – LADIES'
FASHIONS (1ST FLOOR)

Jess pushed inside so eagerly, she tripped on the mat. Scents of ammonia and hot curling irons hit her. Humming dryers and the clink of metal curling pins being dropped onto a tray overwhelmed her voice as she asked if she might, please, come through.

A girl in a white coat glanced up from the head she was stripping of curlers and sang out over the noise, 'If you're my next lady, take a chair.'

Jess went right up to her. 'I need Madame Renée. Should I go straight up?'

The girl dropped another curler onto her tray. 'Rene's away.' She pronounced the name in the English style, 'Ree-nee'.

'Oh. How long for?'

'Couldn't say. The guns going off scared the daylights out of her cat and she's taken it to a relative in the country. She might have decided to stay put herself, but all her stuff's still there, so she'll be back at some point. Since you're here...' The girl offered her a two-bob wash. Jess's hair, held back with her blue Alice band, probably told its own story. 'I don't reckon my next appointment's coming so if you sit over at the sink, I could do you.'

It was tempting... only, she was here for a more urgent purpose. She glanced at her watch. Only forty minutes left of her lunch hour. The hairdresser had combed out her client's curls and was pumping setting lotion over them. Fragrances of lavender and rose petal took Jess back to Friday evenings with Charlotte. Coaxing curls into the dead-straight Gresham hair had become a ritual. Her sister had liked to look her best for her forays into London. What would Charlotte say now?

Darling, have you glanced in the mirror recently?

Jess went to the sink telling herself that it wouldn't hurt to make a relationship with the hairdresser, if it meant she could pop in again to ask if Madame Renée – *Rene*, a far more plausible name – had returned.

The girl, who introduced herself as Doreen, spread a towel around Jess's shoulders. 'Lean back.'

Though the water was lukewarm, Jess almost groaned in pleasure as strong, soapy fingers rubbed and massaged, lifting the last remnants of Colman Street grit from her scalp. Staring up at a cracked ceiling, she imagined Charlotte's coat hanging in the room above.

'What've you been doing?' Doreen asked cheerfully. 'Rolling in rubble?'

'I was caught out in that bombing in August.'

'What, the one that took out the church in Cripplegate?'

'A ceiling gave way in the house I was in. I've been trying to get rid of the traces ever since.'

'Blimey.' Doreen rinsed, and Jess felt something drain away with it. The feeling of being dirty, the fear of becoming an outcast.

'You're lucky,' Doreen commented as she applied a second blob of rose-pink shampoo.

'I suppose.' Jess still thought of Rafe, wondering where he'd spent the night after he quit his house. Since she was never likely to know, she gave herself up to the bliss of the girl's fingers. It was as Doreen swaddled her head in a towel that she realised she'd be returning to work with wet hair. 'Can you do something?' she pleaded. There was a dryer free now.

'That's an extra shilling, love.'

Whatever it took.

Lowering the hood over Jess's head and switching on the motor, Doreen shouted, 'Want something to read?' The dryer sounded like a sea-going barge backing into port. 'I've still got last Thursday's fashion news, if you're interested.' Not waiting for an answer, she fetched a copy of *The London Mercury*'s Thursday supplement. *The Mercury* was where Charlotte had applied for work. There must be an address...

There was. Fleet Street. The editor-in-chief was Mr

Oswald H. Young, OBE. The Thursday Supplement's editor was Miss Jean Treadgold.

It felt like a reproach: *Why haven't you been there yet, asking if they have a Charlotte Gresham on the staff?*

'I caught a cold,' she muttered, 'but I'm going to. I'll do it after work, I promise.' Catching Doreen's puzzled glance, Jess turned pages at random and her eye landed on a column headed, MISS TOUCHWOOD, OUR QUIZZICAL EYE ON THE WORLD OF FASHION.

Miss Touchwood had very firm views.

Showing our calves is patriotic; showing our knees is bad form.

If good perfume is unavailable, the only acceptable substitute is none.

There was a warning to women who wore tweed to musical recitals: *An entire row of dog-tooth check absorbs sound and ruins the acoustics. I have seen a world-class violinist reduced to tears.*

Was she serious, this Miss Touchwood, or simply bossy and absurd? There was something of Miss Hillingdon in the tone. Jess closed the supplement – and her eyes – and let the hypnotic thrum of the dryer take over.

It blurred the disappointment of finding Madame Renée absent from town. At some point, the woman had to come back, and business couldn't be brisk with the city half-evacuated. Which meant Charlotte's coat might still be hanging up there, among the unwanted items. Waiting for Jess.

Jess was hurrying back along Grafton Street, hair shining and loose, when the uneasy sense of being followed stole over her. She stopped and turned, but no one halted or slipped into a doorway. She told herself she was imagining things, though it didn't stop her mind from leaping to the man whose face still haunted her sleep. Whelan, he'd called himself. Cormac Whelan.

This wasn't the first time she'd had the sensation of footsteps behind her. It had happened several times on her morning walks to work; whoever was trailing her turned left when she turned left. Right when she turned right. She was never quick enough to see whose shadow was behind her, but who could it be other than Whelan, who'd tried to get on the train with her, who had called her Charlotte and laid hands on her? The idea of him tracking her to Senate House was frightening.

She couldn't think how he'd picked up her trail but each time she neared work, or home at the end of the day, queasy butterflies hatched in her stomach. What if he worked out which was her bedroom window?

Or leaped out on her in the dark as the days grew shorter?

She needed somewhere else to live and not next week or next month, but *now*. Somewhere safe where there were people who'd notice if one day, she failed to come home.

15

She reached Senate House with time for a gulp of canteen tea before taking her seat.

The first letter of the afternoon seemed almost designed to unsettle her. The writer, 'D', had the rounded hand of a woman. D was imploring 'Dear L' to leave her alone.

> *I told you, I'm joining the ATS and they asked if I'd consider going overseas. I said I would. Best thing for both of us is to let each other go. Who knows who we'll meet before this war's over, eh? So please, no more letters and no more calling on me at work. They don't like it and I hate seeing that side of you. Don't write back. This letter is goodbye, and I wish you the best of luck.*

Jess resealed the envelope and stamped it with her censor number. There was nothing to cut, nothing to black out in this plea for freedom.

That phrase, 'I hate seeing that side of you', gave her a shiver. Whelan had said something similar when he'd cornered her on the platform. *I know I've got a side to me, but we can talk, can't we?*

He'd been looking for Charlotte, who, Jess believed, was out there somewhere, perhaps on the run from him. A man with 'a side'. But did she really know anything for sure?

Other than her visit to Alder Grove, she'd yet found nothing tangible to suggest that Charlotte really was alive. Nor had she faced the agonising dilemma: whether to tell her father what she knew.

He hadn't written, but then, he didn't know her current address. He'd have received the postcard full of cheerful lies about the Girls' Friendly hostel, and if he telephoned there, he'd be met with a blank 'Who?' It would hit him hard, the fear that he'd lost another daughter.

He knew where she worked, of course. He could reach her here if he really wanted to. She had to assume he didn't.

Still, she ought to call home. Confess. Make him listen. He had a right to know that Charlotte, far from lying in a common grave near St Mildred's hospital, had been taken, very much alive, to Alder Grove.

Or did he already know?

She closed her eyes and pressed her knuckles to her temples. Her thoughts kept going round like a carousel: the golden pony, the pink elephant, the painted dolphin. The same doubts, endlessly spinning. The only way to make it stop was to make the call. On Tuesdays, he was usually home by six. She'd do it, she decided, once she'd carried out her second task of the day.

When Miss Cartwright asked for late volunteers – a routine request now that their workload had swelled – Jess kept her hand down. Normally she'd have welcomed the free meal that came with the overtime, but she knew she had to act while her resolve held, or she'd lose courage.

She reached for the next letter to open, glad she had a plan.

Fleet Street first. Father second.

Taking the Tube to Charing Cross, she climbed back to street level into the fading light. The Strand crawled with buses, headlights masked, the pavements lined with sandbags. Every shopfront and basement window was padded against blast and flying glass. Fleet Street was no different, the hum and glow of busy pressrooms leaking through barricaded windows. White arrows stating PUBLIC SHELTER pointed down into the underbellies.

She reached the offices of the *London Mercury* to find the revolving door creaking with staff eager to get home before the sirens that sounded most nights now. Jess pushed her way inside and crossed to the reception desk.

A youth in shirtsleeves, phone clamped to his ear, glanced up. Spotting the satchel over her shoulder, he brightened. 'Artwork delivery? You're late.'

'I'm not – I mean, I'm looking for a Miss Charlotte Gresham. She might have come here for a job interview. Would you know her?'

'What?' He slammed down the receiver, giving up on whoever had been on the other end. 'I'm not the Lost Property Office.'

'I'm not after lost property,' Jess said patiently. 'I'm searching for my sister. I think she might have come here, you see.'

'And I'm supposed to know?' But when Jess didn't back away, he sighed and pulled a ledger towards him. After flipping through several pages, he said shortly, 'No one of that name on the staff.'

'Do you have a visitors' book?'

'What?' It came out as a reflex of irritation.

Jess repeated herself. Another sigh. She thought he was

walking off, but he turned on his heel, thumping down a gilt-edged, leather-bound book, asking, 'When for?'

'Last Christmas,' Jess said, leaning closer. 'Could you look at December last year?'

'Won't be in this one, will it?' He swapped the book for one marked 1939 and pushed it towards her. 'Be my guest.'

Jess flipped to the year's end. Charlotte had written to the *Mercury*'s editor on the twenty-third of December, asking about a newsroom typist's post. She'd been taking her shorthand and typing course in Charing Cross Road, a short walk away; it wasn't impossible she'd also come in person.

A tingle ran through Jess's feet. Charlotte might have stood here, hands resting on this desk, her smile fixed on this very clerk. Confident she'd soon be working in Fleet Street.

Jess scanned every visitor through November into December last year. No Charlotte Gresham. Dejectedly, she shut the book. 'Thanks.'

The young man studied her more carefully. 'You've no idea how many girls come through here looking for jobs. Or husbands.' A dry laugh made his views plain. 'They're replaced faster than the ribbons in their typewriters. It's the hours, see, and the journos can be bast—' He broke off as a tall woman stepped from the lift, fastening her coat. She moved with purpose. There was something regal in the set of a velvet hat worn high at the front, a spotted veil shadowing her face. She carried a handbag, hard-shelled and glossy, in the crook of her arm.

Her glance snagged on Jess. 'Why are you here again?'

Again? 'I've never—' Then it struck Jess. 'You know my sister.'

Behind the veil, something shifted. A flicker of awareness followed by a denial. 'I don't know you from Adam. Or Eve, for that matter.' The tone was educated, with a faint husk. 'If you'll excuse me...?'

Jess stepped into the woman's path and repeated what she'd told the desk clerk. Charlotte Gresham. Here, chasing a job last winter. 'You'd remember, because she'd be wearing a bright red coat and matching lipstick.'

The woman hesitated and Jess sensed a quick mind turning on a sixpence. *Throw the silly creature a crumb or I'll be here all night*, she seemed to be thinking. 'Dark-haired girl, brought a waft of Shalimar with her?'

'Yes, but – Shalimar? I don't know that.'

A smile, more cruel than sweet, lifted the carmine lips. 'Perfume by Guerlain. Unobtainable now – unless you have a Parisian lover with diplomatic privileges.' The woman stepped around Jess, moving for the door.

A second time, Jess got in her path. Nothing, not shyness nor politeness, would stop her now. 'My sister's name is Charlotte Gresham. She was abducted, and I will not rest till I've found her. Have you seen her recently?' She gestured to the clerk, who was pretending to study a phone book while straining to hear. 'He says there's nobody of that name on the books.'

'Then there isn't.' The woman shifted her handbag to the other arm. 'I'd like to go, please.' Her tone was acid now.

Jess stepped aside but followed her out onto Fleet Street. This moment wouldn't come again. 'You were right,' she called, 'she has dark hair like me. We're quite alike. When I said, "red coat," you blinked. It meant something to you.'

'Did it, indeed?' The woman turned, a hand on the clasp of her bag, as if she half-suspected Jess to be a street thief with a good story. Still, something made her hesitate. 'Gresham, you say. Perhaps I do remember. She was looking for work.'

Jess nodded eagerly. 'She wanted to be a staff writer. News, politics.'

'God, she was ambitious. Or mad.'

'Whatever she was, she was willing to start in the typing room.'

'Which is where ninety-nine per cent of them end, chewed up and worn out.'

'Did she get a job?'

The pause that followed stretched as the woman lifted her veil revealing a pale, powdered face and finely arched brows, a foil for the vibrant lipstick. 'She came here hawking her writing, as I recall. Character sketches. Country reflections. Not our style. But on the strength of the coat and the Shalimar – what a nerve – I took one of her pieces up to Miss Treadgold.'

Treadgold. The name strode through Jess's mind on expensive heels. The Thursday Supplement's lady editor. 'Did she get a job?' She knew she was repeating herself but feared she was being toyed with. Tossed crumbs while a crust was withheld.

'No. Miss Treadgold only employs male writers. Can't abide female competition.' The woman slid her handbag up her arm. 'I'm going now and *do not follow*.'

Jess watched her set off in the direction of the Strand, the velvet hat visible above the heads of other pedestrians for about a minute. Once it vanished, Jess looked down at her scuffed shoes. *Do not follow*. What you'd say to a mangy dog. Even so, she needed an audience with this Miss Treadgold.

Back inside the building, she marched up to the desk. 'I don't care how important Miss Treadgold is—'

'You were just with her,' the young man interrupted.

'What, the lady in the hat?' Jess stared at the motionless door, its curved panes dark with advancing night. 'Why didn't you say?'

He leaned his elbows on the polished desk. 'Ever worked in a place like this? Thought not. Editorial staff are divinities. We're what washes past their feet.'

'Make me an appointment to see her. Tomorrow. She met my sister and I have to talk to her again.'

The young man gave her a look that said, *Why not ask for the moon on a stick?* 'Miss Treadgold edits the Thursday Supplement—'

'I know.'

'—which goes to press overnight on Wednesday. Which makes today and tomorrow,' he added to help her grasp the magnitude, 'hell on earth. All copy's due in, and I get it in the neck when people miss deadlines.' He glared at the silent telephone. 'Anyway, I bet she told you she doesn't employ women.'

'She did.'

'Then she wouldn't have given your sister a job in a million years.' He sounded adamant – but what about that ridiculous Miss Touchwood column? *If golf is a good walk spoiled, checked jumpers with plus-fours is civilisation destroyed.*

'You're not telling me Miss Touchwood is a man in disguise,' Jess cried.

'Course not. *She's* Miss Touchwood.'

Miss Treadgold – again? 'She writes it?'

'Got it in one.' He rolled his eyes. 'Look, you could try the other papers. There's five along Fleet Street, plus the Sundays. *The Times* and the *Observer* are on Printing House Square, just up the way.' The phone shrilled. He pointed vaguely toward the street and turned his shoulder.

Jess left, heading back towards the Underground. It was too late to start knocking on new doors. She wanted to lie on her bed, listening to the trains, and digest what she'd learned in the last half hour.

Shalimar by Guerlain. Charlotte had never had the wherewithal for luxuries like that. Nor a French lover, or a rich admirer to buy it for her. None that Jess knew of, anyway.

Her stomach rumbled.

Dinner tonight? Salmon mousse with duchess potatoes,

petits pois and lemon sauce, followed by – who was she kidding? A chunk of cheese and an apple, water biscuits and cocoa. If nobody had stolen the milk she'd left in the cold box that morning.

Still, better than no food and no home at all.

She remembered then her promise to call her father, who would likely be sitting quietly at home right now. *Do it now*, said her conscience.

Or leave it a day or two, muttered the pit of her stomach.

She was passing a black-and-white building, its quaint diamond-paned windows whispering of Dr Johnson and Dickens and the comforts of gin and hot water. A little shot of courage wouldn't hurt.

It was called The George. Blackout blinds were down, but a man stepping out told her it was open, only—

Jess walked past him, crossing the threshold. She'd never been inside a public house before but Miss Treadgold's dismissal spurred her. If Charlotte could force her way in where nobody wanted her, so could Jess. She edged up to the bar, trying to decide what to ask for when the man standing behind it waved her back.

'Sorry, miss, we don't serve single ladies.'

'I – I only want an orange squash. I've been at work all day.' She added for emphasis, 'War work.'

He checked around. It was evident nobody had seen her come in. 'Just this once, then.' He poured the squash from a bottle, topped it with water from a jug. 'Twopence, drink it down, then go, yes?'

'Would you put a gin in it?'

He blinked. 'Gin, you sure?'

'Quite sure.'

'A single?'

Jess took a flying guess. 'No. A double.'

16

'Father – it's me.' She was standing in a phone booth at Charing Cross station, pennies lined up for what she hoped would be a meaningful conversation.

'I know it's you. Who else would put in a trunk call at this hour?'

'I suppose.' The line wasn't too bad, just the usual fuzzy hum. 'How are things with you?'

'Oh – you know. Hard. Sad. What about you?'

She caught the strain in his voice. Love and pity coiled around the emotions stirred up by her brush with Miss Treadgold and an injection of Booth's gin. A fearsome taste but effective. Whatever needed to be said, she was ready to say it. 'I'm all right. Did you get my postcard?'

When he answered, 'I did. Thanks for taking the trouble,' she knew he hadn't telephoned the Girls' Friendly hostel to check up on her. 'Glad you're doing well and making friends. Things aren't so joyful here,' he went on. 'Thirty-one dead in a single raid. ARP reckon five hundred bombs were dropped on us, and frankly, that feels about right.' St George's church in the town centre would have to be pulled down, he said, adding darkly, 'My congregation has tripled.'

'And the parish hall?' she asked tentatively. 'Still the town mortuary?'

'No, that was temporary. We're now a tearoom and a provider of clothes, blankets and shoes. And advice. We're also a dormitory. So many are homeless.'

Homeless. The word found its mark. 'I suppose you're getting no sleep either?'

'Is anybody?' he barked, half affection, half temper. 'I'm glad you're out of it, Jessica. Why the call?'

Small talk was over. *Take a breath.* 'Father, there's something—' She sensed she'd lost his attention and knew it when she heard a crisp schoolmistress voice in the background. Miss Hillingdon. What was *she* doing at the vicarage at this hour? Jess had made the call with the best intentions, to be kind and dutiful, but her temper flared. 'Father, don't you dare ignore me! I need you to listen. Stop talking to that woman!'

He was back with her. 'Sorry, were you saying something? Be quick. The church hall sink is blocked again. Miss Hillingdon popped over to pick up a plunger.'

'She's a plumber as well now, is she?'

'What? I don't know. She puts up notices telling people not to rinse the tea leaves down the plughole but she might as well be writing in Chinese. What d'you want to say?'

This was it, no going back. 'Father, I know Charlotte's alive.' Silence dropped. Even the hum on the line seemed to fade. 'Did you hear me?'

'I heard you, Jessica. I would rather not have.'

'I have evidence. I met a man who knows her.'

'You met a man?' The way he said it, she might have just told her father she'd danced naked for a crowd.

'I went to Alder Grove too.'

A sharp intake of breath carried all the way from Kent. 'You went where?'

'Alder Grove. The asylum. Tell me who took her there. Father, please. No more lies.'

His whisper came back, menacing as fingernails on glass. 'What did you accuse me of?'

Her courage drained away. Gin was notorious for being a false friend, wasn't it? Egging you on but leaving before the fight. 'I'm sorry, but you haven't told me the truth. What you said about Charlotte being buried at the hospital... I hoped you believed it, but it isn't true, is it?'

'How. Dare. You.'

Jess knew this was her cue to back down and beg pardon. But she was beyond that. Gin be damned. It was anger and eleven days of growing up that pushed her on. 'A man accosted me, because he thought I was her.'

'What man?'

'Never mind. I have the letter Charlotte wrote after you said she'd died. *Two days after*.'

'Then you broke rules and looked where you should not.'

What rules? Truth wasn't knocking; it was battering down the door. 'Charlotte is alive somewhere in London. She's in trouble, and I'm going to find her. Did you deliver her to that place – to Alder Grove? Tell me!'

A sound of profound disappointment travelled down the line. *Oh, my child.* 'Your words are an abuse of kinship. An abuse of kinship.'

She thought he'd hung up, but then a different voice came on the line.

'Jessica. This is Miss Hillingdon. What have you done?'

Jess gave the gist. 'You must know plenty, since you marched me off to your sister's after Charlotte went in the ambulance.' That miserable Christmas in Faversham rose before her, the older, sourer, Miss Hillingdon deflecting her questions, chaperoning her to church. 'You told me Charlotte died of a brain haemorrhage.'

'As she did.'

Jess knew her next words might destroy every hope of a homecoming, but she ploughed on. 'She did not, and that makes two liars. You and my father.'

'You little serpent! Beg my pardon at once.'

'When I have found Charlotte, we will come to Ramsgate together, Miss Hillingdon, and you may beg ours.'

The Northern line platforms at Charing Cross were deep ones. Though the authorities frowned on people sheltering in the Underground, there was quite a crowd when Jess arrived, gin on her breath, fury in her soul.

They were buying the cheapest tickets and heading down to pass the night protected from enemy attack, bedding and rolled blankets over their shoulders. Thermos flasks poked from baskets. Children gripped their grannies' hands. Mothers cradled babies, or clutched cat cages with mewing occupants. Jess bought a penny ticket and peeled off towards the Bakerloo line, which would take her home to Paddington.

At the top of the escalator, she planted herself squarely and gripped the handrail. Double gin, what had possessed her? It didn't amount to much in the glass, but she wasn't used to alcohol of any kind. Had she slurred on the telephone? If so, Miss Hillingdon would waste no time damning her name. The escalator began its long descent. The concourse below seemed to ripple like a concrete sea. Nausea swept in, bright polka dots in front of her eyes. Oh Lord, don't let her be sick. She couldn't afford to be ill again.

Her gas mask slipped from her shoulder, bumping down the slatted steps until it stopped behind the legs of a girl in a summer dress and an apple-green cardigan. The girl turned.

God, no.

It couldn't be—

Charlotte met Jess's eyes, then turned away.

'Charlotte! It's me – Jess!'

Everything went grey. Jess knew she was falling. She felt a blow to her head, her knees striking the hard edge of a stair, the burning scrape to her back. She was tumbling into her own screams. After that, nothing until a voice came from far away, cutting through the pain.

'Are you still with us, dear one?'

'Charlotte?' she croaked.

'I'm Mrs Kesgrave,' said the kindly voice. 'Who is Charlotte? I don't see anyone.'

A man's voice followed, a London one, brusque. 'See if she's got an identity card, Madam. She looks young to be drunk.'

'Yes, that satchel's hers. And the gas mask. Drunk, you say? Well, perhaps, but let us not judge. I'll wait while you call an ambulance.'

The voices faded.

When Jess came to, she was lying in a bed. A high, yellow-painted ceiling and grey metal lamps shouted 'hospital'. Her head throbbed like a basket of hammers. Yet despite it, she was certain of what she'd seen: Charlotte, twenty steps ahead. Briefly meeting her eye.

And turning away.

The rejection cut deep, opening up an ache that no anger could fill. Jess knew she was totally alone now, cut adrift. Nobody wanted her. She shut her eyes against the light and whispered into the emptiness, 'Oh, Charlotte. Why did you leave me behind?'

17

MRS KESGRAVE

Thursday, 5 September 1940

So now she had two occupants for the room upstairs. One bed left to fill.

Following the sudden departure of her three previous lodgers, No. 34 Hill Street had felt sadly under-populated. Their leaving had nothing to do with the quality of accommodation, or the rent. Nine pounds a month between three ladies was an absolute snip by Mayfair standards. Mrs Kesgrave knew of one poor girl paying almost that on her own for a room in a basement off Farm Street.

No, it was the war. These days, young women worked hard yet still earned little, living lives that could change by the hour. Gloria Kesgrave remembered a time when the world stayed steady for months at a stretch. Two vast upheavals in twenty-five years had spun the globe faster.

New lodger No. 1 was a delight, an Irish nurse named Grace. Forthright, eager to please, and if Mrs Kesgrave sensed correctly, chock-a-block with secrets. Not to mention the remains of a nasty black eye. Best not to ask.

Lodger No. 2, who'd arrived to see the room minutes later, was another matter. Betony Styles – the Honourable Betony Styles to give her the full bugle blast. Mrs Kesgrave knew the family by reputation. Knew *of*. Heaven forbid they'd ever ask her to tea. Lord Styles was a grandee at the Ministry of Supply, Lady Styles one of those women who seemed to glide straight from the pages of *Debrett's*, all coiffure and ancestry. Charming to everyone, caring for no one.

Miss Betony, alas, looked cast from the same mould. She'd arrived in a flurry, demanding the room immediately, or she'd be forced to sleep on a friend's spare mattress. The horror. She had floated upstairs on a perfume cloud, eyeing the room as if awarding marks out of ten. It hadn't dawned on her that Gloria Kesgrave would be the one doing the choosing.

'I shall have this side,' Miss Styles had declared, perching on the salmon-pink eiderdown of a bed tucked into a niche. Grace, first-comer, had already claimed it, rather than one of the side-by-side beds.

'I need my sleep,' Grace had explained. 'I'm on my feet all day, nursing.'

Miss Styles brushed that aside. She simply couldn't lie down so close to another person. 'I also have to get a good night's rest, to be at my best for work. In my line, it's not permitted to turn up looking a fright.'

'You mean it is in mine?' Grace had showed her teeth.

In the end, Betony won. They'd agreed terms and moved in, but tension simmered. Two such different creatures would never blend. Grace – East End, trying to pass as Mayfair. Betony – Mayfair as a mink hat, trying to pass as a working girl. Both acting their socks off, in their way.

Mrs Kesgrave's sympathies leaned toward Grace, trapped in what amounted to licensed servitude as a private nurse to the appalling Lady Ventnor of Upper Brook Street. Betony, meanwhile, worked for *Practical Modes*, a fashion journal edited by yet another titled lady. As far as Mrs Kesgrave could tell, her working day consisted of standing upright, draped in other people's finery. For five pounds a month. *If there isn't an allowance rolling in from Mummy and Daddy*, she thought, *I'm court astrologer to the Queen of Sheba*.

One bed remained empty. It had to be filled.

Making a living as a 'discreet correspondent' – her own invented title – was a fragile trade. Gloria Kesgrave played the part of 'the other woman' in divorce cases, allowing respectable wives to keep clear of scandal. There was work about, but after paying travel expenses and declining the more unsavoury engagements, little profit remained. She couldn't afford to lose No. 34. The house belonged to the Grosvenor Estate, and rent must be paid on the nail or she'd be doing what her late father used to call 'the bailiff two-step' at the door.

Or hiding behind the sofa whispering 'shh', which had been her mother's method of avoiding debt collectors.

A third occupant was essential. And soon.

Mrs Kesgrave was standing at the drawing-room window, drafting an advertisement for the newsagent's window on Curzon Street...

Shared room available for a young lady

... when she stopped mid-sentence. Someone was crossing the road from the direction of Farm Street, wearing a print dress, smart jacket, coral-pink umbrella. Betony Styles, who else? And running faster than a few drops of drizzle required.

Ah. Now I see.

Grace was close behind, coming up handy – as they said on the racecourse – on the inside. Amused and exasperated, Gloria pressed her cheek to the glass to watch.

Betony made it across first, but Grace saw her chance,

helped by a nurse's A-line tunic and sensible shoes. Through the window came Betony's furious cry—

'Don't you dare!'

Grace's hair had come loose, a halo of rain-misted auburn. She usually wore a starched cap for work. Gloria hoped it wasn't lying in a gutter like an upturned yacht.

A key jabbed the lock; scuffling followed. The front door slammed and Gloria winced for her Clarice Cliff vase, picturing it rocking on its stand. One did not wish to be the iron hand, but really, this was no civilised entrance.

She set down her pencil. The newsagent would be closed by now anyway, and perhaps fate didn't need her help. She was still hoping the third lodger would be the one she'd already chosen. The hurt, bewildered girl from Charing Cross. The one with eyes like crushed violets and gin on her breath. Gloria had seen something of herself in those eyes... her long-ago self. Once, someone had reached down and lifted her up. It was time to do the same for another.

Upstairs, she found Grace and Betony locked in combat over a bed.

I saw it first.

No, I *saw it first.*

Order was restored with a single glacial *ahem*.

'My paying guests at each other's throats? You'll both have to go.'

Two gasps, perfectly synchronised. Good.

'I have decided,' Gloria went on smoothly, 'neither of you will have this bed. Whoever comes through that door next – lodger number three – will take it. And if it's the person I hope, she'll need it.'

'Why?' demanded Betony. 'Does she snore worse than Grace?'

'You're talking about snoring?' Grace roared. 'You're so loud, most nights I'm thinking there's a pig in bed with you.'

'She's been hurt,' Mrs Kesgrave said, ignoring the outbursts. 'She'll need rest and privacy. Now' – she gave two brisk claps – 'supper in twenty minutes. Remember the rota. Grace, you're cooking. Betony, dear one, go down and set the table.'

They glared. Gloria Kesgrave smiled on.

Somewhere out in London, the girl with the violet eyes would be wondering where to go next. If fate played fair, before the week was out, she'd find her way to the smart black door of No. 34 Hill Street.

18

JESS

She'd been brought to Bart's Hospital, she discovered, as it had a reputation for treating brain injuries and neurological disorders. Jess didn't need to be told that she'd struck her head hard. Or that she'd been gabbling to an invisible person as she was carried up to the surface on a stretcher.

Dosed with codeine, she slipped in and out of sleep, teetering between reality and dream. The dreams were clearest: she relived one in pin-sharp detail. It was a conversation she'd had with Charlotte a month or so before her sister disappeared.

A dark November Sunday in 1939, the rain splashing off the guttering. Lunch had been cleared and washed up, their father was preparing for evensong and she and Charlotte were sprawled on the saggy velvet sofa in the snug. Charlotte writing, Jess reading.

Charlotte had nudged Jess with her foot. 'How's your work-in-progress?'

She was referring to Jess's stage play, which hadn't yet developed beyond the first scene. Jess liked making up characters and dialogue, but what Charlotte called 'the dramatic arc' eluded her.

She admitted as much. 'New ideas keep jumping in and I lose track.'

'Because you're obsessed with froth and romance. It wouldn't happen if you tackled something important. For instance, how the war will affect young women like us.'

Jess remembered answering that nobody cared a jot for young women.

Exactly, Charlotte had come back, which was why girls like them needed to speak up. 'Start a new play. Call it *The Window with the Blue Vase*. Make it about a girl who has fallen passionately in love with a man who drops her cold.'

It didn't sound very appealing. Jess wanted to know where the vase came in. 'Is it symbolic, as in "I'm feeling oh, so blue"?'

'Be serious, Jess. This girl... she's in deep trouble and what she does next...'

'Yes?'

'That is your play. Stop trying to please everybody, including yourself, or you'll just write mush. You'll become one of those dabblers who churn out birthday card verses.'

That touched a nerve. 'Unlike you, the first woman leader writer on a national newspaper?'

'Yes,' Charlotte agreed smoothly. 'Before I'm thirty. They won't hide me on the women's pages. I'll write about politics Monday to Friday, and pen novels on my days off, sitting by a sunny window in the London Library.'

And that, Jess thought, stroking the hospital-blue blanket spread over her, was the last serious conversation they'd had before Charlotte vanished.

On her third day at Bart's, she was woken for dinner and told that a telephone call had come in for her.

Her heart gave a violent jolt. Father, Miss Hillingdon? Did they know she'd fallen down drunk?

'A Miss Cartwright from the Ministry of Information,' the

sister said. 'You were missed at work. We gave her a run-down of your condition.'

Oh, heavens.

The trolley came round with stewed mince and mashed potato. Jess turned her face away. 'How does Miss Cartwright know I'm here?'

'The kind lady who stayed with you after your fall found your ID and door pass and made some calls.'

Worse and worse. She'd be disciplined for letting her Ministry pass fall into a stranger's hands. 'Did, er, Miss Cartwright know why I fell?' Jess asked cautiously.

'You mean, your inebriation?' Sister answered through tight lips. 'I didn't mention it. We on this ward take the view that you will have learned your lesson.'

Jess meekly agreed that she had. 'Please don't tell anyone.'

The following morning, she was presented with yesterday's *London Mercury* supplement, and told, 'If you can read it without the words swimming off like tadpoles, we'll know you're ready to leave us.'

She was desperate to get back to Senate House. She was still in her probationary period, and if she appeared unreliable they might sack her. So, taking her time, she read her way through an article on women auxiliary firefighters. After that, a letter from a mother 'To My Son on the Atlantic Convoys'. Heart-rending.

She skipped over a short story entitled 'Blessings in Disguise' as the lead character somehow acquired Miss Hillingdon's voice. Finally, she turned to the fashion pages.

Once again, there was Miss Treadgold in the guise of 'quizzical Miss Touchwood'.

> New shoes with wooden soles saves valuable leather for fighting men. Wear them with pride, knowing you're giving beetles a mercifully quick death.

Is your man possessive or just too much in love... with your Victory lipstick?

Jess frowned, wondering if Miss Treadgold had ever had to choose between a man's burning need of her and her freedom. Because Charlotte had.

The following day, after an early breakfast, Jess was discharged. The air was misty with smoke, as the bombers had visited again last night. Fires glimmered to the east. Jess thought of Colman Street, of Rafe, but with nothing to feed on, the feelings quickly withered. She had one immediate goal: to reach her desk and prove she still belonged in Section C.

Her arrival, with bandages over the worst of her cuts and grazes, caused a small stir. Colleagues looked up, smiling. Her neighbours, Phyllis and Rosa, clucked over her.

'We thought you'd given up and gone home. Glad you haven't.'

Even Miss Cartwright came over to say she'd been missed.

The first batch of letters landing on her desk was more welcome than any words. Here, in the familiar basement among the Saturday shift, Jess felt safe. Despite the pain of bruised fingers, she worked solidly until eleven o'clock tea break.

Phyllis and Rosa saved a place for her in the canteen. They prised the story from her.

'No! All the way to the bottom?' Rosa gaped. 'I bet someone pushed you. People are getting so impatient, rushing to get down to shelter.'

Phyllis offered Jess an aspirin with her tea. 'Take a couple extra, for later, and have my sugar,' she insisted. 'Bet you'll never use the Underground again.'

On the contrary, Jess thought, she would ride that 'down' escalator at Charing Cross as often as she could. It might be

Charlotte's regular station. Next time, Charlotte would not evade her.

As Jess returned to her desk, Miss Cartwright approached, saying, 'Fetch your things. I'm letting you go.'

Her devastation must have been plain because Miss Cartwright tutted sharply. 'I mean, for the day.'

Jess almost doubled over in relief. 'I'm all right, honestly.'

'Don't argue, Miss Gresham. I've been watching and you're no use to us half-conscious. Take the weekend off and come back Monday morning.'

Flashing her pass at the door as she left, she blinked in the afternoon light. Now almost a week into September, it was a little too damp and cool for the park and too early for the cinema. What to do with this gift of time? Not sit in her rabbit hutch of a room and feel dismal.

How about, visit an accommodation agency and find somewhere better?

As she walked towards Tottenham Court Road, where agencies of all kinds clustered, she put a hand in her coat pocket and felt the stiff edge of card.

It was white, embossed, with a bevelled edge and belonged to a Mrs Gloria Kesgrave:

Discreet Correspondent. 34 Hill Street, Mayfair

What on earth?

She'd never set foot in Mayfair, nor had she ever called on the services of a 'discreet correspondent', whatever that might be. Had it been slipped into her pocket on Fleet Street? If so, it would have to have been the grumpy desk clerk or lofty Miss Treadgold. Neither had come close enough, though.

But – wait. Written along the bottom of the card was, *Room at the inn, if you require.*

If she required… could life really be this simple, this generous? The nurses at Bart's had spoken of 'a kind lady' who had stayed with her when she fell. She remembered the voice. A warm, comforting alto.

Where was Hill Street? Jess could hardly open her map. Hope had invaded her fingers, making them clumsy.

Reaching the address after a roundabout pilgrimage – getting lost several times – her optimism had dimmed. People who offered help in a crisis often had second thoughts. Braced for a brush-off, she climbed the steps to a glossy front door and lifted the brass knocker.

After a moment, a voice floated out. 'Whoever you are, possess yourself in patience. I never run. *I sweep*.'

The door opened and a tall woman with black hair and emphatic eyebrows stood on the step. A long silk robe embroidered with pink and yellow peonies was belted snugly, satin lapels making a grand statement. 'Hello,' said the apparition. 'I think I know you.'

Behind the grand vision, Jess saw a chequer-tile floor, potted ferns, a yellow vase on a stand. Ornate picture frames. Something akin to recognition flowed into her. The voice, the interior, even the smell of orange flowers and beeswax – it was what she'd always yearned for without knowing. Artistry. Peace. And above all…

'Are you – are you Mrs Kesgrave, discreet correspondent?'

'A many-layered question is that. Are you Jess?'

'Um, yes.'

The lady moved back, making a gesture of invitation. 'Then I am Gloria Kesgrave. The rest can wait. Congratulations on surviving your awful experience and having the gumption to find me.'

Jess felt herself drawn into a sloe-dark gaze. There was humour, curiosity and speculation. And above all… kindness.

Mrs Kesgrave looked at Jess's satchel and the battered gas mask box. 'No suitcase, dear one?'

'No. Well, not yet. I'd have to fetch it and it's heavy.'

'As all the best luggage is. You are here; that's the important thing. Welcome, Jess. Welcome to the lodging house.'

19

Saturday, 7 September 1940

Mrs Kesgrave's sitting room was crowded with antique furniture, age-softened textiles, lamps and bookcases. It fulfilled every expectation. There was a radiogram with a brass horn. Surfaces were polished to a gleam yet the room felt lived-in, capable of sparking conversation and ideas. Charlotte would have loved it. *Would love it*, Jess corrected herself.

No doubts remained. Her sister was within the encircling streets. This would be the perfect place to call home, to continue her search.

Only, what if she were judged too plain, too dowdy? And could she afford it? There was still the matter of her fall. And its cause. Her fear grew when Mrs Kesgrave came in with tea, pouring from an Art Deco pot into cups painted with crocuses. Jess's fingers still felt clumsy – too much so for costly china.

'Are you a Jessica or a Jessamine?'

'Jessica. But Jess is fine.'

'And what do you do, when not swan-diving onto the Bakerloo line concourse?'

Oh dear. She should have rehearsed this moment. 'I, um, work for the government, in Censorship.'

The teapot spout jerked. 'Censorship? You spy on our mail?'

'I'm afraid so,' Jess admitted, launching into a defence. 'It has to be done because people write the most extraordinary things to each other. I opened a letter from a mother to her son doing his military training on the South Coast. She didn't name the camp, but she named places nearby. Anyone could work out the location from that.'

'Would it matter?' Gloria Kesgrave offered a sugar bowl.

On that occasion, majestic Mr Brinkworth had come in person to scrutinise the letter and had introduced Jess to the concept of triangulation.

'Yes. Very much,' she said, 'if the information reached saboteurs or anarchists. Or a Nazi here under cover radioed the co-ordinates to Berlin. It would make the camp a target for bombing.'

'But, really, would it happen? Has it happened?'

'Not to my knowledge,' Jess admitted, 'but it could. In Censorship, we are guarding against possibility as much as probability. A year ago, we didn't think we were going to be bombed at all, but we have been.'

'"Guarding as much against possibility as probability",' Mrs Kesgrave repeated. 'What a startlingly intelligent phrase. I am impressed.'

Jess didn't mention that she'd been quoting Mr Brinkworth. 'You don't mind about my work? It won't put you off me?'

'Not at all. You will find I have frank views on many matters but I do not judge. All I ask is the same in return.'

It was on the tip of Jess's tongue to ask what a 'discreet correspondent' did for a living, though she'd been brought up never to question her elders. The moment was missed as Mrs

Kesgrave offered a plate of shortbread and suggested they get down to business.

The rental here was three pounds a month for a bed in a shared room. 'I'll take you upstairs to view, when you've had your tea. Hot water's included. As for meals and cooking, we operate a rota. We cook by turn to foster a communal spirit. I already have two young women in situ. You would complete the nest. I like No. 34 to feel like a home from home. Does it sound acceptable?'

Jess nodded eagerly. Home from home. She explained that she was used to cooking and running a house. 'We lost our mother early, my sister and I. For a few years, we had a housekeeper but when she turned fourteen, my sister Charlotte took up the reins. She disliked... *dislikes* cooking, so I did it while she did the household accounts.'

'Excellent. I would need your ration book.' Mrs Kesgrave urged her to take another biscuit. 'One is never enough. That won't be a problem?'

If she meant shortbread, no. Jess took a second piece readily. If she meant handing over vital documents to a stranger... not so sure.

'Both my other lodgers have given me theirs,' Mrs Kesgrave told her. 'And they no longer spend their lunchtimes queuing up as I do the shopping. It would be awkward not to buy your allocation at the same time.'

'I'm registered at shops in Paddington.'

'We would re-register you locally. You seem unhappy, Jess.'

Jess drank her tea. Fragrant, delicate and nothing like the canteen brew at Senate House. When Mrs Kesgrave dunked her shortbread, Jess followed suit, feeling she ought to explain her quietness.

'I came to London thinking I had somewhere to stay, but I was turned away at the door. On top of everything, my purse was stolen.' She hesitated. There were darker reasons for her mistrust.

London's big, but you can't hide from me.

Forcing the voice away, she went on, 'I've had... a difficult couple of weeks. Please don't be offended if I seem cautious.'

'Dear one, I don't blame you in the slightest. And you had your horrible accident. I promise, I will take utmost care of your documents and account for everything spent. Did I mention? It's seven shillings a week extra for breakfast and your evening meals.'

Jess drank her tea. Even with the subsidised meals at Senate House, that sounded excellent value. Except, she now had only one pound and ten shillings in her purse.

Fares, food and gin. Father would be appalled. Everyone else would think it impossible. *Jess Gresham, throwing off the reins. Surely not.*

She longed to say yes. Two housemates sounded like fun. Weren't shared meals the best way to make friends? And with Mrs Kesgrave at the helm, it also felt safe. If they accepted her, she might start to feel part of something again. If they liked her, perhaps she wouldn't feel so very lonely.

'Are you wondering if you can afford me?' Mrs Kesgrave spoke through her shortbread, shielding her mouth with her hand.

'I can afford it, once I'm paid at the end of the month.' So long as she kept her job. 'I told you that my purse was taken...'

'And since then, you've scraped by on what you had in your pocket?'

'Not exactly. A friend advanced me a few pounds. But I still don't have quite enough.'

'Until you're paid. In that case...' Mrs Kesgrave took a pencil and paper from one of her capacious pockets and wrote out an IOU. 'Make good at the end of the month. I trust you.'

Jess felt something shift in her throat. The kind of gratitude that could unleash tears. She managed a nod and steadied her voice enough to ask, 'Who would I be sharing with?'

'With Betony Styles and Grace Wheeler. Betony is what the French call a mannequin and we over here call a "house model". She works for a fashion magazine, and her job is to make clothes look lovely while an artist sketches her. Her other role is to get up late in the morning and go out to swish places with unfeasibly handsome men, as far as I can tell.'

Jess could hardly have received a more daunting word-sketch. All she heard was 'fashion', 'lovely', 'handsome'. 'And, um, Grace?'

'Grace is a nurse who works for a Mayfair family. Like me, she speaks her mind – though I must say, she's evasive about her background. Let me tell you a secret. When she handed over her ration book, I found a discrepancy between the name she gave me and the one printed inside.'

'Oh?'

'She *calls* herself Wheeler.'

'Not her real name?'

'No, it's Whelan.'

Jess felt the blood drain from her face.

'Irish, of course. My dear?' Mrs Kesgrave's tone sharpened. 'I do hope you're not one who judges others. As I said, I like No. 34 to be a home from home. A happy one.'

Jess opened her mouth but the words tangled. Silence stretched until she could almost hear the doors of this refuge being slammed shut.

'You are making a lengthy perambulation of the mind, Jess,' her hostess observed at last. 'Have you reached your destination?'

Yes, thought Jess. And it was a hard one to reach.

'I'm sorry,' she said quietly. 'I'm not... It isn't the Irish. It's just—' She cast around desperately for a way of explaining her gut-terror of Cormac Whelan. As her gaze darted about the room, it snagged on a painting above a dresser. It was a portrait of a cockerel, golden-brown with a red comb like a ducal coronet.

'You are looking at Imperator,' said Mrs Kesgrave. 'My father's pride and joy, who won every show he was entered into.'

Jess seized the chance to talk about something she understood. 'A Buff Orpington, isn't he?'

'Every inch. You know your chickens?' Mrs Kesgrave smiled warmly as she waited for Jess's response.

'I have a little flock of five... had, I should say, before I left home. My father promised he'd get someone to come in to do the outdoor work now I've left. Someone to feed and collect eggs, but I worry for them. Will they love my girls like I do?'

'The hardest question,' Mrs Kesgrave replied. 'Do they have names?'

'The Sussex fowls are Eglé and Eglantine. The Rhode Islands are Eggitha Christie and Edith Sitwell and my Black Dorking—'

'Let me guess. Egberta.'

'Henrietta.'

Mrs Kesgrave laughed.

'My sister and I spent hours thinking up egg names each time we added to the flock. I so miss—' Jess nearly said 'her', substituting 'them' at the last moment. 'The way they run towards you when you come out with scraps.'

'I know. I have only four now, having lost poor Mary earlier this summer. Come and see.'

Mrs Kesgrave took Jess through a small kitchen to a back yard where herbs in pots had been moved aside to make room for a turf-roofed Anderson shelter.

Hitching up her silk hem, she led Jess to a wire chicken coop where three brown hens and one black one scratched in the dirt. 'They're named after the Bennet sisters.' Mrs Kesgrave pointed to each in turn. 'The Buffs are Jane, Lizzie and Kitty and the little Dorking is Lydia. Mary was a barnyard hen, a crossbreed with a terrible squawk. Fitting, really.'

'How did poor Mary die?'

'Fox. We have a few. One must have scaled the wall from the mews behind. In broad daylight, too, but he's the least of it – I'm certain the bombs will scare the poor creatures to death. I wonder if I could build their own Anderson?'

'Would you be allowed to, just for hens?' Jess gave the coop a tentative push and it moved more than she'd expected.

'I see what you're thinking. No wonder the fox got in.' Mrs Kesgrave had misread her expression. She'd been comparing her own tenuous existence to that of the chickens.

'Are you any good with hammer and nails?' Mrs Kesgrave glanced towards a rickety shed. 'I've some spare wood and tarpaper. We could make some running repairs.'

'I'm not very handy,' Jess confessed. 'Charlotte and I made our own henhouse but she did most of it. I just held the ends of things.'

'Not practically minded, then.'

Jess said she'd like to be. 'My mother was a farmer's daughter, and she could birth a cow while harvesting turnips. Charlotte inherited that side, though she's glamorous too,' Jess added emphatically, not wanting Mrs Kesgrave to imagine her sister in wellingtons. 'I take after my father, who's hopeless on the nuts and bolts of life. He's a vicar, so there's always somebody ready to help out.'

'A vicar?' Mrs Kesgrave studied Jess for a moment, then nodded. 'It doesn't surprise me. You possess an unforced innocence.'

Jess pictured a gin bottle tilted over a glass. *Give me a double.*

An hour spent hammering, patching and reroofing – Mrs Kesgrave leading the way – and the hens had a sturdier enclosure, including a covered area where they could retreat if the skies became loud.

'If there's bombing here,' Jess said, 'we could just bring the Bennet sisters into the Anderson shelter with us. I mean, if you want me to stay.'

Had she really decided to come here, despite the coincidence of Grace being called Whelan? There were lots of Irish in London, she told herself. Many named Whelan, no doubt. But what about Mrs Kesgrave, who after all was the landlady? She would choose, not Jess.

'It's a delicious idea,' the lady said, 'though I dread to think of Betony's reaction if I ask her to share quarters with chickens.' Her mouth twitched as she watched Jess dust off her hands. 'Perhaps we can find you a corner here after all.'

By four, Jess was ensconced in her new lodgings. By supper time, her suitcase had been fetched. She'd mentioned again how heavy it was, how she dreaded having to lug it down two flights of stairs and onto the Underground.

'Then there is only one solution,' Mrs Kesgrave had cried. 'We will fetch it by taxi and have the driver do the heavy lifting.'

Mrs Kesgrave said Jess must have the bed that stood alone, in the niche beside the chimney breast.

'Grace and Betony have been fighting over it, but you need peace and quiet, and to be near the door, in case you have to get up in the night.'

'I don't want to upset them.' She didn't want to get off on the wrong foot.

'Those girls can work out a truce between themselves.' Mrs Kesgrave pointed to a mahogany wardrobe. 'That is a shared resource, though Betony hogs it. I've never met anyone with so many clothes. Grace has very few, which I suspect is a bone of contention.' She cocked an eye at Jess's suitcase. 'Are you a Grace or a Betony?'

'If you mean clothes, I've hardly any.' Her clean ones were in a cotton bag. She'd been using a laundry service where they washed, dried and ironed for a shilling a go. 'I've brought plenty of reading matter, however.'

Mrs Kesgrave pointed to a bookcase of the same dark wood as the wardrobe. It was bare but for a pot of face cream and a pamphlet entitled *Your Gas Mask and How to Use It*.

'You won't find much competition for those shelves. I'm glad you're a reader as I adore literary conversations. It was such a relief when I mentioned the names of my chickens, and you didn't ask if the Bennet sisters were an American close-harmony group.'

'*Pride and Prejudice* is my favourite,' Jess said earnestly. 'It's where I go in hard times.'

'I visit *Mansfield Park*,' said Mrs Kesgrave. 'Shall I leave you to unpack in peace?'

All Jess wanted was to crawl under the salmon pink eiderdown, but the rising note of an air raid siren killed that hope. She followed her landlady out to the Anderson shelter.

The afternoon raid lasted just over an hour, detonations coming thickly but muffled and distant. When the two of them emerged, one side of the sky had a brazier glow tarnished with rolling black smoke.

'Thames Estuary,' Mrs Kesgrave said curtly. 'Dear God. I wish it would stop.'

It was almost seven o'clock when Jess finally got under the covers. Mrs Kesgrave was cooking that night and had sent her upstairs for a nap, promising to call her down when supper was ready.

Jess plunged into so deep a sleep, when hands on her shoulders began violently shaking her, the face of Cormac Whelan gate-crashed her dream.

In dream-reality, she tried to run away but her legs wouldn't work.

A voice penetrated. 'Wake up, wake up.'

Jess fought away the bedcovers and opened her eyes. A young woman was leaning over her. In the brassy evening light, she resembled a figure from a stained-glass window. Auburn-gold curls, white collar, a blue tunic buttoned up the front, eyes the same colour. It was the eyes and the shape of chin that sealed it for Jess, who let out a horrified scream.

The girl recoiled, then leaned forward, peering equally hard at Jess. 'You!' she said, as if she'd seen a ghost.

Only then did Jess realise the air raid sirens were wailing. She pushed herself upright. 'What time is it?'

'Doesn't matter.' The nurse gave herself a shake, which seemed to snap her back into a state of efficiency. 'Get some warm things on and come down to the shelter. Quick – they've already set the docks alight, and they'll want to finish the job.'

The accent was careful, BBC-perfect. Nothing like Cormac Whelan's.

But the eyes were. Fierce, undiluted blue. Jess had thought fate was kind, bringing her here. It now felt more like a cunning manoeuvre.

In under ten minutes, Jess was inside the Anderson shelter where Mrs Kesgrave introduced Grace as, 'Our hard-working nurse.'

Jess managed a pallid smile, a brief nod. Grace did much the same, but Jess could feel those eyes on her. Studying. Interrogating.

'Where's Betony?' Jess asked, wishing the fourth member of the household were here, someone else for Grace to focus on.

'She's been working today as well,' Mrs Kesgrave said, ignoring Grace's snort of derision. 'She's probably stayed late at her magazine—'

A distant explosion cut her off. The anti-aircraft guns gave answering thunder. Mrs Kesgrave said they sounded like the ones in Hyde Park. 'We're very much on a war footing here, however it looks on the surface. Let's hope Betony is sheltering with her colleagues and won't try to make it home.'

Grace said she doubted it. 'She's tucked up tight with the two men who are in love with her. I saw them both go into her office. What wouldn't I give to be a fly on the wall,' she added, so caustically, Jess knew the tension ran deeper than a quarrel over a bed. A bed she would happily give up if it would soften the acrimony, but which housemate would she choose?

Mrs Kesgrave poured tea from a thermos, and produced a board game, one entirely new to Jess. It was called Monopoly and involved you shaking dice and pushing a coloured button in a clockwise direction around London streets. You were meant to buy them, make sets and charge other people rent when they landed on them.

She could hear her father weighing in with, 'Blatant racketeering.'

Some names she recognised, such as Mayfair and Regent Street. And Coventry Street where there was a Lyons' Corner House. She made a poor start, her throws of the dice turning up the lowest numbers. She wasn't sure what she should buy either. Her instinct was to conserve the paper money Mrs Kesgrave, as banker, had dealt out. When she landed on Fleet Street, she snapped it up. It made her think she should go back there in real life and ask to speak with the *London Mercury's* editor-in-chief. Oswald somebody. After all, Charlotte had addressed her unfinished letter to him. It led her to wonder where Charlotte was right now, if she was in a shelter or in danger. Alone, scared.

'Your turn, Jess. Throw the dice.'

Jess rolled and landed in jail.

Grace was still casting covert glances her way. Jess had no

idea what Grace suspected or thought she knew. What had 'you!' meant?

It had sounded like a trap snapping shut.

Could this woman know Charlotte, or have met her?

The raid went on and on, exhausting the tea in the flask and their appetite for Monopoly. It was the longest, hardest raid so far. They sat slightly apart, the sustained attack and the returning fire making conversation hard.

At last, the skies quietened and the relief as they waited for the all-clear brought a revelation from Mrs Kesgrave that perhaps explained her reaction that afternoon when Jess described her job in Censorship. She did not own No. 34 Hill Street, she said. It was rented from the Grosvenor Estate. 'The Duke of Westminster's my landlord.'

Moreover, it was not her name on the legal agreement, but that of her former husband. 'And he doesn't know, so you must never mention it.' Then came another revelation.

Gloria Kesgrave was a divorced woman.

Father would be horrified, Jess reflected, so he'd best never know. Nor would he, since she'd been all but disowned. The raid started again. With high explosives falling on some as-yet-unidentified part of the city and the dreadful lottery of death unfolding, the rift with her father felt minor. It hurt, the way a thorn in a finger hurt.

During the next lull, their landlady explained her job. 'I spend nights in hotel rooms with gentlemen.'

Grace gasped, though Jess supposed that as a nurse, she'd seen all kinds of things. For her part, she was shocked but determined not to show it.

'Are – are you saying—' she began.

'I absolutely am not, dear one,' said Mrs Kesgrave briskly. She explained that she acted as the so-called adulterous party when a married couple wished to divorce. 'I share a hotel room with the husband, and in the morning I'm "discovered" in compromising circumstances. Adultery proved, no fuss, and nobody's reputation harmed.'

'Apart from yours,' Grace remarked.

'Oh, mine's up to the job – double-reinforced and riveted.' Mrs Kesgrave gave a bright smile. She'd started out in life as a bit-part actress, she said. 'Usually the understudy, or a party guest with no lines', before making a disastrous marriage of her own.

Being paid to play 'the other woman' turned out to be a steadier living.

'And I don't have to learn lines. I like to think of it as a social service.'

Jess was still reeling. Father would have a seizure. Miss Hillingdon would stagger off to write to the bishop.

But as the shock ebbed, it struck Jess that nothing more clearly marked her break from her old life than this: she was sharing a house with a nurse, a fashion model in love with two men, and a lady who pretended to be a scarlet woman, for a fee.

For one bizarre moment, she felt she might laugh.

Not for long.

Out of nowhere – perhaps taking her cue from Mrs Kesgrave's confiding tone – Grace announced quietly, 'My name's not really Wheeler.'

'It's Whelan,' said Jess before she could stop herself.

Grace froze. 'And you know that how?'

'I – don't,' Jess faltered.

Grace was seated on the bench opposite and leaned forward to peer into Jess's face. 'Either you recognise me, or you've been asking about me. I'm going to wager... the first. You know me, or someone closely related to me.'

'No.' Jess knew she sounded frightened. Hounded. 'It just slipped out. Someone mentioned the name Whelan to me and, um, it's an Irish name and—' She was floundering like a duck. Webbed feet in deep mud.

Grace's voice hardened. 'Course. There are a lot of us about, after all.' She gathered up the hair that had fallen forward and tucked it into her collar. 'I wasn't born in Mayfair, if that's what you're wondering. West of Ireland. Came over on a boat. The family settled in the East End. Whitechapel. And yes, you may tell Betony the hideous truth.'

'I won't do any such thing. It's not my business.'

'What is your business, if I might ask?'

'Jess works for the government,' Mrs Kesgrave said, the peacemaker.

'Which part?'

'Ministry of Information.' Jess named Senate House. Section C, Censorship.

'God save us.' Grace almost spluttered. 'Will you be taking notes if I talk in my sleep?'

'Only if you're muttering in German,' Jess replied, then wished she hadn't as Mrs Kesgrave said firmly that everything that went on beneath her roof was confidential.

'I'll add that secrecy isn't necessarily wrong,' Mrs Kesgrave continued. 'It depends what's being hidden.'

Grace snorted. 'I'm sure we only have respectable secrets in this shelter.'

'Just as I'm sure that Jess will leave her work at the door each evening so you may say and think whatever you choose. Though there are limits,' Mrs Kesgrave said with perfect calm. 'I've no tolerance for spies, ration cheats, black marketeers or' – she glanced up at the shelter roof as if into a past visible to her alone – 'for able-bodied men who dodge their duty while others fight and die.'

Grace had started fiddling with her collar at the mention of black marketeers. Now her hand stilled. Jess saw a pulse beating in her throat.

'Everyone agreed?' coaxed Mrs Kesgrave.

'Entirely,' Grace said, her voice edged with something Jess couldn't interpret.

Mrs Kesgrave turned to more mundane matters. No onions at the grocer's that day. 'Still, I got the last leek. And what a beauty.'

The earth shuddered. Somewhere above the turfed roof, glass rattled. A far-off blast rolled through the night.

'Definitely the Hyde Park guns,' Mrs Kesgrave said with a sigh. 'Have you seen them? They're gargantuan beasts—'

A single blast tore through the night, the reverberation hanging in the air for over a minute. Grace put her head in her hands, and Jess suddenly realised that if she came from the East End, she must be terrified for her family.

She leaned across and touched a starched white cuff. 'I hope they're all right.'

Grace lifted her head. 'They'd better be.'

Another Titanic explosion made the shelter quiver. Nobody breathed as they waited for an impact. It came, but not on Mayfair.

Today – Saturday, 7 September – the Germans had finally come in numbers.

In the early hours of Sunday, the all-clear sounded. The guns quietened. Jess, Mrs Kesgrave and Grace emerged into a world on fire. Towards Soho, towards Holborn and the square mile of the City, the view was of a vast, low-burning pyre. Wordlessly, they inhaled the stench of cordite and smoke, scorching and burning oil. Grace began to cry.

Mrs Kesgrave pulled her close. Jess stood quietly by before going inside and filling a kettle for tea.

Before going upstairs to bed, Grace touched Jess on the shoulder.

'We need to talk,' she said in an undertone. Then, when Jess didn't answer: 'Soon as you're ready.'

20

On Sunday night, 8 September, the bombers returned and turned their fury once more on the battered East End.

Monday morning, Jess walked to work with a handkerchief tied over her mouth. The air was thick, the sky set like egg yolk from the heat of fires. You had to tread carefully, streets and pavements littered with razor-sharp fragments of shell casings. And the smell... London's newest perfume was melted rubber and toffee apple. Somewhere, a sugar warehouse had gone up.

Queuing to pass through security, Jess saw the same shock and weariness on every face. At her desk, waiting for her first batch of letters, she counted twenty empty places. Neither Phyllis nor Rosa were in. It didn't have to mean they'd been caught in the bombing – perhaps their buses simply couldn't get through. Even so, the silent desks pressed on her nerves.

Miss Cartwright herself pushed the letter trolley this morning, offering no comment on the absences. Later, she addressed the gathering.

'Mr Brinkworth asks that we work doubly hard today as we're thin on the ground. He also says, don't rush. Be as meticulous as ever.'

Jess wondered how they were meant to obey both orders at once.

By staying at their desks, it turned out. Instead of morning tea break, water jugs were brought in. The clink of glasses stood in for tea and laughter.

She tried to concentrate, but a memory of last night kept sliding into her thoughts.

Grace's eyes across the shelter. The voice that had called her from sleep before the sirens drowned everything. The sudden tenderness when she'd said of her family, 'They'd better be.'

Why couldn't Grace stick to being Miss Wheeler? Whelan was the name that chilled Jess's blood. The name that had pursued her through the Underground. Leaving Hill Street this morning, she'd felt the house was holding its breath for the moment she and Grace let their secrets slip.

At around eleven, Miss Cartwright left the room, and someone behind her hissed, 'I'm bursting for the loo.'

The whisper brought a ripple of subdued laughter – a moment of normality that steadied Jess more than anything else. Miss Cartwright returned with Mr Brinkworth, who began his unhurried stroll around the desks. When they halted a short way from Jess, she paused to listen. Perhaps at last some drama, a spy ring uncovered, planned sabotage exposed.

Mr Brinkworth caught her looking and came over. A gold fountain pen was clipped to his breast pocket. His oiled, grey hair was precisely parted down one side and today, as always, he was turned out within the bounds of wartime austerity in a smart suit with false pockets. Usually, he wore a neatly knotted tie with a boat-sail pin. Today, he seemed to be wearing clothes from the previous day. He must have been in a shelter all night, like the rest of them.

She liked him the better for being human. Prepared for a

ticking-off, to her surprise, he told her to put the letter aside. 'I'd like you to look at this one.'

Jess took the handwritten note, noting the blue ink, the quality writing paper. Pre-war stock as nothing this smooth was produced now. An address engraved top right showed it had been sent from Pinner, Middlesex. 'Anything in particular to look for?'

'You were on about flash burns not so long ago,' Mr Brinkworth said. 'A friend of yours suffered them, I believe.'

Jess gaped. He meant Rafe, but when had she said any such thing? Certainly not to Mr Brinkworth or Miss Cartwright. Then she remembered. During a tea break with Phyllis and Rosa before her accident, Phyllis had mentioned a nephew in the Navy who had been rescued from the water. Jess had spoken of Rafe. Though not by name. 'A friend, someone I know.' She'd described his one-sided injuries and Phyllis had said, 'That'll be flash burn. Vapour catches light and travels faster than a blink. The poor devils can't get away.'

Had Phyllis reported their conversation, or did the tables have ears?

Mr Brinkworth was waiting. 'Read it, Miss Gresham. I want to see how you approach this.'

She asked, was it a test?

'Of you – no. Of our training, yes.' A faint smile broke his earnest expression. 'Give me your thoughts, uncensored.'

She began to read.

6 September, 1940

My dearest Margaret,

I know you're upset but you're being sensible. Your engagement was all very well before, when he was a promising young officer. But you can't possibly tie yourself to him now. You're only twenty-one. Those dreadful burns!

I heard the Basilisk went down off Dunkirk (not supposed to know, of course), fuel stores caught and lit up the sea. Flash burns don't heal, so you'd be condemning yourself to years of nursing a lifelong invalid. Lieutenant Taverner, RN, standing tall in his uniform, was what any girl would want. Now he's a charity case.

Lieutenant Taverner. Rafe had said he'd been in the Navy but never named a ship. Were there other Taverners injured this way? Could be. Her head buzzed.

'Give me your reaction, Miss Gresham,' Mr Brinkworth prompted.

Jess couldn't answer. Her lips had gone stiff.

Mr Brinkworth tried a different question. 'What will you do with this letter?'

She got a grip on herself. 'I can tell you what I'd like to do, sir. Go to Pinner, Middlesex, and punch this woman on the nose.' The letter was signed, 'All my love, Mother'. 'Then I'd do the same to her loathsome daughter.'

Charity case. How dare they?

Mr Brinkworth cleared his throat. 'I meant, within the bounds of our duty.'

'I'd flag it,' she said firmly. 'Definitely flag it.'

'Not send it on, redacted?'

'No. Pass it upstairs, Mr Brinkworth. This reveals dangerous, classified detail. It damages morale and could put others at risk. The author ought to be visited by the police for aiding the enemy.' Her voice sharpened. 'I'd prosecute this woman under the Official Secrets Act.'

Jess wondered how many men on the *Basilisk* had lost their lives. This woman didn't seem to care. 'That part about the water being lit up… imagine how anyone with a son at sea would feel, reading that.'

Mr Brinkworth did not comment except to say quietly, 'I hope never to inspire your displeasure, Miss Gresham. "Though she be but little she is fierce".'

Am I? Jess wondered. Nobody had ever had cause to steer clear of her before, but now her blood boiled. *Lifelong invalid.* What did they know? 'A man has his health ruined in the service of his country, and his fiancée drops him cold.'

'I'd say he was well rid, but thank you for your opinion, Miss Gresham.' Mr Brinkworth took the letter. 'I will navigate things from here.'

Lunch, Spam and cress sandwiches and tea, was served at their desks, to the muted accompaniment of an air raid warning. In their bombproof basement, they worked through until the all-clear at two thirty. At which point, they were told to go.

'Don't hang around, get home fast, be back tomorrow.'

Jess stepped out into an afternoon that seemed to quiver in shock. Dust swam in the air and above the rooflines, smoky foxtails dirtied the clouds. She was making for Tottenham Court Road, taking a chance on the Tube, when the feeling of being followed crept over her once more.

More than a feeling: she could hear footsteps keeping pace with hers. Instead of spinning round, she continued on, stopping to look in the half-boarded window of a printer's shop. Slowly, she turned her head. The shoulder of a man disappeared into a tobacconist's she'd just passed. Jess went back and this time, it was emotion and not gin that made her bold. She strode inside.

'Show yourself, Cormac Whelan,' she called to the man who stood at the counter. 'Come outside now while I'm angry enough to batter you with my shoe.'

The tobacconist gawped. The man at the counter swung round, startled.

A complete stranger, old enough to be her father, buying a tin of Virginia Leaf tobacco.

Not yet having her own key to No. 34, Jess knocked. She heard brisk footsteps, and had just time to think, *Mrs Kesgrave never runs, she sweeps*, before the door was tugged open.

A willowy young woman with the glossiest fair hair Jess had ever seen regarded her in disappointment. The impression was so profound, Jess apologised. No prizes for guessing that this was the Hon. Miss Styles. The graceful figure, the swan neck... Besides, Jess had seen her dress, pale yellow with a pattern of hollyhocks, in the wardrobe.

Betony glanced past Jess, down the street as if expecting someone else. There was nobody, just a tabby cat dashing across the road. With a sigh, she said, 'Come in. You must be Jess.'

'You're Betony?'

'The same, though certain people have forgotten, it seems. Still, not your fault.' The voice rang like cut crystal, though with a slight drag to it, as if life were too, too tedious. Perhaps it was, for a girl who spent her life standing still, being sketched.

Walking in, Jess blurted out, 'I've been at work today in a dark basement.'

'Snooping for His Majesty. Ogling our post. Mrs Kesgrave told me. Isn't it terribly sinister?'

This morning, when Mr Brinkworth had mentioned flash burn, she'd had exactly the same thought, but she rushed to defend her role. 'I suppose to outsiders it might seem...'

Betony had walked off.

Jess trailed after her. In the kitchen, they found Mrs Kesgrave at the pine table, slicing runner beans.

'Get your apron on,' their landlady said. 'Not you, Jess.'

'I'm cooking tonight.' Betony sounded mildly astonished by the fact. 'The rota has spoken.'

In which case, why is Mrs Kesgrave doing the veg? Jess wondered. She asked after the chickens. Were they all right after the afternoon raid?

Mrs Kesgrave shook her head. 'No eggs this morning. Then again, I wouldn't lay after the hammering we got last night. I wish I could send them to the country, like the children and the pregnant mums, but I doubt they'd survive long. The pot would be their fate.' She went back to her stringing and slicing. 'If you're asking where these beans come from, Lurking Larry, sixpence.'

'Lurking Larry?'

'Our neighbourhood vegetable poacher,' Betony explained. 'He wheels his barrow through lanes wide and narrow, stealing from the allotments. Shameless. Filches people's produce, then sells it back to them.'

'I thought you hated black marketeers,' Jess said to Mrs Kesgrave.

'I do; they're the lowest of the low. But some of the beans are probably mine. I rent a neglected allotment a few streets away.'

Jess fetched another peeling knife and sat down opposite Mrs Kesgrave, taking beans off the pile. They worked in silence as Betony sorted through a basket of provisions in a desultory way. The telephone rang in the front passage, and with a cry of 'I'll get it,' she dropped the paper-wrapped fish she'd been peering at and ran out.

'I don't hold out much hope for dinner,' Mrs Kesgrave said. 'Girls like dear Betony are taught to dance the polka with a Bible balanced on their head, but can they make a jug of parsley sauce?'

Jess didn't answer. She had dragged her day at Senate House home with her, two faces in her mind – a serving Naval officer, burned and cast off by the despicable Margaret; and Cormac Whelan, clinging to her like a strand of spider silk.

Mrs Kesgrave gave her a searching look. 'I couldn't help overhearing some of what you and Grace were saying the other evening, in the shelter. I rather put my foot in it saying what I did about black marketeers. Rumour has it, her brother is deep in that game.'

Jess's knife stopped midway through a cut. 'How d'you know?'

'What the brother's up to? Gossip. He sometimes drinks at the pub on Farm Street and I know the landlady. Young Cormac is a wild card, I'm afraid. Jess, have I upset you?'

'I'm fine.'

So, there it was. Cormac Whelan was Grace's brother. Now she knew Grace's secret, it was only a matter of time before she'd have to tell Grace hers.

'That's enough beans.' Mrs Kesgrave gathered up the trimmings. 'Let's take these out to my girls.' Betony came back into the room and with a wry smile, their landlady asked, 'Anybody interesting?'

'What? Oh... no. It was the Grosvenor Estate asking if you'd had any damage to the roof after last night's fireworks.'

'The roof? Do they imagine I've been up there on a ladder?'

Betony shrugged. The expression in her eyes said it all. She'd dashed to the ringing telephone, hoping for one voice and been let down by reality.

'Come out with us and feed the hens, dear one,' Mrs Kesgrave invited. 'You strike poses all day then go night-owling with your admirers, or droop around looking sorry for yourself. It won't do.'

'It wouldn't be so bad,' Betony drawled with a pointed glance for Jess, 'if I still had my own bed.'

'You can have yours back,' Jess said hurriedly. 'If you really want it.'

Mrs Kesgrave got in first. 'Absolutely not. You are the solution to territorial hostilities, the buffer zone. I forbid you to yield.'

'Buffer zone, like Belgium?' Poor little Belgium had risen up as a neutral state between Germany and France. At the start of the last war, it had been invaded and flattened. 'That doesn't sound promising.'

'I mis-spoke,' Mrs Kesgrave acknowledged. 'You are Switzerland.'

'In that case,' Betony said languidly, 'may I have some chocolate and a bank loan?' But she was at least smiling.

'Come out and judge our handiwork with the hen coop,' Mrs Kesgrave urged. 'Otherwise, you'll spend all night willing the phone to ring and forget dinner. I maintain the telephone,' she explained to Jess, 'for my work. You may give the number to family and important contacts.' Then, raising an eyebrow at Betony, 'Lovers too, but not too many at once.'

To Jess's surprise, Betony came out with them, though not before changing her dress – to one that still outshone anything in Jess's possession. She even daubed varnish on the sides of the coop while Mrs Kesgrave offered encouragement and Jess shone a torch.

'What fun,' said Mrs Kesgrave later as they washed their hands at the kitchen sink. 'Grace has missed out, but she works such long hours. The relief nurse always arrives late, apparently. At least it's a short walk home for her.' Ventnor House, where Grace was employed, was the grandest property on Upper Brook Street, five minutes north of Hill Street across Grosvenor Square. 'Shame about its occupant. Lady Ventnor is unpleasant in every way though her husband, Sir Gideon, is a dear. Ever seen him? Handlebar moustache, Home Guard uniform.'

Jess didn't think she had.

'He secretly hopes we'll be invaded, just so he can fire a gun in anger again. But he's the kindest man alive and deserves a better wife. He's got a nephew he's terribly proud of. Handsome boy, Spitfire pilot. Ever met him, Betony? He's been dogfighting with death since June, though still in one piece, thank God. Can't think of his name... is it Howard? Or Stewart?'

'Owen. Flight Lieutenant Owen Henderson.'

The fierce correction told Jess and Mrs Kesgrave all they needed to know, and probably much that Betony hadn't intended to reveal.

Mrs Kesgrave announced she was going upstairs to rest for a while. 'Betony, don't forget, you're *chef de maison* tonight. The fish in the package you were poking earlier needs to be cooked, or it'll go off.'

Betony's expression was priceless and gave Jess a warning what might appear on their plates at supper. Ought she offer to help?

Mrs Kesgrave read her hesitation and said firmly, 'You must rest too, Jess. You still have the look of a girl who's been through the wringer. An hour, horizontal with a book, will do you no end of good.'

Jess complied, but as she left the room, a shadow seemed to detach and follow her: Cormac Whelan. You'd almost think he'd moved into the lodging house with her.

21

Jess hadn't read many lines when Betony came in, making a beeline for the wardrobe. 'What does one wear to the office on a Monday night? One isn't working but it's not social either.'

'You're going back to work? You're meant to be cooking.'

'Don't fret. I've put the potatoes on to boil and I'm only nipping out for a couple of minutes. My office is literally five hundred steps from here.'

'You mustn't let the pan boil dry...' Sensing her advice was falling on stony ground, Jess laid her book aside and said, 'What do the fashion pages say about going into work late on a Monday? Suit, dress or slacks?'

'Good point.' Betony went to her bedside cabinet and took out a tabloid newspaper. Jess recognised the flash of a masthead as Betony turned to the back.

'"What, pray, is a girl to wear when he or she-who-must-be-obeyed orders them in on the Sabbath?" That means Sunday, doesn't it?' Betony consulted with Jess over the edge of the page.

'Correct.'

'"My advice? A skirt and jacket, enlivened with a scarf in a cheery shade. Crimson if you dare, navy if you must. Hats – forget 'em unless you're going on to church or wish to impress a sulky lift attendant. And for heaven's sake, ladies, keep a powder compact close at hand. The war has stolen our weekends, but that's no excuse for a shiny nose."' A smile broke through Betony's gloom. 'I adore Miss Touchwood. Ever read her?'

'In more ways than one,' Jess replied, and to change the subject, said, 'The dress you had on when I came home was lovely. Wouldn't that do, with a cardie, now it's chilly?'

Betony went back to the wardrobe and took out the hollyhock dress. 'It's nice enough,' she said. 'All right.' She tossed it onto the bed and undressed to a baby-blue slip and champagne-coloured stockings. 'It's only an old thing from Debenham's, but I'm hoping to go out on a date later.'

From an evening bag she took a gold tube of lipstick and used the wardrobe mirror to burnish her mouth deep red.

Go out? 'Betony – what about your cooking?'

Betony swung round, making a face. 'Thing is, I've met this man. Owen, the one I spoke of. I'm head over heels. And my cooking isn't... you know.' Her expression shifted, an idea blooming. 'I don't suppose—'

Jess knew what was coming.

'—you'd take my turn tonight in the interests of true love? I'll do your next two for you.'

'I don't know.' It felt too soon to be changing the terms of their contract with Mrs Kesgrave.

'How about a shameless bribe, then?' Betony rubbed the gloss from her mouth. 'This lipstick isn't my colour, but it will look smashing with your dark hair and eyes.' The gilt tube was thrown.

Jess caught it, flustered now. Out of her depth. But she knew when she was being taken advantage of. 'The rota's the rota.'

'Oh, flip. All right.'

'Sorry.' Jess held out the lipstick for Betony to take back.

'Keep the warpaint. I knew it was wrong, but I still bought it. Next question...' Betony selected a different dress from the rail and held it against herself. 'Is this one better?'

It was shin-length, silk georgette in peach with a draped neck and a flared skirt. 'Teamed with an off-white jacket. What d'you think?' Not waiting for Jess's response, Betony glanced down and muttered, 'Oh, no.'

'What's wrong?'

'Chicken coop varnish on my hands. I can't get it on this dress. It's a Vionnet.'

That meant valuable, Jess supposed. She'd handed Betony the varnish earlier, rather clumsily.

Betony seemed to agree, saying, 'Do you really like chickens, or are you currying favour with our landlady?'

'I adore them. If I like something, I say so. If not, I stay quiet.'

Betony rehung the peach-coloured dress. 'Have a word with Grace, then. You never saw such a work of fiction when she's trying to be lah-di-dah Mayfair and making a hash of it. "One was born within the sound of Hanover Square's doorbells." She sounds like Thingummy from the play that fellow wrote. You know. "Not bloody likely."'

'Eliza Doolittle, *Pygmalion*. I feel sad for Grace,' Jess said. 'From what Mrs Kesgrave says, she's got a lot on her plate. She's frightened for her family too.'

'Oh, the family. *Gor blimey*. Why doesn't she just own up to coming from the East End?'

'She has, actually,' Jess came back. 'And why should she "own up"? None of us choose where we're born. We don't choose our relations, either.'

'I won't argue with that.' Betony shut the wardrobe. 'Has Mrs K mentioned what Grace's brother does for a living?'

'Sort of. But I'm not going to discuss it.' Against the odds, she instinctively liked Grace. Who didn't like a nurse? But it was more than that. Whoever her family was, Grace had a heart, whereas Betony seemed to live and breathe only for herself.

'What are you thinking?'

'About those potatoes,' Jess said pointedly. 'They'll either be pulp by now or boiled black.'

'Be a darling and sort them out? Mash them or something.'

Jess shook her head.

'But I gave you my lipstick.' Betony sounded genuinely wounded.

'Because you don't want it. That's not a gift.' Jess hated conflict, but Betony Styles was a gilded steam engine and would roll her flat if she let her. Whereas Grace, in the shelter on Saturday night, had offered comfort though she must have been demented with worry for her family. Playing their board game, Jess had landed on Bond Street, which Mrs Kesgrave owned. It had a hotel on it and Jess would have gone bankrupt, only Grace, with a wink, moved her on a square. Jess tried to explain this. Betony stared.

'Mrs K has a hotel on Bond Street?'

'Monopoly,' Jess explained. 'I was in trouble and Grace nudged my button on, saying I'd miscounted.'

'Cheated, then. Sounds about right.'

Had she read too much into that tiny act of friendship? Jess wondered. Perhaps, but Grace had as much reason to worry as she did, with a brother dealing in illicit goods and dodging call-up. They'd have to talk soon, properly, and the thought unsettled Jess. In her anxiety, she fell back on a lecturing tone. 'We have to get on with sharing this room. Respecting each other is the only thing that'll work.'

'Here endeth the lesson.' Betony dropped the hollyhock

dress over her head and went to the door. 'Don't worry about the potatoes, though if you do happen to pop into the kitchen...'

She thinks I'm a prig, Jess thought as Betony's footsteps trailed downstairs. *And she doesn't know yet that I'm a vicar's daughter. Honestly, thinking she could bribe me.*

Even so, she couldn't resist trying the lipstick.

It looked gorgeous... and frighteningly like Charlotte's favourite shade.

Kneeling by her bed, Jess pulled out the suitcase and shone her torch on the Remington typewriter that had made the case such a brute to carry.

She didn't lift the lid of the machine. She wasn't ready to see the letter still trapped in its mouth. *Dear Sir, my name is Charlotte Gresham...*

Give it time. When she had something solid to guide her towards Charlotte, she'd read it again. For now, all she had were fragments that didn't yet fit together.

Jess rocked back on her heels, chasing memories through her head. During the autumn and winter of 1939, with the war young and the skies still quiet, Charlotte had seemed her usual sparky self. Her job at the bookshop could never satisfy her restless soul, but as a stopgap she'd liked it and she'd been popular with customers. Taking her typing and shorthand course on the side, going to London every Saturday, had fed the bigger dream.

Of escaping. Forging a career in the hub of things.

She'd visited the *London Mercury* at some point, wearing her distinctive coat, and offered them samples of her writing. How had Miss Treadgold described them? 'Character-sketches and country reflections.'

That didn't sound remotely like Charlotte. Maybe she'd given up on being a serious journalist and was willing to try any angle. She'd dropped her sights even lower after that and applied for the typing pool.

They'd not bitten, it seemed, or she wouldn't have written to the editor. Jess hadn't thought it before, but did the letter in the typewriter have the savour of desperation?

I'm so, so keen to start a career in journalism.

By Christmas, she was gone. Dead, or as good as, shut away in Alder Grove. From where she'd escaped, while the staff were toasting in the New Year. Now, *that* was Charlotte to a 'T'.

And then?

I'm the fool who put clothes on your back and kept you from the gutter on the coldest night of the year.

Joining the dots, Jess saw her sister trudging through ice-cold London streets in cast-off clothes and terrified – as she herself had been on her first night in the city. Like Jess, Charlotte had reached for the only hand extended to her. In Jess's case, it had been Rafe Taverner's. In Charlotte's, that of a hard-eyed criminal. Cormac Whelan. Jess's new shadow.

'Grace's brother,' she whispered.

'Hey, who's been talking?' came angrily from the doorway.

Jess jerked to her feet and saw Grace standing there. In uniform, cape over her shoulders. Their eyes locked. Jess read cold fury, and something of fear. Grace was waiting for her to speak. Jess made a beginning, gave up. What to say, what not to say?

In the end, she chose the simplest answer. 'I already knew. You see, I met your brother Cormac. Or rather, he came after me.'

Grace shut the door and sat down on the end of Jess's bed. 'Came after you, because you ran away from him, yes?'

Jess nodded. 'I was terrified. He... he had this look.'

'I know. It's how he gets. How long were you together?'

Odd question. 'Um, about five minutes. Maybe ten.'

Grace shook her head. 'No, I mean, how long were you lovers?'

Jess blinked, sat down on the bed too, making it bounce. 'We were never that. Good God. I wouldn't—'

'What, touch an Irishman with a barge pole?'

'I mean, I wouldn't go with anyone. Unless I loved the man...' An image of Rafe appeared, then fled. 'I've never had a lover, nowhere close.'

Grace studied her. Her eyes seemed glazed as if she'd just learned harrowing news. 'Then who are you, Jess?'

'Jessica Mary Gresham, daughter of Reverend Ian Gresham of St Saviour's Ramsgate, Kent.'

'Vicar's daughter, then?'

'Steeped in ordinariness.'

Grace made a sound, as if satisfied. 'Probably the safest thing. You're saying my brother came after you.'

'Thinking I was someone else. Mistaken identity.' Now it was Jess's turn. 'Grace, when we first met, who did you think I was?'

Grace got up and began unbuttoning her uniform. 'I thought, here we go. Lodger number three, very sweet and needing a good meal. Did I stare at you? Bad habit. I suppose I needed to see if you'd fit in. Two's company, they say, and three can be hell. But I knew you'd do, after a while.'

'You didn't look at me and mistake me for somebody else?'

A faint pause, then Grace shook her head. 'Not for an instant.'

'And Cormac, running after me, threatening me, you don't know of any reason for that?' Jess saw the jolt, the momentary panic in Grace's expression.

Grace dredged up a smile. 'He's a bit of an arse, I'll admit. He's got the family hot temper. But Cormac's all talk. Really, he's a gent.'

Jess walked over to Grace, pointed and said, 'That black eye...'

'Didn't I walk into a lamp post. This damn blackout.' Grace

pulled off her tunic and put on warm, comfortable things in preparation for a probable dash to the Anderson shelter later. With her back to Jess, she said, 'Did I smell burned potatoes as I came in?'

Jess was left with the impression of a conversation that had backed itself into a corner, then clawed free. They'd had their moment to clear the air, and Grace had looked away first.

22

Betony had returned from her dash to the office, to judge by the sound of clashing saucepans in the kitchen. From her expression when Jess looked in on her, the rota had won and romance had come second.

At least they would sit down to a meal.

'I suspect neither of her swains have been in touch,' Mrs Kesgrave whispered to Jess as they laid the dining room table. 'We imagine being beautiful is the greatest gift, but it can be a burden.'

'Nobody invites her out because she's so lovely?'

'It restricts the field. Only highly confident, attractive men dare ask.'

Jess thought of Rafe Taverner, who had seemed to like her, briefly. Was that because he was disfigured? It must be awful to have good looks ruined. Worse than never being good looking at all. In 'normal life' Rafe wouldn't have glanced twice at Jess Gresham. Somehow, it made his abrupt vanishing more hurtful.

Grace joined them, putting out water glasses. She looked dreadful, the bright hair loose from its pins. Had she been crying?

'Grace?' Mrs Kesgrave asked softly.

Jess braced herself, expecting blame for forcing a conversation Grace had plainly not wanted. 'I went home today.' Grace spoke in a monotone.

She glanced at Jess, who asked, 'Your family's all right, though?'

'They are, but they're frightened. Look, I wasn't going to say, but on Saturday night, there was a direct hit on Columbia Road market. An incendiary piled through a ventilation shaft, into the air raid shelter.'

Jess gasped. 'With people inside?'

'Hundreds. I knew something bad had happened when I went past the Royal London Hospital the next day and saw the ambulances queuing. Someone gave me a lift on a motorbike... It's where I trained.' Her thoughts seemed to be rambling. 'I should have been there. Why ever did I walk out?'

Betony appeared briefly in the doorway but left without speaking.

'We make choices, which at the time seem perfectly sensible,' Mrs Kesgrave soothed.

'They were going to make me redo a year,' Grace came back, 'so I slammed out. It's what I do.' Her eyes flashed at Jess. *The family hot temper.* 'Now, when I'm needed, I'm stuck in a stupid job looking after a spoiled old lady.'

'You could go back,' said Mrs Kesgrave.

'I'm trying.' That was said through gritted teeth. 'Sadly, the hospital system is as pig-headed as I am. Once you get a reputation...' She shrugged. 'At least I was able to read my family the riot act. They said they were never going in a public shelter again. They'd hide under the table when there was a raid.'

'Oh, no. Madness.'

Grace's pale smile implied agreement. 'My sister Immie, who's old enough to know better, says, if a bomb has your name on it, you're going to get it anyway. I asked her, did the bomb that flattened the market have forty names painted on the side? It makes me mad.'

'Sit down. Betony's cooking.'

Grace's response was a mutter that Jess interpreted as *God save us*. But she slumped in a chair. A moment later, a call rang out.

'Dinner's up!'

The meal Betony served was indescribable. The cod for which Mrs Kesgrave had queued an hour on Saturday had the texture of old cork sandals. The skin had dissolved in the cooking liquor, which had caught on the bottom of the pan. Betony had used the same liquor to make parsley sauce and their fish sat in a glutinous puddle speckled green, grey and black. The runner beans were boiled a strange shade of khaki, while the potatoes were black on the bottom, raw on top.

When the siren went at a few minutes past eight, relief surged around the table. They jumped up, and while Mrs Kesgrave made a thermos of tea, Jess and Grace spread golden syrup on chunks of bread.

The all-clear finally went at 3 a.m. the following morning.

They crawled into bed. Jess was woken at some indeterminate hour by a fierce, whispered conversation between the room's two other occupants.

'Whose motorbike did you hitch a ride on, then? I heard you saying you got a ride home.'

'Eavesdropping, Betony?'

'I came to check you were all ready to eat. Anyway, sound carries.'

'I know. We all heard you murdering the fish. It was Owen's bike, all right? He was at Ventnor House, and heard I needed a lift. He offered as it was on his way back to his base.'

'On his way... really? I thought home was Mayfair.'

'Whitechapel, as I'm sure you already know. He was going back to Hornchurch.'

'I know where his airbase is. You don't seem to realise, Grace, I've known him far longer than you. And don't call him "Owen".'

'It's his name. What else should I call him?'

'Flight Lieutenant Henderson.'

'Fine. I'll call him that if you will.'

Betony forgot to whisper. 'Don't be silly. He and I are a couple. You may not like to think it—'

'You don't know what I think. I'm not interested in any man of yours, all right?'

'What does that mean?'

'It means shut up and let me get some sleep. Unlike you, I have to work in the morning.'

'I work too!'

'Standing around looking half-baked in next year's fashion? That's not work. It's not even pretending.'

The argument eventually ceased. Jess let out her breath. In the dark, you could deduce a lot from tone and pauses. Grace had said, 'You don't know what I think,' after a clear hesitation suggesting, to Jess – the aspirant playwright, quietly reading between the lines – that she had something to hide. *Something else* to hide.

Jess hated being piggy-in-the-middle, but there was one advantage to her housemates waging war: neither would be watching her too closely. She could slip in and out as she did at Senate House: shy Jess Gresham, the girl no one really saw.

Her plans for the rest of the week were simple: go to work, steer clear of Cormac Whelan, keep searching for Charlotte – and stay close to shelter when the sirens started.

23

Tuesday, 10 September 1940

'Not falling asleep on your chair, I hope, Miss Gresham?'

Jess jerked to attention as Mr Brinkworth approached. The hours in the Anderson shelter had left her stiff and dull eyed. 'Not at all, sir,' she stammered. 'I was concentrating.'

'Peering through the portholes of your mind?' Today he was neat as a pin in his austerity suit.

'Er, yes. I was.'

'Let us hope the tide of your thoughts is running in the right direction.' He brought news. 'The letter from the concerned mother in Pinner was escalated as per your suggestion. Both mother and daughter have received police visits. Friendly warnings. No more loose talk, no more classified gossip.'

'I'm glad to hear it, sir.'

'As for the young man they were discussing, I'm told he is recovering, privately, at the home of a family member. Flash burn is extremely painful and there is a high risk of infection. A period of rest and confinement is advised. You understand?'

Could he see her blush? How could he know?

Mr Brinkworth nodded at the letter in her hand, which she hadn't yet opened. 'Will this one set the world alight, or merely smoulder, Miss Gresham?'

She blushed harder and sliced into it, reading quickly. 'It's, um, from a gentleman, writing to the lady who was his fiancée during the last war, suggesting that as he is now a widower, she might like to meet.'

'Ah. Where, Berlin?'

'At the Lyons' Corner House on Piccadilly. He will wear a spotted tie and carry a copy of the *Radio Times*.'

'Let me stop you.' Mr Brinkworth flattened his palms, discouraging her. 'When I ask if a letter is "interesting" I mean, should we send it to the Intelligence services? The wistful hopes of lonely gents and jilted spinsters fall not into that sphere.'

Fall not into that sphere. Jess wondered if Mr Brinkworth spoke like this at home, or if he assumed a character at work. Just as she did. Meek, dull, obedient. As soon as it was lunchtime, Jess was going to Grafton Way to see if the owner of Elegant Exchange had come back. The Jess who had brazened her way into Alder Grove and called her father a liar would, for an hour, come to life. And, hopefully, take a step closer to Charlotte.

She muttered, 'It's not of interest to Intelligence, of course, but has the man with the spotty tie been waiting twenty-five years to write to his long-lost fiancée?'

Mr Brinkworth cleared his throat. 'Miss Gresham. Were you not listening during your initial induction?'

'I was, hard as I could, but there was a lot to take in.'

'Then allow me to reprise. We, the Postal and Cable Censorship Office, do not inspect every letter, cable or telegram sent through the mail since we'd need fifty times the workforce.'

'Mail is picked out at random. I know that, sir.'

Mr Brinkworth's gaze brushed the rows of desks. 'Your job

is to read the ones allocated to you line by line, with a detached yet gimlet eye, may the goddess of metaphor forgive me. You are not reading public correspondence to feed your curiosity. Most of what you censor will be careless gossip. Folk saying too much, in all innocence. You are unlikely to net a spy. It doesn't mean they aren't out there.' He raised his voice, as others around paused to listen. 'Be alert for anything that looks like code or a clandestine message. Do we have clarity, ladies?'

'Yes, sir,' came a general, muttered reply.

'Miss Gresham?'

'Totally, sir.' She took an envelope from her in-pile. It was addressed to a Reverend C. W. Loftus in North Yorkshire. Mr Brinkworth was watching. Did they really need to inspect letters to ministers of the church? She could only imagine her father's wrath, if it happened to him.

Mr Brinkworth took the envelope and sliced into it with his own letter opener. 'You are the daughter of a vicar, I understand?'

Jess nodded. Somewhere behind her, someone muttered, 'Should have guessed.'

'From Ramsgate?'

She nodded. He'd looked at her file. Did he study everyone's?

'Let me ask you a question.' Mr Brinkworth handed the letter back to her. 'Imagine, this is written by your father to a friend... let's say an old university chum. An Oxford man.'

Jess felt her eyes widen. Her father had studied theology at Oxford, but that wasn't in her file. 'Let's say the letter reveals something alarming,' Mr Brinkworth continued. 'Let's say... the precise co-ordinates of Ramsgate's excellent public shelters. You cannot imagine why your father would want to pass on such details.'

The room had fallen still, waiting for the next question.

'This is your revered father,' he continued. 'A man above reproach. Describe your next action.'

Jess knew a critical choice was being thrown at her. Would she put her black censor's pen through her father's words? Or reseal the letter and send it on its way? She expelled a breath. Everything hung on what she said next. Her job. The pay packet at the end of the month. For an instant, she resaw Charlotte on an escalator ahead of her, once again moving out of reach. Then the moment she keeled forward and tumbled... Some falls were physical; others were symbolic. Both could break you. 'I would call Miss Cartwright over,' she said.

Mr Brinkworth narrowed his eyes. *Go on.*

'I'd explain my relationship to the sender and ask if, in future, I might not be given letters from Ramsgate.'

Laughter burst out and Jess peered around, confused. Had she said something stupid?

Mr Brinkworth wasn't laughing. 'That, Miss Gresham, shows a misunderstanding of your role. You signed the Official Secrets Act.'

Miserably, she nodded.

'Which binds you to discretion and confidentiality, yes?' He shook his head, saving her the trouble of answering. 'No. Signing the Act, you assumed the duty of putting personal relationships, even the love of your life, second to the interests of this country.' He addressed the room. 'In the hypothetical situation that anybody's beloved father betrays this nation, each and every one of you will not only report it – you will volunteer to be the first line of scrutiny.' He tapped Jess's desk. 'You would ask for letters from Ramsgate. As many as we can give you.'

She understood. Spy on her father, if required. Report him. See him punished. She couldn't remember whether it was Betony or Mrs Kesgrave who had described her work as 'sinister'. And hadn't she already been accused of an abuse of kinship by her own father? So perhaps she was made for this work.

'Gimlet eyes, Miss Gresham. Clear-headed detachment.'

'Yes, sir.'

'In particular, look for anything written in invisible ink.'

Jess frowned, hearing suppressed giggles. 'How would I—' She stopped, noticing the smile on the chief examiner's lips. He was teasing.

'Read on, reseal it and move to the next. The unforgiving trolley approaches.'

Jess found nothing to note in the Reverend Loftus's letter and bumped her rubber stamp down on the envelope. PASSED BY CENSOR. Into her out-tray, on to the next.

Within minutes of the lunch bell sounding, Jess had escaped and was walking into Doreen's hairdressing salon.

Doreen was seated behind a desk, sipping tea and flicking through a magazine as the dryers thundered. Jess called out, 'Hi, it's me again,' so as not to make her jump. 'Has Madame Renée come back?'

Doreen took a couple of seconds to recognise her, then shook her head. Standing up, she spoke right into Jess's ear. 'I don't think she's going to, from what she wrote.'

Jess's spirits dived. Not another brick wall.

'But she sent me this…' Doreen leaned down to open her desk drawer. She took out a key. 'She asked if I could check on things once or twice a week.'

Jess only just stopped herself snatching the key from Doreen's hand. 'Could I go up and look? I won't take anything. It's just, there's a coat I'm hoping she has. I really want it.'

Red as a London bus. Glossy cherry buttons.

Doreen looked unsure. 'It's not for me to say. Rene rents the space, like I do.'

'If I find what I'm looking for, I promise I'll send her the money. You have her address.'

'I suppose.' It was permission enough. Doreen clearly wanted to return to her tea and magazine. Key in hand, Jess went through to the back. She had one foot on the stairs when the siren began.

That low wail from the lungs of doom. *Oh no, not now.*

Ignore it.

Jess started up the stairs.

Doreen was behind her. 'Come with me; we'll go to the Tube station, get down to the platform.'

'I'll only be a minute,' Jess said, her eyes on the dim passageway above.

'Or ten. My dad's an ARP warden, and every day he risks his life rounding up stragglers.'

Her elbow grabbed, Jess had no choice but to give up. In the salon, Doreen flicked off the dryers, releasing her clients, and handed out silk scarves to cover the curlers as they dashed off to find shelter. Doreen locked her cash box in the desk.

Jess closed her fingers around the key which Doreen seemed to have forgotten. In a moment, she'd be gone too...

'I've got eyes in the back of my head.' Doreen's voice cracked like a whip. 'I'm not having them digging your body out of the rubble, not after I've spent years building this business up.'

Jess accepted defeat and waited while Doreen locked her front door. The sirens had reached their top note. It burrowed into the ears, made your heart pound.

'Right, let's run like greyhounds,' Doreen urged, but Jess couldn't. Her fall at Charing Cross was still there, in the deep bruises. Knees, pelvis, ribs.

'You go ahead,' she told Doreen. 'I promise I'll follow.'

A pub a few doors up, the Crown and Harp, was emptying, men bundling out, some still clutching their pint glasses. And they weren't all old, either. The younger ones couldn't all be servicemen on leave. They must be in reserved jobs.

A wiry man with red hair ambled out. He looked to be in his late twenties, his lean frame swallowed by a wide-shouldered suit. Another one not in uniform... Then she noticed the limp.

A moment later, a second man joined him – same cut of suit, brown pinstripe, laughing from under the brim of a homburg. *Him.* Following her even now, in broad daylight.

A mist descended over Jess. She took a stride towards the pair.

'What are you up to, you daft nitwit?' Doreen was back, catching her arm.

Jess pointed. 'That man, the one who thinks this is all so damn funny – I'm going to tell him what I think of him.'

'No, you don't.' Doreen's voice was sharp with fear. 'That's Cormac Whelan. We don't mess with him unless we want our faces redesigned. I'm not joking.'

Cormac turned, looking straight at them. He'd stopped laughing.

Jess let Doreen pull her away. She hadn't got what she'd come for. Maybe she'd made things worse. But she still had the key.

24

The raid was a false alarm, and Jess returned to Senate House conscious that her lunch hour had stretched to two.

The guard at the door laughed at her expression.

'Don't worry, miss, half the building got caught. You won't get a carpeting.'

He was right. When Jess returned to C Section, she saw only a peppering of staff and even Miss Cartwright swept in a few minutes later, pink-cheeked, pushing her spectacles up her nose in agitation.

'You can't collect a pair of shoes from the mender's without an alert,' Jess heard her mutter as she gave her glasses an extra shove and a long-threatened sneeze arrived. Jess blessed her under her breath.

False alarms kept coming. They worked on, trusting in the building's bomb-proof reputation. That evening, she left at 6.30, having worked through a short attack at 5 p.m. Taking the Tube to Green Park, she emerged for the short walk to Hill Street to find the air stinking of gunfire and fresh shrapnel on the ground.

Mrs Kesgrave opened the door to her, saying, 'I'll get your

key cut but, Jess, come into my sitting room; there's something I need to tell you.'

She found Betony there, waiting. The blackouts were drawn, wall lights casting a glow over Betony's silk blouse and the blonde hair that fell in sculpted waves. Betony didn't answer Jess's quiet 'Hi,' and her heart dropped like a lift in freefall.

Maybe Hill Street, the room, the companionship, had been too good to be last.

'Sit down, dear one,' Mrs Kesgrave said. 'I've made tea and put out an extra cup as I had a feeling you were on the way. While I pour, Betony will break difficult news.'

That's it. I'm being chucked out. They've had a confab and my face doesn't fit.

Jess sat and saw Betony's throat contract as she said, 'It's about Grace.'

'Grace?' Jess replayed their conversation in the bedroom. Grace insisting she'd never mistaken Jess for anyone else. The flicker of panic when Cormac's name was mentioned. *I pushed her too far. Now she wants me gone.*

'There was a bomb,' Betony was saying. 'High explosive. Last night, in the East End.' Betony sent Mrs Kesgrave a helpless look. 'I'm not very good at this.'

'Something's happened to Grace?' Jess didn't dare say it: *Killed?*

Mrs Kesgrave handed her a cup of tea. 'Grace is all right. It's her family and it's dreadful. A bomb fell on a block of flats in Whitechapel near where Grace lived before she came here. Her mother and brother were caught in it.'

Grace's brother. Jess had seen Cormac laughing outside the Crown and Harp... she worked it out... just six-and-a-half hours ago. To her horror, she felt relief. Cormac Whelan, whom even Doreen the hairdresser feared, whom Charlotte had escaped by the skin of her teeth, was dead. She was free. Charlotte was safe. Then she thought of Grace. 'Poor girl. How is she, do you know?'

Mrs Kesgrave invited Betony to explain.

'She's at the scene, I think. I was at Ventnor House when the news came. A friend... well, my sweetheart, Owen, is her employer's nephew, and I was there trying to...'

'Track him down because he hasn't called.' It slipped from Jess's lips.

Betony's eyes opened in alarm. Incomprehension. 'I heard you arguing,' Jess said. The rest, Betony would have to work out for herself. She asked Mrs Kesgrave, 'Will Grace know that we know?'

'Not yet. We'll have to be very gentle with her but something tells me she won't want sympathy ladled on.' Mrs Kesgrave took a sip of tea. 'We can't pretend nothing has happened, so it's a case of treading carefully. My experience of grief is that it stalks you. You think it's given up—'

'I tried to say how sorry I was,' Betony cut in fiercely. She'd been sending Jess little, uncertain glances, no doubt trying to work out how much of her quarrel with Grace had been overheard. 'She as good as told me to shut up, said my life is all tied up nicely with a ribbon, I've got everything I want, so how would I understand?'

'Grief lashes out,' Mrs Kesgrave counselled.

'So does Grace.'

Jess drank her tea, relieved she wasn't being evicted and that the world had rid itself of Cormac Whelan. The first emotion was allowable, the second, plain wrong. What could she do or say for penance? Then she remembered the rota. 'It's my turn to cook.'

'Indeed it is,' said Mrs Kesgrave. 'There's a cauliflower and a knob of cheese in the cool box.'

Jess escaped, glad of an occupation until she found the pan Betony had used to cremate her parsley sauce face down on the drainer. Unwashed. Oh well. She'd asked for penance. She began to scrub.

After so many false alarms today, another felt inevitable. It came just as she'd put the cauliflower cheese under the grill to brown. She took it out, gathered plates, knives and forks, pepper and salt. She and Mrs Kesgrave were piling up trays to take into the back yard when Grace came in, her face haunted. Dirty too, except where tears had scoured away the dust.

'Darling girl.' Mrs Kesgrave broke the tension, drawing her close.

Grace pulled away. 'Thanks, I'm all right. If you don't mind...?'

'Of course. We won't speak of it until you're ready, but we won't pretend either. You've lost a mother and a dear brother, which is all we need say for now.'

Grace dashed fresh tears away. 'Yes, Mam's gone. And Granny Driscoll, her best friend. And...' She battled a sob. 'And my best friend too.'

'Your brother,' Mrs Kesgrave prompted gently.

Best friend? Jess couldn't understand how. Still, family was family.

'Ricky,' Grace was saying. 'He and Cormac were twins, but Ricky was a thousand times the better man. I've spent the whole way home wishing one was dead instead of the other, God forgive me.'

And I've spent an hour wishing the same thing, Jess said to herself. *God help me.*

25

WEDNESDAY, 11 SEPTEMBER 1940

Jess's journey that morning took three times as long as usual with Tube lines closed, bus routes blocked. In the end, she walked the whole way, resigned to being late. Rain had fallen overnight and as she side-stepped puddles and shattered glass on Tottenham Court Road, she felt grateful for her sturdy shoes and gabardine coat. Smoke curling from the roof of a furniture store was as stark as a news headline: the bombing was getting closer. Sandbags that had been neatly piled were now blast-damaged, their contents turning the gutters yellow.

When she finally made it to her desk, her colleagues' drawn faces had her wondering if she looked the same. Having got up in semi-darkness, she'd not so much as glanced in the bathroom mirror.

The morning brought the usual stack of mail and a new word. Letter after letter quoted it.

'They're calling it the Blitz, which is "lightning" in Jerry-speak, least I think so.'

'The newspapers are talking about "the London Blitz",

whatever that means. I don't want to open my morning paper and read bloody German, thanks very much.'

Mr Brinkworth explained that Blitz was short for Blitzkrieg, or 'lightning war'. 'Whether it's a reference to its speed or the way it lights up the sky, I cannot say. Let's hope, like most storms, it blows itself out, preferably over the North Sea and by the end of the year.'

Whether it was a sign of his confidence in her, or innate mischief at work, Mr Brinkworth arranged for Jess to receive a pile of letters from Ramsgate. It hurt to read what people there were writing about the destruction of their town. She was forced to use her black pen more than usual.

Air raids came almost on the hour. Hammer blows, relentless. They couldn't leave at the end of the day and were fed in the canteen before lying down on camp beds brought in for emergencies. The following day, after breakfast served by bleary-eyed staff, they were given leave to go home and catch a few hours' sleep.

Jess walked out into a drizzling dawn whose colour came from new fires on the skyline. She wondered how Grace was feeling, waking up and remembering afresh that her mother was dead, and the brother she'd loved. Crushed under a mountain of rubble. Grace had told them, again and again, how she wished Cormac had died, not Ricky, and then accused herself of being wicked.

Jess had assured her she wasn't. 'You're in shock. You're not in charge of your emotions.'

It was too early for buses, and Jess doubted the Tube would be running freely so she set off to walk the two-and-a-half miles to Hill Street. On Gower Street, she became aware of another person keeping pace behind her, but it was hard to make him out in the misty light. He wore a coat, and Jess got the impression that he'd pulled his collar up high. As you would, she supposed, if you wanted to tail someone, incognito.

She walked faster but after a night on a camp bed mattress, her muscles had locked. Whoever it was needn't be much of a bloodhound to keep up with her.

From Gower Street, she turned down University Street, then Huntley Street in a bid to throw him off. That brought her to Grafton Way where she paused. She could hear the hum of early traffic on Tottenham Court Road and pigeons cooing from the rooftops. No footsteps now.

Hoping she'd outpaced whoever it was, she passed the Crown and Harp. Shut, of course.

At Doreen's, Jess stopped and read the card that was still stuck to the window. ELEGANT EXCHANGE – LADIES' FASHIONS (1ST FLOOR). Someone had added, CLOSED UNTIL FURTHER NOTICE.

Nothing new, then. Sighing her frustration, Jess was about to walk away when she realised that Doreen's salon door stood slightly open.

26

It had been forced; the lock had given way. Jess slipped inside and saw at once that Doreen's desk had been pulled from the wall. The drawer where she put the cash box gaped open.

'Looters.' The Blitz might be less than a week old, but robberies had rocketed, according to hearsay. Mostly, they happened in the dead of night when householders were sheltering. Certain men were willing to risk the bombs, because the pickings were good.

Whoever it was had come in and taken the most valuable item. Money. Nothing else seemed to have been touched. The trays of curlers, the hand mirrors and the bottles were all neatly in their place.

What about the rooms upstairs? Jess still had the key. She could look for Charlotte's coat. If she was quick, who would know?

She moved past the spot where Doreen had stopped her before, and kept climbing.

At the top, a door bore a neat sign: ELEGANT EXCHANGE.

The key fitted and Jess stepped into darkness. Black felt

swathed the windows keeping out the street- and daylight. There was a smell. Not unpleasant, and one she recognised but couldn't name. Turning lights on revealed rails shrouded in holland covers. Removing these sheet by sheet, she uncovered a hoard of garments. Quality stuff, to her eye at least. Day and evening wear, stoles, jackets, coats. Hats and handbags on shelves. Every sleeve or strap carried a manila label, stating a date, initials – of whoever would be owed commission? – and a price in shillings. It seemed a well-organised enterprise.

A desk was piled with unopened mail, suggesting Madame Renée – Rene to friends – hadn't meant to be away so long. What had stopped her coming back... bombs? A needy cat?

Jess made a slow circuit, accompanied all the way by her reflection in a huge cheval mirror.

She was stringing out her disappointment, of course. There was no red coat, no flash of daring colour, just black, grey, camel and brown. The ghosts of other people's lives. She should go.

If she was caught, they might think she'd forced the door. Wandering onto the landing, she went up a second flight of stairs to the under-eaves where a line of wooden crates lured her into another disappointing search. They contained blackout cloth impregnated with mothballs, a stash of glycerine soap, the kind that was mixed up into shampoo, and a quantity of rags, hand-stitched into curlers. This must be where Doreen kept stuff she didn't want in the salon. The soap's rose scent took her back to the moment Doreen had washed her hair. *Funny*, she thought. *I'll probably still remember that when I'm ninety.*

Picking her way down, rose-otto was replaced with the resinous smell of Madame Renée's stockroom. Jess had left the door open.

It came to her: 'Cedar wood.' A dressing-up box from her childhood had been full of Edwardian dresses and hats, which she and Charlotte had paraded about in. Cedar shavings at the base had kept moths away. She found its source, a sea captain's chest with a key in the lock.

Jess opened it, and there it was. Lying on top of other winter coats, a gleam of red. Lifting it up, shaking out its folds, she put her nose to the inner lining and her breath caught. Threading through the spicy base notes was the perfume Charlotte had worn the last night they were together.

Charlotte had been vague when Jess had asked what it was.

'Oh, just something they sprayed on me in a department store.'

Really... or Shalimar by Guerlain?

Jess dragged off her gabardine coat and pushed her arms into the red sleeves, closing her eyes as she fastened buttons one by one.

In front of the mirror, she lifted her hair and secured it on top of her head with a slide. From her skirt pocket, she took the lipstick that had been tossed her way and applied it with the confidence she'd seen Betony use. She met her reflection full on.

'Hello, Charlotte. I've found your coat.'

'Well done. I suppose you know they took it from me at that vile institution.'

'Yes. I keep discovering where you've been, Charlotte, but every time, all that's left behind is a hint of perfume.'

'Poetic, darling. How's the playwriting?'

'Given up. What's the point? I was only writing to be like you.'

Below, the street door clicked against its frame, too controlled to be the wind. Jess went very still, catching a murmur of men's voices, moving closer. A laugh quickly snuffed out. Framed by the mirror, Charlotte's coat was a dead give-away. Too red, too smart for morning. Too obviously not hers.

She should fling it off, put on her dowdy school gabardine. Only the footsteps had reached the stairs. She'd stayed too long and there was no way out.

27

It was two men, speaking low but not in whispers. Jess recognised one voice only too well. She had little doubt who had jemmied open the door to get at the cash box.

'Might as well take that soap,' the voice said. 'It'll go quick on Petticoat Lane.'

'Will do. Mikey will take it off our hands.' A different speaker. Irish, more nasal.

'I like a quicker return than that—' The first voice broke off. Perhaps he'd noticed the light Jess had turned on at the top of the stairs. 'Has that been on all night? Christ alive, Frankie, we'll have the sodding ARP down our necks.'

Jess waited, her heart going like a blacksmith's mallet. She could have hidden under one of the white holland covers but there was an inevitability to the confrontation with Cormac Whelan. It had been beckoning for days.

She fancied she knew what he would say. What he might *do* was the un-guessable bit. Moving to the window, she drew back the blackout by a few inches. In case she had to shout.

She then turned to face the open door.

Cormac was through first. He stopped dead. His voice came in a rasp. 'Charlotte!'

The other man – Frankie, was it? – pushed past. Jess recognised the red hair just visible under his hat. Cormac's friend from the Crown and Harp. It was the limp that made her certain.

Pushing up his brim, Frankie peered at her. Shook his head. 'It's not Charlotte. It's the one who was on the street, yesterday, staring. Jesus, Cormac, will you not learn to tell them apart?'

Cormac swore. His anger was directed at Jess.

'I'm wearing Charlotte's coat,' Jess said, trying to sound in control. 'I came here to find it.'

Frankie got in first. 'Nice colour. Red, like a whore's.'

Cormac told him to shut his mouth. 'It's not only the coat,' he said. 'It's the lipstick. She wore red to outshine a fire engine. You don't carry it so well.'

'Because I'm not her, Cormac.'

'I'll never feckin' get it,' Frankie muttered, a tic tugging at his cheek. An old scar ran down one side. Earlobe to chin. 'What is it with these stuck-up girls, all starch and prayer books at bedtime? But I forgot, your Charlotte was used goods.'

While Jess choked on her fury, Cormac drew something from his jacket pocket. It looked at first like an old paintbrush handle, the bristles pulled out, but as Frankie was pushed up against the wall, she saw it was some kind of handle with a narrow groove at the top. Into the space was wedged a razor blade, ground thin as paper.

Frankie's reaction suggested he'd seen it before. 'Put it away, Cormac. You wouldn't want to slip.'

'Wouldn't I?'

'Sorry – all right? My big mouth. I've nothing to say against your lady. Wherever she's gone.'

'You called her "used goods". Who put those words in your big, ugly mouth?'

'Nobody, I swear. I'm saying what I heard. That she came from some place, barefoot in her night clothes, and a strange, mad look to her.' Frankie knocked Cormac's hand away and gave Jess a nasty grimace. 'This one's her sister, right? You can see the same in her.'

Cormac waited for Jess to answer. She inclined her head. 'I'm Jess Gresham, Charlotte's younger sister.'

'So, Jess Gresham,' Cormac said drily, 'how did you know the door downstairs would be open today?'

'I didn't,' she said. 'I've been trying to see this coat for a while. I was told it was here, and I was walking past.'

'Just happened to be walking past.'

'Yes. I've been at work all night.' She could have added, 'As have you,' but held back. Maybe Frankie guessed her thoughts because he shot out a feral grin.

'Keep the coat, lady. You say nothing, we'll say nothing. Everybody's happy.'

'I'm not taking it,' Jess insisted, shocked they should think so. 'I needed to know it existed and I'm going to pay for it.'

Frankie looked at Cormac and tapped the side of his trilby hat. It had greasy dents either side of the crown from lifting on and off. 'This one's not right upstairs,' he said. 'It's the father I feel sorry for – two daughters off the rails. One a runaway, this one a thief.'

Cormac regarded her with brooding resentment. It wasn't Frankie who was provoking him, she realised, but her. She buried her hands in her coat pockets to hide their tremor, felt her lipstick... and something else, a scrap of paper. Left there by Charlotte?

Something to check later. If there was a later.

'What do we do about her?' Frankie's manner changed, as if he'd woken up to the fact that they were at the scene of an earlier crime, with the morning advancing and a witness. 'She can identify us.'

She won't, Cormac's shrug suggested.

'Her kind,' Frankie persisted, 'they go straight to the police.'

Cormac said nothing. His gaze was fixed, but his focus had gone. Jess had almost forgotten – he'd lost his mother and twin brother only a few days ago. Grief hadn't stopped him breaking into a shop, though.

He said, 'I'll let you go once you tell me where she is.' The pad of his thumb tested the edge of his blade. Jess's mind went numb. What she'd assumed was grief was a void.

'If you mean Charlotte, I don't know.'

'You're lying. It's in your face.'

How could anything be in her face beyond terror? Because he felt nothing, he assumed the rest of the world was the same. 'I'm desperate to find my sister. I'm chasing every shadow and I get nowhere. You saw her last, not me.'

Cormac nodded to Frankie, and in a flick of an eyelid, Jess had her arms dragged behind her back. Cormac undid the top two buttons of the coat and spread the collar wide to expose her neck. Frankie pulled her head back and the razor blade kissed her windpipe.

Please. She'd walked into this trap. Earlier, she'd spotted one or both of these men following her and had thought she'd shaken them off. This was the price of naivety. The vicar's daughter who thought she'd become streetwise but actually knew nothing. Violence was in a day's work for Cormac and Frankie. That she was Charlotte's sister and half their size meant nothing, except it made their job easier.

Only... was Cormac giving her one last chance?

'Tell me where she'd go, Jess. Give me something and you can leave. No, button it, Frankie,' he hissed as his friend tried to object.

Please, brain, work. What could she drop at Cormac's feet? That Charlotte had ridden the down escalator at Charing Cross? No – because he'd stake the place out. What about telling him that she'd collided with his sister Grace in the lodging house?

Don't. If he didn't know already, it meant Grace didn't want him to. And ten to one, he'd call by. Imagine the field day Betony would have, Grace's thief of a brother on the doorstep. An idea shimmered and she grasped at it. 'Charlotte loved books. Her ambition was to join the London Library and write there, at a window seat. She might already be a member.'

The razor did not move. 'She spent half her life reading books, when she wasn't writing one,' Cormac sneered. 'I told her she'd get a nasty squint. Tell me something I don't know.'

'What I'm saying is, the library would have her address.' Why hadn't she thought of this before, and gone to the London Library herself? And what if she'd hit on the truth, and betrayed Charlotte?

The blade lifted a fraction. 'Can you find out?'

'Perhaps. It's confidential but they would have a record.'

The blade nicked her and Jess cried out.

'I need more.' His voice was coaxing. 'Whatever Frankie says, Charlotte wasn't mad. She called the men in white coats her jailers, and the nurses "the wardresses". She feared them enough to run out her slippers, into the snow. Who were they, Jess?'

The staff at Alder Grove, of course, but if Charlotte had never spoken of it to Cormac, there was only one reply. 'I don't know. At home, they said Charlotte died on the way to hospital. I believed them.'

She looked at Cormac over the razor's edge, trying not to breathe too hard, or blink. 'She escaped from her wardresses at New Year and must have come to London. When you saw me and thought you'd found her, she'd just left you, hadn't she?'

'That morning, before I woke.'

'And that was what...' Time was a blur. 'Two, three weeks ago.'

'Give or take.'

'Then I know less than you, Cormac. It's like being in a tunnel with a pinprick of light, and however fast I run towards it, my sister is always the same distance away.'

Cormac took the blade from her throat. 'Rub that lipstick off your mouth. It makes me sick to see it.'

Jess kept a clean handkerchief in her gabardine, but that was lying by the sea captain's chest. She dug her hands into the pockets of Charlotte's coat, found the lipstick and the paper note, dry and soft.

She dropped the note, not daring to look where it fell, and used the back of her hand to wipe off as much red as she could. Had she got through to Cormac? Would he let her go?

A shout from the street pulled her attention to the window.

'Whoever's up there, get that light out!'

She'd opened the blackouts a few inches before these men arrived, and the light in the room must be shining out into the sulky morning. A passing ARP warden had spotted the breach. 'Shall I close them?' she stammered.

'Get on with it,' Frankie snarled, 'or we'll have flies in the ointment. You squash one, the other buzzes louder.'

Jess moved to the window and pulled the curtain – to the far edge, exposing her figure at the window and the room behind. It was like throwing everything on a roulette wheel. Hammering on the glass, she screamed against the pane. Whoever was below had to hear.

The pavement was deserted. There was nobody there, and no sign there had been.

The room darkened as Frankie turned the light off. Jess waited. She felt so very abandoned, and... strange word under the circumstances... disappointed that she might die in a stranger's office on an unremarkable street, because there was nobody to help. She pulled the lapels of Charlotte's coat together, containing her shivering, her sadness, inside.

Frankie shot a look the door. Put a finger up. 'Someone's coming.'

He was right. Feet were climbing upstairs in a steady, unhurried way. It must be the ARP man, coming to investigate.

She saw Frankie dip his right hand into his jacket pocket. When he brought it out, his knuckles were armoured with a strip of shaped metal. A well-aimed swing would shatter bone.

Cormac took a stance in the middle of the room, knees flexed. *Whoever's on their way*, Jess thought, *they won't stand a chance.*

The door opened and a man stood framed, the collar of a greatcoat drawn up each side of his face.

Jess knew the short, brown hair, the unmistakable shape of the brow and nose. When he glanced her way from beneath dark brows, she gasped, 'Rafe? Is it you?'

He didn't answer but looked from Cormac to Frankie. Reaching behind him, he switched the light back on.

Frankie recoiled as if he'd seen the dead. Burn injuries still marked Rafe's face, but they showed signs of healing. Jess had asked Mr Brinkworth about the *Basilisk*, the ship she believed Rafe had sailed on. She'd learned it had been present at the evacuation of Dunkirk and saved the lives of countless members of the British Expeditionary Force, while under fire. To her, Rafe's scars weren't disfiguring. They represented something this pair would never understand.

When Rafe took off his coat, showing more scars, Frankie swore. 'You look like you've risen from the dead.'

'Maybe I have. There's every chance I died and you're seeing a stumbling ghost who can't face oblivion.'

The low, grazing way Rafe spoke had Frankie muttering, 'God save us. How did you...'

'Die? In the service of my country. What about you?'

'What about me? I'm exempt from the call-up. Injured leg.'

'I meant, how did you get that?' Rafe drew an imaginary line down his face, tracing the shape of Frankie's scar.

Frankie touched the jagged pucker. 'Borstal. Broken bottle.'

'And you?' Rafe looked straight at Cormac. 'Serving your country or serving yourself?'

Cormac tilted his head, like a gambler sizing up a stranger at the gaming table. Jess feared that to Cormac Whelan, Rafe resembled not a ghost but a vulnerable man with no one at his shoulder. She saw him nod, a coded message to Frankie. *At my signal...*

'Rafe' – Jess pointed a warning finger at Frankie – 'look at his fist.'

Rafe did so and raised his hands in surrender. 'You're going to use knuckle-dusters on a ghost?' He took a step forward.

Frankie took a step back, undisguised horror on his face. He must genuinely believe he was staring at a dead man.

Rafe followed him until there came a splintering smack and Frankie flew backwards, landing against the base of the mirror.

Jess looked in awe at the unadorned left fist that had felled him.

Cormac raised his blade and for several beats of her heart, Jess feared he'd leap on Rafe. She imagined blood and lacerated flesh. But to her astonishment, he moved towards the door, never taking his eyes off Rafe. Who let him go.

The last thing Jess saw of Cormac was the hard flash of blue eyes in her direction.

'Honour among thieves,' Rafe said dryly, holding his right hand out to Frankie, who was cradling his jaw. The left, which had delivered the punch, was held close to his body.

Frankie got to his feet, muttering incoherently. Rafe shooed Jess out of the room.

'Wait for me downstairs. I'll deal with him.'

She was halfway down before she registered that she was

wearing Charlotte's coat. Stealing it, effectively. Rafe, who came to the head of the stairs, asked what the problem was.

'I have to give this back.'

'Do it later.'

'My old school coat... I left it.'

'Does it matter?'

'My security pass is in it. There's my satchel too. I need them; it's everything—'

He told her to go out into the street and wait, then turned back. Instead of doing as he said, Jess planted herself at the bottom of the stairs, ears pricked for violence. Though what she'd do if a fight broke out...

It was Frankie who came down first, hanging onto the bannisters. His hat was askew and he regarded Jess with a seething energy.

The blow to his jaw had not curbed him on the subject of Charlotte, it seemed. 'When Cormac found her, she was wearing clothes they give away at the door of a flop house. A ragged, old coat, slippers on her feet. She looked like a drowned rat. You know why she ended up in that state, nowhere to go, begging favours from Cormac?'

Jess shook her head.

Frankie dropped something at her feet. It was the fold of paper from the red coat pocket. He tapped his nose. 'Funny, isn't it, what the vicar's daughter hides from the vicar.'

She stooped, picked up the note, but couldn't look at it as Rafe was coming down with her things. Frankie vanished.

28

Rafe took her to a café on Fitzroy Square. He found a table away from the window as if he didn't want to be looked at.

A waitress asked them what they wanted, saying that the choice was mushrooms on toast, toast and jam or toast and margarine.

Rafe ordered the mushrooms and extra toast and jam. 'Coffee?' he asked Jess.

'Yes, please. You won't mind if I haven't much appetite, only they fed us at work at four this morning.'

'What did you have?'

She smiled thinly. 'Toast and mushrooms.'

'Don't you love this war?'

She searched his eyes for signs of humour but saw none. Hardly surprising. He seemed watchful, still sharp with adrenalin. He also seemed intrigued by her mouth and she wondered if she'd smudged lipstick into the corners as she rubbed it off. When he leaned forward, she thought he was going to tell her.

'May I know how you came to be trapped with that pair of thugs?'

'First,' she said, 'tell me how you found me. I thought I must have conjured you up.'

'Well, I do resemble something half alive,' he said heavily. 'Your friends were ready to believe I'd stepped up from my grave.'

'Not my friends. And that's not what I meant. I was moments from having my throat cut. I thought so, anyway.'

'Perhaps you were,' he said. Their coffee arrived. 'The quiet one,' he said, 'Mr Blue Eyes. I've met his sort, usually around pub closing time in naval ports. They rarely go in with their fists; they pick their battles. Don't want a broken nose or a night in the cells. They leave that to others.'

'You mean, Cormac Whelan only fights when he knows he'll win.'

'That's his name?' Rafe asked. 'Whelan... Irish?'

'A Londoner with Irish roots.'

'Common burglar or worse?'

'Worse. While we're hiding from bombs, Cormac and his kind are out looting.'

'You seem to know him well.'

She shook her head, but the hazel eyes warned her – *I'm too tired, too damaged, to take nonsense from anyone.* 'I know enough to be afraid of him,' she said. 'It's a long story, and I would tell you but—'

'But why would you trust me, after I walked out on you that night.' Rafe lifted one side of his mouth, and she saw him flinch. He'd opened wounds on his hand from delivering that punch, and the way he cradled it in the other struck pity in her. And anger. *Charity case. Lifelong invalid.* That vile letter, those awful women...

'You had your reasons for going,' she said, 'though I wish you'd explained. Thank you for the money.' A blush rushed past her defences. She was the charity case. She had been, then, anyway.

'Glad you found it.' He said it casually.

'I'll pay you back.'

'Jess, I'm not in a rush.'

The waitress approached with a plate in each hand and another balanced on her forearm. 'Dig in, lovebirds,' she said.

Jess waited until she'd gone to ask, 'Why did you leave? I thought something awful had happened to you.'

'It had – a ceiling fell on my head. Remember?'

As if she'd forget. 'Are you saying it made you go a bit strange?'

'I was already, I think. Out of hospital only a few days. I was meant to go to a convalescence place but I couldn't face it, so I broke into my great-aunt's house.'

'So, you're a housebreaker too?'

'Technically, yes. But it wouldn't stand up in court. My great-aunt Beatrice is in a nursing home on the South Coast. I had her permission, over the telephone, and she told me where to find the key, but when I arrived somebody – who knows, your friend Cormac? – had already forced the door. I lived like a hermit in the dark, wondering what the hell happened to my life.'

'You were at sea and your vessel was attacked,' she said, making it sound like an educated guess.

He nodded, spearing a mushroom. 'In the Channel. We were standing off from the beach at La Panne, waiting to pick up more men. Planes came over dropping bombs like hailstones. One caught the boiler room and the fireball killed our engineers. I can't describe the sound. We lost power and I went down to see – when a second bomb hit.' He lifted his burned left hand to the injured side of his face. 'They kept coming. The planes. They have thousands. After we'd saved those we could from below deck, we abandoned ship and I was pulled out of the water.'

Jess could only imagine how much he'd left out. He'd gone

down in the bowels of a steel-hulled ship under fire. *Into* fire. How must it be to be stranded in the cold swell, waves breaking over your head, your skin seared? The cries of your crew mates in your ears?

It wasn't surprising if he'd 'gone a little strange'.

For a while, they ate in silence. She could see Rafe had difficulty in chewing. His left hand made heavy work with his fork. Except that she feared offending him, she'd have offered to cut up his toast. 'Tell me why you went without a word.' She wanted to know, even if the truth was hurtful. 'Did the bomb falling so close bring everything back, or was it me? I know I can be trying. Dull. Everyone thinks so.'

He didn't rush to reassure her. 'I sent you out to make me a drink, I seem to recall.'

'Barley water. The electricity was off, so I couldn't make tea.'

'I wanted you out of the room.'

'Getting rid of me.'

A brisk nod answered. 'The pain was getting too much. It can subside for some hours, and then, usually at night, it hits a peak. It gets so bad, it can make me pass out. I thought I'd got over that stage, but that bloody ceiling... Great-Aunt Beatrice let the place go. I'd seen ambulances in the street when I peered out. They stopped, had a look round, then reversed back to the end of the road. I knew I had to get myself inside one.'

'They came back?'

'No. I staggered down to the corner because I knew if I didn't get proper treatment it would be the end.' He indicated his injuries. 'If this goes septic, it's...' He made a two-note sound, implying 'end-of'. 'I didn't want you to see me being hauled into an ambulance, my teeth bared in pain.'

'I'd have helped. I wouldn't have judged you.'

'Really? Everyone else does. Poor old Rafe, not a shadow of the man he used to be. Oh well, throw him on the scrap heap.'

She almost said, 'You mean your fiancée, Margaret?' She stifled the impulse, because referring to that odious letter would break the Official Secrets Act. Rafe would feel his privacy had been violated. Instead, she said, 'Not everybody thinks it.'

'No? I'm sorry I bailed out on you.'

'You left me some money, and gosh, I needed it. I can't pay you back just now, but I will. In fact, I'll write you an IOU.' She reached for her satchel.

He stayed her with a gesture.

'Jess, I'm on half pay from the Navy and my brother is putting me up – or putting up with me, as he sees it – and won't let me contribute. I don't need a promissory note. I trust you. It means a lot that I can do something for someone.'

The waitress came and asked if they'd like a refill of coffee. 'It's on the house, considering.'

'Considering what?' Rafe asked, politely.

'The time you've had, love. Navy?'

'How did you know?'

'I've a brother in the service. Navy barbers only have one regulation cut, don't they? My brother says the officers have a way of speaking, too. Short sentences that carry over a howling wind.'

'I use short sentences because long ones hurt.'

'You can still have another cup of coffee, can't you? You, miss?'

'Yes, please,' said Jess.

The waitress gave Jess's coat a quick once-over and smiled. 'Red suits you. Matches your lipstick... what's left of it. Victory Red? I saw a tube in Selfridge's. Couldn't run to it, but that colour could chase the blues off any face.'

Jess smiled her thanks, cheeks warm. No wonder Rafe had been staring at her lips. There must be more left on than she thought. Red coat, lips to match.

'I need to take this back,' she said anxiously, indicating the garment.

'You'll have to explain,' he said.

'It's complicated.' Her story would sound like nonsense but she had to say something. As she didn't know how to begin, she started at the end. 'It isn't mine.'

'You're saying you took it?'

'Not intentionally. I found the front door open...' This wasn't going well. She cleared her throat. 'This coat belonged to my sister, who is missing.'

Rafe edged back in his seat, memory dawning. 'You said when we met that you were looking for a missing person. I assumed it was a man.'

'Her name is Charlotte. I haven't seen her since December last year. I keep finding her footsteps but they lead nowhere. Like this coat – I knew it was above the hair salon, but the woman who owns the business left town. When I walked past and saw the lock had been forced, I went in. I found it, put it on. I put on lipstick too and suddenly, it was as if she was inside me. I know she's in London. Somewhere.'

'Lots of girls run away to London.'

'You don't understand. She was here *after* she died. Supposedly died.'

A tremor in Rafe's face suggested he hadn't expected that.

'Then those two arrived. Or returned, I should say, and I was caught, which made me a witness.'

'No wonder you were scared.'

'I thought I'd die up there.' The image of a man in a trilby flying backwards flashed through her mind. 'Did you learn to strike out like that in the Navy?'

'No, school. Amateur boxing taught me a valuable lesson. Let your opponent think you're right-handed and lead with the left.'

'Frankie didn't see it coming.' She added, 'I shouldn't have walked out with this coat on. I've no excuse, really.'

He agreed. 'Technically, you have stolen it. What now?'

'I want to keep it and pay for it. The business owner calls herself Madame Renée, but really, she's Rene.'

That almost drew a laugh. 'I wonder if Parisian *modistes* give themselves English names. "Mrs Featherstone of Rue de Rivoli."'

'I shouldn't think so.' Jess bit her lip. Being thought a thief, even if unintentionally, weighed on her. 'The hairdresser on the ground floor knows where to send money,' she said, 'only I don't know how much Rene wants.'

'Seventeen shillings.'

'You think?' He'd sounded remarkably confident.

Rafe pointed to Jess's left-side cuff where a price tag was stitched to the underside. 'I keep seeing it when you lift your cup. Jess...'

She waited for him to finish, but he looked away. Perhaps he still suspected she was mixed up in something unsavoury. They'd first met when she blundered into his house, off the street. He might be forgiven for having doubts. The moment felt fragile.

One of them must speak. 'Was it you who shouted, "Put that light out"?'

He shook his head. 'ARP warden. I saw him yell up at the window and walk on. Probably wanted to get home.'

Someone had been shadowing her. She'd suspected Cormac but now she wasn't so sure. 'Rafe, how come you were in the right place at the right time? I asked if I conjured you up, and you haven't answered. Were you – you couldn't have been...'

'Couldn't have been?'

'Following me?'

'Why would you suppose that? I mean, why would I set out to see you again?'

'It was a stupid question. Ignore me.' Since that short-lived romance with the boy on the beach at Ramsgate, no man had ever gone out of his way to meet her.

Only, Rafe seemed set on teasing her. 'You wouldn't suppose I'd slip out of my brother Frederick's flat, walk down Tufton Street each night, hiding my scars behind my coat collar, pretending I needed the exercise... and see if I could spot you?'

'No. Course I don't think it. Obviously, it was a coincidence that you walked into that room today, when I needed you.'

'Course it wasn't coincidence,' he said, almost angrily. 'I made it my business to find you. I'd walk for hours through Westminster, St James's, Mayfair, Knightsbridge, sometimes ending up in Soho, searching, searching.'

'For me?'

'More, for an idea. A mind-worm. A face imprinted.' He placed his hand over hers. 'The night we met, I slipped away like a thief. I left money like a bastard. Clean. Final. No room for questions. It's who I've become, Jess. I can't bear to be weighed down, but I hate what I've turned into. So, I search.'

This reminded Jess how Charlotte would talk sometimes, when she wanted to expand an idea while giving nothing away. 'Are you saying you were looking for me, or for a way to feel better about yourself?'

'You're astute. Both. And I found you sooner than I thought I would.'

'And it was you on my heel all these times?'

'It was, and clearly I need to brush up my skills if you spotted me. You told me you were in the Civil Service, Section C. "Emergency Intake." I did some delving and discovered that in all probability, you worked at Senate House. The mausoleum, lucky you.'

Did some delving where, how?

'My brother Frederick works for Naval Intelligence. He has so many strings to pull, he's practically an orchestra. It took him an afternoon to get the information. So, yes, I've been tailing you on and off since I was released from hospital again.'

Should she be appalled? Scared? Flattered? What she was, was bewildered. 'All because you felt guilty?' she pressed.

'At first I just wanted to see that you'd survived, but then it became more. I felt I'd been handed the job of protecting you. It helps me make sense of my injuries. To have a role in life.'

'I see.' Jess understood what Rafe was telling her, but it didn't hit home. Cormac Whelan had chased her because he wanted Charlotte. A man following her to make sure she was all right... that felt unlikely. 'I only saw you on my tail this morning,' she said. 'Before that, it was footsteps. Shows you are quite good at it.'

'Not really. You and your map make an easy target. You do a lot of walking around, stopping and flapping pages.'

She had to laugh. It was true.

'I tried to work out a pattern, but there didn't seem to be one. A couple of times I lost you on the Northern line. After that, the trail went cold – until today.'

She wasn't ready to tell him about her plunge down the escalator. He misread her silence.

'Don't worry, now you know my secret, I won't shadow you again. Let's be glad it put me where I needed to be this morning. Duty discharged.'

Did that mean he'd cured his guilt and she wouldn't see him again? For a moment, she'd believed that someone really cared about her. 'What – what will you do now?'

'Oh, lounge about, be bad tempered and impossible to be around. Get better, rejoin a ship if they'll have me.'

'Go back on active service?' A chill wrapped itself around her heart. Of course he would. Next time, he might not be lucky.

Rafe called for the bill. 'Where is home now, Jess?'

She told him. Thirty-Four Hill Street, Mayfair.

'Might I call on you? Only if you want. I'd like to know you better. Drink tea in a sitting room with a clock ticking on the mantel shelf, discussing the weather and the misery of rationing. As ordinary people do.'

She'd like that too, but a picture formed, of Betony peering in, locking onto Rafe's burns, recoiling. Then recovering herself, as Betony always did, with a smile like a perfect pen-flick, a gracious phrase on her tongue. The finishing-school-certificated social recovery. Unbearable.

Grace wouldn't flinch. She'd take Rafe in her stride, or say, 'What are you putting on those burns?' Or not notice him at all through the fog of her own grief. But if Grace ever heard how her brother had put a razor to Jess's neck, what then?

Jess realised she had absolutely no idea what Grace's response would be. She might defend her brother. She might not – but for a certainty, it would distress her and Grace Whelan had enough to cope with right now. 'I'm not sure when would be the best time to come,' she said, trying to work out when Grace and Betony were least likely to be home.

Rafe's voice cut in. 'Forget it. I shouldn't have suggested it. Why would you want me in your home?'

'No, it's not that—'

He copied her apologetic tone. 'No, it's just, it's only, it's really rather...' His voice dropped back to its usual level. 'Spare me.' Taking out his wallet, he laid coins on the table. He added a generous tip and got to his feet. 'I'm glad I was in the right place this morning but I'm the wrong company now. Goodbye, Jess.'

He left, and this time, she couldn't blame the war, her father, or fate. As she stared at his empty chair, she felt a tearing loss. And deep remorse that she'd added one more wound to a man already scorched by fire. He'd mentioned Tufton Street. She could turn the tables, seek him out, follow him, talk to him.

Or perhaps it was best that they go their different ways. Rafe had the steep climb to recovery; she had her own mission.

With half a cup of coffee still in front of her, she stayed at the table and drew the folded note from her pocket.

'What the vicar's daughter hides from the vicar,' Frankie had sneered.

It was a small square of thin paper, the kind waiters used to jot down orders. 'No. 6' was printed in the top right corner. A table?

Three lines followed in purplish-grey pencil:

Viaduct near Stoney Street, brick terrace. First house, blue vase behind a lace curtain. Call in the afternoon. Ask for Mrs Munday and say you've come about the laundry. Never, ever give your real name.

Two words leaped out. *Blue vase.*

Call your play *The Window with the Blue Vase*, Charlotte had said during their last happy conversation, before she vanished. 'Make it about a girl who has fallen passionately in love with a man who drops her cold.'

Jess whispered the rest. 'She's in deep trouble. What she does next – that is your play.'

Was Mrs Munday's house where Charlotte had gone next?

The waitress came to clear the plates. It was on the tip of Jess's tongue to ask if she'd ever heard of Stoney Street. She stopped herself and gathered her things. She had her map of London and all the hours until one o'clock, when she must be back at her desk.

29

Stoney Street was in Southwark, on the south bank of the Thames. Jess took the Tube, got off at London Bridge, and followed her map past the cathedral towards Borough Market. Warehouses of soot-blackened brick and rank gutters told her plainly that she was as far from Mayfair as a fishmonger's apron from a lady's glove. Even the railway arches smelled of stale cabbage.

Stoney Street ran straight through the market. Traders glanced at her as she passed, wearing the red coat. Her gabardine was over her arm, and she wished she'd put that on instead. She felt too noticeable. A rag-and-bone cart creaked past her as she paused, scanning for a brick terrace and a house with a vase in the window. Its driver stared, as if he knew what she was searching for.

There was a snag. Most windows in the mean, flat-fronted houses were blanked out with layers of newspaper, perhaps because the occupants were too poor to buy blackout fabric.

A train clattered above her eyeline. At least the viaduct was unmissable.

She walked towards it, the unease in her chest growing with each step. Here was the terrace. In the window of the first house, a blue vase with a chipped rim sat on the sill between two lengths of black cloth, the fabric carefully tucked around it. After a hesitation – did she want to know? Could she bear not to? – Jess knocked. An elderly woman in a housecoat, hair gathered up under a duster, peered out.

'Yes, dear?'

'I want to speak with Mrs Munday.'

Guarded eyes took in her face. The coat. 'What for?'

'I've come about the laundry.'

A quick side-to-side check, and a crooked finger beckoned Jess inside. 'You're early. We don't normally admit before two.'

'Sorry. I'm due back at work this afternoon and I had to come a long—'

'Shh!' cut the excuses short. 'Keep it to yourself, love. Follow me.' The woman led Jess up uncarpeted stairs. On the upper landing, a single knock on a closed door was followed by two short raps. Code, Jess presumed.

At a shout of, 'What is it, Mother?' Jess was admitted into a room with a lino floor, a table, a sink and a bed. The blinds were drawn, a bare bulb for light.

A woman in a green cardigan stood at the sink, elbows working as she washed something by hand. Without turning, she asked over the slosh of water, 'Who sent you?'

'Um, a friend.'

'Hm. What's your age, love?'

'Nineteen.'

'First name?'

Jess nearly let slip her first name, catching herself in time. 'Mary.'

'Another Mary.' The woman pulled out the plug. As the water gurgled away, she dried her hands on a scrap of towel.

The older woman, 'Mother', peered at Jess's waist beneath the coat's cinching belt, measuring it. 'How far along?' she asked.

The question caught Jess unprepared. 'Um...about two months.'

'You're not showing much,' came the reply. 'Still, makes it easier. Which friend sent you?'

This time, Jess had an answer ready. 'Charlotte.'

The woman in the green cardigan turned finally, giving a visible start as she saw Jess. 'Blimey, you've not gone and got yourself knocked up again, have you? I thought I gave you a talking-to.'

It was enough. The secrecy, the long table and these words of recognition said everything Jess needed to know. Everything she'd feared.

'You were here a few days before Christmas, up from Kent, as I remember.' The younger woman came over and looked right into Jess's face. Her cheeks were heavily powdered, lipstick leaching into the creases of her mouth. She smelled of cigarettes. After a while, she nodded. 'Last time, you were calling yourself Joan. Still, what's in a name? It's still two pounds, up front. No shortcuts down the staircase this time, eh?'

'I'm sorry?' Jess didn't understand. 'Shortcuts?'

'Maybe you banged your head too hard to remember. Explains a lot. Right, Joan. Mary. Whatever. Mother will give you an appointment.'

The woman returned to the sink, put the plug back in and ran more water. The old lady took a dog-eared diary from her housecoat and opened it, pencil poised.

'Sooner is better than later.' A date was suggested; Jess nodded. It didn't matter. She wasn't coming back.

At the street door, the old woman detained her for a second. 'You know the drill, dearie. Not a word. Not to your mother, your sister, or your best friend. If we go down, you go down. Understand?'

It had taken so little time, she was back at her lodgings by eleven, with two free hours before she needed to report back at Senate House. Jess went straight upstairs. All was quiet. Mrs Kesgrave had mentioned visiting a friend and Grace, of course, would be at work – she was always out by eight o'clock in the morning.

There was a chance Betony might be in bed; her working day began somewhere between ten and noon.

Not today, though. It was a relief to hang up the red coat in an empty room. Jess kicked off her shoes and with a groan, flung herself down on her bed.

You've not gone and got yourself knocked up again?

In that mean little house, she had met the ghost of Charlotte. On the stairs, in the room, on the table Jess hadn't been able to look at. Her sister's last days at home finally made sense. The last time Jess had seen her sister in good spirits, with colour in her cheeks, had been the morning of Saturday, 16 December last year. Charlotte had been setting off for London, for a day at the typing college. Red coat, matching lipstick, chic black hat and court shoes.

Off to the city to push on with her Fleet Street dream. She had returned that same day but on a much later train than usual, and something felt off. She was quiet, went straight upstairs and locked herself in the bathroom.

Four days later, Wednesday the twentieth, she had skipped work and gone to London again. 'It's exam time,' she'd told Jess and their father over breakfast. 'Typing tests in the morning, shorthand in the afternoon.' She had to reach sixty words per minute on the typewriter, and a hundred at shorthand to get her certificate. It explained her mood. The tense looks, the quick slam of the door as she left. That night, she'd come back even later. After eleven. Father was out, fortunately. A church council meeting that overran.

Charlotte had looked ghastly. Pale, shivery. 'Going down with something,' she'd muttered, shaking her head when Jess offered to heat some soup for her. 'I'm going straight up to bed.'

She'd been asleep when Jess came up. She was breathing deeply, at any rate, and didn't respond to Jess's whispered, 'Are you warm enough?'

Next morning, Charlotte wouldn't get out of bed. 'Will you call in at Pickering's?' The bookshop. 'Say I'm laid up with flu. I won't be back till after Christmas.' She'd refused food again, though she allowed Jess to bring her a cup of tea. Later, Jess had found it on the beside cabinet, untouched.

Jess had gone to work as usual that day, returning home in the dark at six. She'd gone upstairs to check on Charlotte and discovered the bed empty, the covers pushed back. In the bathroom she'd found her. Lying on the floor like a bent nail, knees drawn up.

At first, Jess couldn't make sense of the dark mass beneath her sister's hips, for a moment taking it for a shawl laid on the floor. Her attention was on Charlotte's pallid face as she knelt down, and the parted lips moving with shallow breaths.

And then her hand met something warm and thick. She looked down, saw the truth, and screamed. Once, twice – before running down the stairs just as her father came in.

What did she know now, Jess asked herself, with Stoney Street fresh in her mind?

That Charlotte had almost certainly undergone a termination of pregnancy during that midweek London trip. That it had gone dreadfully wrong, leading to catastrophic blood loss a day later. Who had put Charlotte in that position?

A man...

Not him, please.

A man who dropped her cold. Who bought her expensive French perfume – Guerlain's Shalimar – and, who knows, a red coat and a smart hat.

Jess rose from the bed and went down on her knees.

Not to pray, but to drag out the suitcase. She was ready to read the letter once more. She snapped the catches and lifted the lid off the Remington. Imagine. If she'd taken Miss Hillingdon's advice to pack only warm clothes, this precious machine would be mouldering in the box room at the vicarage. The keys still gleamed like sweets, the gold cyphers on the 'e' and the 't' worn smooth because Charlotte had been a proper writer. Unlike Jess. Dedicated, driven, never satisfied.

Writing, planning, keeping secrets. Tap, tap, tap. Carriage return. Tap, tap, tap.

The last letter was still curled around the roller.

23 December 1939

Dear Sir,

My name is Charlotte Gresham and I wrote to you over a month ago in response to your paper's advertisement for a newsroom typist. I am so, so keen to start a career in journalism…

The twenty-third of December had been a Saturday, two days after Charlotte had supposedly died on the way to St Mildred's, a hospital outside Canterbury.

Jess had been sent away, escorted to the railway station by Miss Hillingdon. A deliberate ploy she now realised, designed not to protect her, but to blind her.

Charlotte must have been discharged from St Mildred's and brought back to the vicarage, or how else could she have typed these lines? Jess imagined her sister tapping away in their old bedroom, hunched over the Remington, teeth gritted.

Dear Sir, my name is Charlotte Gresham. I have to get away. I'm pleading for a job. You see, I've been dropped cold and I'm in awful trouble—

Charlotte wouldn't have heard feet on the stairs over the rattle of the keys. Or the bedroom door opening, a looming figure on the threshold.

'Charlotte, who are you writing to? Stop at once.'

'You can't make me, Father. I'm grown up now.'

He could, of course. Charlotte would have been so weakened, she could never have withstood what came next.

'A brain haemorrhage,' Miss Hillingdon had called it. But the blood had pooled under Charlotte's hips and thighs.

Jess had kept the note with its directions to Stoney Street and now tucked it up against the letter. Really, she ought to burn it, but something told her to hold onto it. To show her father, wave it under his nose?

After all, he must have known. The hospital would have examined Charlotte and reported the results, either the same night or the morning after she was admitted. It explained Father's brooding grief, his frantic need to bury the truth. Abortion was illegal and a mark of shame.

She would be like her father, she decided. Bury the truth. Tell no one. Her new friendships in Hill Street were too fragile. Betony would recoil. Mrs Kesgrave might understand – *might*. But Grace, a nurse, and almost certainly Catholic with her Irish roots... she would be appalled. Illegal. Dangerous. *It's murder*.

'Oh, Charlotte, why didn't you tell me?'

What the girl does next, that's your play.

What this girl would do, Jess decided as she replaced the lid on the typewriter, was help Charlotte start her life again. Once she'd found her.

Of course, she could see no more of Rafe while she carried this burden. He'd walked out on her anyway, and Charlotte would need her. Nothing else mattered.

Not even the faint, splintering sound of something giving way inside her.

30

BETONY

The cranberry dress clung like sauce to a scoop of ice cream.

Betony stood on a dais in the upper room of 54 Farm Street, holding an imaginary urn in her arms, chin tilted towards the small window. *Practical Modes* extended its no-fuss philosophy to its offices. White walls, rugs on floorboards and minimal heating. It had turned glum outside and silk rayon had no warmth in it.

Ambrose, their sketcher, frowned at her, pencil hovering. 'Could you stop fidgeting?'

'I will if you can find where that draught is coming from.' Georgian houses were lovely to look at, but you'd think consumption and chest infections had been designed into them. Three flights of stairs to the top kept her slim, which was the best one could say. A week's worth of Blitz dust lay on the window glass. Outside, a distant all-clear sounded. Had they just worked through another raid?

Ambrose sat back, huffing irritably. 'The light can't decide what direction it's coming from and that fabric's too shiny.' He glared at Betony as if she were to blame. 'Whoever came up with "on the bias" ought to have my job. Could you move?'

'Now I'm to move – where?'

'I don't know. Out of the glare of an unforgiving day.'

Stepping off the dais, Betony patiently retook her pose. 'Better?'

'Not much. Arms higher... the left one. Drop the right a touch. A touch. And stop twitching! When I was in Paris, the mannequins stood for hours without needing food, water or breath.'

'Then they must be thriving under Occupation.' Betony angled a shoulder. 'Like this? Oh, don't snap my head off. I'm paid to stand and you're paid to draw.'

'For now,' he muttered and before Betony could ask what that meant, he pointed with his pencil. 'What's that on your left arm? Has someone written your name and address there for you?'

Betony flashed him a look. Trust him to notice. She'd tried to get that telephone number off by scrubbing at it, but it must be some kind of indelible ink. As if she wanted to be reminded that she'd made a complete fool of herself. She'd dialled the number and the phone had rung at the Canadian High Commission. Winter Macpherson's lair, not Owen's. Wasn't that typical of life? One man was so keen he'd used her as a notepad in the dark while the one who kissed like a dream had gone on to ignore her. Worse, actually.

Betony had a suspicion that Owen had turned his eyes towards Grace. Course, Grace nursed his aunt, and he used the house as an overnight stop when he was up in town, so they'd be thrown together. Grace had ridden pillion on Owen's motorbike the other day. 'He offered me a lift.' *Ha. And I bet you clung very, very tight.*

Grace Wheeler. Sorry, Whelan, with the Titian hair and grief-filled eyes. Betony knew she shouldn't hate her. After all, her family had been killed and Grace was a nurse. Nurses were sacred, weren't they? Whereas she, Betony Styles, was next to useless. One up from a shop dummy. One down, if Ambrose's expression was anything to go by.

An office door banged open and a woman in slacks and a shirt strode up to Betony and, without a word, adjusted the cranberry gown's sweetheart neckline.

'Finished?' she asked, turning to Ambrose. 'Only, I've just had the designer on the phone. He wants it back by five this afternoon.'

Sybil March – the Hon. Sybil March – editor, publisher, saleswoman and, since August, staff writer at *Practical Modes*, leaned over to see Ambrose's work. 'You haven't caught how the light caresses the drapes,' she said. 'Oh, don't growl like a bear. We've got to catch the magic of this one. It's not every day we get a dress of this calibre.'

Ambrose ripped out the page. 'The window's filthy and I'm given third-rate materials.' He jabbed at his sketchbook. 'This lousy paper... it's like trying to draw on a pair of damp cotton drawers.'

Betony stifled a groan. The shorthand version of Ambrose's rant was that she'd now have to stand for another hour. Holding this pose.

'I can't get better paper,' Sybil was saying. 'Not for your purposes, nor at the printer's either. August's issue was the last of the good stuff. The sample they've sent me for the October print-run and the Christmas issue... put it this way. Before the war I wouldn't have used it to line a parrot's cage.' She frowned at Betony.

Who lifted her chin higher to avoid eye contact. Betony had sensed something amiss when she arrived for work that morning. She'd come in early, hoping Sybil would be out so she could use the phone in the office. Bad paper stock, or worse? Sybil was all angles and energy today. Her ash-grey plait, draped over her left shoulder, was tied with yesterday's ribbon, suggesting she'd slept in the office again. Bombs were falling, windows were rattling, cracks were appearing.

As if Betony had spoken out loud, Sybil pulled up a chair and sat down facing the wrong way, folding her hands over the back. 'Two days ago, Lux Soap pulled their advertisement.'

'Oh, no, why?' Betony dropped her arms. No point getting cramp if Ambrose was on a go-slow. Lux Soap was their biggest revenue source... and they were generous with free samples.

'They're focussing their advertising more strategically,' Sybil said bitterly. 'Apparently, they're doubling their spend with *The Mercury*'s Thursday Supplement.'

Ambrose growled again, deep in his throat. 'The traitors. Our journal has more reach.'

'But it doesn't have a Fleet Street address or a board of wealthy directors. Jean Treadgold will be dancing her victory dance,' Sybil said wearily. 'We, meanwhile, struggle on, defending our right to exist.'

'Bet they're getting decent paper to print on,' Ambrose muttered.

'Yes. Which brings me to the next disaster. Whitworth & Pritchard's were hit in the Mile End raid two nights ago and lost four of their presses. They're limping on at half strength. Which means, the Christmas issue has to be print-ready two weeks earlier than I hoped.'

This time she glared at Betony, who stammered, 'Sorry, what have I done?'

'You, dear, nothing. It's your father I'm angry with.'

'What's he done?'

'Absolutely nothing. That's my grievance. I met him the other day, asking please, please, could we be given an allocation of printing paper. Nothing special, just decent quality. And he said—'

Betony knew already he'd have said 'No'. Her father, a rising man in the Ministry of Supply, had no time for anything, newspaper, pamphlet or magazine, that did not contribute directly to the war effort. Lord Styles had little time for Sybil March either, considering her a bad influence on his wife and daughter.

'Let me guess. He said *Practical Modes* is pointless frippery, more deserving of a good bonfire than precious paper stock.'

'God, were you in the room?' Sybil got off her chair and stretched, her spine clicking. 'My office, ten minutes, Betony. Ambrose, get the dress drawn. You're a fashion sketcher, not Botticelli with a commission from the Pope.'

Keeping his response behind his teeth, Ambrose turned to a clean page and set to work. Five minutes later, the cranberry dress – and Betony – were captured in sharp lines of grey, red and black. Betony peered at it.

'I look as if I'm going out to a party having just murdered the neighbour's children.'

'You used the telephone this morning while I nipped down to the loo,' were Sybil's first words when Betony, still wearing the cranberry dress but with a jumper on top, entered her office.

'Sorry. I had to call someone.'

'It's what phones are generally for. Next time, use a public box or the one in the pub. I'll take the cost out of your wages.'

'You're upset, Sybil.'

'Not upset – frantic. Can't you tell the difference? Since I let Alison and Marjorie go, I've been doing everything: writing every word, selling ads, dealing with printers and distributors, on almost no sleep. You, meanwhile, come in late, mooning like a Juliet without her Romeo, and cheek Ambrose.'

That last bit – cheeking Ambrose – was essential, as Betony pointed out. 'He'd be unbearable otherwise.'

'He's twice your age, has an invalid for a wife and without him we'd be sunk. No more lip.'

'No more,' Betony conceded. 'Unless he really provokes me.'

'And keep your love life out of the office. I'm guessing you're in love—'

'I am.' Betony seized the chance to mention the man who was never out of her thoughts. 'His name's Owen.'

'Owen?'

'Oh, don't say it as though it's a social disease.'

'I'm thinking what your mother will say. "Betony, couldn't you fall for a man called Edward or Henry?"'

'Mummy doesn't know yet. He's a Spitfire pilot.'

Sybil groaned. 'You're in love with a man your parents will loathe, and who may be shot out of the sky by teatime. Why do you do it?'

'Nobody chooses love. It lands like Cupid's arrow fired in the dark.' Actually, a power cut in the Café de Paris, a kiss she could still feel when she closed her eyes.

'You're right. Nobody chooses love. What they choose, if they're born into our world, is a viable marriage partner. Ask your mother.'

'Are you saying that Mummy was in love with someone else, but picked Daddy?'

'She picked the heir to a title. I'm not saying any more. All I will add is, don't fall for someone who is being sent off daily to die. Find a nice chap who writes memoranda in some safe Ministry basement, who will keep all his limbs. Meanwhile' – Sybil rat-tatted on her desk with inky fingers – 'the Christmas number. We'll lead with the gown you're wearing, so think of a heading. Something that'll give the Thursday Supplement and Touchy Treadgold reason to gnash her teeth.'

Having devoured everything Miss Touchwood had ever written, Betony was stunned to be asked. Delighted, too. 'Alison always came up with creaking puns. Marjorie's were even worse.'

'Then do better.' Sybil tapped a finger. 'They'd have heard me refer to the colour as cranberry and come up with something like, "Berry Merry Christmas!" "What's Sauce for the Gander"...'

'Sacking them was radical,' Betony said, 'but spares us the *pun*ishment.'

'It saves money,' Sybil said curtly. 'I'd no choice.'

'Like Caesar burning the bridges his army needed to cross.' Ambrose, standing in the doorway, had ditched his sardonic expression. He looked rather sad. The Botticelli remark must have got under his skin. Betony remembered her promise not to cheek him. She was going to try and be nicer to people from now on.

If the best way of helping in this crisis was to come up with a headline or two, then that's what she'd do. She gave a twirl, her skirt swishing. What would Touchwood say... '"When the sirens wail and the stockings ladder, put on a fearless colour. Cranberry for a brave heart."'

'That's a strapline, not a heading,' Ambrose griped.

'All right – "Christmas is rationed, but glamour need not be."'

Sybil said, 'Not bad.' Then, 'How about, "One dress for all season"?'

'Ungrammatical.' Ambrose lifted a lip, turned to Betony. 'How about, "One dress, two lovers, no phone calls"?'

'You're a bastard, Ambrose.' So much for being nice.

'Enough, children, enough.' Sybil's fingernail tapped harder. 'Listen, Betony, write a page. We're doing gloves for Christmas, remember? A pair to last, a pair to mend, a pair to make. Give me five hundred witty words.'

'You're hiring her to write?'

If Ambrose rolled his eyes any harder, Betony thought, he'd be reading his own mind.

'Why not?' Sybil shrugged. 'I can't take on a professional

and I'll hurl myself under a bus if I have to draft another jolly piece about turning your husband's old coat into a kilt. Betony spends most of her time here yawning, so she might as well do something useful.'

Ambrose spread his hands. 'You're going to pay her?'

'Well...'

Betony got in quickly. 'If I'm doing extra duties, I should get something.'

'Darling, you already owe me a hundred years' work for the times you've been late.' Sybil frowned at the ceiling as if numbers had appeared up there. 'You're on what, six pounds a month?'

'Five,' Betony corrected. 'My rent's three and I have to eat and buy stockings.'

'You have an allowance, though. That's why I can get away with it.'

'Not anymore.' September's four pounds had not appeared in her post office account. She'd hoped it was an oversight. 'I called Daddy's office and his secretary told me he's stopped paying. Unless I join Mummy in Somerset, I can shift for myself.'

'Oh, the tragedy.' Ambrose threw his arms apart.

'It will be if I end up homeless,' Betony snapped. 'What if Sybil replaces me with one of your precious Parisian types, who flounces out in a rage three times a day and tears into you if you don't make her look like Venus or Greta Garbo? Or brings in a friend who draws like a dream, for half what you earn? Oh, look at your face. The worst I do is drift off to sleep and move my arms.'

Ambrose looked at Sybil. It was obvious Betony's words had found their mark. 'Five pounds a month is rather stingy.'

'Not for a silly deb who can't get up in the morning.' Sybil March sat back, folding her arms tightly. 'I'm wishing I hadn't begun this conversation.'

'What if she starts taking her job seriously and turns out some decent writing?' Ambrose suggested. 'As you said earlier, "When the sirens wail and the stockings ladder", isn't bad. Touchwood without the weary cynicism. If you want Jean Treadgold to spit nails, do what she does, only nicer.'

'Nicer...' Sybil gave Betony a thoughtful look. 'Miracles do happen. All right. Six pounds a month.'

'Eight,' Betony said. Her father's voice intruded at once: *Betony, were you a son, I'd have sent you to the colonies to acquire a backbone. As a girl, you have one job. To be a credit to your mother and me and marry well.*

'I could prove myself on eight pounds,' she said.

'Six.' Sybil was implacable. 'Unless you persuade Lord Styles to turn wheels on our behalf and procure me some paper fit to be printed on. Think you can do it?'

'No. Daddy never moves wheels unless they've been greased by six committees and signed off by a cabinet minister. If I ask him, he'll find an excuse to shut us down.'

Sybil sighed. 'All right. Your first commission, then, is to make the cranberry dress the talk of every front parlour from Surbiton to Salford. I want shopkeepers knocked off their feet by women waving coupons. Do it, and I'll pay you seven pounds a month.'

'Deal. "Cranberry: the colour with courage and sauce. Pair it with a slick of lipstick, and no blackout can dim you."'

'Write that down before you forget it. No – type it and have it on my desk by morning.'

'Type... I can't.'

'I'm deaf.' Sybil briefly covered her ears then waved Betony and Ambrose out.

Leaving work shortly after, the commission burning in her brain, Betony walked the short distance back to Hill Street. Seeing Jess leaving as she turned the corner, she got a vision of a leather suitcase under a bed. Betony had peeked inside it, of course, taking the chance when both Jess and Grace were at work.

There was a neat black Remington inside that never saw daylight.

With luck, the house would be empty and a few hours of two-finger typing would see her complete her first professional piece of writing.

Betony Styles, fashion journalist. 'Miss Touchwood, but nicer'.

'I'll save you a piece of humble pie, Daddy.'

31

Charlotte must have had a love affair, or she wouldn't have got pregnant. Jess was back at work, late afternoon tea break over. During the fifteen minutes' recess, she'd had time to work out dates. Charlotte's baby couldn't have been Cormac's. The timings were all wrong. No, her sister must have met somebody in London during the autumn of 1939. Jess could easily imagine Charlotte dashing to the National Gallery, or the Wigmore Hall, in her college lunch hour, getting a quick fill of culture between classes. Meeting someone fascinating.

Perhaps while gazing at a Landseer painting.

'I do so admire his line,' Charlotte might have said.

'And I admire how he makes you feel the air around the form,' the stranger would answer, in a voice low and amused. 'As if one might step inside the frame and breathe in the light.'

That would draw Charlotte in. Sensual, illicit. Ah, but what about that perfume, the Shalimar? The gift of a Parisian lover with diplomatic privileges, according to Miss Treadgold.

'As if one might breathe in the light, *non, Mademoiselle*?'

Strangely, that afternoon, amid a slew of letters with Ramsgate postmarks, Jess had been given one from a French refugee to another. She'd struggled through, leaning on what she remembered from school, before finally sending it upstairs to the foreign language section. One phrase had stood out – she'd translated it as 'having the courage to trust'.

If you had left your home carrying nothing but a bundle of clothes and a false identity, trust would be hard to hold onto. Yet the writer had spoken of rekindling it, like a candle flame, guarding it with his hands until it flared bright.

If he could, then surely she could too. Trust that Charlotte had found her way in London and survived. Trust that her sister had made choices which, at the time, had made sense.

Jess had hurt Rafe because she hadn't trusted her housemates to treat him with respect. Likewise, she had assumed her housemates and Mrs Kesgrave would despise her if they knew about Stoney Street. But what proof had she? Nothing – only fear and prejudice.

'I must stop living as if everyone lies to me.' She too must gain the courage to trust.

It was growing dark when she left, kept late because the department was falling behind. On the step of the lodging house, as she lifted her hand to knock, Jess heard her name being called.

'Hold fire, I'll let us in.' It was Grace, torch wavering, her cape on over her uniform.

'Lovely to see you,' Jess said, exercising her resolution to be open and trusting. 'I've had a difficult day but hope you've had a better one.' Now she sounded as if she was addressing a gathering.

'Oh, the usual.' Grace didn't seem to notice. She plonked down her large black bag, which Jess knew contained spare caps, a pair of black stockings – just in case – and a rolled copy of her favourite reading material, *Peg's Paper*, unashamed romance. And a love letter or two from a certain pilot? It wasn't Jess's place to pry. 'Nine hours on my feet,' Grace complained.

'Being mentally and physically abused by my ghastly ghoul of a patient and the night nurse late yet again. Still, there are compensations.'

'Oh?' *Don't pry, Jess.*

'Certain family members are, shall we say, more to my taste than Lady Ventnor.'

That would be Owen, Jess thought, *who is also to Betony's taste.* Perhaps being too open, too trusting, wasn't wise under the circumstances. Still, she had vowed. 'Is Lady Ventnor the ghastly ghoul?'

'She's an angry, spoiled, ill-tempered, gout-ridden malingerer. And that's on a good day.'

'And you can't leave?'

'Not yet, and not easily. I didn't take my final exam – I'm not an SRN.' Grace closed the door behind them and hitched her gas mask higher on her shoulder. 'You heard me saying to Mrs Kesgrave how I blotted my copybook at the Royal London? I don't think they'd trust me not to do the same again. Walk out, slam doors, all that.'

That word, nosing its way in again. Trust. *All right, message received*, Jess told it silently. *I will reignite the candle flame and guard it with my hands.* She was about to answer when a noise from upstairs caught her ears. 'Shh. What's that?'

She knew even as she asked. The sound had lived too long in her memory. *Clack. Clack. Clack.*

The keys of a Remington typewriter, echoing down the stairwell. Her heart seemed to hang, suspended, in her chest. It couldn't be—

'Charlotte,' she rasped.

'Who?' said Grace.

'My sister.'

'Your – wait, you've got a sister?'

But Jess was already flying up the stairs two at a time.

32

She burst into the bedroom to find Betony kneeling beside her bed, the typewriter denting the eiderdown. She was pecking at the keys so intently, she didn't notice Jess, open-mouthed, stricken.

The typewriter lid lay on Jess's bed. Beside it, torn nearly in two, was Charlotte's last letter.

Jess gave a wild, ungoverned cry. Rage and grief. Grace came in behind her. Betony jerked round, eyes wide, hands hovering above the keys. For once, she had nothing to say.

Jess picked up the letter between shaking fingers. Her voice sounded unrecognisable, even to herself. 'What have you done?'

Betony got to her feet, eyes moving to the letter. 'I don't think that was me.'

'How dare you? I don't want your excuses.' Jess felt words frothing in a frenzy to be released. 'Keep your lies. These are my things; they're mine.'

'But it's only a typewriter.' Betony glanced at Grace, searching for support. It was clear she found none because her gaze snapped back to Jess. 'I'll buy you a new ribbon, all right? I'm writing something for work. We had to sack both our staff writers and my editor can't do everything. People are always accusing me of being a pointless clotheshorse, so I—'

'Shut up, Betony.' Grace stepped between them, her voice hard. 'Nobody cares, and this is about something other than you. It's about our right to privacy. Our right not to have our things pawed over by a self-indulgent brat. How would you like it if I took one of your lovely frocks, or your curlers, or your stockings?'

'I wouldn't mind if you asked.'

'And if I didn't? You're not queen of this bedroom. Take whatever drivel you're writing, put the typewriter back, then beg Jess's pardon.'

Whether Betony did so, Jess didn't wait to find out. Cradling Charlotte's unfinished job application to the *London Mercury*, she ran down and locked herself in the bathroom, sat on the edge of the bath and sobbed. What had made her scream like that? Now she'd made an enemy of Betony and probably worsened the ill-feeling between the other two girls. It was almost laughable. What happened to trust and openness?

'But she shouldn't have touched your typewriter, Charlotte. I never did because it was yours. Your world, your precious hope. Everything was stacked against us, and that was your way out.'

A tap at the door roused her. Wiping her eyes on her towel, Jess opened it and found Betony standing on the other side.

'Darling, I'm so sorry. Will you forgive me?'

Fresh tears came.

'Grace is right, I'm an absolute stinker and need to be told. The typewriter's back in its place. I'm now going downstairs to massacre another meal. Macaroni cheese, with cinders and scorched-earth topping.' Betony attempted a little smile. *Are we all right?*

Jess wiped her eyes. 'I'll come and help.'

'You don't have to, honestly.'

'I'll help. It's a crime to burn cheese with a war on. I'll join you when I've changed.'

Peace resumed. Only Jess feared that what she'd thought was fragile before was now shattered, beneath the surface.

In their room, she found Grace in front of the wardrobe in her slip, holding an emerald-green dress on a hanger.

Grace looked over her shoulder. 'Did she apologise?'

Jess nodded. 'Did you make her?'

'Sort of. She isn't that bad. There's a heart there. It just hides behind layers of inherited privilege. I think I was rather mean to her. Drivel, and all that.'

Jess agreed. 'Even if it is drivel, she has a right to try.'

'Mm. Betony is a bit too inspired by her heroine.' Grace laid the green dress on her bed and took something from beside Betony's pillow. She cleared her throat.

'"Autumn, or 'fall' as our American cousins call it, is a sort of in-between time when a girl must be both prepared for sunshine and sudden icy blasts. Brr! The summer frock leaves for the Riviera (in its head) and out comes tweed and the trusty cardigan. Preferably cashmere though lambswool will do if you're not flush. Pair light fabrics with sturdier ones, but never, please, sheer silk over a vest. The French call it 'transition dressing' and it's something we British do instinctively. Do it with style!"'

'It's not bad,' said Jess, once again hearing Miss Treadgold's clipped, confident voice. Red lips and calculating eyes behind a demi-veil. 'I take it that's a Miss Touchwood piece?'

'No, Betony's, including spelling mistakes. I suspect it's mostly copied.'

'I think it's called plagiarism.'

'Well, imitation is the sincerest form of flattery, isn't it? Betony should watch out, though.' Grace put the page back and held up the dress. 'What d'you think – will this do for my important date?'

Jess considered it. The emerald dress was simple, certainly not new, but the colour would sizzle against Grace's hair and peachy skin. 'What's the occasion?'

'Meeting somebody's mother.'

'Owen's.'

Colour flooded into Grace's cheeks. 'How the hell?'

'I have ears.'

'Oh, crikey, does Betony know?'

'Not from me,' Jess assured her. 'Nor will she.'

'You're right, it is Owen,' Grace said, glancing at the door as if she feared Betony stood on the other side. 'It's early days. We hardly know each other. I suppose we just clicked.'

'It happens.' She and Rafe had. Or she had, anyway. Could you click only on one side? Probably not. Jess went to her bed, peering under it to check her suitcase was back in its place. She'd take Charlotte's letter into work and mend it with Sellotape. There was no harm done. Not really. She doubted Betony had even glanced at the page and even if she had—

Oh, no. No, no.

She pulled out the suitcase, fumbling at the locks.

'Jess, what's up?'

Jess didn't answer. She lifted the lid, searched, moved clothes, books. It wasn't there. *It wasn't there.*

Behind her, Grace murmured, 'Jess, you're worrying me.'

Leave me alone. She'd tucked the directions to Stoney Street against the letter, like mother and child. Now it was gone. 'I'm all right,' she said in a monotone. 'I've lost something...' She stood up, looking around wildly.

'D'you mean this, perhaps?' Grace fetched something off Betony's pillow. 'I thought it was hers, though it did seem odd. I mean, I can't think the Honourable Betony goes south of the river too often.'

'Grace, no.'

Grace didn't hear and started reading: '"Viaduct near Stoney Street, brick terrace. First house, blue vase behind a lace curtain. Call in the afternoon. Ask for Mrs Munday and say..."' Her voice slowed and she met Jess's eyes.

Jess couldn't speak. Couldn't find a mask to pull down over her distress.

'"... Say you've come about the laundry,"' Grace continued heavily. '"Never, ever give your real name." Oh, God love you, girl, what is going on?'

When Jess shook her head, Grace gave her waistline a moment's professional study then waved the piece of paper. 'If you're in the family way, I can help. I know how these things work – I've met girls in trouble, any number. And seen the aftermath. Darling...' Grace held out her hand.

Come, sit on the bed; I'll put my arm round your shoulder and listen as you cry.

But Jess couldn't. She couldn't trust Grace, nor herself with Charlotte's secret. Instead of taking the offered hand, she snatched the note from Grace's hand, saying, 'I'll thank you to mind your own business. You said it yourself: if we don't respect each other's privacy, we can't live in the same house, let alone the same room.'

She ran out, tearing the paper into little pieces. On the floor below, she flushed it down the lavatory.

33

WEDNESDAY, 18 SEPTEMBER 1940

Ramsgate letters piled in front of Jess. A line in one of them cut through her numb misery:

Darling Sue, why aren't you writing to me? Have all my letters gone astray?

She felt the lonely ache behind the words. She'd come to London to find her sister and failed. She had made, then lost, a friend in Rafe. Grace and Betony were treating her with kid gloves. Who could blame them? They must think her eccentric: quiet one minute, spitting fire and fury the next. Only Mrs Kesgrave remained the same, placid and kind as ever. Oh, and the Bennet sisters, the chickens. Small mercies.

She opened another letter, her fingers working mechanically.

Nicky keeps asking where his rabbits are. I've said they've gone to live on a farm but now he wants to fetch them home. I haven't told him our house has gone too. Sunday night. Thank God we were in the Tube, at Bethnal Green. What can I tell him? He's only six.

Another, from a young man to his godfather, brought distress of a different kind. The writer had just received his call-up papers.

Mum can't stop crying and I'm scared I won't be able to fire a gun and you'll all be ashamed of me.

Cormac Whelan would look dashing in uniform, but would he ever assume the quiet courage of an unwilling soldier, or would he prowl the streets with his razor blade on a stick, until they caught him?

'Flash and menace,' she murmured.

'They sound like comic book characters.' It was Mr Brinkworth, doing his rounds. 'Any mackerel today among the sprats, Miss Gresham?'

'Only sprats so far, Mr Brinkworth.'

'Keep fishing.'

Her next three pieces of correspondence were love letters, one of them so passionate, her cheeks were burning even after she placed it in her out-tray. It had the effect of erasing her resolve never to see Rafe again. She'd already looked up his street on her map and during her lunch hour, she dashed to the post office and wrote him a note, explaining that she hadn't meant to insult him. She'd been afraid how others might react to his injuries.

I see now how small-minded I was. If you can brave the world, why should I shrink from it?

She addressed the letter as best she could. Rafe Taverner

RN. Tufton Street, London W1. And because it was suddenly so vital he get it at once, she paid for it to go by bicycle messenger.

'No house number?' asked the clerk. When she said no, 'But his brother's a resident in the street,' he nodded, saying, 'Don't worry, our chap will find the right place.'

During the afternoon tea break, she picked up someone's Thursday *Mercury* and turned straight to the Touchwood column. Its content was remarkably apt.

> A working girl's budget needn't condemn her to *drabbity* dressing. One well-cut frock in a flattering shade will carry her from munitions bench or typewriter to a table for two. Remember, it's not the size of the purse, it's the size of the *poise*.

Drabbity, Jess thought. What a strange, but oddly familiar word. Before she could chase the thought, the sirens went. The raid dragged on into early evening, and Jess was grateful for the solid embrace of Senate House. Only yesterday, a bomb had torn through Marble Arch Underground, killing those who'd thought themselves safe below ground. Grace had been in running distance, and she'd helped some of the casualties. Owen had been with her; Jess had heard Grace telling Mrs Kesgrave, but she doubted they'd mention it to Betony.

Grace was brave as a lion. The hospital that had thrown her out needed its head examining. *As do I*, Jess thought. *I was so nasty to her. I won't blame her if she can't forgive me.*

When seven o'clock arrived, she'd dealt with almost three hundred letters, and her fingers were swollen. It was her mistake to glance up as Miss Cartwright came around asking for overtime volunteers.

'You will, won't you, Miss Gresham? We're so behind.'

Jess hid exhaustion behind a smile. Maybe it beat going

home, where she'd only sit wondering if Rafe had got her letter, and what he made of it.

At nine, the bombers were back, turning Senate House into a temporary prison, forcing those within its walls to work a nightshift. The all-clear went a few minutes after five the following morning. Jess was given leave to go home and report back at 1 p.m.

Gower Street had not yet suffered a direct hit, but the road was littered with jagged shell casings, presumably fired from Regent's Park. Prolonged battery always brought roof tiles tumbling, and people rushing for shelter would abandon bicycles, suitcases and handcarts by the side of the road, or on the pavement, creating a hazard for those going home before it was fully light. Jess moved hesitantly, keeping to the middle of the road whenever she could. She reached Hill Street just after seven.

She now had her own key and was putting it in the lock when she heard her name called. She spun around.

Cormac Whelan had melted out of sight many days ago, but the memory of him was as sharp as ever. For a moment, cold terror gripped her. Had he tracked her down? Then, seeing the outline of a military coat and turned-up collar, her emotions flared in a different direction.

'Rafe! You got my letter? What are you doing out so early?'

'Coming to see you,' he said. 'Actually, I called last night but you weren't in. Mrs Kesgrave and I reckoned you'd be let out of jail this morning.'

She took him inside, saying, 'I'll make you a cup of tea in the kitchen, but we must be quiet. The others will have spent the night in the Tin Palace' – the Anderson shelter – 'and they'll have crawled up to bed just before dawn.'

He wouldn't stay long, he said. 'You need to sleep too. I just wanted to be sure you were all right. And to thank you for writing. For being so frank.'

Putting the kettle on the hob, she told him she'd thought about that moment in the café on Fitzroy Square every day. 'I could have kicked myself. I should have run after you.'

'That would have been nice.'

The kettle would take five minutes at least to come to the boil, and Jess went to Rafe and took his hand. The uninjured one. 'I'm sorry.'

'You're not wearing your red coat.'

'No.' She used her grey gabardine for work. She wouldn't risk leaving the red one in a cloakroom with dozens of other women coming and going. 'I wrote to Madame Renée, by the way, promising to send seventeen shillings by postal order the moment I get paid.'

'I never doubted you.' He declined her offer of toast. 'I'm not eating your rations. I'll go home in a minute, but I had to see you. Tomorrow...'

An invitation to dinner? Her heart leaped. A foolish smile made a home on her lips. 'Yes?'

'I'm leaving London.'

Why did this keep happening? Pick her up, smile into her eyes, drop her flat? 'Why must you go?'

'So I can heal. The doctors say my recovery has hit a plateau. The Navy thinks I'm taking too much time growing a new skin.' He indicated his jaw, where the flesh seemed rougher, scalier than before. Healing was never a beautiful process. Things often got worse before they got better.

'Where are they sending you?'

'Oh, some old manor house in East Sussex. One road in, no roads out. I'm to report on Saturday, first thing. Travelling tomorrow.'

'Then what?' A layer of her heart was being torn away. 'Will you come home when you're recovered?'

Even before he spoke, she knew the answer. He was letting her down gently, not dropping exactly. It felt somehow worse because it showed he'd thought about it.

'I'm to be redeployed. Wireless, map and cypher work.'

What did that mean?

'Intelligence – though not officially.' He looked away, evading the next question, and Jess wondered what exactly they planned for him, unofficially. With the Official Secrets Act standing between them, she couldn't ask. Instead, she touched his good cheek and held his gaze until he looked away.

'Don't, Jess.'

'Don't what?'

'Look at me as though you're seeing into the void. I don't know what'll happen to me. Where I'll be six months from now.'

'And you won't come back and see me.'

He shook his head. He looked so tired.

'Why not? You'll get leave.'

'Not necessarily.'

'Everyone gets leave.' It came out in anger, though it was only fear.

'Not everyone, Jess. Not on classified ops. I don't know when I'll get back to London, which is why I wanted to call and say goodbye.'

She couldn't see his expression through her tears but heard the flatness in his voice. A finality. Once, she'd have accepted it as her due, her fate. Not now. Not when everything that mattered was teetering on the cliff edge. 'Not so long ago, you followed me across London because you feared for me. You went out in the dead of night. Where's that gone, Rafe? That concern – or were you just bored and missing life on board ship?'

'I wanted to make sure you were safe. And you are.'

'But why was it important?' She made him meet her eyes.

'It's your turn to be frank. Why did you have your brother find where I worked? Why follow me for days? Why take on Cormac Whelan?'

'Because,' he said, through his teeth, 'who the devil else was going to?'

Right. His truth. She'd hoped for so much more. 'Thing is, Rafe, I love you. I can't help it, and I wish I didn't.'

'Come on, Jess.' He stepped back, the gap of an inch feeling a mile wide. 'We've met three times. It's too soon.'

She shook her head. *Not for me.*

'I like you,' he said gently. 'You're a dear, sweet girl. If there were more time, and no bloody war—'

'You'd take me out twice, realise how ordinary I am, and not call again. I know how it goes. My tragedy is, when I love, I give all I have but it's just not enough. I know that.'

She gave him a moment to deny it. He didn't.

She thought fleetingly of the boy on the beach, who'd vanished without a word after she'd offered him her fledgling heart. At least Rafe had explained. She wouldn't let him go away remembering her on the verge of tears, pleading. Forcing a smile, she went to check the kettle, which was doing its job perfectly well and needed no interference from her. When she turned back, her eyes were dry. 'Can we at least write?'

'Course. There'll be a post-box address. I'll send it.' A faint smile. 'Expect your letters to be opened, though.'

'Feels like divine retribution,' she said, trying to match his tone.

They embraced, cautiously. She could feel his heart thumping.

'Be safe, Jess. Don't cross paths with bad people. Promise?'

'I can't do that.'

He touched her chin, lifting it gently. 'That's what I like about you,' he said. 'You don't give up.'

'You do,' she whispered.

He bent his head. It wasn't a lover's kiss but something quieter. Not a promise. More as if he was releasing her. His lips were warm, hesitant, and so were hers. She breathed him in, knowing she'd return to this moment again and again.

'You'll be fine after a while, Jess. You'll forget me.'

Never, she thought, but said nothing and forced another smile because pride was all she had left. She was sure he would have left then, but a commotion broke out in the yard behind the kitchen. They rushed out in time to see a fox on top of the hen coop, tugging at the tarpaulin. The chickens were running about, clucking in panic.

'Shoo! Get away!' Jess hurtled across the yard. The fox fled, scaling the rear wall in a flash.

'He'll be back,' Rafe said quietly, watching her. 'Soon as you go inside.'

'Don't,' she pleaded. 'The poor Bennet sisters. They've already lost Mary to the fox.'

'I love the way you go into battle, Jess,' he said, smiling faintly. 'I'll take that image with me.'

Why not take hold of me, she thought with wrenching sadness, *then you wouldn't need an image*. She folded the tarpaulin back over the coop and looked up.

He'd gone.

34

Thursday, 19 September 1940

Coming home in the rain, Jess felt a change in the atmosphere of the lodging house. Though Rafe had only visited once, his presence had seeped into the fabric. He'd be packing for his trip into the depths of the English countryside. Fixed on the next phase of his life.

Walking into the kitchen, she found Betony at the table, staring at a notebook.

'Are you cheffing tonight?' Getting no answer, Jess checked the rota on the cupboard door. 'It's Mrs Kesgrave's turn. Is she in?'

'Don't think so,' Betony said vaguely, not lifting her eyes.

Since the explosion over the typewriter and Betony's apology, they'd both been treading on eggshells around each other. Now, it seemed, it was back to normal, Betony lost in her own concerns.

'What are you working on?' Jess asked.

'Sorry?' Betony looked up to see Jess peering down at her

notebook. 'I'm writing an article. Or trying to. Does "hemline" have a hyphen in the middle, or is it two words?'

'It's one word. Should we get cooking?' Jess prompted. 'The siren might go and we won't have had anything.'

'Oh, would you mind?' Betony tapped her temple. 'I'm cudgelling grey matter, for something on skirt lengths for October's issue. We had to pull an article on gloves because the factory making them got bombed. I need something that'll knock my editor's socks off only I can't keep to one idea. That's how you write something, isn't it? Start and finish with the same idea?'

Jess pulled out the chair opposite Betony at the table. 'You start with one and develop it. Taking the reader on a little journey.'

'Right...' Betony chewed at her lip.

'Sometimes it helps to just let it flow.'

'Flow... my life's flowing.' Betony threw down her pencil. 'Down the plughole. My parents have all but disowned me. I'm broke. I had two gorgeous men in love with me and now they're both ignoring me.'

'They're probably busy,' Jess said awkwardly. 'There is a war on.'

'If man wants to see you, he'll find a way. Unless he's stranded at the top of Ben Nevis or in a submarine. Nothing from Owen. Not a call, not a postcard.'

'Read me what you've written.' Jess moved her chair round to Betony's side of the table. Anything to stem this confessional. Grace had returned glowing from her meeting with Owen's mother. Betony was pining for a telephone call that would never come.

Self-consciously clearing her throat, Betony read her piece on hemlines. They were in a state of flux. Bless them, they so wanted to stay down, but through fabric shortages and the need for women to 'stride through the blackout and clamber across bombsites', they were being forced upward against their will.

Jess perceived the germ of an idea, but it was lost in Betony's wild punctuation and her determination to be funny.

'I've written it out fifteen times already,' Betony sighed. 'I'm desperate to show my editor that I deserve her faith in me. And I need the pay rise she promised. I'm sure Owen dropped me because he thinks I'm frivolous. Winter loves me as I am...'

'Winter?' Was Betony referring to the upcoming season?

'Winter Macpherson. Canadian, works at the High Commission.'

'He likes you as you are?'

'Mostly. He hates that I flirt with other men.'

Jess waited to see if Betony was joking. Apparently not. 'Fancy that.'

'Perhaps that is all I am. As my father says – a useless coat hanger.' The blonde head sank, and Jess felt a wave of pity. Maybe Betony wasn't so different from herself or Charlotte, wanting to make something of her life. It sounded as though she, too, was battling a repressive parent.

Jess pointed to the potatoes and a floppy-looking cabbage on the chopping board and said, 'You get peeling and I'll give this a rewrite.'

Twenty minutes later, Jess read her version.

'"Hemlines are in a state of flux. With cloth in short supply and so many women out at work, a hem that hovers an inch below the knee is simply more serviceable. No more catching on rubble or steps. You can stride over the crater that appeared overnight outside your home and move more safely in the blackout. A plain wool serge or gabardine wears well for daytime. For evenings, longer lengths can still be managed. Your wardrobe should have one in a neutral colour, but please, not black. No cloth in the shops? The women looking their best are those who dress in clothes that let them get things done, while keeping their own style. A good skirt is one that works as hard as you do."'

'Gosh.' Betony had almost peeled one potato while Jess rewrote her piece. 'I love it, only I wanted to sound... I don't know... a bit more...'

'Like Miss Touchwood?' Jess put the notebook down. 'Thing is, Betony, you're best at being yourself. Your magazine is *Practical Modes*, so be practical.'

'Could I give this to Sybil and say it's mine?'

'You may.' Jess found another potato peeler and fetched the vegetables to the table.

After they'd made inroads, at very different speed, Betony said, 'About the other day. Your typewriter. I was a beast.'

'You apologised and I hoped we'd left it all behind.'

'Even so, I wanted to atone.' Betony fetched her handbag, removing a sheet of paper. It only took Jess a couple of seconds to realise it was Charlotte's last letter, the raw edges miraculously fused. She'd been looking everywhere for it, planning to take it to work and mend it there. She'd assumed it had somehow been thrown out with the rubbish.

'I had our studio artist do it,' Betony said. 'Ambrose is a craftsman, but more importantly, he knows how to get double-sided tape.'

Jess thanked her, adding, 'I suppose you read it?'

'Couldn't stop myself, but it's only a job application. I assume Charlotte Gresham is your sister... Did she get the position?'

'Yes, she is and no, she didn't.' Jess put the letter away in her satchel. 'Thank you. Now we're even. No more apologies.'

'Got it. Grace can't call me a thankless cow again.' Betony's expression shifted. Casual. Too casual. 'Who's she seeing? I presume there's a man... you can usually tell.'

'Grace and I don't know each other well enough to have heart-to-hearts about love,' Jess said carefully. She could feel Betony's confusion. Even in an old shirt, cardigan and trousers – regulation attire for an evening that would probably end in the Anderson shelter – she looked impossibly glamorous and the obvious choice for a footloose Spitfire pilot. Yet he preferred an Irish East Ender.

Betony's eye in turn fell on Jess's red coat, which she'd brought down that morning, to restitch a button that was working loose. 'That is a lovely thing,' she said, stroking the shoulder. 'I wouldn't have imagined you in red, but it really suits you. Where did it come from?'

'Debenham & Freebody. It was my sister's. She... left it behind.'

'Bought at Debenham's?' Betony shook her head. 'Not a chance.'

'Charlotte said so.'

Betony lifted the coat up to display the hem. 'Three inches deep, blind-stitched by hand. British ready-mades, even from good stores, never go to those lengths. This coat is Paris couture, pre-war. A Lelong, I'd lay money on it.'

Lelong meant nothing. 'My sister could never have afforded a Paris coat.'

'She might, second-hand.'

'Oh?' Jess mentioned Elegant Exchange. 'On Grafton Way.'

'I think I know it but' – Betony was shaking her head – 'there's only one place in London you'd see something like this. I could take you.'

'No.' Jess said it too fast and Betony blinked.

'Fine. Only offering.'

Jess left the room, taking the coat, but hadn't reached the stairs when the sirens signalled ten minutes to get to safety. Time only to rouse Mrs Kesgrave, fast asleep on her bed, check that Grace was not doing the same, fill a basket with provisions, make a thermos of tepid tea and stumble out into the dark.

Friday, 20 September 1940

Betony had left to go on a date with her Canadian. Grace was going out on the town too, with Owen. There had been a really upsetting exchange between the two of them earlier: Betony had finally got a letter from Flight Lieutenant Henderson, telling her he'd met someone else.

She hadn't made a scene. Surprisingly, she'd been calm, but clearly furious and in no doubt who had pinched her man. Jess, by now an exhausted piggy-in-the-middle, had been thankful to see them both leave. Mrs Kesgrave had come upstairs not long ago to say goodbye too. She had a professional engagement. A divorce lawyer who sometimes booked her had called last minute, asking her – *begging me, dear one* – to take herself to the Sea View Hotel, Brighton.

'It's a ticklish divorce case and the woman who would have acted as correspondent broke her leg in the blackout. Should you need me, phone the hotel and ask for Miss Violet Banks – my alias when I'm at work. If there's a raid, you *will* go into the shelter. Promise?'

Jess promised.

'And, er' – a light cough – 'my girls?'

'I'll take the hens in with me. Now, go, please don't worry.'

Jess planned an evening in bed, with a cup of cocoa and a book. Luftwaffe and the sirens willing, of course. She selected a novel she hadn't read before, *Dangerous Liaisons*, translated from the French. It had been Charlotte's, bought second-hand on Charing Cross Road and left behind at the vicarage. The price was written in the flyleaf, two shillings and sixpence.

Someone had written – not Charlotte, it wasn't her hand – *To survive, one must know how to play.*

'Hm,' Jess muttered, turning a page. 'To survive, one needs to sniff out when somebody else is playing.'

The novel was written as a series of letters. She was engrossed in Madame de Volanges' warning about the antics of the dangerous rake Valmont, thinking how nothing really changed, when the cadences of eighteenth-century France were overtaken by a rising moan. Sirens.

She was about to experience her first air raid in the Anderson, all alone.

Ten minutes later, she was heading out into the yard, torch in hand and *Liaisons* under her arm. Anxious clucking from the hen coop reminded her of her promise. Since their near miss with the fox, the Bennet sisters had been restless.

'Chick-chick,' she said gently. 'Come on, girls, we'll huddle together.'

Hens for company beat squabbling housemates and star-crossed lovers any night of the week. She could wrap all the blankets round herself and think about Rafe, who must by now have arrived in East Sussex, or certainly be on his way.

Thinking about her? Jess had no such faith. That brief farewell kiss was unlikely to be as memorable for him as it was for her.

The shelter door shut and sealed, the hens settled, the attack began. The impacts felt close but lacked the ferocity of the raids that had devastated Oxford Street two nights earlier. Perhaps the Germans were losing momentum. A piece in the *London Mercury* had implied an invasion had been stopped 'by determined resistance from our RAF fighter squadrons'.

Was the tide turning, or was it just what they all wanted to believe? With luck, tonight wouldn't be a long raid, if the Germans were changing tactics. 'They won't want to lose more aircraft,' she told the hens. Three were perched on the bench beside her; the fourth, Lydia, was cradled against her chest and she could feel the beat of her tiny heart. The little black

Dorking displayed none of the wild spirits of her namesake in *Pride and Prejudice*.

'Lydia fell in love with all the officers of the militia,' Jess said, needing to hear her own voice alongside the growing din of the raid. 'She couldn't resist a man in uniform.'

Her thoughts veered. Would Rafe write and provide her with an address? Letters weren't always bringers of joy. Her imagination took a little path of its own:

Dear Jess,

This is very hard to write, but I'm afraid that having thought things through—

Don't, she told herself. Something landed close by. The shelter gave a sharp shudder and the detonation rolled on, lasting a minute or more. She couldn't place where the bomb had struck. Course, it could be miles away. Sound travelled.

She restarted her one-way conversation with the black hen. 'Charlotte and I had one just like you... perhaps a little bigger. Crow black with longer legs than usual, and she used them to take on the bigger birds. We called her...' What was it they'd called her? It was something to do with a rhyme she and Charlotte would chant.

No. The name had flown.

Another violent crump made the shelter shake. What if it couldn't hold? What if a bomb landed right on top and it became a burial pit? Would anyone know she was here and try to rescue her? The awful irony was that she was only here in London at all because she'd set out to rescue Charlotte.

Her busy, frightened mind took her back to her bedroom in Ramsgate. The wallpaper with the faded roses, the hard floor and home-made rugs. If she'd never opened the box room door and found Charlotte's Remington, she'd still be sleeping in her single bed there, the vicar's daughter. Working at Hedgley's, filing and typing, being ignored. Helping out in the parish and keeping house for her father. Instead, she'd rushed to London, headlong into a series of mishaps far beyond her experience. Cripplegate. Rafe. Cormac Whelan... the escalator at Charing Cross.

Charlotte twenty steps in front of her, then gone.

Miss Treadgold.

Mrs Munday of Stoney Street. *No shortcuts down the staircase this time, eh?* Whatever that meant.

'I just wanted the truth, even if it meant absolute proof that Charlotte was dead.' The hens settled as if the admission soothed them. Jess made a conscious effort to breathe steadily and not give in to fear.

It became hypnotic and after a while she began to see faces. Charlotte's first. Black hair, crimson lips, skin too pale. Then Mrs Kesgrave in her fabulous silk robe. Betony next, asking, 'How do you spell "hemline"?'

And lastly Grace, the wounded soul whom Jess had pushed away. It would have been easy to say, 'It's not me who's in trouble; it was Charlotte. She went to Stoney Street, and you probably know the rest.'

The bombs kept falling. The guns encircling London boomed at the top of their voices, aiming at the darkness to destroy the incoming planes before they opened their hatches.

All at once, they fell silent and into the lull came a thin, sinister whistle.

Jess had just time to think, *This one's got my name on it. God help me.*

The blast was volcanic, the earth folding in on itself. The sky seemed to crash down on her steel ark and the roof sagged inward, making lights explode behind her eyes. Her torch toppled over and went out. She fell into the suffocating dark, unsure if the world still existed or if everything above her had been erased. Her lips formed a cry she knew nobody would hear.

Would anyone realise she was alive, beneath the suffocating weight on this roof?

Would Mrs Kesgrave, Betony, Grace think of her – the difficult, secretive girl who never quite let them in?

Fear closed in and all she could do was wait to see which would fail first: her oxygen or hope.

35

GRACE

At around midnight, the taxi dropped them short of Berkeley Square; the driver could get no further. Getting out, Grace saw that the junction with Hill Street was barricaded by ARP wardens. There were fire engines on Hill Street too. Buildings were ablaze somewhere past the midpoint. Their end. Not good.

She'd got a lift home in with Betony and Betony's date, Winter Macpherson. Had she been the sort to keep a diary, Grace would probably have written, *The strangest of nights, Owen and I, Betony and Winter, bumping into each other at the Savoy. Can't get away from it, real life beats fiction. But maybe it all ends well? I'm engaged!*

Only, the night wasn't ending well. Grace could hear the hiss of water under pressure and hoarse shouts from the crews. Roaring flames, spitting sparks. She watched Winter pay off the cabbie and help Betony out.

Together, the three of them approached the barricade.

'God.' Betony clutched her white velvet jacket to her bare shoulders. 'It's definitely our end of the street.'

Grace went up to an ARP warden. 'What's happened?'

'Bomb, miss. Hit a house.'

'Which house?'

'Not sure. Near the top.' He'd been here pretty much since the fire crews arrived, he said. 'It was a direct hit but all I know, it has "thirty" in front of it.'

Grace and Betony exchanged glances. Two night-owls, rivalry forgotten, they looked towards the barricade.

'Hey – wait—' the warden yelled as he saw what they were about to do. 'You're not to climb over. There's a rescue going on.'

Winter shouted at them too. 'Don't even think about it. The building might collapse on you.'

They ignored him. Betony's long legs and wide skirt made easy work of a sandbag barrier. It took Grace a little longer to struggle over and slither past the ARP warden but she'd grown up on rough streets. She knew how to dodge a man wanting to catch her.

Winter gave up shouting and came too.

All three halted where the smoke thickened and auxiliary firewomen stood in a line.

'You lot need to skedaddle,' one of the firewomen shouted.

'Is it us?' Betony's voice was ragged.

'It's... not,' Grace said. It was the house two doors up from theirs. Flames roared above its chimney pots, its roof and upper floor gone. It resembled a giant tea chest into which somebody had poured fuel and thrown a match.

The house right next door had flames in its upper rooms, glittering behind shattered windows. Into these gaping vents, the fire crew were concentrating their hoses.

A firewoman came up to them. 'You're hindering the rescue. You, sir,' she barked at Winter, 'take them away before they get under our feet.'

'That's more than I can promise,' Winter replied. He turned to Grace and Betony. 'Is anyone else in the house – your landlady?'

Grace told him that Mrs Kesgrave should be safely in Brighton by now. 'She was getting ready to go when I left this evening.' But Jess... She grabbed Betony's arm. 'Was Jess staying in tonight?'

'I think so. She doesn't go out much, does she?' Betony tugged the auxiliary firewoman's sleeve. 'Our house—' She pointed. 'We have to get inside. It's—'

'What, your fur coat and your second-best dress?' The fire-woman's voice rang with disdain. 'Give up. We don't want three more bodies to dig out.'

'You don't understand. Please listen—'

Grace took over. She knew how to pitch her voice when she needed to, coming from a big, noisy family. 'There's an Anderson shelter in the back yard is what she's trying to say. Our friend Jess will be inside it.'

An ARP warden approached and they repeated the information.

'She'll have survived, won't she?' Betony's voice held a pleading note.

'Depends,' said the man.

'On what?'

'Where the shelter was positioned, where she was sitting and which way the stack fell.'

'Stack? What stack?' Grace demanded. This wasn't the moment for a man to be technical, or cautious. They had to find Jess, pull her out.

'That stack.' The warden pointed to the house next door, which, Grace saw, had lost its chimneys. She heard Winter swear under his breath.

'Which way did they fall?' he asked.

The warden shook his head. 'Can't say till it's safe to go in. Nothing anyone can do till the fires are under control.'

Wait? Stand around till the flames were doused – was he

joking? Grace tried to push past him but found herself gripped in a wrestling lock by the auxiliary firewoman.

'For your own safety,' she told Grace. 'I've seen whole houses fall in with a second's warning. You don't want to be stuck under tons of burning rubble, do you?'

'But that's what's happened to Jess.' Grace struggled to get free. 'She'll die if we leave her.'

'Better one than four,' the woman said coldly. 'Now get back, or I'll find a copper to arrest the lot of you.'

Winter looked sick, but he seemed to agree. 'She's right. Listen, those shelters are designed to take a hell of a weight before they crush. If the chimney came down on top of her, she'll be trapped and feeling very alone. But not dead. Soon as it's daylight, we'll get her.'

'By then it might be too late.'

It was Betony who said it, echoing Grace's thoughts. Moments later, the roof of the house next door fell in.

Grace heard herself keening and made herself stop. It was like Ricky and Mam again. Granny Driscoll and all the other poor sods in the shelter at the Peabody Estate... a direct hit. They'd suffocated in the dark or died in the crush. 'I won't leave Jess to the same thing. I'll go through the house. Downstairs isn't burning.'

'They won't let you,' Winter said. Tall and with the presence of a man used to taking charge, his words checked her. He was right. His arm came round her waist and his other went around Betony and he kissed them one after the other on the brow. 'But they might let me.'

His mistake was to consult the senior ARP man, who said, 'Try it, squire, and I'll arrest you.'

'You have no power of arrest,' Winter said angrily.

'No, but I have a bloody loud voice and there's a pair of special constables guarding the top of the street... should you fancy a night in the cells.'

'Bellow away.' Winter turned towards the house. The warden grabbed one arm; an auxiliary firewoman took the other. In the tussle that followed, Betony and Grace locked glances.

'Got your key?' Grace mouthed.

Betony tapped her evening bag. 'Now, while they're not looking.'

A moment later, they were through the door, dashing down the chequered hallway of the lodging house.

36

BETONY

She led the way to the kitchen. Both women carried slender torches, but even pulling away the brown paper muzzles over the glass made little impact on the dense dark.

'No point putting the lights on,' she heard Grace mutter.

'God, no. We'd probably electrocute ourselves.'

They ran up to their room, out of breath by the time they punched open the door and found all three beds empty.

'Looks like she's in the shelter. Back down again,' Betony said.

They hurried into the kitchen but when they pulled open the door to the back yard, they were greeted with a wall of tumbled brick, mortar and broken slates. More was piled outside the kitchen window. 'We can't get out this way,' Grace rasped. 'God love her, Jess has to be under that lot. Oh, heavens, the poor chickens.'

Betony felt sick. It wasn't only Jess and the chickens who were in jeopardy. Should flames engulf the front of the house, she and Grace would be walled up in here. She was about to suggest they retreat, when from the front passage came urgent footsteps, and a man's voice. Not Winter's.

'Bet it's a bloody special constable,' Grace muttered.

Betony felt a guilty relief. Instantly, she thought of Jess under that landslide and wanted to slap herself for even thinking of escaping.

'Ladies?' came the voice.

They prepared for a severe dressing-down. Into the beam of their torches stepped a uniformed figure. Not a special constable, nor an ARP man with armbands and buttons... this was a man in full naval uniform, gold rings on the sleeve cuff. He was capless, his hair darkened from the mist of fire hoses. The apparition stared past them. 'Is she out there?'

'Who the hell are you?' Betony gasped when the stranger turned his face, revealing the sheen of fragile skin.

'I'm Rafe Taverner, Jess's friend.'

'How did you know to come here?'

'No idea. Something pulled me back.'

'There's a problem,' Grace said in her matter-of-fact way, pointing to the back door. 'Door's blocked, window too. We don't know what to do.'

Rafe took her torch and shone it through the glass, nodding because he saw what she meant. 'There's another way.' He reached for Grace's hand, indicated Betony to follow, and led them back to the street. Outside, they saw Winter in urgent conversation with a pair of constables. He turned as Betony shut the front door of the house.

The special police officers followed his glance. 'Don't tell us you've been inside?' one of them yelled. 'Orders are clear – nobody within a hundred feet of the building until all fires are out. And who might you be?'

The policeman who came up to them gave Rafe an uncertain look. 'You've been burned. If you've been looting...'

'I was bringing these two women to safety, and my burns are old ones,' Rafe answered. To Betony and Grace, he whispered, 'Follow me.' He nodded to Winter, and though the two men had never met before, Winter fell in beside him. They went back down the street towards Berkeley Square until Rafe took a left, stopping almost at once at the entrance to a passage. 'This is Waverton Mews, which runs behind the houses. Ladies, wait here.'

'With respect,' answered Grace, 'not a bleeding chance.'

Betony wholeheartedly agreed. 'We go together.'

'All hands on deck,' added Grace.

'Overrated,' muttered Rafe, but he didn't argue.

The mews had once housed the horses that pulled the carriages of the rich and the lads who tended them. It had granite setts and a gutter down the middle, which provided a useful guide in the dark. Adopting a hunched walk to avoid breathing the smoke rolling over the walls, they made their way along. The closer they got to Mrs Kesgrave's rear wall, the greater the heat, until it struck them like a shovel.

'This is it...' Grace croaked. 'I think.'

Rafe agreed. 'Those are her coping stones on top. Some are missing, where the fox gets over.'

'How the devil d'you know that?' Grace demanded.

'Never mind. Who'll give me a leg-up?'

'Me, I guess,' said Winter. 'When you're over, wait for me, right?' He cupped his hands for Rafe's foot. 'One, two...'

A moment later, Rafe was over the wall, dropping down the other side. They heard him give a grunt of pain then call, 'OK.'

'Me next,' said Grace.

'You don't need to,' said Winter.

'We've had this conversation. Leg up, please.'

Grace was pitched up, and she clung for a moment to the top of the wall, legs kicking. 'Bloody hell. Stupid going-out dress.'

They heard Rafe promising to catch her and a moment after came a thud and another 'bloody hell'.

'Me now.'

'Oh, Betty,' Winter groaned. 'You aren't cut out for this, sweetheart.'

'Don't you "sweetheart" me. Think of little Jess, hoping someone's coming to save her. I know you think I'm feeble, but I'm not some frilly milksop.'

'I don't even know what that is.'

'I'm saying, I'm fed up of people thinking I've nothing to offer.'

'I've never thought that, Betty.'

'Good. Leg up.' She set a gold-toed sandal into his palms. 'Go!' She'd have cleared the wall with panache, but her long skirt snagged on the coping stones, held her for a heartbeat, then tore. One of Lucien Lelong's finest creations gave its life in a valiant cause. Betony dropped onto her backside in the yard. 'Ouch.' She was up at once. 'I'm fine.'

A moment later, Winter proved his broad shoulders were muscle, not tailor's padding. He hauled himself over, landing beside her.

'So, what have we got?' he shouted over the tumult.

'We've got a mess,' Rafe shouted back. 'Neighbour's chimney stack down along with a slice of roof and guttering. We can shift it brick by brick, but we'll be here till Christmas. We need Heavy Rescue.'

'Any chance they'll come before the fire's out?' Winter asked.

'Minimal to none while that blaze is going,' Rafe said. 'Nobody moves till the fire officer says.' He cast a dispirited glance over the piled debris. 'Unless we can pull rank.'

'Can we? Can you?' Winter prompted.

'My brother might, but he's out of town for a couple of days. You?'

'Me? Terribly important – in Ottawa or Canada House.' Winter's tone was dust dry. 'Otherwise, no.'

'Grace?' Rafe sounded tight.

'Oh, come off it,' she snapped. 'My only kin this side of the Irish sea is a sister with three kids and my brother. If you want beer, nylons or dodgy petrol coupons, ring Cormac Whelan. Anything else, forget it. Betony – your old man's in government, isn't he?'

'Ministry of Supply.' Betony, sensing the truce with Grace was about to fracture, held up her hands in defence. 'He's no use here. And we aren't speaking.'

They fell silent, all of them measuring the depth of the wreckage between them and Jess. A neat yard turned bombsite, chicken coop gone, kitchen door unreachable.

'Hang on – what about Owen's uncle, Sir Gideon Ventnor? He's a bit of a noise in Mayfair and you work for the man,' Betony threw at Grace.

'He's Home Guard,' Grace came back. 'He won't have any pull with the fire brigade.'

'Wasn't he in the Royal Horse Guards, the Blues, years ago? I'm sure I remember Daddy saying so once, at a reception somewhere. He'll have friends; men like him always do. Grace, fetch him. Get him to make calls and if he balks, tell him you'll stop pandering to his ghastly wife.'

'I couldn't—' Grace began, then something seemed to click and she said, 'You're right. Sir Gideon came with me after the bomb at the Peabody Estate. He can talk his way past a line of uniforms. And he commands a band of volunteers—'

She ran back to the wall. Winter laced his hands, Grace hitched up her dress and a moment later her feet were slamming on the cobbles. 'Be quick as I can,' they heard her shout.

That left them free to start the job of lifting segments of wall and roof away from the place they believed Jess lay buried.

Betony prayed the Anderson was doing the job it was

designed for – sheltering the life inside. Poor little Jess. She'd been so kind, rewriting that piece on hemlines. Sybil had loved it. Betony had glowed... and taken full credit.

Which meant, she owed Jess.

37

JESS

She could smell smoke. The darkness was complete, and every breath tasted of soil. At least the chickens were alive, the black Dorking still cradled under her arm. Soft rustling suggested the chickens were more at ease in this cocoon than she was, except when one of them gave a wary croon as if they, too, were testing whether they were still alive.

'Spirits up, girls.' Though with the passing of time, escape felt ever less probable. Someone had to realise she was here first. If Grace and Betony had come back to Hill Street and found disaster, they might think she'd either died outright – or taken shelter somewhere else, like the Tube. What if they never came home at all, and she lay here while the fire burned itself out and a hoarding was put around No. 34 to deter looters?

'Please don't let me die.' It felt an unreasonable thing to ask, because bombs didn't discriminate. It might be her this time. Her name on the list. Why not?

Jess murmured, 'I'm sorry, Charlotte. I won't ever find you, unless there's a heaven and I'm sure there is. I swallowed their lies. I should have made a fuss and demanded answers when they made up stories. Father, Miss Hillingdon. Now you'll never know I did my best to find you.'

She began to hum, threading words into a tune. An old rhyme about a black hen...

'... *she lays eggs for gentlemen. Sometimes nine and sometimes ten, something-something, my black hen.*'

A memory was knocking against the inner skin of her mind. The way Charlotte used to tap the bucket of kitchen scraps and sing that as they walked to the hen coop in the mornings. 'Chick-chick, come and get it.'

They'd had such fun, making up names for their girls though Charlotte was always the inventive one. The lovely white Sussex she'd christened Mary Shelley... Jess let out a shaky breath. 'You were the clever one.'

The rhyme that had been tugging at her resurfaced and this time Jess sang—

'She lays eggs for gentlemen.

Sometimes nine, sometimes ten—

Tiggy-Tiggy-Touchwood, my black hen.'

Touchwood.

Miss Touchwood, our quizzical eye on the world of fashion.

'Charlotte,' Jess whispered. 'I see you. I've finally found you.'

Please don't let her die here. Not now. Jess began to thump the shelter's roof. 'I'm down here. Grace – Mrs Kesgrave – Betony, down here.'

38

GRACE

By the time she'd led Sir Gideon Ventnor to Waverton Mews, the cobbles were running like a shallow stream. Despite the constant spewing of hoses, fire still burned like a forge two doors up but steam from next door's shattered roof suggested that building was on its way to being doused.

She'd known as she ran to Upper Brook Street that Sir Gideon would be sheltering in his cellar with his wife, the butler and the cook. She could knock till Judgement Day, and they wouldn't hear her. But she also knew that four days earlier, her brother Cormac had forced his way in to steal valuables from Ventnor House. The front door had been repaired, two locks now instead of one, but Grace knew her brother.

No housebreaker worth the name would leave himself only one way out of a house he was doing over. One of the windows overlooking the street had a sliver of wood driven into the frame, leaving space enough to push the fingers in and lift.

She had roused Sir Gideon, and he had sprung to action, already in uniform from an evening drilling his platoon. He made three telephone calls. The first to the duty officer at Hyde Park police station, the second to the fire brigade's divisional office. The third to a local greengrocer, one of his Home Guard men.

'Gather the lads, Horace, quick as you like. Waverton Mews.'

What it is to have influence, Grace had thought as he rammed on a tin hat and accompanied her out of his house.

Grace had left him talking to the senior fire officer and now, with no way of getting back over the wall, she waited. For twenty minutes, until a band of Home Guard men in steel helmets, service dress pulled on haphazardly, came and beat down Mrs Kesgrave's backyard wall with sledgehammers. They made a gap wide enough to pass through. Red Cross volunteers arrived, carrying steel-framed stretchers. Grace had seen those before, most recently as she waited for Mam and Ricky to be dug out of the rubble at Peabody.

She tried to shut out the memory.

'Help us find Jess, please God, she's never done a wrong thing in her life.'

Heavy Rescue volunteers shouldered in with ropes, picks, shoring timbers, jacks and crowbars. They must have come from another emergency as their faces were sooty. Grace, edging through the gap in the wall, watched them survey the fallen masonry, conferring among themselves.

'Right-o.' Sir Gideon's voice carried over the throb of a diesel generator powering an arc light. 'We're not many in number, so it's all hands to the pump. We'll form a chain. Rubble can be laid along the mews, against the walls. The heavy stuff can be piled up to the right.' He pointed. 'I've been given charge and I answer to the duty fire officer, who has told me he'd rather not have to fill in any accident reports at the end of the night. Watch your fingers. Nobody move anything large until our Rescue colleagues give the word. Go to it.'

Grace expected to be told to stand back. They'd surely tell

Betony in her silk-jersey dress and ruined velvet jacket to buzz off.

Oddly, they didn't. Perhaps it really was all hands to the pump.

Rafe was staying close to the house where bricks and broken guttering formed the densest heap. He'd rolled his sleeves, and his hands were caked with dirt. Winter stood next to him, then Grace, then Betony. Grace saw Betony glance at her fingernails and give a slight moan.

Oh well, let her have her vanity. She was doing all right, on this occasion.

'We lift, we pass, we don't throw.' Sir Gideon's voice remained crisp. 'Call "hold" if anything moves.'

First went the loose slates and splinters of lath, then the bricks of the chimney stack and the shattered pots. They worked in rhythm. Reach for the next chunk, take the weight, pass it on. Every time Grace heard masonry landing in the mews, she thought, *That's an inch closer to Jess.*

She had cut her hand and grazed her arms, she didn't remember when. She'd scrunched her hair into a bun and used one of her stockings to secure it. Betony's red Paris gown was hitched above the knee. Her gold sandals were orange with brick dust. They worked as steadily as any man on the line, giving nobody the excuse to say, 'Get those girls out of here.'

Only once did they pause, when Betony took a chunk of concrete from Grace and noticed the brand-new ring on Grace's left hand. Fourth finger. The concrete crashed to the ground.

'You and Owen?' Betony said in a voice stripped of feeling.

'Yes. His idea. He wants to feel he's got someone waiting on the ground. Says it gives him something to stay alive for.'

'Well then. That's good.'

Grace felt Betony physically pulling in her emotions and said, 'You and Winter, you've patched things up? It suits him, the new garb.' Winter had come out to meet Betony dressed not in his customary dinner jacket and black tie, but in Air Force blue. CANADA at the shoulders, wings stitched over the pocket. 'You wanted a man in a uniform,' she teased, 'and now you've got one.'

'So I have, and it took me until tonight to realise he was the man who kissed me in the blackout at the Café de Paris as if the world were a minute from ending. At the time, I thought it was someone else…' Betony wiped her forehead. 'Come on, stop slacking.'

Winter matched Rafe lift for lift while Sir Gideon strode about, keeping the chain tight.

'Hold!' Rafe's hand went up. Everyone went still. 'Thought I heard something.' He pointed to a gap in the rubble. 'I thought I heard a faint knock and look, there's grass.'

The shelter roof had been piled with soil and turf.

A volunteer slid a shoring pole into place, tapping it home to stop the debris shifting.

'Carry on,' ordered Sir Gideon. 'I think we're close.'

They worked their way down. At a signal from Heavy Rescue, Rafe got onto his knees, pushed his arm down into the void and tapped on a patch of exposed steel roof. They all waited, silently praying for the answering knock.

None came.

'Jess, darling? Knock if you can hear me.'

Again, they waited.

'Jess, love, can you hear me? I came back.' After a minute, he got up, looking utterly wrung out. 'Nothing.'

One of the Heavy Rescuers took his place, knocking with the end of a spanner. 'Miss, miss?'

'It's Jess,' Grace told the man. 'Her name is Jess Gresham.'

'Are you down there, Miss Gresham?'

For long seconds, still nothing. And then they heard as if from the depths of the earth:

'I'm here. Tell Mrs Kesgrave, I've got the chickens.'

39

A comment between nurses told Jess that she had been sedated, and that she was in a women's side ward but would soon be moved to the main one.

She didn't need to be in hospital; she needed to be out, searching for Charlotte on Fleet Street. Searching for Miss Touchwood.

Only, they wouldn't let her go yet, and her head was aching badly.

She remembered virtually nothing of the moment she'd been brought out of the twisted Anderson shelter. They'd cut through the metal with blades, lifting it away piece by piece. It had felt like hatching from an egg. She did remember begging them to be careful of the hens. And then, coming up on a stretcher, the strangest thing.

She'd seen Rafe, staring down at her, his face streaked with dirt. He was in uniform, gold stripes, and had looked so stricken, she'd tried to reach for him, but her hands had been under a blanket. And she'd heard Grace's voice.

And Betony's. Or had she dreamed it all?

A nurse helped her sit up and drink a cup of tea. Jess asked which hospital it was.

St George's, she was told, on Hyde Park Corner.

'What day is it?'

'Tuesday, dear. The twenty-fourth of September.'

'What?' Her clearest memory was of taking a book down to the shelter on Friday night. She'd lost four days! 'I should be at work,' she said anxiously.

The nurse laughed at her. 'Enjoy a rest, I should. Work can wait.'

Hovering still between dream and waking, Jess asked, 'Did you see a naval officer when I was brought from Hill Street... did he come with me?'

She'd been brought in by ambulance, the nurse said. 'Red Cross staff came with you, that's all I know.'

'Have I had any visitors?'

She had, three ladies while she'd been asleep, and they'd been advised to come back later.

Of course Rafe hadn't come. He wasn't even in London. She'd dreamed him up, a mirage to meet a need. Thanking the nurse, she turned her head into her pillow and let a tear fall unseen.

The following morning, Jess was discharged. Mrs Kesgrave was waiting in reception, a taxi outside. Jess stumbled into her arms, unable this time to control her emotions.

'I thought I was going to die – oh, are the girls all right?'

'Hens or housemates? All are in good health, dear one. And you?'

'Bump on the head and my ribs hurt, but I think that's old bruises brought back to life. I can't wait to get back to Hill Street.'

Mrs Kesgrave turned Jess to face her. 'My dear, we can't go back. The street is still cordoned off; the house that was hit is still smoking. Our windows are broken and there's water damage. Who knows what else. I might never be able to go back at all.'

Never go back? It hit like an iron punch. Homeless, again? Split up from Grace, Betony and Mrs Kesgrave, the only people in London she knew? *Oh, please, please don't let it be the streets again or bunking down in the Tube.*

Mrs Kesgrave was telling her that right now, they were all staying above the pub on the corner of Farm Street. 'Only temporary, till we all go our separate ways, I suppose.'

The remembered rhyme dropped into Jess's head and she began to recite it. '*Tiggy-Tiggy-Touchwood, my black hen. She lays eggs for gentlemen. Sometimes nine, sometimes ten, Tiggy-Tiggy-Touchwood—*'

'*My black hen,*' Mrs Kesgrave finished for her. 'Are you all right, Jess?'

'I think so. While I was trapped, I realised I know where to find Charlotte.'

'Charlotte... oh, your sister. The one who didn't like cooking, so did the household accounts after your mother died.'

'You remembered. Yes, and she's been missing almost a year.'

'Dear one, you never said.'

There was a lot Jess hadn't said. 'And I want to, because I know what you all did for me. You got me out and saved me.'

'Not I,' said Mrs Kesgrave as she ushered Jess into the waiting taxi. 'Shepherd and Flock, Farm Street,' she told the driver. 'I only arrived back the morning after. It was Grace, Betony and Betony's delicious Canadian you have to thank.'

'Three heroes, then.' And one hallucination.

'Four heroes,' Mrs Kesgrave corrected. 'We mustn't forget the other one, the naval officer who called to see you a week or so back, when you were held up at work. Rafe, isn't it?'

Jess went still. How on earth could he have been there?

He'd been on his way to East Sussex. 'I was sure I'd heard his voice, but I told myself I was imagining it. Is it true?'

'Well, I don't believe Betony or Grace would invent something like that. And actually, I can shed some light.' As the taxi crawled around barriers and diversions, Mrs Kesgrave she told Jess how she'd caught the Brighton train from Victoria on the Friday evening, for her appointment at the Sea View Hotel.

'At Lewes, we were ordered off. Troop trains needing priority, apparently. I disembarked, and there was your Rafe, on a bench with a bag at his feet. He'd been waiting hours for a connection which kept being cancelled. We chatted and when I mentioned you were at home, alone, he became agitated. When it came over the Tannoy that a London-bound train was being let through, he was off. Last I saw, he was pounding over the footbridge to the other platform. And thank heavens, as I believe he was the only one who knew the back way into my yard.'

'Because he chased a fox.' Jess wanted to laugh, cry. Above all, to see him. 'He'll be in such trouble. He was supposed to be reporting to some naval intelligence unit.'

'Don't worry,' Mrs Kesgrave said. Someone as resourceful as Rafe would be bound to think up a plausible cover story. 'And remember, it was his choice to come back, Jess.'

His choice to return, but yet again, not to stay. 'He didn't come to see me in hospital. He didn't call or send a note.'

'No.' Mrs Kesgrave agreed it was a little odd. 'Grace said that after you'd left in the ambulance, she tried to find him to thank him, only he'd sort of melted away.'

It was what he did, Jess reflected. Vanished. In hospital, foggy with the sleeping draughts they'd given her, she'd started to wonder if Rafe Taverner wasn't another of her ghosts. Wanting to touch normality, Jess asked after the chickens.

'Quiet yet resolute, in a makeshift coop behind the Shepherd and Flock. I'm so thankful you took them in with you, otherwise—' Mrs Kesgrave pressed a crumpled hanky to her eyes and it was Jess doing the comforting for the remainder of the journey.

Mrs Kesgrave asked the cab to let them out on Hill Street. Someone had made a gap in the barricade, and as it was unmanned, they went to look at the house. At the devastation.

They found Betony standing just outside the roped-off area. The front door had DANGEROUS. KEEP OUT chalked on the paintwork.

After Betony hugged Jess and asked how she was, she admitted she'd been hoping to get in and collect her things. Her clothes, mostly. 'Thieves will love them and one or two aren't even mine. They belong to the magazine.'

'What can we do?' Jess thought of her books and of Charlotte's typewriter. The idea of it being stolen, or left to rust, was unbearable. She'd dragged it all the way to London. It was her beacon of hope, that one day soon she'd unveil it in front of Charlotte and say, 'Ta-dah!'

'We'll go in, soon as the ARP chappies give the go-ahead,' said Mrs Kesgrave. 'We'll have to don tin hats, but it's vital we salvage our valuables. Anything that isn't smoke damaged.'

Jess saw then that the window – *their* bedroom window – was shattered, blackened fragments still attaching to the frame.

Mrs Kesgrave continued, 'Sir Gideon – my new favourite Mayfair neighbour – has offered us a van and a driver. We can load up as much as it will carry.'

'Where will we take it?' Jess doubted the pub would want their boxes. And from the sound of it, it was a very temporary billet. Jess hadn't missed Mrs Kesgrave's comment, that they'd 'go their separate ways'. It chilled her.

Betony informed her that Sybil March, her boss at *Practical*

Modes, had offered cellar space. She peered more closely at Jess. 'You look awfully sad.'

She was fine, Jess assured her. Grateful to be alive. 'I shall never complain about anything again.'

'You had a close shave,' Mrs Kesgrave remarked. 'Apparently, had the chimney stack not broken into pieces before it fell – well, let's not dwell on that. Clearly, you are blessed among mortals.'

But what about No. 34? Could it ever be repaired?

'The Grosvenor Estate will have to decide,' said Mrs Kesgrave.

'Not in a hurry,' was Betony's view. 'Building materials are only for public use these days, even if you can find workmen. Assuming the place isn't condemned altogether.'

'I shan't despair,' Mrs Kesgrave declared. 'I will create visions of myself, walking back in and touching all my precious things as I go.'

On Farm Street, Jess was taken through the main bar of the Shepherd and Flock – the 'Bo Peep' as it was known to locals – and up narrow stairs. It dawned on her then that she had only the clothes she was wearing. Everything was off limits behind a rope barricade and a KEEP OUT sign.

She reported for work the following day in a dress and jumper from *Practical Modes*. When Miss Cartwright came up and asked rather sharply where she'd been, Jess said simply, 'I got bombed.'

'I didn't realise Westminster was hit,' Miss Cartwright replied, and Jess realised they still had her listed at the Girls' Friendly Society hostel. She had broken a rule: 'All alterations in personal circumstances to be communicated without delay.'

At morning break, she followed Miss Cartwright to her

office, explaining that she was now lodged above a public house, 'While my current address is repaired.'

'Please keep us informed of all changes, Miss Gresham.'

'I will.' Her eye fell on a GPO bag. Goodness, that was her name on the tag. 'What is this, please?'

'Your work for this week,' Miss Cartwright said. 'Waiting for you like Greyfriars Bobby.'

'Sorry, like who?'

The faithful terrier who'd kept vigil at his master's grave, she was told. 'In his case, for fourteen years.'

Jess took the bag, promising to storm through it. She wasn't going to volunteer for overtime today. Come six thirty, she'd be on her way to Fleet Street. For a reunion, she hoped.

Or if not, for a confrontation.

Last night, in the pub lounge over fish and fried potatoes, she'd told Mrs Kesgrave, Grace and Betony about Charlotte.

Not everything. Not about Stoney Street or Alder Grove. She hadn't mentioned Cormac either and neither had Grace. Jess had kept things simple, describing a rift with their father, how Charlotte had run away to London to pursue her dream to write. She'd gulped a breath, and said, 'I think she's Miss Touchwood.'

Betony had instantly poured cold water on that. 'Are you suggesting that your sister is a columnist for a national supplement and nobody's told you? It's Jean Treadgold's baby. Everyone knows. Honestly, I've met the woman. She talks like the column, and anyway, did your sister know anything about fashion?'

'You mean, because I don't?' Charlotte had certainly loved good clothes and aspired to them. They'd just never had the money to indulge. 'She wore Shalimar perfume,' Jess had informed Betony. 'And – if you were correct – a Lelong coat too.'

Betony didn't look entirely convinced, but something in her

expression shifted. Could Charlotte really be the acerbic Miss Touchwood, writing about clothes with such deft confidence? Tweed, cashmere, the relative merits of silk or satin to line an evening coat?

Yes, Jess told herself now as she emptied the postbag onto her desk. Miss Touchwood's columns boiled down to sharp comment, humour and opinion. 'And,' she repeated last night's clinching argument, 'we had a hen once that we called Tiggy. Tiggy-Tiggy-Touchwood. A black Dorking.'

At that point, even Mrs Kesgrave had looked doubtful. Betony and Grace had exchanged glances. *She's knocked her head, poor girl.*

In the basement of Section C, it was easy for Jess to fear that she was deluding herself. Tiggy Touchwood was a chicken who laid small, brown eggs. Miss Treadgold wrote the column and Charlotte was as lost as ever. Even so. It wouldn't stop her visiting Fleet Street and the offices of the *London Mercury*.

With over a hundred letters to and from Ramsgate to sort through, she forced herself to concentrate on her job. Around midday, she took out a letter with a London W1 postmark. The name on the front made her rock in her seat.

The Reverend Gresham
St Saviour's Vicarage
Ramsgate

She picked up her letter opener but instead of slicing through as she normally would, she angled the blade. With the subtlest flicks of the knife, she released the gummed flap. Checking no one was watching and using a pencil, she eased out the contents.

The hairs rose on the back of her neck, as if the edge of a razor had touched her.

40

London, Monday, 23 September 1940

Dear Reverend Gresham,

Allow me to introduce myself. I am a friend of Charlotte's.

I finally tracked down your address at the library. First time in years I've been inside one of those, but I liked it. The silence is refreshing. It was your daughter Jess who told me her sister Charlotte had an ambition to sit in the London Library and write. I paid a visit to ask if she was a member.

They wouldn't tell me at first. It was a patient business, following a librarian home and engaging him in conversation in an alley. He gave me the address Charlotte gave them. Yours.

Why am I writing to you? Firstly, I'd like to find her but I don't suppose you know any more than Jess does. Seems we all have the same goal, to track down the prodigal, though with different intentions.

I know why you put Charlotte away, locked her up. A short while back, I learned about a house in Southwark where a Mrs Munday practises. Someone I know well gave me the name, and how to find it. I went and after a little persuasion, the woman there was clear enough. Your elder girl went to rid herself of an infant.

But you know this and I reckon that's your business, so now to mine.

I found Charlotte last New Year crouched in a doorway near where I live, almost frozen. I took her home, fed her, clothed her at my own expense for months. I trusted her but she left without a word. Ever since, she's hidden herself but Jess is circling. I have every faith she will find Charlotte and lead me to her.

When I have Charlotte in my grip, you can have her. Once I've evened the score. To learn she destroyed an unborn child, even another man's child, tells me what a worthless harlot she is. Meantime, the cost of supporting her has to be addressed. Make me a suitable offer, and this matter will remain between us. Otherwise – VICAR'S DAUGHTER DISPOSES OF BASTARD CHILD in the *Ramsgate Gazette* is not something you would want your parishioners to read over their teacups.

Write to me at the Ring and Rabbit, Smith's Court. I am certain we shall come to an understanding.

With all respect,

'Cormac Whelan,' Jess breathed. Turning the letter face down, she ran to the toilet, where she bolted herself in while her pulse steadied. It was brazen blackmail; it ought to be reported. She should do so at once. In signing the Official Secrets Act she'd sworn to place her country before personal loyalties. But the nation's safety wasn't at stake. Charlotte's was.

It sickened her to the core that she'd pointed Cormac towards the London Library. She'd stuttered it out with a razor to her throat, certain he'd never follow up. Naively convinced that, if he did, the library staff would keep confidentiality.

Who would do that, in an alley, with the same blade glinting?

And the other betrayal that led Cormac to Mrs Munday's? Someone had given him the name. The directions. Someone he knew well, the letter had said.

Grace, of course. She'd read the note in the bedroom at Hill Street. After that show of sympathy and kindness, she had sold Charlotte to her brother.

Betrayed Jess, then helped save her life. How to make sense of that? *I thought she cared about me. I liked her so much.*

Letting herself out of the toilet, Jess went to the sink. By the time she had washed her hands, she'd made a choice.

Back at her section, Jess shifted the GPO postbag to shield her actions. Turning Cormac's letter over, she uncapped her black pen and added a postscript in a hand that mimicked his.

> *Why don't we meet, Reverend Sir? Let's say this Saturday at 9 p.m., somewhere we can be sure nobody will interrupt us.*

Where?

Miss Cartwright was beginning her slow walk-around the lines of desks. Where would be guaranteed private?

Of course.

> *Meet me at 34 Hill Street, Mayfair.*

Would Father come? Jess thought so. A man who had tried to bury a daughter in an asylum to guard his name would act now to silence a scandal.

She must think of a way of luring Cormac to the meeting.

She resealed the letter so that only the sharpest eye would

suspect it had been opened. Into the out-tray, no censor's stamp. If anyone in Section C had been watching, God help her.

As evening fell, they were told they could leave unless volunteering for extra hours. Jess packed up her desk, keeping her eyes down. The moment had arrived: the final yes-or-no, waiting for her on Fleet Street. She checked her satchel for the copy of the Thursday Supplement borrowed this morning off Betony. Still there, folded into quarters.

Outside it was raining, and a chill wind cut through the thin mackintosh from the cupboard at *Practical Modes*. Her red coat was a prisoner again. In a wardrobe in a bedroom too hazardous to enter.

She took the Tube, getting out at Charing Cross and walked, head down against the wet, to the *London Mercury*'s offices.

She stalled. What on earth...

On the pavement stood two people who had no business to be there. Unless it was to tell her she was mad. It was Mrs Kesgrave and Betony, both wearing black coats and hats, looking as if they'd been waiting in the rain for some time.

'You can't stop me,' Jess said, pushing past them through the revolving doors. She felt them fall in behind her. As they drew level, one on each side of her, she felt ridiculously small, a pawn flanked by two queens from opposing boards. 'What are you doing?' she hissed.

'Guarding you,' said Mrs Kesgrave quietly.

'Guarding Miss Treadgold, you mean.' Jess turned on Betony. 'She's your friend.'

'She absolutely is not,' Betony said hotly. 'We can't stand her at *Practical Modes*. I heard today that she jumped the queue at the paper warehouse and took the stock set aside for us. She's not someone you confront alone, Jess. Not unless you've claws of your own, or a powerful family behind you.'

Jess's throat tightened. 'You think I'm living in cloud cuckoo land.'

'No,' said Mrs Kesgrave, her voice low. 'We think you're brave. That's why we came. Shall we confront the tigress? You believe she employs your sister and refused to help when you came before, so let's find out.'

'All right.' Privately, Jess was glad to have these two beside her. She just wasn't ready to say it.

The young clerk she'd met before was behind the desk, same telephone jammed to his ear. Seeing her, he raised an eyebrow, implying, *You again?*

'I wish to see Miss Treadgold.'

He shook his head, turning away to speak into the telephone receiver. 'Sorry. Someone wandered in off the street. You were saying?'

'I must talk to her,' Jess said, raising her voice. 'I will talk to her.'

The young man covered the mouthpiece. 'Not a chance. She's in a meeting with the editor-in-chief and board members. Nobody's allowed in.'

He went back to his phone conversation.

'Let me.' Betony advanced to the desk, cleared her throat and when that got no response, rapped with a knuckle.

'For pity's sake.' The young man cut the call, saying in a wrung-out voice, 'You're not going up there. It's more than my life's worth.'

'Do you know who I am?' asked Betony.

He gaped slightly. 'Er, no.'

A business card was placed in front of him. 'The Honourable Betony Styles, fashion writer.'

'Oh. Sorry, ma'am. Miss.' He blushed. 'Only—'

'And this is Mrs Gloria Kesgrave, senior fashion editor of the *Washington Post.*'

'In London for two days,' said Mrs Kesgrave in a creditable American accent. 'And an old, old friend of dear Delia.'

'Who?' asked the young man.

'Miss Treadgold.'

'Her name's Jean.'

Mrs Kesgrave threw out a laugh. 'Not if you were at school with her, dear one. Which floor?'

The young man muttered, 'Fourth, door marked "board members only". Just don't say it was me.'

Mrs Kesgrave took it on herself to knock. She didn't wait for an answer.

Jess shuffled into the boardroom behind her, Betony at the rear. A table large enough for twenty held three men in pinstripe suits and two women, one of whom was Miss Treadgold.

The man at the table's head, in a starched stock collar, old-fashioned jacket and narrow tie, asked who the devil they were.

Jess opened her mouth. As so often in situations like this, nothing came out. Five pairs of eyes dismantled her. What they'd see was a face made tense and thin by her recent ordeal, straight hair flattened by rain, an old school satchel and gabardine.

'Which one's the tigress?' Mrs Kesgrave asked out of the side of her mouth.

'Velvet hat,' Betony whispered back.

The figure at the head of the table had a name plate on a stand. EDITOR-IN-CHIEF. This would be Oswald H. Young, whom Charlotte had so hopefully written to. Vain hope, Jess thought.

He repeated his question. Who the devil were they?

'The rather more important question,' Mrs Kesgrave said, 'is, where is Miss Touchwood?'

'Right there.' The editor pointed to Miss Treadgold. 'What's your business?'

Without a word, Miss Treadgold went to side table and dialled three numbers on a telephone. 'Security to the board-room, please.'

Jess felt a spongy, sick feeling. All she wanted was to be told that Charlotte wrote for this newspaper, and to be given an address. Then she'd go quietly. She didn't want trouble. She certainly hadn't envisaged being frogmarched onto the street. 'Please, just hear me out,' she cried, in a voice already stamped with defeat. 'I know you met my sister, Miss Treadgold. Charlotte Gresham. She brought work for you to look at, but you said it wasn't your kind of thing.'

'Oh.' Miss Treadgold looked at Jess more fully. 'I remember. Charlotte, yes. Red coat. Shalimar.'

'I don't think you told me the whole truth. I think you employed her, but for reasons of your own, didn't tell me. I just need to find her. Please, please say where she lives and I'll never bother you again.'

'Unfortunately,' Miss Treadgold said crisply, 'I have never employed your sister and have no idea where she might be.'

'*Tiggy-Tiggy-Touchwood*,' Jess shouted, desperate now. '*My black hen. She lays eggs—*'

'That's enough, Jess, dear.' Mrs Kesgrave put a hand on her arm and squeezed. 'Let me.'

'No, let me.' Walking to the table, Betony rested her gloved fingers on its edge. 'Our business here is simple. To put an end to deception.' Betony's voice rang with confidence, every word perfectly placed. 'It is one thing to write behind a pseudonym. Everyone does that. What is unacceptable is when that pseudonym belongs to another.'

Miss Treadgold regarded Betony stonily. She seemed to

have forgotten Jess was there. 'I don't know what you think you know, young woman,' she said icily.

'I am Miss Styles,' Betony came back. 'Writer at *Practical Modes*.'

'*Practical...*? Oh, that.' Miss Treadgold's sneer was a masterpiece. 'Sybil March's rag. If you're here trawling for inspiration, have some free advice. Go bankrupt and save yourselves embarrassment.'

'Actually, our circulation is climbing.' The way Betony's fingers tightened suggested Miss Treadgold's claws had drawn their first blood. 'But that's not the point.'

'Have they finished?' the other woman at the table snapped. 'Only I have a train to catch. Oswald,' she addressed the editor-in-chief, 'see them out.'

Oswald H. Young OBE came towards them in a way that was courteous yet subtly threatening.

'Thank you, ladies,' he said. 'If you're done, I'll see you to the lift.'

Jess knew she had seconds before this venture turned into a humiliating scramble. She cast around for courage... and her eye went to the empty end of the board table where two volumes of the *Shorter Oxford English Dictionary* had been placed. She padded over and picked up *A to M*.

It came down on the table harder than she intended, with a hefty smack.

Now they could see her.

'My name is Jess Gresham and my sister, Charlotte, came here last year wanting a job. You turned her away, Miss Treadgold.'

Miss Treadgold shrugged. 'Perhaps I did. She wouldn't be the first. They all troop in, desperate to write. Few have any talent.'

'But you remember Charlotte, not only because of a coat with cherry buttons, French perfume and talent to burn. You let her show you her work. You were impressed. It wasn't country ramblings, or character studies, as you told me. That wasn't Charlotte's style. It was clever, satirical social comment. Politics. Maybe a bit of fashion. Enough to whet your interest.'

Miss Treadgold's lips tightened. 'Be careful, child,' she said quietly.

'No, that's the point,' Jess replied earnestly. 'I'm always careful and I wouldn't dare say this if I wasn't two hundred per cent sure. Let me hear you swear that you, and only you, are Miss Touchwood.'

'I am Miss Touchwood. It's known the length of Fleet Street. Oswald, tell her.'

The editor-in-chief dipped his head. 'It's her. She writes it. Fiendishly clever too. Worth its weight in gold ink.'

'Clever, yes. But this is the thing. Every Thursday, Miss Treadgold, you publish my sister's writing under your name. How do I know?' Jess took Betony's copy of the supplement from her satchel and opened it at the Touchwood column. 'Let me read a few lines: '"A working girl's budget needn't condemn her to *drabbity* dressing. One well-cut frock in a flattering shade will carry her from munitions bench or typewriter to a table for two."'

She looked straight at Miss Treadgold. '"Drabbity".'

'What?' said the woman at the table. 'Tell her to speak up. What's she saying?'

'"Drabbity",' Jess repeated. 'I suppose it means dull. Plain.'

'Exactly,' said Miss Treadgold. 'If you've finished—'

'It was the name of a pet rabbit we had, years ago. He was browny-grey and never did much, just ate. Charlotte made up the name. When I first read it in the column, I thought – how extraordinary. Perhaps it's a real word after all. But of course, it isn't. It's Charlotte's mind at work, her sense of fun. She knew, as I never did until now, that to survive, one must know how to play.'

'Oswald' – Miss Treadgold proffered the telephone receiver – 'call the lawyers.'

Oswald H. Young hesitated.

'Call them,' Jess invited. 'I want it on record. My sister's skill, her talent, is what makes Miss Touchwood and it's not yours to steal. I want that in writing. More than that, I want my sister's address.' She flattened her palm flat on the table with its boardroom sheen and held Miss Treadgold's eyes. 'I will find her. Touch wood.'

As they crossed the reception, Jess paused, meaning to thank the desk clerk. Reluctant or not, he'd put his job on the line for them.

He was back on the telephone, jotting a message one-handed, eyes fixed elsewhere. Numbers, hurried scrawl, a broad pencil. He tore the top sheet free, but the flimsy under-copy came loose and fluttered towards Jess. She caught it automatically.

The colour of the writing stopped her. An odd grey-purple... she'd seen it before.

It was carbon ink, she realised. The pad held a top sheet, a slip of carbon and the duplicate beneath. They were numbered. At the top corner of this was printed: No. 6.

The directions to Stoney Street had been written on an identical scrap. Written here.

By Miss Treadgold? By a secretary? Or by this young man?

Jess's stomach twisted. She didn't want to know.

'Sorry, did you...?' he began, reaching out to take the paper. Jess turned her back and walked out.

41

Mrs Kesgrave had written down the address for Charlotte that Miss Treadgold had muttered in a furious undertone.

Shepherd Market, Mayfair.

When Jess gaped in disbelief, Mrs Kesgrave explained that it was not *their* Mayfair, but a small enclave tucked behind Piccadilly.

'Cheap rents,' she said, adding with forced brightness, 'beloved of artists and writers.'

'And professional ladies,' Betony put in, then checked herself. 'Not that I'm suggesting your sister—'

They took the Underground to Piccadilly and lost their way almost immediately in a confusion of narrow streets and passages. A policeman eventually set them straight.

White Horse Street, he told them. Far end. If they could smell the beer from the King's Arms, they'd gone too far. They were to keep to the left and look for Market Court.

They overshot it and had to retrace their steps, nearly back to Piccadilly. Betony remarked grimly that they seemed to be searching for that most dispiriting of needles: the one in the haystack.

This time they examined every gap between buildings, looking for the entrance to Market Court.

'There,' Jess breathed, lifting her torch to a nameplate screwed crookedly to a wall.

The alley was too narrow for a vehicle – indeed, for anything wider than a barrow or a bike – and darker even than the street behind them. They walked in single file, their footsteps dull on uneven cobbles, their breath loud in their ears. The air reeked of coal smoke and rubbish left too long.

Jess stopped before a building that must once have been a factory or a foundry. Bars on the lower windows and exterior bolts securing the front door were as good as a Keep Out sign. *No.3* was daubed on the bricks in white paint. 'It can't be this place,' she muttered.

Mrs Kesgrave shone her torch on her scrap of paper and said, 'I'm afraid it is. Still, outside is no indicator of inside.' She reached up and clanged the bell.

A woman of indeterminate age came, gripping a darned cardigan against a sunken chest. 'Yes?'

'We're looking for Charlotte Gresham.' Mrs Kesgrave's tone combined warmth and authority. 'May we come in?'

The woman stepped back, invitation enough.

Once the door was shut and the blackouts drawn, the light flickered on. 'Outside' was every bit a predictor of inside, it turned out. Damp wallpaper, lino worn to the boards. The hallway reeked of town gas. Or tomcat. Hard to say. Something Jess didn't wish to identify skittered for cover beneath the skirting. The woman who had let them in folded her arms tightly. 'Are you family?'

'Charlotte's? Yes,' said Jess breathlessly. 'Is she—'

'I haven't seen her for a few days. The landlady says she's been slow paying her rent so maybe she's scarpered.'

'Which room?' Betony asked.

'Right at the top. You can go up, but don't make a noise or

you'll have the old biddies in Room 5 bawling at you. They can hear a mouse piddling in a corner of the coalhouse. Good luck.'

'How many rooms are there?' Jess wondered as they climbed the stairs.

'As many as can be crammed in, I should think,' Mrs Kesgrave muttered. 'Brr. It's colder inside than out. If your poor sister can't even pay her rent here...' She left the rest unsaid.

Betony finished for her. 'Then that Treadgold woman is downright exploiting her. I'll report her.'

'Let's find Charlotte first.' Jess wasn't sure what she would do if Charlotte had slipped away again. If she'd missed her by days or merely hours...

The stairs creaked violently and on the first-floor landing, a door flew open.

'No noise after eight o'clock! You know the rules. I'll have you thrown out— Oh.' Seeing more than one culprit, the angry figure on the threshold faltered.

'Are we going right for Miss Gresham?'

The woman pointed upward. 'Keep going.' Jess measured her in a glance. Aged, and more defeated than spiteful.

The next set of stairs led up to a short landing with a single door at the end. Jess tapped.

'Charlotte? It's me. Jess. Charlotte?' She tapped again. There was no answer. The knob turned, but the door was locked. 'There must be a key.'

'Undoubtedly, as there's a keyhole,' Mrs Kesgrave said. 'What if the key's in the other side?'

'We won't know till we try. We'll have to find the landlady.'

Mrs Kesgrave glanced behind her to the narrow staircase they'd just laboured up. She was a little out of breath.

Betony volunteered. 'Stair climbing is wonderful for maintaining the stomach girdle.'

'You should write about that,' said Mrs Kesgrave.

Betony began the trudge down. Jess tapped again at the

door, calling Charlotte's name through the keyhole. But she feared the worst. 'The room's empty. I can't hear a thing.'

Fifteen minutes dragged by before Betony reappeared with a key. 'I can report that the lady in charge of this establishment is all kindness, her concern for Charlotte's welfare quite touching.' The words dripped acid. 'If your sister has gone and we clear her stuff out tonight, she won't be charged another week's rent. I even had to pay for this.' She passed the key to Jess.

'I'll refund you.'

'Don't think you can, darling. The price was my stockings.'

In the dull gleam of an unshaded bulb, the sight of Betony's bare legs made Jess feel humble.

The key fitted.

No light came on in the room when she flicked the switch.

'Did I mention,' said Betony, 'the landlady turned off the supply when Charlotte missed her rent last Friday?' She switched on her torch and Jess did the same, revealing a sloping ceiling and a tiny window. On a wall peg hung a poor-looking coat – the sort Frankie O'Halloran had sneered at as 'the kind they give away at the door of a flop house.' Jess frowned. The coat fitted the room, not her image of Charlotte.

But the scarf beside it – a twist of vivid silk – was unmistakeably her. 'A scarf in a cheery shade. Crimson if you dare...' So said Miss Touchwood.

Just as telling were the sheets of paper spread over the floor, a scattering of pencils, a sharpener and an eraser. Jess shone her torch at a scuffed little writing desk, then at an iron frame bed. At first, she thought the bedding had been piled on top, a sign of abandonment, of flight – until her beam revealed an outline.

She gasped, seeing a hand almost as pale as the bedsheet it lay on. When she crept closer and touched it, it was ice cold.

Mrs Kesgrave stepped up beside her. 'Let me.' She drew down the covers and Jess saw an emaciated girl, dressed in skirt, blouse and jumper, curled in a foetal position. Dark hair cut so short, a patch of scalp was visible above the ear. The eyes were open. Liquorice dark, staring from bruised hollows.

'It's not Charlotte.' This tragic creature was nothing like the girl on the escalator at Charing Cross, in a summer dress and bright cardigan. 'It's not my sister.'

'Yes it is.' That came from Betony, who had picked up one of the pages from the floor. She began to read:

'"After last night's bombardment, London calls on the Fashion Front to shoulder arms. Defiant lipstick, a pocket clothes-brush and an iron determination to out-smile the Luftwaffe, ladies. Nothing unsettles those Messerschmitt boys more than the thought of two elegantly gloved fingers raised in an attitude of victory."' She looked at Jess. 'Miss Touchwood. I'd know the voice anywhere. "Powder your nose, sisters, straighten your seams and let Berlin gnash its teeth."'

A voice hardly audible said, 'Not "sisters", that's not right. Only I can't think... I can't think...'

They clustered at the side of the bed. Jess fell to her knees, stroking a tuft of black hair. 'Charlotte, is it really you?'

42

Thursday, 26 September 1940

'I need to get inside No. 34 to rescue the typewriter.' Jess had just finished reading the latest draft of the Miss Touchwood column, rescued from the floor of Charlotte's room. Having vowed Charlotte would never submit another word to the *London Mercury*, her sister's agitation at missing her deadline had won out.

This was next week's column and must be submitted by Monday, latest.

Jess would dictate it, over the telephone, to one of Miss Treadgold's secretaries. An uncashed cheque from Charlotte's desk for seven shillings and sixpence, drawn on the *London Mercury's* bank, proved that a contract between Jean Treadgold and Charlotte existed. The woman had traded on Charlotte's talent, taken everything and given back a pittance. Of all the people Jess had cause to despise, Miss Treadgold stood at the top of the list.

'Miserable bloodsucker,' was Betony's verdict. 'Ought to be publicly shamed.'

But Charlotte was frantic to keep her job, to keep writing, and Jess would do nothing to distress her sister.

It was evening, and they were above the Shepherd and Flock. In a while, they would go down for their dinner. Jess had put in a normal day's work, though not for a moment detaching from thoughts of Charlotte, who had remined here, sleeping. One cause for relief: nobody had approached Jess that day to accuse her of tampering with the mail. She could be confident that Cormac's letter to her father would have landed on the mat at the vicarage. Waiting for her father to open it.

Or for Miss Hillingdon to get there first.

'Could Charlotte manage to come down for dinner?' Betony asked. 'I want to feed her up.' To Betony, Charlotte Gresham was a heroine. The tenth Muse, a writer so talented, Miss Treadgold had stolen her voice.

Jess didn't think Charlotte was ready either for stairs or to appear in public. Grace agreed, having given Charlotte a thorough check and taken her pulse.

In Grace's opinion, Charlotte wasn't only malnourished and dehydrated, she was severely anaemic. 'Girls often are, if they have heavy monthlies. Or from blood loss. Such as, say, a miscarriage?'

The look that accompanied the comment was loaded and brought back what Jess had momentarily pushed aside – Grace's likely part in passing Cormac the Stoney Street address. She felt a rush of anger. 'I think you know perfectly well what happened.'

Unimpressed by Grace's confusion, Jess went downstairs to call the *London Mercury*, dictating her sister's words over the telephone. Miss Treadgold, who came quickly on the line, appeared not to detect the substitution. Nor did she refer to Jess's visit the previous evening. Just said smoothly at the end, 'Thank you. Sterling effort. Same next week. Goodbye.'

Cold-blooded parasite, Jess thought as she replaced the receiver.

Grace was waiting for her when she left the booth. 'No – don't walk past me. I don't know what you think I've done or said, but this is about Charlotte, not you. She needs to be in hospital. I can make some calls.'

'To your brother? Sell Charlotte again, to the most violent man you know?'

'Jess, what are you talking about? I'd never sell Charlotte or any woman to my brother. You have to be joking. Cormac chills me, if you want the truth.'

'He wrote to my father.' Jess quoted Cormac's letter, though misremembering all but the gist. 'It's blackmail, and I'm sure he means every word. He wants to hurt Charlotte, then send her back home so she can be locked up again.'

Grace didn't argue. 'I'm sure he does want to hurt her.' She touched her eye, healed now. 'He's a monster and that's why I warned Charlotte when I saw her in his bed.'

'You saw her...'

'At his place.' Grace nodded. 'Smith's Court. Edge of Soho. I went to see him and she was there sleeping beside him.'

Jess stared at Grace and could hardly speak. 'And you said nothing?'

'I didn't know what to think. First off, I thought it was you I'd seen. I supposed you were embarrassed and didn't want to talk about it. You can be very buttoned-up, Jess. You make it hard. I said nothing even when I thought you were planning... you know.' Grace glanced at Jess's stomach. 'To get yourself seen to on Stoney Street. I thought it must be Cormac's baby. I should have said something but it wasn't my business.'

'You made it your business, though,' Jess said hoarsely, her voice rippling with anger. 'When you told Cormac, a man you say terrifies you, about Mrs Munday. He went there. He got the truth out of the woman and he's used that to threaten my father.'

'I see.' Grace looked mortified, haggard in a way Jess had never seen before. 'I'm sorry but how did he get your father's address?'

The question was asked innocently and it drained the fight out of Jess. 'That was me,' she said limply. 'I let something slip when Cormac – when he—'

'Jess, say it. When he...?'

She told Grace about being caught in the room above Doreen's salon. The razor blade. The touch of it against her skin. 'I thought he was going to kill me. Him or Frankie—'

'Frankie O'Halloran was there?' Something flickered across Grace's face. 'That son of a bitch. He's the reason I never qualified as a nurse. Cormac brought him to our door, just as I was leaving for my final exam. Frankie had been stabbed in the leg in a fight, and he was losing blood. I wasn't given a choice; I had to patch him up and I got blood all over me. By the time I'd washed, changed and caught the bus, the exam was half over. They wouldn't let me retake. Those men ruined my life. For a while.' A secret thought brought light back into Grace's eyes. 'Frankie is Cormac's partner in crime, and you know what, I think they crawled out of the mouth of hell as a matched pair.'

Jess remembered Frankie coming down the stairs at Doreen's place, sneering, the scar on his face puckering. He'd enjoyed her fear in that upstairs room, and her humiliation. He'd tossed that piece of paper at her feet. The directions to Stoney Street...

Someone I know very well gave me the name, and how to find it. Frankie had told Cormac. Of course he had.

Jess put her hand to her face. She'd fallen into prejudice and blame without a thought. 'I'm sorry. Forgive me.'

Putting both hands over her face, she began to weep.

'Jess, don't cry, love. I should have told you that I saw you at

Cormac's. Well, your sister, I know that now. If I'd told you, it might have helped. Or would it just have scared you witless? Why didn't I say… because I'm ashamed of my brother. I try so hard to be the know-it-all nurse, living in "Mayfair, don't-you-know". But you can't leave twenty years of life in Whitechapel behind. Just as Charlotte couldn't be anything but what she was. A vicar's daughter, way out of her depth. When I saw her in Cormac's bed, she looked terrible, like a whipped puppy. I told her to leave him, said he was bad. And you know what? Later I found out she did just that. Got up, packed a bag, flitted before he woke. He, course, went into a rage, fit to kill.'

'I know. He chased me.' Jess wiped her eyes on her sleeve. 'It's possible you saved Charlotte's life. Like you saved mine at Hill Street. Thank you. For both of us.'

Grace nodded. 'Poor Charlotte. I wish I'd helped her more, because it put her on the run again, living on a pauper's wage.'

'And they say being a writer in an attic is romantic.'

'Nothing's romantic, not even romance.' Grace glanced at her new engagement ring. 'I'm more scared and worried for my man now than I was a week ago. It's why I read *Peg's Paper*. You know what the ending will be to every story. Only, guess what? They've stopped printing it.' Grace laid a hand on Jess's arm. 'Your sister needs care. I know I touched a chord when I said "miscarriage", and if it was – induced – botched – that explains a lot. I also suspect bronchitis. You've heard her breathing.'

Jess nodded. 'It's noisy.'

'That will get worse as winter comes.'

'I'm going to take care of her.'

'No, Jess, you've got a job to go to. It won't do Charlotte any good if you end up broke too. Besides, she can't keep going into air raid shelters, into the damp, night after night. Ideally, she'd leave London.'

'I don't think she will.' Besides, where was the sanctuary where nobody would ever winkle out Charlotte's story and make a telephone call to St Saviour's vicarage? 'I can't risk her falling into my father's hands.'

The conversation lapsed, returned to at bedtime. Charlotte's breathing was like a hacksaw on wood. It couldn't be ignored.

'She needs hospital followed by convalescence,' Grace said.

'She'd do best in the countryside,' said Mrs Kesgrave. 'Clean air.'

'Like the air at Alder Grove,' Jess said caustically.

'I won't go there.'

Nobody had seen Charlotte struggling to sit up. In the light of a low-watt bulb, she was paler than Jess had ever known her, the once-glossy hair reduced to scrubby clumps because Charlotte had shorn it, she said, fearing she'd get fleas off the mattress in Market Court.

She rasped, 'I won't go. They lock you up. For years.'

Jess went to her. 'You're never going back; you have my word. But I agree with Grace, you need nursing. Good food, sleep. We'll think of somewhere.'

'How would Ealing suit?' Grace said. 'A nice, leafy road?'

'Owen's mother's, you mean.' Betony came in, catching the end of the conversation. She'd been down to the bar and was holding a glass of beer, black with a creamy head. 'You were invited to meet Mrs Henderson. I never was.'

A silence descended, chilly enough for Jess to imagine battlelines being drawn. Hostilities resuming.

Then Betony gave a sigh. 'Then again, I phoned her one time and mistook her for her own charwoman, so it's not surprising I was frozen out. Is it, really?'

They all laughed in relief. 'Not really,' said Grace.

'I won't make the same mistake with Winter's mother.' Betony put the beer down. It was for Charlotte. 'Stout is packed full of iron.'

When she'd found somewhere to sit, Betony asked if

Owen's mother might really be willing to take on an unexpected guest.

'I think so,' Grace said. 'She's kind, and she already has people staying, refugees, one from Poland. A doctor. I think it might work.' Grace went over and crouched by Charlotte's bed. 'Would you consent?'

Charlotte turned the full force of her gaze on Grace and answered a different question. 'Yes,' she said. 'I had a miscarriage. But it was not a botched abortion.'

Jess intervened. 'It's all right, Charlotte. I went to see Mrs Munday. You don't have to say anything.'

'Why did you go there?'

'Looking for you. I found the note Miss Treadgold wrote.'

'Oh, that. "The window with the blue vase".'

'It was in the pocket of your red coat.'

Charlotte seemed to droop. 'You found that? They took it off me.'

'I know.'

'Alain bought it for me. He was my very good friend. I met him in a second-hand bookshop on the Charing Cross Road.'

Dangerous Liaisons, Jess thought. *It would be a bookshop, wouldn't it?*

'We were both looking at plays by Racine. Love. On my side, anyway. Later, when I realised I was in the family way, I tried to contact him. He'd given me a false address.'

'Charlotte, why didn't you tell me?'

'What could you do, little sister? I was pregnant and I knew how Father would react. Why burden you? I was managing things. Being the elder daughter of the vicarage, doing my shop work, going to church on Sunday, nipping to London to learn how to be a typist. Some women get sick and faint when they're expecting, I never did. I met Miss Treadgold and she gave me a job on the spot. I was to leave home and start straight away.

She'd find me a little flat. I trusted her.' Charlotte's voice darkened. She began coughing.

'Don't, if it hurts,' Jess urged.

'I must.' Charlotte coughed again into a hanky. 'I told her I was expecting, and suddenly it changed. She changed. I don't know how, exactly. I felt suddenly like a fly in a spider's web. I was hers. She had me.'

'Did she tell you about Stoney Street?'

'One of her secretaries put the note in my pocket. And the money to pay. Mrs Munday was waiting for me. "How far along are you, dearie? Two months? You're not showing much, still, that makes things easier."' Charlotte's face contorted. She coughed, violently this time.

'Twentieth of December 1939,' Jess said. 'You got home very late.'

'I believe you're right,' Charlotte gasped. 'I climbed those greasy stairs. Mrs M was washing her hands, and said without looking round, "Take off your under things and lie on the table." I couldn't. I just couldn't. Even though I knew I'd lose my chance to write. I'd have to go home and face Father. I ran – only I fell down those bloody stairs. Bump, bump, bump, the whole way to the bottom. Her old mother screaming, thinking I'd done it to avoid paying. "You get back up there, young woman." I got the door open and ran. All the way to London Bridge and onto a train home.'

'You didn't come in till gone eleven.' The events of those late December days would never fade from Jess's mind.

'When I reached Ramsgate, I made a telephone call. I was trying to reach Alain.'

'The father.'

'It was a false number. Oh, someone answered. A complete stranger. It was mortifying. I hung up and walked for miles, and thought of wading into the sea, getting it over with. Alain used to say' – she adopted a smoky, French accent – '"You can survive life if you know how to play." I hadn't realised I was the toy. Anyway, I began to feel ill. My belly was cramping. I came home and you were waiting up, bless you. I was praying a miscarriage would hold off till next day, when you'd all gone out. Prayers answered.'

'Only you nearly died. I screamed for Father to call an ambulance.'

'It was the right thing.'

'So – wait,' Grace intervened. 'If you were taken to hospital in an ambulance, how come you ended up at Alder Grove? That's in a different county.'

Jess and Charlotte exchanged a glance.

'Our father, Reverend Gresham, removed me,' Charlotte said tonelessly. 'After two days. He drove me to Epsom in the Austin 7, with Miss Hillingdon, and signed the papers. Had me committed.'

'Two days?' Grace echoed. 'Discharged from hospital after a traumatic miscarriage... That is criminal.'

'I wish I could hear you say those same words to his face,' Jess whispered.

43

'Do you believe her?' Grace asked Jess when they were alone.

They were at a table in the bar, cheese, tomato and onion flan in front of them. They were eating in two shifts so Charlotte wasn't left alone.

'That she fell downstairs and miscarried?' Jess picked a morsel of pastry off her plate. Charlotte's revelations had badly dented her appetite. 'I do, yes.'

'It's just that I've heard every imaginable story,' Grace sighed. '"I fell off a bus" or "I tripped over the cat". The procedure is illegal, and so often fatal. When they're in hospital, being questioned, they'll come up with anything.'

Even so, Jess completely accepted Charlotte's story. *What the girl does next, that's your play.* 'I believe she decided on the spur of the moment not to go through with it. To have the baby, damn the consequences. That's Charlotte, every inch. And when I went there and they thought I was her, one of them said, "No shortcuts down the staircase this time."'

'Then it's true and she made the right choice,' said Grace. 'All but two of the patients I've looked after who got botched up died with sepsis. Every time, I had to tell the ward sister and she called the police.'

They ate in silence for a while. Grace's mention of the police was an unnerving reminder of another crime unfolding in the here and now. Father might already be planning his trip to Mayfair on Saturday, expecting to confront his blackmailer – and Jess still hadn't the faintest idea how to draw the other party in.

She had baited the trap: writing to Father in Cormac's name, telling him to come to No. 34. But how to get Cormac there?

Could Grace be persuaded to act as go-between? Get a letter to her brother purportedly from the Reverend Gresham, agreeing to the meeting?

Jess couldn't bring herself to ask. Not yet.

She chose the easier path, enquiring after Owen. 'He crash-landed his Spitfire a while back, didn't he?'

'He's all right. Few bruises still. He's being sent up to North Yorkshire to rejoin his squadron.' Grace gazed at her ring. 'I'm hoping to take some time off and visit him. I've never been up north. How's Rafe?'

'I have no idea. He might have gone to his brother's in Tufton Street or be in deepest Sussex by now.'

'But he's all right, yes?' Grace tried to spear a tomato.

'I hope so.' Jess felt the soft brush of foreboding. 'What are you saying?'

'After we got you out, I thought he looked... you know.'

'No. I don't.' Jess's voice shot up. Fear seemed to live in her pocket, coiled and ready to leap out. 'Grace, tell me.'

'I thought his colour was bad. Yes, I know, he has burn injuries, but his whole face was... odd. And he was having difficulty breathing.'

'Why didn't you do anything? For pity's sake, Grace!'

'Because he disappeared. I went to check where the ambulance was taking you and by the time I'd got back, he'd just gone.'

Jess put down her knife and fork, too sick to eat another thing. Why was Grace only now telling her that Rafe might be ill? She'd been imagining him safe and sound in an old manor house, starting his new life. Should she knock on every door on Tufton Street? She might have done so, but Grace spoke the one name that had the power to push even Rafe out of her mind.

'There's something else I need to tell you, Jess. Cormac won't let go of this blackmail against your father. He's got jaws like a terrier. I told you how I stopped Frankie O'Halloran bleeding to death?'

'And missed your final exam.' Jess nodded.

'Well, afterwards, Cormac held that over me. Frankie had been knifed during a violent break-in, and by tending him, I'd aided and abetted a criminal. For months, Cormac had the thumbscrews on me. Whatever he did, I would have to be his alibi. It only stopped when I told him I'd rather go to prison. Have you warned your dad what he's like?'

Jess shook her head. Hardly. She told Grace about the post-script she'd added to Cormac's letter. 'I set up a meeting, at No. 34. I felt they deserved to argue it out.'

Grace gaped. 'Jess, are you mad? You've seen how Cormac argues!'

'Yes,' Jess said resolutely, 'but they're as guilty as each other when it comes to abusing Charlotte and it has to end. Only... I need to get Cormac there too.' She waited, letting her eyes speak for her.

Grace let out a low groan. 'You want me to lure him into the trap?'

'It needs to end,' Jess repeated.

A long silence followed. Grace seemed to turn everything over, weighing loyalties, reliving things she'd never said aloud.

At last, she drew in a breath. 'All right, I'll do my part. With Mam and Ricky gone, I've nobody to protect apart from myself. I've a sister, Immie – she's close to Cormac. Something she said makes me think he's planning a flit to Ireland to lie low. The army's after him.' Grace's voice dropped. 'I went to the police a little while back, to report him. Theft, dodging his call-up, carrying false papers. He slipped the net: I think his landlady at the Ring and Rabbit tipped him off. He always gets away with it.'

Jess swallowed. 'If I were to give you a message, supposedly from my father… would you pass it on?'

'To Cormac? I'll do more than that,' Grace said quietly. 'I'll go back to the police. This time I'll make sure they get him.'

Jess nodded. Arrest and imprisonment would erase the threat of Cormac Whelan very neatly. Charlotte would be free of him for ever, as would she. 'In that case, tell him it's this Saturday, nine o'clock. No. 34 Hill Street. I'll be there. Will you come with me?'

'No.' Grace shook her head, harder when Jess asked again. 'If you think I'm walking into a house with no back exit, and my brother anywhere near it, you're mad. If he ever guesses I grassed on him, or that it was me who told Charlotte to run…' She drew an invisible blade across her throat. 'I've got too much to live for. Sorry.'

Jess said no more. The die was cast. When her father and Cormac met, she'd be there making it three.

This, she supposed, was the courage Miss Hillingdon had accused her of lacking.

44

Saturday, 28 September 1940

No raids all day. Hopefully, the peace would hold overnight.

Jess supposed she was now a fully fledged criminal, having entered a house under cover of night, one the authorities had declared off-limits. She'd walked upstairs while daring the ceiling to fall down on her head. Everything reeked of smoke. The higher she went, the stronger the smell but their bedroom wasn't the cinder-shell she'd feared. The firemen's hoses had doused the flames next door before they breached the walls. The rugs would have to go, the curtains and their bedding.

But the wardrobe had held good. Jess put on the red coat and pulled Charlotte's typewriter from under her bed and carried it down to the kitchen.

She lit a candle and checked her watch. She'd invited her father for nine. Ten minutes to wait.

Charlotte had once told her that drama happens when one person wants something, and another person stops them. A drama was in prospect then, as Cormac would come wanting money, and her father had none. Reverend Gresham would want assurances that Cormac would never reveal what he knew, and Cormac was as trustworthy as a cornered rat.

She heard the front door bumping open. The wood had swelled because the fire crew had soaked the building's façade.

Feet in the hall, a firm tread. Two sets of footsteps.

Jess heard her father, clearly reassuring himself that this was the correct address. 'It seems very strange. A condemned house. Not sure we should even be in here.'

'What else would you expect from a man like that, Ian?'

Oh. Her. Predictable.

'You're right, Clara, as always.'

Ian and Clara. No longer 'Reverend' and 'Miss Hillingdon'. It made Jess fear them less. As if she'd caught them with their fingers in the sweetie jar. She straightened her shoulders and called, 'In here.'

They entered, two out-of-towners in overcoats, Miss Hillingdon in a hat which – as Miss Touchwood might put it – declared war on charm. Jess's father wore the familiar battered trilby, his coat collar pulled up so she couldn't tell if he wore his dog collar. Jess was wearing the red coat, her hair pinned up in a chignon. She had deliberately adopted her sister's look and her father stepped into the trap.

'Charlotte.' His voice was soft, almost tender. 'At last. You've caused more ruin than you know. What game is it now?'

'No game, Father. I'm here to witness a transaction. The reckoning begins.'

'The reckoning began long ago—' Reverend Gresham broke off at a nudge from Miss Hillingdon.

'It's Jessica.' Miss Hillingdon came right up to Jessica's shoulder. 'Where did you get this coat? Do you know where your sister is?'

Jess shook off the grip. 'I do. Am I telling you? Hell will freeze over first.'

'You will tell us. We'll make you.'

'Abduct me and lock me up at Alder Grove?'

It was impossible to know in candlelight how her words landed, except that Clara Hillingdon took a quick in-breath.

'How is it you're here?' her father asked again.

Jess explained that this had been her home – until an incendiary landed on the roof two doors down.

'Nonsense,' Miss Hillingdon snorted.

Jess had briefly forgotten the woman's capacity for arrogance. 'It was an incendiary.' Grace had been told so by Sir Gideon.

'What I'm saying,' Miss Hillingdon snapped, 'is that you cannot live here. You're staying at the Girls' Friendly hostel in Westminster.'

'Actually, I've been all over the place, but never there.'

'You lied?'

'Shamelessly. The difference between us… Clara… is that I have the guts to admit it.'

'What do you know of this unsavoury business, Jessica?' Reverend Gresham, though an educated man, seemed unsure of himself. That booming tone was absent. He couldn't be afraid of her, surely.

'I know you're here to pay off Cormac Whelan,' Jess answered. Ah. She'd shocked him. He was thinking – how could she possibly know? 'Charlotte's former protector,' she continued. 'A euphemism, of course. He's tired of being the rejected lover and is willing to settle for hard cash. How much have you brought?'

'Nothing,' said Miss Hillingdon.

'Forty pounds,' her father said at the same moment.

Jess advised him to be like the Duke of Wellington. 'Tell the man to publish and be damned.'

'He's threatened—'

'—scandal in the *Gazette*. I know. Pay, and he'll be back for more next month.'

'Are you behind this, Jessica? Is this your petty revenge because I didn't pander to your hysterics?'

When had she ever had hysterics? Or was that how her father translated 'grief'? Her voice hardening, she told him she'd read Cormac's letter to him. 'I won't bore you with how I got hold of it, but you're right, I saw my chance. I've brought you here so you can own up to what you did, Father. To admit, face to face, what you did to Charlotte.'

'It's simple,' her father said, without hesitation. 'Nothing but my duty.'

'I'm afraid that isn't true,' said a fourth voice.

Jess froze. For an instant she thought she'd imagined it – until she saw who had stepped into the light. 'Grace!'

Her throat tightened. She'd come after all, despite her fear, and it changed the atmosphere. It brought static to the air. 'I didn't expect you.'

'I wasn't going to come – then I thought of you, on your own somewhere that must still scare the bejaysus out of you.'

'Mind your language, young woman.' Miss Hillingdon drew herself up. 'Who might you be?'

'No names,' said Grace. Her voice was steady, almost gentle. 'I don't need yours, and you're not getting mine.' She turned to Reverend Gresham, without any trace of deference. 'I take it, you're the father?'

'I am Jessica's father, yes.'

'I heard you say you did your duty by Charlotte.'

'I do say it.'

'Then tell me, Reverend – how does dragging a patient out of her hospital bed after a traumatic miscarriage count as duty?'

Reverend Gresham had no answer, but the turn of his head told a clear story. He was answerable to nobody.

Grace had more to say. 'You tore her out of bed while her body was in shock, her womb raw, blood still seeping. She needed rest, comfort, a hand like mine on her pulse. Instead, you hauled her out in her night things because you feared shame more than you cared for her life.'

'It was for her good.' Jess's father leaned two large hands on the table. His face was tight. 'How could I ever have held my head up if it got around that my daughter had conceived a child out of wedlock?'

Grace drew back her lips. 'All about you, then! Do you understand that blood poisoning could have set in? Charlotte might have died outright. God love her, she might never carry a child to term because of it. All to hide her from the eyes of your churchy chums. Shame on you, sir, shame.'

'How dare you speak this way to a man of the cloth?' shouted Miss Hillingdon.

Jess thought Grace would tell the woman to go to hell. But she continued with terrible calm. 'Jess tells me you're the ever-present handmaiden. Did you stand by while he forced his own daughter from a hospital bed? Did you help drag her to Alder Grove, to begin a life sentence behind walls? Don't answer, for I know you did. You colluded. Whatever religion you profess, the pair of you' – Grace looked from one to the other – 'that night you abandoned it.'

Miss Hillingdon looked around for some defence. Her eye fell on the typewriter. 'That's Charlotte's Remington. We locked it away.'

Jess agreed, it was.

'Now I understand why lifting your suitcase hurt your father's back.' Miss Hillingdon shook her head. 'Another lie, Jessica. How can we ever trust you again?'

'I lied by omission. You lie outright, Miss Hillingdon.'

'Ian?' Miss Hillingdon demanded an intervention.

Reverend Gresham made it, moving closer to Miss Hillingdon. 'Clara is the soul of truth.'

'Really?' Jess was incredulous. 'Two words. Brain haemorrhage.'

Her father pushed out his chest, and informed Jess that she would travel home with them in the morning. 'I want you under my eye. I'll make enquiries to see if your old job is still vacant and Clara will chaperone you until I deem you fit to be trusted again.'

Jess explained that her father would first have to clear things with her boss.

'I'll write his name and address for you.' She scribbled quickly and handed him the paper.

He dug out his spectacles, squinting. '"His Majesty King George, Buckingham—" Your idea of a joke, Jessica?'

'No. I work for King and country, so in theory he is my employer.'

She was rather pleased with that. Too pleased to notice the sound of boots in the passage. The realisation who it must be came only when Grace pressed herself flat against the wall, as though she'd vanish through the plaster if she could.

The door flew open. The candle flinched.

Cormac Whelan had arrived.

45

Cormac looked at her with hope. *Charlotte.* It died and reality was a silent snarl. *Cheated again.*

It was the coat. Always this coat. Jess thought, *He loves Charlotte, yet he's here to sell her out.*

She introduced her father.

'Father, this is Cormac Whelan, your blackmailer.'

Disgust crossed Cormac's face. 'Well, well, Jess. And Grace too.' He turned to face his sister. 'Would you know it, the police tried to nab me a few days back.'

Grace managed a hesitant shrug. 'I heard a rumour.'

'Wonder how they knew about Smith's Court.'

'Oh, you'll have been seen sneaking in and out, I dare say.'

'You dare, do you?' He gave his sister an ironic salute. 'A crowd I wasn't expecting. You, sir,' he addressed Reverend Gresham, 'all I'm asking is recompense for taking care of Charlotte, over many months. But for me, she'd have been on the streets or worse... and now, I've a fancy to go travelling so I'm thinking—'

Reverend Gresham cut him short, placing a thick envelope on the table. 'Forty pounds. All I'm able to get without notice.'

He ignored Jess's objection and surveyed Cormac, who was wearing another of his generously cut suits, hair slicked with an oil containing some kind of glittery frosting.

Jess tried again. 'Father, his threats are bluster. Do you really imagine the *Gazette* would print a scurrilous story? Even if he spreads rumours, who'll believe him? Your parishioners respect you. They all think Charlotte is dead. He'll sound like a rambling lunatic or the desperate conman he is.'

Don't get in my way, Cormac's blue eyes projected coldly.

She had no choice but to prevent her father, in his mania to protect his standing, from signing up to a lifetime of blackmail. She told him again to put the money back in his pocket.

'Charlotte took his help, yes, but she feared him. People do. Ask Doreen, my hairdresser. Ask Grace, who knows better than any of us. He's been using me to lead him to Charlotte but I don't fear him anymore and neither should you. Going to Ireland, he says. What's he running from? Do you see a uniform? This is a man who will do anything but his duty. Do not hand your hard-earned money over to him.'

Reverend Gresham spoke but without emotion to spare. 'If he's so worthless, why did Charlotte end up in his home?'

'Because those she should have counted on betrayed her. You might call it "an abuse of kinship". You are the cause.'

'Me?'

'You all but handed her over to him.'

Her father nodded wearily. 'You are right. Charlotte has one true ally. You girls were always bound together. And because of that bond, I cannot bring either of you home. I must be master in my vicarage, or no master at all. So be it. After tonight, I have no daughters.'

Jess felt the claw of tears. The instinct to throw herself at the familiar, solid frame brought her to her feet. In that moment, if she could have found forgiveness, she would have.

It was Cormac who stopped her by choosing that moment

to reach for the envelope of cash. Her father's attention swung away.

Reverend Gresham tried to protect his money, but the swift lick of a razor edge made him snatch back his hand with a cry of pain.

Grace lunged at her brother.

'This is for all the times you threatened me, and beat me, and Ricky – and for getting between me and my dreams, you bastard!'

For a horrifying moment, all Jess could see was brother and sister locked in struggle – Cormac easily deflecting Grace's blows, the wooden tool with its glint of steel flashing between them.

The door burst open. Boots clattered on the tiles, and blinding torchlight cut through the gloom.

'Cormac Whelan? Police. We're arresting you for identity card fraud and evasion of military service. Hands where we can see them.'

Cormac bolted past Jess, hurling away his weapon. He got the door to the yard open – and found it blocked by tons of masonry.

He turned to face the two burly uniforms, his wrists held out. As Rafe had told Jess, Cormac Whelan was a man who picked his battles.

He spared his last words for Jess and Grace. 'I don't forget and one day, I'll be out.'

46

Sunday, 29 September 1940

Showing her card as she went through the double doors, Jess came out of Senate House into thin autumn sunshine. The gleam on wet cobbles made her believe for an instant that London – and life itself – was at peace. Another shift done, and her thoughts were with Charlotte, whom she'd once again left sleeping.

A long talk last night had cleared up two riddles. Firstly, how Charlotte had escaped from Alder Grove and made it to London. The truth was brutally simple. She had lain quiet in her bed, feigning passive acceptance, until the staff were bringing in the New Year with drinks in their common room. Someone had forgotten to lock her window. She'd climbed out, made her way to the station and crept into the guard's van of the night train.

'And nearly froze to death. I got out at Vauxhall where there's no ticket barrier after hours and just kept walking. I collapsed somewhere... Cormac almost stepped on me.'

And Jess's sighting of her on the escalator at Charing Cross Underground?

A mirage. At the time, Charlotte had been down on her luck, living on tap water and stale bread in Shepherd Market – moments away from Jess, if only they'd known it. Whoever Jess had seen, it wasn't her.

Charlotte knew nothing of the drama at Hill Street and Cormac's arrest. It was too soon to tell her. Jess was wondering what she might pick up on the way home in the way of a treat – a bag of Victoria plums from the grocer's, perhaps – when she heard someone calling her name.

'Miss Gresham, wait up.'

She turned to see one of the security men hurrying towards her. 'Nearly forgot. There's a message come for you.'

Her heart gave a small leap, hoping it might be from Rafe. The note was brief, written in haste:

Urgent. St George's Hospital, Hyde Park Corner. Come at once. I'll wait for you there. G.W.

The world, so briefly righted, tipped again into shadow. Grace wouldn't write 'urgent' unless something dreadful had happened. Cormac, free? Had he gone on the attack… found Charlotte?

She raced to the Underground, her mind leaping ahead, forming ideas she didn't dare put into pictures. Perhaps Charlotte had taken a turn for the worse. Grace had warned how weak her lungs were, how she needed proper care.

Perhaps she'd begun one of those coughing fits and brought up blood… *No, don't think it. Don't.*

She flung herself between the closing doors of a train. Four stops, one change, her reflection in the window pale and stricken.

She got out at Hyde Park Corner and ran.

Grace wasn't waiting. At the desk, she was told to go straight to Ward 5. 'Side room at the end.'

Her shoes squeaked on the polished linoleum as she hurried past rows of beds, inhaling air sharp with disinfectant.

At the far end, another corridor. Halfway along, she saw Grace, instantly recognisable in her cape and uniform. She was talking with a man whose height and colouring made Jess's heart stumble.

'Rafe?'

They both turned. Grace called to her but Jess's eyes were on the tall figure wearing a coat with its collar turned up high. She gasped.

Rafe, with his face miraculously healed. He seemed older. There were faint lines at the corners of his eyes, a breath of grey at the temple. When he spoke, it broke the illusion. This wasn't Rafe.

Jess stammered her apology. 'I thought you were someone else. It's the coat – he wears one the same.'

'Course he does; it's Navy issue.'

Grace took her arm. 'Jess, this is Rafe's brother, Frederick Taverner. Mr Taverner, this is Rafe's friend Jess.'

'Friend?' It was said with fastidious disdain. 'Hardly the correct designation for someone who wrecks another person's life. Have you come to coo at his bedside?'

Jess looked from him to Grace. 'I thought I was coming to see Charlotte.'

'No, she's being looked after by Mrs Kesgrave.' Grace steered her towards a room marked OBSERVATION, HIGH DEPENDENCY. 'Jess, I did something I shouldn't. Instead of going into work this morning, I went to Tufton Street.'

Rafe's brother followed them, saying, 'She knocked on my door like a military policeman and demanded to see my brother.'

'You'd told me where he lived and I couldn't stop thinking I should have checked on him earlier,' Grace said, ignoring the interruption. All the dirt they'd shifted rescuing Jess, well, nobody who'd suffered burns should have been anywhere near it. 'And the effort of heaving those blocks and bricks. Then he lay on his stomach in the muck, to call your name.'

'Oh, Grace.' Jess knew none of this.

'You're damn right he should never have been there,' Frederick Taverner said roughly.

'If he hadn't, I'd still be under that rubble.'

'Some might wish you were. I'm sorry, I'm sure you're very nice but my brother went through hell. Ever burned your thumb on a candle flame, or spilled boiling water on the back of your hand? Imagine that over half your body. And then a worthless drab of a fiancée throws him over. "Dear Rafe, I'm sure you'll agree it's for the best." Bloody women.'

'Not all women,' Grace said firmly. 'Jess is steadfast. She's the best.'

'Huh,' was Frederick Taverner's opinion.

The door they stood beside had a square of glass and Jess peered through. She could see a patient, in a high bed, wearing a pyjama top, propped up on pillows. The side of his face closest was bandaged with gauze, as was the hand on the coverlet.

'May I go in?' she asked.

The brother snorted. 'Will it make any difference if I say no?'

'Of course. Because then I'd have to elbow you aside.'

With a glower followed by a cynical half-smile that Jess found heartrendingly familiar, Frederick Taverner opened the door. 'Five minutes. Starting now.' He lifted a wrist that bore an impressive-looking watch.

Jess hadn't taken more than a stride inside when Grace came after her, touching her arm. 'Don't get too close. Infection risk.'

Grace retreated and Jess heard her saying, 'Five minutes from now. Start counting again.'

Jess crept as near the bed as she dared. Rafe could see her and she him. She'd know anywhere the flop of brown hair trying to outgrow its regulation cut. His hands and wrists were swathed in bandage. The skin on his face and neck, and under the collar of his pyjamas, shone with some kind of salve.

'It's me,' she whispered.

'I know.' Rafe's voice grated.

'Am I allowed to be here?'

'Course. Did you meet Freddie?'

'Yes. He gave me a lecture. All women are worthless, apparently.'

'He's hurt. For me. He takes things hard. Ignore him.'

Jess ventured a step nearer. 'I take it, Grace insisted you come to hospital?'

'I think so. I wasn't in good shape. Someone got bossy and called an ambulance. I think it was your Irish housemate.'

'And my friend.' Jess heard pride in her voice, that she could say that and know it to be true. 'I feel ashamed, though. I should have come to find you.'

'Why?' He lifted his hands an inch, then let them drop. 'I've made it nigh on impossible for you to care about me.'

And yet I do, she answered silently. *Very deeply*. She couldn't voice it but said, in a stiff, little voice, 'Thank you for coming to my rescue when I was trapped. If you hadn't known the way to the back of Mrs Kesgrave's house—'

'He wouldn't be in this state now.' Five minutes had flown by. Frederick Taverner was in the room. 'I've told him he's a bloody idiot and likely to be court martialled for returning to London without leave. Unless I pull strings.'

'Which you will,' Jess shot back. 'Or what kind of useless brother would you be?' She wasn't sure which was the sweeter, Frederick's astonishment or Rafe's chuckle.

'Now you know why I love her, Freddie.'

Had Rafe really said that? Jess fought the urge to run forward and grab his hand. Standing three feet away was torment. 'Do you mean that?' was all she could say.

'I do. Hope I'm not being a bore.' It hurt him to speak, she could tell, so she answered in the simplest way she could.

'You couldn't bore me if you tried. I love you too. So very, very much.'

'And one day, Frederick will adore you, too.'

'Pigs might fly,' muttered the brother.

'Jess, take this man away and buy him a coffee. Inform him that pigs everywhere are being granted their certificates of air worthiness. Go, both of you, before Sister throws you out.'

Some minutes later, standing awkwardly on Hyde Park Corner, Jess was relieved to learn that Frederick Taverner had no desire to share a café table with her or Grace. A bus grinding by and a fleet of motorbike despatch riders passing in convoy made conversation, thankfully, impossible. Jess had one last request to shout.

'Will you lift the ban on me visiting Rafe?'

'No.'

'Oh, please, Mr Taverner.'

'Commander Taverner, actually.'

'Sorry. I'll try and remember.'

'You don't need my permission. All I will say is, take care of my brother. No more dramas or collapsing buildings. And no deciding halfway along you'd rather marry somebody else.'

'You're galloping way ahead. So far, Rafe and I have only had coffee, toast and mushrooms.'

'Good. Keep it that way.' Commander Frederick Taverner stepped out into the traffic. An imperiously raised arm brought everything to a stop.

. . .

'God save us,' Grace said as they watched him go. 'I'm glad you're in love with the other brother... did he really say marriage?'

Jess nodded. 'It's madness. Including today, Rafe and I have only met four times. Five, if you count him knocking on the top of the Anderson shelter. Nobody talks about marriage this soon.'

'When there's a war on they do.' Grace flashed her ring. 'Escaping the clutches of death speeds up the timetable.'

Jess laughed. 'You mean, one collapsed ceiling equals two dinners out and a bomb through the house next door is six dinner dates and a dance?'

'Something like that.'

They linked arms and walked to the Underground, chased by autumn leaves swept on a brisk wind.

On Farm Street, they separated, Grace continuing on to Ventnor House, to explain her absence that day. 'Wish me luck as I fall on my knees and grovel at the bunions of Lady Ventnor.'

Jess went upstairs at the Shepherd and Flock and found Charlotte sitting up in bed, a notebook open on her lap.

'Hello, Jess darling.'

She sounded tired and was blinking as though she'd been reading too-small print.

'Grace says you need iron tonics, and sleep,' Jess said gently, picking up the notebook. There was a single line of hesitant writing. 'Can't you rest for once?'

'I was writing you a note, actually, in case I dropped off again.' Charlotte clasped her hands together. 'We're being booted out.'

'Out?' Jess sat down hard. 'From here?'

''Fraid so. The landlady's been up. She's got to billet some social welfare workers. Their place in Westminster was hit last night.'

Not homelessness again. Why did this keep happening?

Betony came in, grey-faced from the office. After the

briefest hello, she said, 'Sybil's shutting *Practical Modes* after October. No Christmas issue. By hell or high water, we'll get one more out, then that's it. No paper, the advertisers are fleeing now the word's gone round. We're finished.'

A moment later Mrs Kesgrave arrived with a basket of groceries, sighing as she sat down. 'I walked past Hill Street on my way back. An ARP warden told me we can't go in until they've done safety inspections.'

'How long with that be?' Jess asked.

'He didn't know. Could be weeks.'

'Weeks?' Betony's expression suggested she was picturing her wardrobe being pawed at by looters.

The mood sank, nobody with anything uplifting or even hopeful to say. Until Grace's tread sounded on the stairs. Firm, decisive.

'I'm losing my job,' she announced.

A universal groan rose.

'Anyone would think it's Friday the thirteenth,' said Betony. 'Soon we'll be sitting in line in the gutter, fighting over the last sardine in the tin.'

Jess wanted to cry. 'What absolutely rotten luck.'

'It's not,' Grace said, flinging her cape over the back of a chair. 'Frankly, I was either going to leave or smother Lady Ventnor in her sleep. My being away today gave her time to think, she said. She's decided she needs a change of scene. The Blitz is too much for her nerves and she's off to Devon, where she has cousins. They, poor souls, have no idea what's coming their way.'

'What about Sir Gideon?' Jess would always have a fondness for the man who had marshalled her rescue forces. 'Will he mind?'

'Mind?' Grace snorted. 'He'll probably break into a Morris dance the moment her car turns the corner.'

Mrs Kesgrave still looked downcast. 'He'll rattle around that place, all on his own. I wouldn't be surprised if some government department doesn't commandeer it for their staff.'

'They won't,' Grace said, eyes alight, 'because he's offering the upper floors to us. Same rent, same terms as with you, Mrs Kesgrave. A bedroom each, and two bathrooms. What do you say?'

Jess stared. *What did she say?* 'All of us? Together?'

'All of us.'

For a moment no one spoke. Then Betony gave a small, breathless laugh. 'I won't have to share a wardrobe ever again.'

Mrs Kesgrave seemed almost overcome. 'I could walk past No. 34 every day and check it's all right. Oh—' A doubt struck. 'What about my girls?'

'There's a yard at the back, and he's keeping the butler and the cook, so they'll be fighting over the eggs.'

'They can have omelettes every day,' Mrs Kesgrave gasped. 'We've been granted a miracle.'

Jess's throat felt too tight for words. A roof. Friends. Safety. She imagined going into Miss Cartwright's office and saying, 'I thought you should know, I have a new address. It's on Upper Brook Street, Mayfair.'

'So?' prompted Grace.

'Yes. Telephone him now,' cried Betony. 'And bring some beer up to celebrate.'

Afterwards they all hugged – all but Charlotte, who had drifted softly into sleep. Jess looked from one woman to the next: fair, dark, red-haired, each marked in some way by loss, by fire, by fear, and felt something stir. Not despair, not even relief. Something steadier.

The moan of the siren cut through their laughter, ending the moment. There was nothing for it but to make for the public shelter in Grosvenor Square. With Charlotte wrapped in coats, they hurried into the blackout. Searchlights crossed against the sky as the guns began to bark.

That feeling stayed with her as they ran, Jess laden with blankets, Mrs Kesgrave carrying a hamper in which she had placed her chickens and Charlotte stumbling between Grace and Betony, who were the tallest and strongest of the group.

They had survived bombs, betrayal and heartbreak. And whatever came next, Jess believed, they would face it the same way.

Together.

A LETTER FROM NATALIE

To my dear readers,

I want to say a huge thank you for choosing to read *The Vicar's Daughter at the Lodging House*. If you did enjoy it, and want to keep up to date with all my latest releases, just sign up at the following link. Your email address will never be shared and you can unsubscribe at any time.

www.bookouture.com/natalie-meg-evans

Thank you for reading *The Vicar's Daughter at the Lodging House*. Jess's journey is one of the quiet miracles of wartime London: a shy young woman who steps into the city with naïve expectations, and discovers, through heartbreak, danger and unexpected love, the strength that was inside her all along. I hope her courage and her search for truth have stayed with you now that you've turned the final page.

Throughout Jess's story, the Lodging House family – Grace, Betony, and Mrs Kesgrave (and not forgetting the chickens) – has continued to draw together, setting rivalry and mistrust aside. Grace, tested by love and loss; Jess, stepping into her own power; and Betony, whose glamour and sharp edges hide much deeper uncertainties. Their friendships have become the heartbeat of the series, each young woman shaping and steadying the others as the Blitz rages around them.

And now, we come to Betony.

Many of you have written to me about her: a girl who appears privileged and self-possessed, yet whose world is far more fragile than it seems. In the next book – the final part of the trilogy – Betony's life will be turned upside down. Swept from the bright lights of London fashion into a world of factory work and 'make-do', she learns, sometimes painfully, how courage, compassion and authenticity matter far more than appearance or ambition. And when the man she loves falters beneath the weight of his own doubts in the heat of battle, it falls to Betony to lay aside romantic ideals and show a steadier, more mature form of love. Hers is a story about how war forces the young to grow up, and how the bravest acts are often the quietest.

I am deeply grateful for your company through this trilogy. Your kindness, your messages and the way you recommend these books to friends mean more than I can say. If you've grown attached to the Lodging House and its young women, I hope you'll join me next for Betony's story, the most challenging journey of all.

With warmest wishes,

Natalie Meg Evans
Suffolk, 2026

www.blythe-evans.com

facebook.com/NatalieMegEvans
instagram.com/natalie.meg.evans

PUBLISHING TEAM

Turning a manuscript into a book requires the efforts of many people. The publishing team at Bookouture would like to acknowledge everyone who contributed to this publication.

Audio
Alba Proko

Commercial
Lauren Morrissette
Hannah Richmond
Imogen Allport

Cover design
Lesley Worrell

Data and analysis
Mark Alder
Mohamed Bussuri

Editorial
Natalie Edwards
Imogen Allport

Copyeditor
Jon Appleton

Proofreader
Becca Allen

Marketing
Alex Crow
Melanie Price
Occy Carr
Cíara Rosney
Martyna Młynarska

Operations and distribution
Marina Valles
Joe Morris

Production
Hannah Snetsinger
Mandy Kullar
Nadia Michael
Charlotte Hegley

Publicity
Kim Nash
Noelle Holten
Jess Readett
Sarah Hardy

Rights and contracts
Peta Nightingale
Richard King
Saidah Graham

RAISING READERS

Books Build Bright Futures

Dear Reader,

We'd love your attention for one more page to tell you about the crisis in children's reading, and what we can all do.

Studies have shown that reading for fun is the **single biggest predictor of a child's future life chances** – more than family circumstance, parents' educational background or income. It improves academic results, mental health, wealth, communication skills, ambition and happiness.

The number of children reading for fun is in rapid decline. Young people have a lot of competition for their time, and a worryingly high number do not have a single book at home.

Hachette works extensively with schools, libraries and literacy charities, but here are some ways we can all raise more readers:

- Reading to children for just 10 minutes a day makes a difference
- Don't give up if children aren't regular readers – there will be books for them!

- Visit bookshops and libraries to get recommendations
- Encourage them to listen to audiobooks
- Support school libraries
- Give books as gifts

There's a lot more information about how to encourage children to read on our websites: **www.RaisingReaders.co.uk** and **www.JoinRaisingReaders.com**.

Thank you for reading.

hachette UK

Printed in Dunstable, United Kingdom

83464970R00190